MATERIAL GIRLS

MATERIAL GIRLS

Elaine Dimopoulos

Houghton Mifflin Harcourt
BOSTON   NEW YORK

For Gail and Dimitri Dimopoulos,
ever wise, ever fashionable

www.hmhco.com

The text of this book is set in Arno.

Library of Congress Cataloging-in-Publication Data
Dimopoulos, Elaine.
Material girls / by Elaine Dimopoulos.
pages cm
ISBN 978-0-544-38850-5
[1. Celebrities — Fiction. 2. Fashion — Fiction. 3. Singers — Fiction.
4. Popular music — Fiction.] I. Title.
PZ7.D598Mat 2015
[Fic] — dc23
2014009171

Manufactured in the United States of America
DOC 10 9 8 7 6 5 4 3 2 1
4500522225

"The first purpose of Clothes . . .
was not warmth or decency, but ornament."

—Thomas Carlyle, *Sartor Resartus*
(The Tailor Retailored), 1833

Chapter One

Late, late, late, late. Julia was going to kill me.

I hopped around my room, yanking clothes out of my closet and throwing them on the bed. Like an idiot, I'd forgotten to charge my Unum, so the battery had died overnight. Which meant, of course, that my alarm hadn't gone off this morning. Which meant I'd probably still be sleeping right now if my mother hadn't come in to investigate why I wasn't at breakfast.

Okay. I could pair the yellow Torro-LeBlanc leggings with the blue musketeer tunic — did they really go, though? — or do a black and white combo with the oversize blouse and a belt. That was probably safest. I wouldn't have to change my nail polish, either. But I'd worn black and white last week — the other judges would definitely remember. I chewed on a section of my hair and glanced at the clock. I had to decide *now*, or I'd never make it to work by nine.

Tunic and leggings, fine. I grabbed my silver trendchecking gun from the top shelf of my closet, flicked it on, and pointed the barrel at my clothing tags. As the laser hit the tunic's tag, the gun beeped and the green light stayed green. Same for the tank top. But when I scanned the tag on the leggings, the light turned red. I groaned, hurled the leggings and the gun to the floor, and grabbed my charging Unum. "Sabrina," I said into the microphone.

Sabrina's face, which always looked as if it was concentrating hard, filled my Unum screen. "Hey," she said. From the light smudges of color behind her, I could tell she was outdoors.

"I'm freaking out. I haven't left yet. I have nothing to wear." Panic tightened my voice. "The yellow midcalf leggings expired."

"Yeah. Like last week."

"So what do I pair the musketeer tunic with? Mine's cobalt."

Sabrina thought for a moment. "You have the black leggings from the urban street punk trend, right?"

"I wore them last Thursday."

Sabrina's mouth twisted. "Then I don't know. Would stovepipes work? Or you could do tights the way Olivia —"

"I hate that look," I interrupted.

"Me too."

I dug into the pile on my bed and pulled out my maroon stovepipe pants. I hit them with the trendchecker, just to be safe. Green light — still wearable. I shoved them on the bed under the tunic and turned the Unum to show Sabrina the look. "I like it," I heard her say.

It wouldn't be my best outfit, not by far, but it would do. "Fine," I said, rotating the Unum back so I could see her. I wiggled my fingers in front of the screen. "My nails are yellow, though."

She shook her head. "You are going to be so late."

I stumbled down the curved stairs of our apartment, clutching the handle of my briefcase in one hand and fanning the fingers of the other hand to dry my nail polish. My mother, Karen, stood in the front hall, smiling at me and holding a titanium travel mug. She made two lattes every morning, one for me and one for my father, who was undoubtedly sipping his on the train already.

Even in my rush, I noticed that Karen's hair looked good. She'd finally mastered the four-quadrants-of-the-scalp method I'd shown her. The wavy part in the back was bone straight, tamed by the flatiron.

"Don't worry, honey. You'll make it. And you look great," she said brightly.

I kissed her on the cheek and grabbed the mug of latte, spilling some on the bamboo floorboards on my way to the front door. Pausing to flip the lid cover closed, I nicked my thumb on the plastic, and a streak of clear nail cut through the brown polish. I pursed my lips in frustration.

"Oh, Marla, don't have a big lunch." Karen had grabbed a dishtowel from the kitchen and was kneeling down to wipe the spill. "I'm trying a new paella recipe tonight."

"Sure. Your hair looks prime, by the way!" I called over my shoulder as I yanked the apartment door open and ran to catch the elevator.

Outside, a warm winter breeze rustled the sidewalk palm trees. I jogged past the white and yellow high-rises and held my hand out to stop traffic as I crossed two intersections. My station was just ahead. My coffee sloshing inside the mug, I flew up the railway steps as my train sighed to a stop at the platform. I joined the crowd pressing through the doors and looked around for a free seat.

I didn't bother trying to locate Braxton. I knew he would have caught an earlier train, just like Sabrina. Finding a spot, I laid my briefcase across my lap and released my breath in a loud exhale. I was never late for anything. I hated this feeling. Maybe, for a backup alarm, I could buy a second Unum … or did we have an old alarm clock somewhere in the apartment?

The morning light danced across the domed ceiling of the train, and I sat back to watch it. Out of the corner of my eye, I could see heads turn as a few travelers recognized me. Hoping they weren't picking apart my outfit, I ignored them. I pictured my empty seat on the Superior Court bench — and Julia's look of disapproval — and willed the train to move faster.

Chapter Two

*I*vy let her legs hover in the open door of the urban utility vehicle before stepping out. Even though she was wearing a giant pair of Torro-LeBlanc sunglasses, she squinted in the glare of the camera flashes.

As usual, her bodyguards muscled through the crowd, clearing a path along the sidewalk to the store entrance. Fatima, her publicist, followed, with her Unum to her ear and her head cocked to one side. Ivy was next, surrounded by her nymphs. Madison and Aiko linked arms on either side of her, matching their strides to hers. Hilarie and Naia brought up the rear.

The procession moved slowly, not because the photographers blocked its way, but because it was an arranged photo op. As Fatima always reminded them, there was no point in going to so much trouble for blurry pictures. Ivy pressed her lips together in her signature pout, tilted her chin down, and stared directly into the camera flashes as she strutted forward.

Today she was modeling the Rudolfo label's armed-forces trend. She wore a tube dress in a fatigue pattern, combat boots, and a shiny necklace of dog tags attached end to end. A black leather bag with silver studs hung off her shoulder. Her nymphs were dressed in complementary fashion: Aiko had on a sailor dress; Hilarie wore baggy Gestapo pants and a T-shirt with TELL ME YOUR SECRETS printed across the front; Naia sported a bomber jacket and goggle headband. Madison wore a sleeveless jumpsuit of the same fatigue print as Ivy's dress. Ivy glanced at the bandoleer slung over her nymph's shoulder like a beauty queen's sash. She probably should have traded her necklace for the ammunition belt. It looked so tough and edgy on Madison. Oh, well. Too late now — obviously, she wouldn't debut the trend a second time.

Halfway to their destination, Fatima, who was still on the call, nodded to Ivy. Ivy cupped her hand over her mouth and whispered into Aiko's ear: "Time to laugh, girl."

Ivy and Aiko smirked at each other. Tiny giggles bubbled out of their mouths. Ivy quickly turned to Madison and whispered through a cupped hand: "I am the funniest person you've ever met."

The three girls exploded in laughter. Hilarie and Naia picked up the cue and joined in. All five of them directed their grinning mouths toward the cameras. As always, Ivy was careful not to expose too much gum or crunch her chin into her neck. She and her nymphs kept laughing as the bodyguards held open the doors to the Torro-LeBlanc flagship store and stopped only when the doors were firmly shut behind them.

Ivy relaxed her face muscles and massaged her cheeks. She was used to laughing at nothing, but it always felt kind of stupid. Her gaze rose to the screens that were mounted on support beams. Torro-LeBlanc was broadcasting the Pop Beat channel. Karisma was performing; the band's raw sound filled the vast store, from its cement and sea glass floor to its warehouse-style ceiling, where exposed gray pipes zigzagged in a wild maze. She hoped they would eventually play "Swollen." No matter how many hits she had, it still gave her a rush to hear her tracks broadcast in public.

Her bare shoulders were suddenly cold in the aggressive air-conditioning. "It's kind of freezing in here," she said to the nearest employee, a middle-aged man with a shock of dyed yellow hair.

"I'm so sorry, Miss Wilde. We'll fix that right away," he replied, and jogged to the back of the store. While she stood hugging her shoulders, she watched her entourage of nymphs drift magnetically toward the racks of clothes on shiny gold hangers. Torro-LeBlanc personal shoppers swarmed them, offering to assist. They had the store to themselves for an hour before it would be opened to the general public. Ivy swallowed a yawn — it was on the early side. But she'd be okay as soon as they got started.

Ready, set, shop. The lyric from the old Torro-LeBlanc ad came to mind, and she hummed it. Eyeing the new late-winter styles, she headed toward the racks.

Chapter Three

With about a million other commuters, I got off at the Fashion Row stop in downtown La Reina. I guarded my latte carefully — that was all I needed this morning, to have someone freak out because I spilled a drop on their Zhang & Tsai jacket. Or worse, after making it all this way, to spill it on myself. I turned the corner and, freeing myself from the crowd, ran up the steps of Torro-LeBlanc. I pulled open the design house's heavy doors. Hurrying through the vast lobby of pink marble, I saw that the mannequins in their glass cases had been regarmented. There it was, the plumed velvet hat we'd approved a few weeks ago. Gorgeous, just as I remembered it. There wasn't time to pull out my Unum now. I could order it during the break.

A clog of employees blocked the gold elevators. As politely as I could, I snaked through, slipped into one that was almost full, and barked "five" at the voicebox. I looked at my watch as the doors closed. Eight fifty-eight. I would just make it.

The elevator doors parted on the fifth floor to reveal Julia waiting for me. Immediately, my stomach tightened.

She was wearing a black miniskirt and one of Torro-

LeBlanc's latest pieces, a sleeveless sweater made of dyed-turquoise bear fur. She had one hand on her hip. The taut skin over her cheekbones sparkled in the hallway lights, and shiny gloss covered her unsmiling lips.

My apologies bubbled forth. "Oh my gosh, Julia, I'm so sorry. My Unum died and my alarm didn't go off. I don't know what's wrong with me. It won't happen again. Ever," I said in a gush.

Julia glanced at her wrist. "According to my watch, you're just under the wire, honey," she said in her deep and silky voice. But she still didn't smile. "Come." She cocked her head toward the end of the hall. "Let's walk and talk."

I swallowed and stepped out of the elevator. After working under Julia for nearly two years, I knew that to "walk and talk" was usually not a good sign. And to make matters worse, Julia was in four-inch platform heels today. The higher the heels, the slower the walk.

I prayed my stovepipes looked okay with the tunic.

"You've always delivered for us, Marla," she began, as she strode deliberately along the corridor to the garment-judging room. "You spent, what, only six months as a sifter before you were promoted to selector? Highly unusual, but Torro-LeBlanc believed in your talent."

It was actually five months, but I didn't correct her.

"And I'll never forget that frayed shawl you convinced the court to approve for the bohemian trend in the late fall line," Julia continued. "It remained a hot item for almost three months. You had an *eye* for the hot sellers."

I knew what shawl she was talking about. It had been so soft, its colors warm and rich like blurred chalk in the rain. I had taken a chance on it, and I'd been right. I didn't have the heart to throw mine away when its trendiness expired. I could see it in my head, balled up in the back of my closet at home. Karen didn't even know it was there.

"But for some time I've been wondering about your eye," Julia said. "What's happening with you? Garment lengths, sweater cuts, accessories . . . these days, the court goes one way and you go the other. I'm noticing a lot of dissenting opinions. Or you're the only one sticking your neck out for something."

Was I? Last week, I had fought for a maroon opera cloak embellished with gold embroidery. The rest of the court had called it feeble and overruled my defense, but I had loved its romantic feel. The week before that, I'd been alone in defending a hemp bag that earned gagging noises from two other judges, including the almighty Henry. Okay, that one I might have been wrong about.

Sure enough, Julia confirmed my suspicions. "That cloak you voted to approve the other day. Let's be honest — it was absolutely hideous!"

I knew she wanted me to agree with her. "I guess you're right," I said slowly. "I thought it would align with the musketeer trend, though." The cloak came into sharper focus in my head. I remembered thinking it was charming, thinking the court had made a huge mistake not approving it. Was I really the one mistaken?

Julia looked at me for a moment and shook her head. "*I* don't want to stop believing in you," she said, turning to face me as we reached the garment–judging room door. "I have always told the sixth floor you remind me of a young *me*, during my days on the Superior Court." Her expression grew wistful, as it always did when she spoke of the past. "We made frosted eyeglasses the midwinter must-have before any other design house. It was a golden time." I resisted rolling my eyes. We heard about the eyeglasses approximately once a season.

"*I* have been the one convincing management that they should still believe in you too," Julia went on. "But you should know, Marla, that there are those who think you've peaked. After all, you're almost seventeen. There has been talk of moving you down to the basement . . ."

I couldn't believe what I was hearing. "But I'm only — I'm not — that's not fair!" I stammered. I instantly thought of Winnie. "Winnie Summers was a judge until she was nineteen!"

"Winnie was an exception." Julia sighed. "You knew you wouldn't be on the court forever."

"But the basement? I thought I'd be an event planner or a shoot consultant when I got older. Or a catalog editor." I shuffled through Torro stats in my head. "Holcomb Flax became an editor. Shelley Mardirossian did runway prep."

That was the deal. Judges didn't end up in the basement. Especially judges like me. I remembered going down there on my first day of work, when my floor director gave the new sifters a tour. Hordes of drafters sat cramped together around tables in the dim light, sketching design after design, often going months without seeing one of their ideas endorsed for production. Most dressed badly because they worked on commission and couldn't afford to keep up with trends — but worse still, they were all so pathetically *old*.

Tears brimmed in my eyes, and I blinked them back. "Please, Julia. You can't do this to me. Torro is my life," I said.

Julia's voice grew silkier. "Now, honey, I know that you'll show them all. Get in there and remind everyone why you're on the fifth floor." She smiled, revealing a mouthful of perfectly even, polished white teeth. "I'm glad we had this talk."

I turned the knob and entered the brightly lit garment-judging room, followed by Julia. I was the last judge to arrive, and I could feel the others looking at the two of us curiously. As I sidled to my seat along the semicircular oak bench, I wondered if they knew what Julia had spoken to me about. Gossip traveled fast at Torro-LeBlanc.

My hands trembling, I removed my Tabula from my briefcase, set it on the bench, and turned it on. I opened a fresh template with the heading EARLY SPRING GARMENT REVIEW: NOTES BY JUDGE MARLA KLEIN. I glanced to my left where Sabrina sat. She mouthed the words *Nice pants* and gave me a small smile. Maybe I was overreacting.

"Very well, judges, let's begin," Julia announced. "Our first piece of the day is a knee-length double-breasted trench coat by drafter Kevin Chen."

As soon as the drafter wheeled his dress form into the judging room, I knew this garment would never be approved. No one was wearing knee-length coats these days, and gabardine hadn't been in for several seasons. Looking around at everyone's expressions of disgust, I could tell they all agreed. The coat itself wasn't bad-looking, but I wondered how it had made it all the way to the fifth floor.

Kevin stood next to the dummy, rubbing his hands together. "Hello, everyone," he began. "It's great to see you again. It's been a while." I felt Julia's eyes on me and didn't dare smile at him. He plunged on. "So here I have a piece that could compete with the Rudolfo armed-forces collection. I was going for sort of a classic officer thing." He waved his arms at us. "Imagine the front lines of battle, dirty-faced troops all around. An imposing figure cuts through the mist wearing . . . this." He pulled on the coat's sleeve. "It's got that commanding feel, that mystique. Everyone's going to want one."

I cringed. His pitch was sounding feebler by the minute.

"I know that the trench hasn't been in for two seasons," Kevin continued, "but I thought that if Torro-LeBlanc brought it back before the other houses, we'd have a competitive edge. Plus, gabardine is water-resistant. Perfect for spring!"

Listening to Kevin, I realized how his design had made it upstairs. The sifters and selectors had been afraid that if they let the coat go and trenches came back this season, they'd be in trouble.

On the far left of the semicircle of judges, Olivia spoke first. Even though she was a recent appointment to the fifth floor, she wasn't shy about expressing her opinions. "I don't think there's *any* chance of trench coats coming back *any*time soon," she said. "I don't know what you were thinking. And the cut, and the buttons — it's all wrong."

"I completely agree," said Henry. He was one of the two boys on the court and the only judge who predated me. "No one is buying knee-length anything these days. How can you look at that feeble mess and expect it would sell? I'd laugh if I saw someone wearing it."

"I think that's enough," Julia broke in. "Would any of the judges care to defend Kevin's design?"

No one spoke.

"Thank you, Kevin. Better luck next time," Julia clucked as she ushered the drafter outside. I felt bad for him, but he probably knew the rejection was coming. "Judges, don't forget to enter your formal notes," Julia instructed.

I typed: *Trench coat: Classic design but drafter completely misread current trends.* No one could take issue with that, could they?

The next drafter to enter was a woman named Tess Peterson. Tess was the one who had spawned the bear-fur trend with a fur purse she had designed. I saw her smile at Julia's sweater as she walked to the center of the room carrying her prototype.

"Hi again, everyone," Tess said, her voice betraying the nerves that simmered beneath her confident smile. "As you all know, I love working with fur, and I've been thinking about boots for this spring. Last season, the prime rage was the knee-high flat boot covered in unworsted lamb's wool. So for *this* season, I'd like to propose something that builds on that style. Here is a full-coverage high-heeled boot done in . . ." She paused for effect. "Alpaca fur!"

I heard immediate murmurs of approval from some of the judges. Tess held up the boot and turned it around slowly for us to see. She flexed it at the knee joint to demonstrate the smoothness of the bending mechanism.

Looking around at the grins of admiration, I wondered what the others could possibly be thinking. Alpaca boots for early spring? Seriously?

Utterly ridiculous, I typed. *Are we trying to look like yeti? And what are the things going to smell like when it rains?*

But I hesitated to speak. I listened to the judges flood Tess with praise for her design. Could Julia be right? Was I losing my touch? I sat in silence, my fingers tugging and twisting my tunic hem, as the boot was officially approved for production. My right hand stabbed at my Tabula screen to delete my comment. I retyped: *Alpaca boots: Build well on late-winter trend.*

I took a sip of the latte dregs and tried to clear my head. I had been *chosen* to be on the fifth floor from all the other Taps on the Junior Courts. I *deserved* to be there. Didn't I? I turned to Sabrina. "I really hope those hit big this season, Brie," I said, with as much enthusiasm as I could muster.

Sabrina, who was beaming over the boot, launched into a monologue about the different Torro-LeBlanc miniskirts that would coordinate perfectly. She ticked them off on her fingers. Feeling queasy, I forced myself to nod in agreement.

Tess thanked us profusely and left.

Fortunately, for the rest of the day I found myself in agreement with the other judges on the looks that passed before the court. We spent our final hour sorting the approved garments into various lines and noting where there were holes so we could tell the sifters and selectors what to keep an eye out for.

After work, I got off at my stop but didn't go home immediately. I decided to take a walk in the park near my apartment. I went there whenever work got crazy — it helped clear my head. I loved this park. It was filled with palm and eucalyptus trees. Mothers pushed their kids on the swings, as Karen had pushed me when I was little.

I put down my briefcase and took a seat on a swing. The breeze, sweetened by the honeyed scent of the flowers, refreshed me. As I began to pump forward and backward, the Unum in my pocket buzzed. It was a message from Braxton, but I tucked it away without responding. I could call him later.

I thought about my choice. I did have a choice, after all. Going forward, I could wait for someone else on the court to speak first. I knew this would be what my mother would tell me to do. Once it was clear which way the scales were tipping on any given garment, I could join the majority. Or I could keep arguing for the pieces I felt were special and risk losing my seat. I hadn't gotten as far as I had at Torro-LeBlanc by keeping my opinions to myself. I loved fashion. Maybe my judgment was off now and then, but my bosses had always told me I had good instincts for choosing things people would want to wear.

But maybe it was time to shut up for a while.

Next to me, a little girl squealed as her mother pushed her higher and higher. She looked so carefree it made me feel heavy.

"Your clothes are lovely," the mother said to me as I hopped off the swing. "Do you work for one of the Big Five?"

"Torro-LeBlanc," I answered. Normally I was so proud of the fact, but today I didn't elaborate. I gathered my briefcase, returned home, and tossed quick hellos at my mother, who was scrubbing mussels in the kitchen, and at my father, who was stretched out on the couch, playing a video game on his Tabula. After locking the door to my room, I dug my expired shawl out of the back of my closet and rubbed the soft knit between my fingers. I had convinced a reluctant court to approve it once, and it had stayed trendy for ten weeks. No matter what Julia said, I *did* have an eye for fashion.

Chapter Four

"H old on, girls," *yelled Fatima.* Ivy turned to see her publicist sink into a cushioned bench near the Torro-LeBlanc store's entrance and cross her legs. "Prime shoot. I'm sure they got some good ones. I'll check Maven Girl and the other hotspots in a bit." She began scrolling across the screen of her Unum. "Jarvis sent me your schedule for the next couple of weeks. Here we go. Listen up!" she called out, pausing to confirm that everyone was paying attention. Ivy herself was curious. Except for major events like her tour, she never had more than a vague sense of what was coming. "There's the album-release party," began Fatima, "three promo gigs, the *Entertainment Daily* Correspondents' Dinner, the Belladonna runway show, and four club nights, one ending in a disorderly-conduct arrest."

"Again?" groaned Ivy.

"Sorry, girl, gotta keep you 'Wilde,'" said Fatima with a wink. "Oh, and you'll need looks for a few more shopping photo ops, too." She smiled and tipped her black military cap at the girls. "So go nuts."

"Don't worry," said Madison. "I've already mentally bought half the store." The other nymphs grinned in agreement.

As usual, Ivy went first, pointing to the clothing she wanted to try on: "That top with the plastic stripy things. Those jeans in purple." Attendants grabbed her requests and stacked them over their arms. The personal shoppers held out other garments for her to consider. Her bleariness from the early morning vanished. To shop like this, to be able to choose whatever she wanted, was definitely one of the best parts of being Ivy Wilde. She held a beige safari shirtdress in front of her body and turned to her entourage for input. Hilarie gave her a nod. Ivy was grateful that her nymphs were usually pretty honest. They would tell her when they thought a color or a cut was unflattering but would never try to talk her out of something she absolutely loved. She'd heard stories about other nymphs sabotaging their celebrities by giving them bad advice in order to outshine them during a shoot.

Taking note of her choices, other personal shoppers grabbed coordinating looks for her nymphs, who themselves gathered armfuls of additional pieces that appealed to them. Finally, laden with nearly the entire Torro-LeBlanc late-winter line and giggling with anticipation, the whole group headed to the dressing rooms.

Ivy tugged garment after garment over her head. She loved the freshness and fantasy of each piece. She would emerge from her dressing room and stand on the platform in front of the brightly lit three-way mirror, pouting at her reflection, imagining how a certain halter top would look in her favorite nightclub, how well a pair of denim cutoffs would photograph from behind. She could visualize the moment when she'd wear the clothes, complete with the crowd of people staring at her. She took her time, picturing herself through their eyes.

Not caring if the store staff saw their underwear — it was

designer, after all — the girls ran back and forth between dressing rooms to trade clothing or offer a quick opinion. Sometimes they gathered in front of a mirror to see how they looked as a group. They put their disorderly-conduct-arrest look together with little trouble, though Aiko had to part with a pair of alligator stilettos that Ivy wanted to wear. Aiko was nice about it, assuring Ivy, "Clayton's totally going to think those are hot."

"The higher the better, he always tells me," Ivy said with a straight face. "Even when heels aren't in, he wants me to wear them."

"Isn't that always the way," said one of the personal shoppers, nodding her head knowingly.

"You two are such a great couple, Miss Wilde," said another, beaming. "I'm a huge Clayton Pryce fan. Do you two, you know, *sing* when you're together?"

"Yeah, not so much," said Ivy. "We're kind of busy doing other things." The shopper's eyes widened. "Aiko!" called Ivy. "Can you bring me the black and white boa?"

The girls' "yes" pile grew bigger and bigger. Soon, smiling Torro-LeBlanc employees were recruited to begin packaging the clothes in boxes and garment bags.

Ivy exited her dressing room wearing a gingham babydoll dress she thought looked cute. She stepped on the platform in front of the mirror and inspected herself from all angles. Naia, who was being zipped into a silk dress nearby, watched her.

"I kind of love this," Ivy said to Naia's reflection in the mirror.

"It looks *so prime* on you, Miss Wilde," said one of the personal shoppers as she hurried over to tug on the hem needlessly. "The fit is just right. Torro's anticipating a big prairie trend. You could be the one to launch it."

Naia wrinkled her nose. "It's cute — but is it 'Wilde' enough? You look like you should be milking cows. I don't think —"

"Oh, but what you do, of course, is play up the frontier angle," interrupted the personal shopper, showcasing a shiny plum manicure with enthusiastic gestures. "Have your makeup artist give you a dirty brow. Tie a bandanna around your neck. And the dress can look tougher. Jerry! Grab a pair of those ripped tights from the display case."

Naia shrugged. "Whatever. If you like it, Ivy." She smoothed her hands over her dress and examined herself in the mirror, raising herself up on the balls of her feet. "I'm going to need to see this with some heels," she said to another personal shopper, who nodded and hurried away.

Jerry returned with something that looked like a long, rolled spider's web draped over his upturned palms. Ivy's personal shopper lifted the tights delicately with her manicured fingertips and handed them to her. "Trust me. Just try them on."

Back inside the dressing room, Ivy sat down on the bench. She carefully gathered one of the tights' delicate legs in her fists, stuck her toes inside, and pulled the fabric over her ankle and calf. She was rounding her knee when she caught sight of the price tag dangling off the waistband label. She caught it between her thumb and forefinger to double-check that she had read it correctly.

One hundred fifty-nine dollars. She so rarely glanced at price tags these days. Her record label, Warwick, paid for her clothing; even if it didn't, her salary could easily cover her shopping sprees. But one hundred fifty-nine dollars for tights. Could that be right?

In an instant, she remembered why that number felt significant to her. It had been the price of her first pair of slicers. Her parents had paid for half, and she had saved her allowance for two months to cover the other half. She recalled the moment of finally, *finally* bringing them home from the store, strapping them on, and tottering up and down her sidewalk. After falling hard and often, she'd gotten the hang of it, and had eventually learned all sorts of tricks like skating backward and stopping short. She'd loved whizzing around her neighborhood on those blades full of tiny ball bearings, the pavement smooth underfoot, the wind in her face . . . Ivy sat in the dressing room, half dressed, lost in the memory.

The music changed to a thumping dance beat and splintered her thoughts. She looked down at her leg, now covered in a mess of holes and slashed fabric. One hundred fifty-nine dollars. For one pair of ripped tights. To wear with one dress . . . once. Yes, she could afford it, no problem. Yes, she was a star, and stars had to wear Big Five labels. She didn't think about money much, but every so often, something like the tights reminded her how different her new life was from her old . . .

In a swift motion, she pulled off the tights and removed the dress without looking at its price tag. She fished in her handbag for her placidophilus tin and shook it. It was empty. Cursing, she slid back into her tube dress, then stepped out of the dressing room holding the gingham dress and tights. She thrust them at the personal shopper. "No to both."

"Are you sure, Miss Wilde?"

Ivy nodded. "Positive."

The personal shopper didn't miss a beat. "Well, perhaps you'll be interested in something else from the safari line instead?"

Ivy ignored her. "Hilarie? Mad? I'm out of P pills. Anybody got some?"

"IS THE REIGN OF THE 'WILDE' CHILD OVER?" The

question resounded across the store. Ivy looked up at the nearest screen and saw the source of the voice: a young *Pop Beat Newsbreak* reporter with spiked black hair and lined eyes. He sat behind a desk; a photograph of Ivy hovered above his left shoulder. Ivy recognized her devil's costume from her *Girl Gone Wilde* tour the previous year.

"Ivy Wilde's single 'Swollen' is holding at number one this week, but a new singing sensation is challenging the naughty princess's claim to the pop throne." Slowly, Ivy's nymphs peeled back their dressing room curtains and stared at the screens.

"Newcomer Lyric Mirth debuted at number six this week with 'So Pure It Hurts,'" continued the reporter. "Sources say her self-titled album may go platinum by fall. Furthermore, Sugarwater, which has long featured Wilde in its advertising, is taking a gamble on the new artist with its prominent Rock Row billboard." Ivy drew in her breath as the screen flashed an image of the giant ad. Lyric, dressed all in white, hovered in midair, giant white wings extending from her shoulders. She held a Sugarwater bottle and sipped the brown liquid through a straw, her eyes open in wide innocence. Ivy felt like blackening both of them.

"Wilde and Mirth were both tapped onto *The Henny Funpeck Show*, which launches so many music careers," the reporter went on, interlacing his fingers. "Mirth is quoted as saying that she has always admired Wilde's success and hopes to follow in her footsteps. She may get her wish sooner than she thinks, as certain critics find Mirth's angelic voice and style a refreshing antidote to Wilde's devilish antics. But don't take our word for it. Here's 'So Pure It Hurts,' by Lyric Mirth!"

Not bothering to listen past the opening chord progression, Ivy flew back into her dressing room. She grabbed her Unum and shouted "Jarvis!" at it. Moments later her agent's face appeared on the screen. His look of amusement was maddening.

"Did you see it?" she demanded breathlessly.

"Kiddo, just *relax*." His voice was calm, almost lazy. "We've seen this before. We'll see it again."

"But the poster — and the album sales —"

"Uh-huh. So she's got the spotlight. For a whole fifteen minutes. Let the poor kid enjoy it. Once you release your album and start touring, she'll be buried."

"But —"

"Have I *ever* been wrong?"

"But . . . they said . . ." Her voice dropped to a whisper. "They said my reign might be . . ." She couldn't bring herself to finish.

Jarvis ran his fingers through his gray hair and chuckled. "Let me tell you when you're in danger of fossilizing, will you? I promise, you'll hear it from me first. In the meantime, take a P pill and *don't worry about it*."

"I remember Lyric." Ivy bit her lip, thinking about their brief period of overlap at *Henny Funpeck*. "She's a good performer."

"You're better. Just relax, kiddo. Okay?"

She sighed. "I'll try."

"Oh, one thing. Tell Fatima. We've canceled the Correspondents' Dinner. Not enough coverage. Instead, you're going to be the guest of honor at Millbrook's Tap."

Millbrook. Ivy smiled in spite of herself. She'd been home only a handful of times since her own Tap, far less frequently since her career had picked up. She wondered what it would be like, how it had changed, how her family was doing.

"It's Constantine's year," she said softly.

"Thought you'd like to be there for that." Jarvis winked.

"We'll spruce it up, tons of photo ops, stream the ceremony, the whole deal. Who's the best agent in the world?"

Ivy rolled her eyes. "Cocky, much?" She paused. "No, really, Jarvis. Thanks. I — it'll be nice to go home."

He nodded. "I know, kiddo." Ivy heard two faint beeps coming from the screen. "Whoops — gotta go," said Jarvis. "It's *Pillow Party*. I'm working on a guest spot for you. You getting some good clothes today?"

"Yeah."

"Good. We'll talk soon. Stay young."

The Unum screen went black.

After the day of shopping at Torro-LeBlanc and the other four flagship design stores in La Reina, Ivy was exhausted. The group had a quick dinner at Saltimbocca, and Fatima drove the urban utility vehicle, now stuffed with bags and boxes, back to Ivy's estate. Although her nymphs lingered in the kitchen, blending smoothies for dessert, Ivy announced she was going straight to bed.

In her bedroom, she pawed through her drawers in mounting frustration. She opened the door to her closet and wearily climbed the spiral staircase. Fatima was on the second floor, going through Ivy's rows of clothes with two assistants and a gold trendchecking gun. Little rubies gleamed along its barrel.

The three of them were hanging Ivy's new purchases and getting rid of the clothes that had expired before Ivy had had a chance to wear them. She stared at the giant pile of discarded clothing on the floor. *One hundred and fifty-nine dollars* flew back into her head; she tried not to think about what all those crumpled, unworn items had cost.

"Yes?" said Fatima, scanning the label of a floral pin. She

ripped it off the jacket to which it had been attached and tossed it onto the discard pile. "I thought you were going to bed."

"I'm trying. Where are my Millbrook sweats?"

"Those grimy things?" said Fatima. "I tossed them."

"*What?*"

"What if there was a fire in the house?" demanded Fatima. "You run outside in the middle of the night and get photographed in *sweatpants*? Your image is ruined! Plus, you'd better get used to looking good all the time for the reality cameras. Filming starts again in a few months when the tour begins."

Ivy sighed. "So what do I sleep in?"

"Here." Fatima walked over to the closet bar on the opposite wall. She lifted a shiny black outfit on a hanger and held it out to Ivy.

"You've got to be kidding. What is that made of?"

"It's a new patent leather–vinyl blend. They're calling it 'shale' or 'scale' or something. Bancroft House came up with it. Not exactly cotton, I know, but get over it. You've got to let the world know you're 'Wilde' — even when you sleep."

Back in her bedroom, Ivy snapped the stretchy tank top over her head and pulled it down around her torso with difficulty. She wriggled into the matching shorts and climbed under the covers, squeaking as she moved. Sighing, she fumbled on her nightstand for a placidophilus pill and popped it into her mouth. The scent of strawberries filled her nose. She chewed, waiting for the pill to kick in, for her nightclothes to feel suddenly comfortable, for her day of shopping to turn into a pleasant memory, for her worries about Lyric Mirth to disappear.

Chapter Five

The morning after Julia told me I was in danger of losing my seat on the court, I arrived at the station ten minutes before the train arrived. My nail polish was fully dry. I wasn't taking any chances.

When the train pulled up, I was the first one through the door. Aboard, I pulled out my Unum and used it to locate which car Braxton was riding in. I spotted him in the crowd and waved.

"Hey, babe!" Braxton called, beckoning me over. He was wearing his black Denominator Films baseball cap. In the seat across from him, I could see Sabrina's blond ponytail. I held my latte above my head as I navigated my way down the center aisle toward them.

I slid into the seat next to Braxton. He squeezed my knee and gave me a quick kiss on the neck. I loved the way he smelled, like a fresh shower. "You made it," he said.

"I actually got up at a decent hour this morning." My father had found me a backup alarm clock in our basement storage unit, but the truth was, I had woken before either alarm went off. I'd stared at the red numbers on the clock, my brain buzzing. I hadn't mentioned Julia's warning to Braxton or to my parents. I told myself it was because I didn't want to worry them, but deep down I knew I was the worried one. Besides, it was totally humiliating. Braxton had never mentioned getting a warning like this at Denominator.

"Just get a cat." Sabrina popped her earbuds out of her ears. "Chubbs sits on my head every morning until I yell at my mother to feed him. He's better than an alarm." She crossed her legs so that her foot stuck into the aisle. "Braxton was talking about the summer action season."

Braxton grinned and flicked his eyebrows up and down really fast, just once. I loved that little tic of his. "Just wait for it to start up. All I have to say is: Junie Woo and Kev duPrince. Dismantling an underwater bomb. *While battling electric eels.*"

Another Kev duPrince flick. Much as I wanted to be enthusiastic, it was hard. The last three Braxton had dragged me to had made my head throb — something blew up every five minutes. Not wanting to hurt his feelings, I nodded my encouragement.

"I guess that sounds okay," said Sabrina. "I'm so over Kev duPrince, though." She picked a stray cat hair off her leggings and blew it over her shoulder. "He's kind of fossilized on us by now, don't you think?"

Braxton frowned. "You're making me nervous. Half the court at Denominator wanted to replace him with Jason Steelpacker, but the senior members overruled them. Kev was dominant through the whole *Ghouls of Rockaway* franchise."

He looked so distraught that I waved my hand to dismiss his concerns. "You're the expert, Brax. You've been Denominator's golden boy ever since the Tap. Don't worry about it."

It was true. Braxton and I had been promoted to Superior Court judge at our respective companies within months of each other. We'd met at a release party for a Jennifer Tildy rom-com — Torro had contributed some wardrobe pieces for the film. He'd told me he liked my hat. Next thing I knew, the hat was lost on the floor somewhere and we were making out in a corner.

"I guess," Braxton said. He was still frowning.

A group of girls standing in the center aisle exploded in laughter. I looked up. They were a year or two younger than I was — probably selectors. They were clustered around a single Unum, while one girl scrolled across its screen. From their comments, I guessed they were looking at an online fashion magazine. They pointed to the screen and shrieked like seagulls about the featured styles.

"They Torro-LeBlanc?" asked Braxton.

"No." I noted the mirror ball bag that hung off one girl's shoulder. "Bancroft House, I think," I said, checking with Sabrina for confirmation. She nodded.

One of the girls caught me looking up at her. Her face brightened with recognition. "You're on Torro's court, aren't you?" she said, turning away from her friends.

Before I could answer, Sabrina piped in. "Yes, we are, and no, we don't have any tips for you. We're just trying to ride to work in peace."

"Whatever." I felt the girl's gaze travel up and down my outfit. "Nice pin," she muttered before turning back to the group.

"Nice face," Sabrina shot back.

I looked down at the silk chrysanthemum pin that blossomed on the lapel of my cropped riding jacket. I had remembered to scan it this morning, hadn't I? No way it could be expired. Lapel pins had come in again only last season . . .

"Obsoloser. Don't listen to her," said Sabrina. "You always

look prime, Marla. Here, check out the new single by this Lyric Mirth girl. It's gonna be huge. I can tell already."

Sabrina stuffed an earbud into my ear, and the thumping beat drove the uneasiness out of my head. I listened to Lyric's bright voice belt out the chorus:

> *Don't touch my body*
> *Don't kiss my face*
> *Between our hearts*
> *Leave an infinite space*
> *I want to hurt*
> *Let's keep things pure*
> *So pure it hurts,*
> *So pure it hurts . . .*

My hands were clammy when I took my seat on the bench, but the morning passed well. I found myself in a natural majority on most decisions. The last drafter even tried to push through a suede vest, and I enjoyed deconstructing his argument that suede was really a spring fabric. One of the judges, Ginnifer, had totally backed me up. I was starting to feel comfortable in my chair again.

Julia gestured in the next drafter and introduced her as Vivienne Graves. I couldn't remember the last time I'd seen her. Vivienne was thin with black hair. She wore dark clothes and had dark circles under her eyes. Appropriately, the design on her dummy was a black dress. I inhaled as soon as I saw it. It was one of the loveliest pieces anyone had ever wheeled into the garment-judging room. It fell below the knee, creating a natural silhouette. It was sleeveless with a modest V neckline, and the fabric with which it was made rippled like a dark pond. I wanted to dive into it. I immediately typed: *Black dress: Stunningly simple, comfortable, elegant, the new look of early spring. Yes!*

"I was going for something simple and elegant," Vivienne began. Her voice was strong but raspy. "Everywhere I look I see bright colors and metallics, and they're starting to make me dizzy. I'm not saying that they're bad," she added quickly. "I just thought a return to the black dress might be welcome for some this season."

The silence that met these remarks was uncertain. I looked around at the judges but couldn't read their faces. I wanted to begin my endorsement . . . but what if everyone else hated it?

Finally, Henry spoke. "While *you* may prefer something this simple and dark, I'm not sure other people would. What's fun about it? Where's the trend potential? I just — don't get it."

"Yes," Olivia said slowly. "I think I agree with Henry. It's pretty boring. Maybe if it had a fur-lined collar, or some beading on the bottom — but without any accessorizing I don't see how it's special."

"Totally, Livy," Sabrina said, piling on. "If it were released, its trendiness would probably expire in a week."

One by one, the judges agreed. The dress was dull; it wasn't eye-catching; it needed to be more innovative. Vivienne stood by her creation, listening to everybody criticize it, one after the other. She finally turned her hollow eyes to me. Over Vivienne's shoulder, I saw Julia peering at me intently. I reread what I had typed on the screen and looked up again at the drafter in front of me. My right hand hovered over the delete button. But this time, instead of tapping away my opinion, I clenched my hand in a tight fist.

"Sorry, I love it," I proclaimed. "I think you're all wrong. I'll defend it. Torro will sell a million of these. I just know it."

At 5:03 p.m., Julia told me to stay put. After the other judges filed out of the garment-judging room, a CSS agent materialized in the doorway. We occasionally saw Corporate Security and Surveillance agents patrolling the building in their gray dress uniforms — all the creative industries were big on safety.

Julia informed me that my position on the Torro-LeBlanc Superior Court had been terminated. The following day, I was to report to the basement to begin work as a drafter. "No tears, now," she said firmly and walked out of the room. The CSS agent escorted me out of the building.

I spent the ride home from work with my face buried in Braxton's shoulder. I hated crying in front of him — but I didn't need everyone on the train to know I'd lost my seat. I tried to breathe deeply and swallow my sobs.

"It's just not right," Braxton kept whispering, as he rocked me gently. "You can't let them do this to you. You've got to get them to put you back on the court."

"What am I supposed to do?" I mumbled into his collarbone. "Julia said the decision was final."

"Get your mother to call your boss. She'll fix it."

I wasn't optimistic. Parents of Taps weren't even allowed in the design house. Then again, Karen wasn't the type to go down without a fight. Maybe she'd help me make the case for a second chance? I stoked the faint ember of hope for the remainder of the train ride through La Reina.

I decided to let the bad news out as swiftly as possible. I unlocked the door to the apartment and placed my briefcase on the kitchen counter. "Julia transferred me from the Superior Court to the basement." My voice caught on the word *basement*, and I cleared my throat. "She said I'm a drafter now."

My mother let the roasting pan she was scrubbing fall into the dishwater. She stared at me, wide-eyed. "What happened?"

"I have no idea." I thought of Vivienne's black dress, and my defense, which had been brutally crushed by the other judges. "I tried to push for this amazing dress, but apparently, I've lost my touch. Karen, do you think . . ."

I didn't have to finish the question. Karen was peeling off her soapy gloves and reaching for her Unum. She called Julia personally. I sat on one of the kitchen counter stools, rotating back and forth with nervous energy as I listened to the conversation. At first my mother spoke calmly, reminding Julia of my "gifted fashion instincts" and years of service to Torro-LeBlanc. When that didn't work, she pleaded for one more chance, alleging that the demotion had broken my heart. It was true — it had. Finally, to my surprise, she raised her voice and called Julia an "ungrateful shrew of a manager."

"I'll speak to your boss about this!" she screamed into the Unum before hitting the End Call button. She then called the vice president of human resources, who confirmed that Julia had final say in hiring and firing for the Superior Court. "Outrageous. What kind of show are the Silents running over there?" Karen muttered, thumbing across her Unum for the next number.

Even with my hopes sinking lower and lower, I loved my mother for her intensity. She had always been this way, 100 percent committed to me and my career. Deciding on the best sketches for my Tap page, editing my opinion entries, revising and re-revising the layout until it was perfect. And, after I'd been tapped, listening to my stories from the third floor of Torro-

LeBlanc, advising me on which selectors to kiss up to for a promotion, and on and on, until I'd made it to the top.

I listened as the chief creative officer's assistant deflected a final call to the executive office. Karen repeated her protests but hung up, defeated. We shared a look.

"I'm sorry," I said. I wasn't quite sure why I was apologizing, but I went over and put my arms around my mother. She hugged me back limply.

Dinner was awkward.

"Don't worry, sweetheart." Walter, my father, tried to be overly cheerful. "At least you're still working. Besides, you'll spend only a few more years at Torro. Once you're married, you'll have little ones of your own to take care of. Being a mother is the most important job in the world." He reached over and squeezed Karen's hand.

My mother blinked out of her vague funk and shot a smile at my father.

Marriage? Little ones? Was he for real? "Uh, I'm not exactly ready to get married," I said. I had been taking the train to Torro-LeBlanc since I was thirteen. It felt strange to think about doing anything else. I knew that some of my old classmates a couple of grades ahead were starting to have babies, but I couldn't even imagine that yet. I still felt way too young to give up my own work.

"A *drafter*, of all things." Karen shook her head in disgust. "Wouldn't you rather tell everyone you quit? We have some savings. There's your account, of course, and Walter's network is doing fine."

"We really could use the commissions, though," my father said quickly, his mouth full of the truffle-and-fontina flatbread.

"A prop master's salary isn't going to take us on vacation every year."

Karen ignored him. "You can stay home with me. We'll go shopping tomorrow, or to the salon, if you like . . ." She clasped her hands. "I know. We can make a lava cake together!"

My mother looked so excited that I felt bad letting her down. It *was* tempting. Days upon days of drafting designs like a robot, most of my ideas ending up in the garbage . . . or a long stretch of relaxation? The latter had been my mother's path. Karen had worked for a fashion house when she was younger, the now-defunct Grigoriev label. She'd served as a selector but had never been promoted to the courts. She'd then married my father, another Tap who worked at the Knox Network. Walter had judged for about a year and now handled props for Knox's television shows.

Karen had loved bragging to everyone within earshot about my quick rise to the top within Torro-LeBlanc. Not that I used to mind. I knew it would be a blow to have to tell her friends her daughter was now a drafter, but this wasn't my mother's life. It was mine. And something about Karen's days felt hollow. I was sixteen — could I really fill my next few years with shopping and baking and salon visits? How could I give up work altogether?

Then, of course, there was Braxton. What would he think if I just quit? I wasn't sure if quitting was better or worse than staying on as a drafter in his eyes.

"I'll see how I feel tomorrow morning. But I'll probably go. Even though I practically got fired, I still love Torro-LeBlanc," I said, shrugging. "It's my life."

"This flatbread is delicious, Karen. Really. You outdid yourself," Walter said, reaching for a fourth piece. I nodded in agreement. It was.

The next morning, I took an early train and curled up alone on a seat, avoiding eye contact with the other riders. I navigated the lobby of Torro-LeBlanc with my head down and waited in front of the elevators for one heading to the floor below.

"Hold the door!" Olivia shouted, jogging over. My now-former bench mate grabbed me by the elbow and yanked me into a nearly full elevator heading up. I wondered why her hands looked funny, like little raven's wings. I looked closer and recognized the accessory: she was wearing the feather gloves Torro was about to release. I felt a lurch of jealousy. Olivia had probably grabbed them out of the runway sample room to which the Superior Court judges had privileged access. I would have to wait until they were released now. And I didn't know if the commission from one sketch would even cover them fully. It wasn't fair. I should have grabbed the musketeer hat when I'd had the chance.

"I hear there's a fringe number coming in today that one of the Junior Courts approved unanimously," Olivia chirped. "Can't wait. Let's be honest, is fringe ever not fun?" She took a sip from her travel mug, and a tiny black feather floated away into the elevator compartment.

I should just tell her, I thought. *She'll know soon enough anyway.*

But I rode the elevator all the way to the fifth floor, and when Olivia got out, I mumbled an excuse about having left something in the lobby by mistake. Not meeting Olivia's eyes, I said "lobby" into the voicebox. Only when the door had closed did I add, clearly and quietly: "basement."

It was as depressing as I remembered. Rows of rectangular tables, with three feet of space between them, stretched from end to end. The drafters sat elbow to elbow, three on each side. Along the tables' middles, like centerpieces, copies of every fashion magazine on the market were scattered, along with white paper, pencils, pens, colored pencils, and markers. At least the lighting was better than I remembered — had they fixed that? — but the floor was concrete, and the walls were exposed brick painted a dingy white. The vast room felt cold. I would have to remember to wear an extra layer tomorrow. I tried to remember if any sort of cardigan was in right now.

Helplessly, I looked around as the drafters got settled for the morning. Some of them chatted with one another; a few were opening magazines and beginning to page through them. Others were filling their mugs in the near corner of the room, under a sign that spelled *Coffee Bar!* in pink neon. The sign's enthusiasm was unfounded. On the fifth floor, I had refilled my mug with caramel cappuccinos and mocha lattes that a shiny gold contraption frothed forth at the touch of a button. This was a countertop with some burners on which glass carafes of brown liquid sat, uncovered. Torn sweetener packets spilled their contents on the Formica surface. I couldn't believe how sad it all was.

"You must be the new one." I turned to find a solemn-faced bald man peering at me. He wore a gray pinstriped three-piece suit with a light blue tie. Ties, at least the kind that hung straight down, hadn't been trendy for a few seasons. And the suit — where to begin? Did he actually work for Torro-LeBlanc?

He consulted his Unum. "Marla Klein, is it?"

Did he really not know me by sight? It wasn't as if the Superior Court members were exactly a big secret in the company.

Still, I didn't want to say anything rude and screw things up on my first day. "Yes, I'm Marla."

"Welcome. Godfrey Gibson. Director of Torro-LeBlanc's Drafting Division." He was chewing something as he spoke. I picked up the scent of strawberries. Placidophilus pills. I was surprised, but I felt a little better. If he used, he probably wouldn't be a bad person to work for. Calm, anyway.

"We have your stool set up. My assistant will show you the ropes. Now, you must be here because you have some artistic talent worth speaking of. Have you sketched the human form before?"

I wondered what the right thing to say was. I hadn't tried to draw anything for years — hadn't needed to. I remembered the hundreds of fashion drawings I'd posted to my Tap site. I'd had a ton of hits, so I must have been pretty good back then. But what if my talent had dried up? "I used to be okay," I said, "but I haven't really sketched anything in a while. I've been looking at sketches for years, though, on the Superior Court. It's sort of the same thing, isn't it?"

I could feel Godfrey studying me. The pace of his chewing increased. "Of course," he said at last. "You'll get the hang of it. Winnie!" He snapped his fingers over my shoulder.

"Now we have one rule here," he continued. "Talking about anything other than fashion is discouraged. Run your ideas by your colleagues. Show them your sketches. But if your mind is on other things, you're not imagining new trends, and that's what Torro-LeBlanc is paying you for. Don't think we aren't watching. We are." He winked at me and laughed a high, fluty laugh.

His words gave me the creeps. The familiar face that appeared by his side, however, made me forget my worries. It was

Winnie Summers, the judge who had left the Superior Court just after I had begun serving on it.

"Hi, Marla! Thanks, Godfrey. I've got it from here."

Godfrey nodded and turned away.

"Nice to meet you!" I said as enthusiastically as I could to his back. He swiveled around and gave me a quick wink.

"It's *really* great to see you, Winnie," I told her. It was comforting to be with someone who could actually understand what I was going through. "Godfrey seems nice," I muttered as we walked along one side of the room. "But those clothes . . ."

Winnie shrugged. "He's so old he's just stopped caring. He's really all right, if you can look past the suit. So you're here now!" she said, beaming a bright smile at me. "Welcome to the basement!"

I tried my best to return the smile.

"Trust me, you're going to love it here," she continued. "I mean, the money's not as good as it was on the court, and you don't have the final say anymore, but you're *creating* the trends! You'll see someone walking down the street in your clothing and know *you* drafted the original garment. What's better than that?"

I leaned down to whisper into Winnie's ear as softly as I could. "But we always thought the drafters were sort of pathetic."

"Look around! There's nothing pathetic about your new colleagues."

I looked. Was Winnie nuts? For every drafter who was sketching intently, there was another idly folding a paper airplane or stabbing holes in a magazine page with a pencil point. Okay, maybe *pathetic* was harsh, but lots of people looked tired or distracted. Better coffee wouldn't hurt.

I recognized some familiar faces from the upper floors.

Carín was down here now, as were Bruce and Petra. They still wore trends. But the older the drafters got, the more obsolete they became. Some of the clothing gave Godfrey's suit a run for its money.

I also noticed that substantially fewer of the older drafters were women. The older men were generally the ones combing the magazines and sketching earnestly. This was odd, as girls tended to outnumber boys on the third, fourth, and fifth floors. "I didn't think this many guys worked at Torro," I said to Winnie.

"A lot of the women leave when they have children. Tap preparation becomes more of a priority. But you'll find some of the most inspired workers are the slightly more . . . *mature* men," Winnie said seriously. "The ones that are the principal wage earners in their families are especially motivated."

Desperate was more like it. I began to feel panic creep in. "I don't know if I can do this," I said. "Maybe I should go home today and think about it and start tomorrow."

Winnie faced me and grabbed my shoulders. "Marla, look at me. You're a drafter now, and you need to accept it. Trust me — it's really not that bad. Lots of people quit, but you could be really great. Torro would be sad to lose you. Give it two weeks. Then decide. 'Kay?"

I thought of home and imagined my mother painstakingly measuring the ingredients for the lava cake. I swallowed and nodded.

"Now," Winnie continued, "for the first week, nobody's expecting much. Don't even try to draft your own designs yet. Just copy models out of the magazines. You must have been good at art pre-Tap or you wouldn't be here. Retrain yourself. It'll be easier to communicate your own ideas later if you master some basics."

I thought back to working as a sifter. The sketches that looked elementary — like a toddler had drawn them — were never promoted beyond the third floor. Again, I hoped my artistic ability hadn't left me.

"There are those that believe in quantity," Winnie went on. "They try to maximize their chances by generating as many sketches as possible in a given day. One every half hour or so. Then there are those who work harder on fewer sketches. Either approach is fine. Whatever works for you."

We neared the end of one of the long rows of tables. Winnie gestured to an open stool. "Shout if you need anything. Happy drafting!" With a smile and a wave, she was gone.

I put down my travel mug and looked around at my five neighbors. Directly across from me was a guy with dark wavy hair whom I didn't remember seeing recently in front of the court. But I knew the drafters on either side of him. To his right, diagonally across from me, was the woman who had brought in the black dress yesterday: Vivienne Graves. Not surprisingly, she was again wearing a plain black turtleneck, no embellishments, no texturing. I wondered where she'd even found the piece. Kevin Chen, the designer of the terrible trench coat, sat to the guy's left.

On my own left was a girl with blond pigtails around the same age as I was. To my right sat an older drafter with graying hair.

The ring of faces stared at me. "Hi," I said, sitting down. No one replied. I couldn't think of what to say next, so I grabbed a piece of paper. As I reached for a pencil with my other hand, the drafter across from me spoke.

"Fresh meat, Viv," he said, nodding to his right. He grinned at me, not nicely. "How does the princess feel now that she's out of her little tower? Not so nice to swim in the moat with the fish, is it?"

I didn't respond. I opened a magazine and began to look at it.

"Stinks, in fact, doesn't it?" the drafter went on. He twirled his pencil slowly between all five fingers.

"I bet she owns a luxury trendchecker and scanned every article of clothing she has on," said Kevin, chuckling as he leaned back and folded his arms across his chest.

In spite of myself, I glanced up at Kevin. What was he getting at? Maybe he had an economy model, but it was obvious he scanned too. His blouse and musketeer vest were part of Torro's current line. But there was something different about the vest — something about the proportions of the silver cross, and the way the thread on the border was fraying . . . It hit me. It was a *knockoff*. And this drafter was shamelessly wearing it inside the design house that manufactured the original. Where was his self-respect?

"You'll soon get over that little habit," Kevin continued. "Trendchecking gets too depressing."

"Thanks for the tip," I said, looking down once again at my magazine. My mother was always talking about catching flies with honey, and smiling your way to the top, and stuff like that. I really, *really* wanted to call him out on his outfit, but I bit my lip.

"Want to know how long it took me to get my first sketch approved?" The dark-haired drafter leaned toward me. "Four months. Four months of watching my savings dwindle. Of watching the trends in my closet expire without being able to replace them. Of working day after day in this underground refrigerator, drinking crappy coffee and talking to these obsolosers." He pointed the pencil at the others, who smirked. "Six months is the limit — no approved sketches, and . . ." He sliced his pencil across his neck and grinned. "Want to know how long it's been since my last sketch was approved?"

So much for Godfrey's no-gabbing rule. I returned to flipping the pages of the magazine and tried to ignore him.

"Hey, I'm talking to you, princess." He leaned across the table and yanked the magazine out of my hands. I could feel tears starting to prick at my eyes. I blinked furiously and cast around the room, wondering if Winnie was near enough to witness the exchange. The drafter seemed to read my thoughts.

"You think Winnie will save you? Think again. She likes one quality in people: the ability to make Torro-LeBlanc money. You don't draft trends and she'll fire you with that perky smile still frozen on her face. And, judging by the fact that the powers that be sat you with *us*, I doubt they have much faith in you." The guy inclined his head toward the opposite end of the row. I looked. Tess Peterson, the drafter of the bear-fur purse and those ridiculous alpaca boots, was sitting down there, surrounded by a number of drafters I had seen recently in front of the Superior Court. Was the seating really arranged by talent? I refused to believe it — because that would mean I'd failed before I'd even started.

With a faint rattling sound, the pigtailed drafter to my left shook a tin over her palm. She popped the tiny pill that emerged into her mouth and began chewing.

"Maybe she's here to motivate us," said the older drafter on my right. I looked at him to see if he, too, was mocking me, but his expression was earnest, even hopeful.

"Yes, Randall. Our insecure, shallow child muse. Lucky us,"

the dark-haired guy spat. I pictured Braxton shoving him against the basement's brick wall and telling him off.

Vivienne, the drafter of the black dress, looked up from her piece of paper, where she was sketching something that looked like a hammer or a gavel — an accessory, I guessed. She sighed. "Lay off, Felix."

So that was his name. Felix's face registered his surprise. "She's *Superior Court*, Viv."

"Oh, so what," the pigtailed drafter interrupted. She gave me a wistful smile. "I'm Dido. I was a sifter for three years but never got promoted. You must have been really good."

Finally, someone who *got* how much of a big deal the Superior Court was. I returned the smile willingly. "Thanks. I'm Marla."

"Exactly." Vivienne was looking at Felix. "She's Superior Court. She knows *every member* of the court right now." I watched Felix's scowl slowly dissolve. I wondered what they both were thinking. On the verge of asking, I stopped when Vivienne added: "And she's not full of malice like the rest of those prepubes."

Kevin peered across Felix. "How do you know? Did she say something in the judging room yesterday?"

"Call it a hunch." Vivienne looked at me. Flakes of mascara were lodged in the depressions below her eyes, making them look even more sunken. "But I'd be willing to bet she's entertained the notion recently — maybe just once or twice — that trends are stupid."

The three designers across the table looked at me. I didn't know what to say. Of course trends weren't stupid. A few, maybe, but just the extreme, impractical ones, like hairy boots. A few weird outliers didn't ruin the *idea* of trends. Trends were exciting and dynamic. Trends were what made fashion, well, *fashionable.*

Felix mumbled something to Vivienne that I didn't catch.

"Not yet," she said. "Marla, right? You just work on your sketches. Get good. It's the only way you'll stay here. And despite Felix's histrionics, I think you're going to want to stick around."

Chapter Six

Millbrook.

Ivy peered through the tour bus window at Main Street. She couldn't suppress a small smile. They had done everything they could to scrub and shine the downtown for her arrival. The storefronts were freshly painted, the sidewalks repaved, the crust of loose garbage and debris swept from the curbside. Flags printed with her new album cover hung from every lamppost, limp in the still air of the crisp February morning. The dividing lines in the center of the street had even been resprayed, one red, one black — her *Girl Gone Wilde* tour colors.

Despite the face-lift, not much had changed. The mall they had passed on the way into the city center did have a bulbous new addition. But the closed manufacturing plant still stood, waiting for demolition. The elementary school also looked exactly the same, as did the Flippin' Flapjack House, the gas station, Judy's Hair Paradise . . . and there was the statue of Skip McBrody on the green. Solemnly, Ivy held her breath as the tour bus passed it.

"So you grew up here." Madison plopped down across from

her on the gray velvet seat and grinned. "I bet you couldn't wait to get out."

The comment caught her by surprise, but Ivy was quick to return the grin. "Totally. It's kind of a dump."

"Were you expecting your Tap assignment?" Madison asked. "Mine was a total shock. I thought I was going to be picked up by a television studio. But this is way better," she added, shifting to lie back on the seat bottom and cross her stocking feet against the glass of the bus window.

Ivy remembered the moment her Unum had flashed the words INDUSTRY: MUSIC. Her pulse had begun to race; then: ORGANIZATION: *THE HENNY FUNPECK SHOW*. It had seemed an eternity before the final line appeared: ROLE: PERFORMER. Her Tap videos had been strong, she knew, but still, the last performer to come out of Millbrook had been Skip. It had been such a long shot. But she had done it.

"I kind of thought I had a chance, but I went nuts when I found out. It was a good moment." Ivy put her forehead against the window and stared out at the street as the bus lumbered around a corner. Her thoughts turned to Constantine — he probably hadn't swallowed a single bite of cereal this morning. She couldn't wait to celebrate with him.

"Well, you totally deserved it," said Madison. She yawned. "How many more minutes until we descend on Crustaceousville? Do I have time for a nap?"

Ivy and her nymphs climbed down the bus steps wearing the new space-age trend released by Zhang & Tsai: all shimmering silvers and whites, puffy moon boots, and spandex. Aiko even had on a helmet with a mirrored face shield. None of the nymphs had wanted to cover their faces, despite the saleswoman's entreaty to "Think of the mystery!" They'd drawn straws and Aiko had lost. Ivy found the helmet perfect for checking her reflection out of the corner of her eye.

Fatima hadn't been thrilled about Aiko's face being covered for the shoot. She'd tried to get Madison to switch outfits, but Madison threw a fit at the prospect of not wearing her galaxy hairclip, and Fatima backed down. No one ever came out and talked about it, but Ivy had noticed that the nymphs of white performers usually included one or two girls of different races. Personally, she liked having Naia and Aiko in her entourage. They made her seem more interesting. The five of them looked perfect in publicity shots, too — like a really prime clothing ad. Plus, the two girls were super sweet . . . so the whole thing kind of worked out.

Ivy was glad that the space-age trend was practical; it was brisk out, but her silver down jacket with the puffed shoulders kept her warm. On her head was the best piece of the line: a hat of slanted silver orbitals, as if someone had flicked the rings of a planet askew. At irregular intervals little lights blinked around each ellipse.

Madison blew into her cupped fists. "I miss La Reina," she muttered. "Why would anyone live anywhere not warm enough for palm trees?"

Ivy didn't answer. While she and her nymphs struck their usual poses in front of the photographers and videographers, she looked around at the cordoned-off crowd for familiar faces. She was surprised by the heavy military presence. Was there an orange alert level or something stupid like that?

She saw her parents, standing side by side in front of the rope, next to one of her bodyguards. Both dressed head to toe in fatigues, both beaming.

It hit her. Everyone was wearing the Rudolfo label's armed-forces trend. Well, not everyone — there were a couple of musketeer shirts in the crowd, and some feathered bags and gloves, and some shale bodysuits — but the majority of residents in Millbrook must have seen Ivy's photos on Maven Girl or some other hotspot, gone to the Rudolfo store, and forked over cash for the trend. Because she had worn it once. On a shopping trip. Like a creeping mist, the uncomfortable feeling from the dressing room at Torro-LeBlanc returned.

Unless they were knockoffs. She couldn't tell from here. She hoped they were.

For her parents, it was fine; her salary kept them quite comfortable. As she walked up to them, she could see the giant embroidered *R* on her mother's bag. That was no fake.

The videographer followed her as she approached her parents, his camera inches from her face. Ivy was used to this, but she sensed her mother stiffen. Christina was always awkward in front of cameras.

"Eva!" she said, too loudly, drawing Ivy into an embrace. "I mean, Ivy! Ivy! We missed you." Her mother worked nimbly around the headpiece to give her kisses on both cheeks.

"Hello, sweetheart," said George warmly, hugging her next. Ivy noted that his black beret covered his thinning hair nicely.

Ivy had no intention of going to pieces in front of the cameras and fans. Facing her parents' doting gazes, however, she suddenly felt like clutching them both and heading straight home. She blinked away tears; the videographer's lens came closer.

"Where's Constantine?" she asked, clearing her throat.

"He's already inside the stadium with the rest of the students. He's so excited," said Christina. "He couldn't sleep last night."

"I'm so sorry to interrupt," said Fatima, delicately touching Christina on the shoulder. "But we have to keep to schedule. Ivy will be all yours as soon as the Tap is over. One night at home, no cameras, no entourage. Just a couple of bodyguards outside the house, of course."

Christina smiled and grabbed Ivy's hand. "I've been cooking all day."

"I can't wait," Ivy whispered. Fatima led her to the line of fans holding out pens and Ivy Wilde paraphernalia to autograph.

Backstage, Aiko pulled off her helmet with visible relief. Fatima showed Ivy the stage from the wings. One of the roadies was checking the microphone. There was a giant digital time display upstage right; it read 2:25 p.m. Tap always took place at three in the afternoon.

"Get ready," said Fatima, adjusting Ivy's hat and fluffing up the shoulders of her jacket. "We're bringing up the person who's going to introduce you. It's a Peter Drummond? He seems very eager."

So Peter was going to introduce her. She should have known. Peter had been her sixth-grade drama teacher, and he had no scruples about taking credit for her Tap results. Yes, he had starred her in *Itsy Bitsy Betsy* and worked as her vocal coach. And yes, he had helped her mother film her Tap videos. She was grateful and all, but the truth was, she was now sixteen and an international pop star. She had moved way beyond Peter.

"Evangeline!" Speak of the devil. Peter hustled up to the group, grinning like a puppy. He had gained some weight, and his hair was a darker shoe-polish black than she remembered. "Oh, excuse me, *Ivy*," he said, giving her an exaggerated wink and shaking her hand heartily. Ivy managed an aloof smile. "The proudest moment of my life was when little Evangeline was tapped," Peter announced to her nymphs and Fatima. "Proudest moment. There hasn't been anyone like her since."

"Little Evangeline. That's so cute," said Naia, poking Ivy's arm gently.

"Thanks, Peter," Ivy muttered.

"We go *way* back," Peter continued. "Say, any chance your old teacher can get a copy of the new album? I'm dying to hear it! No leaks, I promise," said Peter, raising his right hand in a pledge.

"Sorry — no advance releases," said Fatima, steering him away and giving him specific instructions for the introduction. Ivy watched as Peter withdrew a folded piece of notebook paper from his pocket and handed it to Fatima. She unfolded it, scanned it quickly, and tore it into quarters, shaking her head. Ivy was relieved; Fatima had probably saved the crowd an earful about Peter's genius for developing young talent — and saved her a certain amount of humiliation as well. Seeing Peter's defeated expression, she did feel a twinge of sympathy for him but quickly shook it away. She had to focus on her performance.

"*Such* an obsoloser," she said aloud to her nymphs. "Can someone get me a Diet Sugarwater or something?"

When he walked to the standing microphone a few minutes later to a steady crescendo of applause, Peter said simply: "To celebrate our Tap this year, we are honored to have a very special guest artist performing today." The applause turned into screeching cheers, and Ivy saw that Peter couldn't resist winking at the crowd. "Put your hands together for Millbrook's very own . . . Miss Ivy Wilde!"

As was their preperformance routine, Hilarie squeezed Ivy's hand backstage, and Aiko held her shoulders. When Peter stepped away from the mike and extended a hand toward her, Ivy took a deep breath, ran her tongue over her teeth, and walked onstage, arms raised and waving. The roar of the crowd, that swollen pulse of sound, throbbed its way into every pore. She never took placidophilus pills before she performed — who needed them when she had this? She reached the center of the stage, gripped the microphone, and screamed, "What's up, Millbrook?" The crowd screamed back.

Fatima had chosen a ballad off her first album for the performance. "Sharpen Your Teeth" was always a crowd pleaser. And perfect for simple gigs on the road because it didn't require a crew of backup dancers. With her middle finger, Ivy pushed in her earbud to hear the accompaniment over the crowd noise. She began to sing:

> *Each time I dream,*
> *I dream of your face,*
> *The only thing beautiful*
> *In this dumb place.*

As she settled into her performance, she looked out into the crowd. Usually, with the stage lighting flashing in her eyes in indoor stadiums, she didn't have the luxury. But it was the middle of the day, and the bright winter sun illuminated the brown-green military garb. She wondered if everyone would run out to the Zhang & Tsai store tomorrow to go space-age. She resisted the sudden urge to fling her hat into the wings like a Frisbee.

The adults sat in three sections of raised bleachers that

formed a U facing the stage. The students had the seats on the lawn, though nobody was sitting. They stood on their chairs, swayed, and sang along as she began the chorus:

> *Sharpen your teeth,*
> *Paint your skin white,*
> *'Cause I'm feeling wild,*
> *Wild tonight.*

> *Roar at the moon with me*
> *Race through the wood —*
> *Next morning, dried bite marks*
> *and blood.*

As usual, the children were arranged in order of descending age. Those closest to the stage were the biggest — the seventh-graders, about to get tapped in a few minutes. As she began the bridge, Ivy scanned their faces, trying to locate Constantine. Not on the right; was he there in the center? No, that kid's hair was too light . . .

Then she saw him, standing off to the left in the second row, a virtual statue between the manic classmates on his left and right. He looked up at her with his mouth slightly open, a look of half awe, half amusement on his face.

She took the mike out of its stand as she finished the bridge, walked across the stage, and, ignoring the other outstretched hands, gave him a high-five. His face broke into a full grin. She watched as his classmates rattled him with hugs afterward.

The song ended. Ivy took a bow and, as Fatima had instruct-ed, ignored the requests for encores. She replaced the mike in its stand and threw up her hands.

"Thank you!" she said, igniting the ovation once again. The power felt so good; she could keep them cheering all day if she wanted. Forget Lyric Mirth — she was adored. She glanced at the giant digital projection off to her right: 2:57. Better get everyone prepared. She held up her palms like a traffic cop. After a moment the cheers started to fade.

"Three minutes till Tap," she announced into the mike. "Good luck, sevens. Make Millbrook proud."

She took a few steps back so she could watch the fun. The crowd noise evaporated as the seventh-graders in front of her took out their Unums. One girl looked sick to her stomach; a boy stumbled off his chair and had to sit with his head between his legs.

She thought of how much was about to change for them. She remembered her best friend Marisa Garcia, whom she had promised she'd stay friends with no matter what happened, whose hand had gripped hers at the very moment their Unums started buzzing, who had been tapped as a nymph for the actress Junie Woo . . . She hardly spoke to Marisa anymore now. The seventh-graders were saying goodbye to school friends, to slicers, to summer vacations. But it was worth it. She didn't have Marisa, but she had her nymphs. And her fans. And Clayton Pryce. It was worth it.

She looked for Constantine. Her brother was in the middle of a breathless clump of sevens, his face stoic. *Please, GameTech or Arcadia,* she thought. *Or even Cathode. Come on.*

"Good luck, Jayden!" a woman screamed from the bleachers. A chorus of shushes reprimanded her.

The clock turned 3:00.

For a few eternal seconds, nothing happened.

Then, about half the seventh-graders' Unums began humming and vibrating in the vast silence like a swarm of angry bees. Lighting up, they began flashing a pattern of green, purple, and pink. Unblinking, the seventh-graders stared at the small screens until . . .

A collective gasp, as the sevens received their industries.

A second, quieter gasp for the organizations. Ivy looked for Constantine, but a tall girl in front of him was blocking his face from view.

Finally, the seventh-graders' roles flashed on the screens.

Whoops of joy, wails of disappointment, tears, screams of "I *got* it!" filled the front of the arena. The seventh-graders battered into one another in their attempts to hug their friends and jump off chairs to run to their parents. Behind them, the sixth-graders watched the mayhem jealously. Celebrations in the bleachers exploded like fireworks as good news was passed upward.

But where was Constantine? Ivy searched the swarming mob for her brother. At last she saw him. Standing by the rail in front of the stage. Shaking his Unum, pressing its buttons.

It was neither humming nor flashing. Even from the stage, she could see that its screen was black.

Constantine looked up at her and began to cry silently.

While George stayed in the car with Constantine, Ivy and her mother ran into the house to pop the balloons that filled the kitchen. From the refrigerator, which was stuffed with celebratory dishes covered in foil, Christina withdrew a cake with *Congratulations Constantine!* scrawled on its surface in orange icing. She held it out to Ivy.

"Trash?" she asked. "It's a crushed walnut cake."

"You made it, right?" Ivy asked, sticking a fork into a yellow balloon. "Just scrape off the writing."

"After you — I never thought he would be an Adequate. Never," her mother mumbled, extracting a butter knife from a kitchen drawer. "The poor thing. It's going to be fine, of course. Your father and I were Adequates and we did just fine."

Ivy nodded.

"Don't talk about work, Evangeline," Christina said, as she shaved off the top layer of frosting. "Not until he's in bed tonight."

"Of course not. I'm not an idiot." She took off her orbital hat and deposited it on the kitchen countertop. The green granite was a new addition, she noticed. Its quartz chips sparkled under the blinking lights.

By the time he entered the house, Constantine had stopped crying. He wanted to go straight to his room, but George insisted that he sit at the kitchen table with the family. As he pulled out his chair, Ivy quickly picked up one of the overlooked balloon skins at his feet and balled it in her fist.

Sitting next to Constantine, she listened as her parents talked about the disappointment they'd felt when they didn't get tapped by one of the creative industries. Her mother described not wanting to get out of bed for a week. "But even though it seems as if the world has ended, it hasn't," Christina said, shaking her head firmly. "You can still carve out a respectable life. Look at me. Everything worked out. I fell in love and had two beautiful children."

"You're a mother," Constantine said after a pause. "It's different for girls. There's not as much . . . shame. Especially if you turn one of your kids into *Ivy Wilde*."

Ivy wondered if she should say something in the silence that followed, but her mother spoke first. "Our fine president is an Adequate. And he is a man."

"Right, like I want to be president. Fun. Bills and budgets.

I hate math." He groaned and rolled his head back. "Can I go now?"

"No." Their father took over. He admitted to Constantine that the film industry's rejection still stung. This had always been obvious to Ivy; every time her family had gone to the movies, her father emerged looking a little dazed and sad. But he described how, slowly, chemical research became the thing he knew he was meant to do. Ivy remembered yawning at these speeches growing up; his work had sounded so boring, so pointless. As she listened to her father now, his work didn't sound any less boring. But she realized that, in a kind of twisted way, George was talking about chemistry the same way she talked — and thought — about performing.

"I know the Adequate industries don't pay as well, but you can live a full life," George said. "A lot of my friends have found personal satisfaction as researchers, reporters, teachers, doctors —"

"George, face it." Constantine exploded. "You sit in a lab all day doing feeble experiments that nobody cares about. I wanted to work on video games that *everyone* would play. It's completely different. And excuse me, a *reporter?* That'll be fun, writing about all the stuff going on in the creative industries. Maybe I can do an article on my sister, the star." He laughed spitefully. "Or a teacher. That's the best. I'll watch class after class of sevens get tapped. Perfect."

Before George could reply, Constantine stood up. "Eva, come look at my Tap page," he demanded. "Maybe you can tell me what went wrong."

Shrugging at her parents, Ivy followed him into the bedroom and watched as he turned on his Tabula. He got up from his desk chair and she sat down in it.

As an ominous chord played, the name CONSTANTINE VASSILIOTIS swelled toward her on the screen. At the crescendo, the red letters burst into pieces and crumbled away, revealing Constantine's Tap homepage. She navigated around it. He'd had 1,158 hits, which was a better than average number. But only about half had rated him a "Trendsetter" or above. There were the usual stills of the video game characters he liked, with blurbs about what her brother thought made them and their weapons appealing, powerful, cutting-edge. She watched his videos, most of which were unrelenting montages of explosions from recent games. He'd picked good ones, and set them to great music, but . . .

"Where's your original content?" she asked, clicking through his files. "Did you come up with new game ideas?"

Constantine shrugged. He lay on the bottom bed of his bunk, his legs crossed on the comforter, combat boots still on his feet. "Didn't think I needed them. I sorta ran out of time."

Ran out of time? This was Tap. Nobody did any homework in seventh grade; even the teachers basically understood that the first half of the year was for creating Tap pages. Some of Ivy's teachers had even let her work on hers during class.

"Will spent months animating original stuff last year and he got overlooked," Constantine said. "So I didn't bother. I wanted to be on GameTech's court eventually, anyway. Judging." He punched the wall. "I can't *believe* I'm an Adequate."

"But . . ." Ivy bit her tongue. Calling her brother lazy, saying he hadn't done enough, wouldn't help anything. "You're right," she said, nodding. "It's completely unfair. Your site rocks. I'm sorry."

Constantine snorted. "I can't believe I have to go to school on Monday. I'd rather die."

"Don't say that. You know George and Christina will be on watch for the next month."

Constantine rolled his eyes. "You're the one with Skip Mc-Brody's career. Make sure *you* don't have a little"— he put two fingers to his temple and flicked his thumb —"*accident.*"

Ivy frowned. Since she'd been tapped, no one in her family had ever mentioned Skip's suicide directly. "Thanks, Constantine. That's kind of sick, you know."

The two sat in silence. "So . . . do you want to talk about the Tap some more?" Ivy asked at last.

"No offense, Eva, but I can't really talk to you about it. You have no idea how it feels."

She looked at his face, the dull eyes, the nostrils still faintly pink. "You're right," she said. She reached into her pocket for her placidophilus tin and shook it. It was full. She removed a single pill, put it in her pocket, and stuck the tin in the top drawer of his desk, closing it softly. "Those will help."

Constantine stared at the drawer. "Thanks," he whispered. "Go tell everyone I'm fine. Good luck with the album release." He grabbed a comic book from his nightstand. "Maybe I'll write an article about you someday."

Ivy walked out, leaving the door to her brother's room open.

Chapter Seven

I *was getting used* to life in the basement.

I was getting used to copying models out of magazines. I made some pathetic first attempts where my people looked like gingerbread men — these I stuffed into my briefcase before anyone could see. But I kept at it, praying that my old technique would come back. After a few days, my people looked more lifelike and less like something Karen would bake for dessert.

Dido would look over my shoulder every so often. "Elongate the torso and the limbs. Here." She would take my pencil and make some changes. "Your designs will look more flattering." I practiced willingly. It helped to concentrate on tiny tasks and not think about the grand dive my life had taken.

"Now work on close-ups of clothing," Dido later advised me. "Sifters and selectors like when you include a detailed view as well as a garment on a body. Well, you remember." I did.

I was getting used to the way a selector stepped out of the elevator every day around eleven a.m. and handed a stack of drawings to Godfrey. He ruffled through them and handed them off to Winnie, who distributed them with a warm smile and a shoulder pat. My second day on the job, Randall had one of his sketches selected.

"Congratulations," I said, looking at the drawing in his hand. It showed shoes whose high heels forked like the tail of a swallow. They were definitely original, but I wasn't sure I would have approved them as a judge. They didn't really fit into any of the major trends right now. Still, I liked their sleekness.

Randall didn't smile as he stood up. "I never get my hopes up," he said. He left to visit Garment Construction on the second floor and oversee the building of his shoe.

When he returned to the basement two days later, he sat down and shook his head sadly. "Sorry," I mumbled at him, and gnawed the inside of my cheek. I'd rejected designs all the time as a judge. I'd felt sympathy for drafters who'd had to leave the room with rejections, but the truth was, I hadn't thought about them as much more than creators of flawed garments. I hadn't thought about them as people. I watched Randall grab a piece of paper and sigh as he began a fresh sketch.

I was getting used to dropping my signed, finished sketches into the gray bins and my day's pile of scratch paper into the green bins on the way to the elevator. Winnie told me that Torro sent its paper waste to a processing plant a few blocks away and bought back its own recycled reams. "Isn't it great to work for such an environmentally friendly company?" she chirruped.

I began to think it wasn't natural to be so perky all the time.

I was getting used to my mother kneading her forehead at dinner. Karen would describe her embarrassing encounters with the other mothers she'd run into that day, to whom she had been forced to reveal my current title at Torro-LeBlanc.

"And everyone asks why you just don't quit altogether. Emma quit Belladonna last year. She and Lorraine have started to look a little seedy, I'll give you that, but they're taking a cruise together this November. A mother-daughter trip. Doesn't that sound like fun?"

I stared at my plate of food and shrugged. "It's sort of fun to be drawing again," I muttered. It was — I had to admit it. I had gotten into the habit of bringing a short pile of paper home each day in case I got an idea while I was sitting in front of the television after dinner. Sometimes the shows inspired me. I could build off the featured trends — add sleeves, or change a hem length, or create a purse that would match a dress some character was wearing. I rolled my eyes one night when I saw one of the Carlottas from *Clone Valley* stomp across the screen in Tess Peterson's yeti boots. That was one trend I wouldn't touch.

"That's the spirit, honey," said my father heartily. Karen shot him a chilly stare. It was in moments like these that I really, really wished my parents had been able to have more than one child. From his nervous budgeting at the kitchen table these days, Walter probably wished the same thing. I felt bad for him — and for my mother. But I didn't see how quitting could help anything.

Fortunately, I had Braxton. He had been totally decent through the whole debacle. The day after I'd been demoted, he bought me the sweetest teddy bear with a satin bow. Although Sabrina no longer joined us, we still rode into work together almost every day. On weekends, we vegged at his place — him playing Larceny IX and me sketching clothes while we ate his mom's latest seven-layer-dip experiment. Braxton told me he'd support me if I stayed on as a drafter or if I quit, either way. It was hard, though, to hear him talk about the court battles at Denominator. I missed my own battles with the Torro judges, even the ones that ended in defeat.

I couldn't get used to the nasty basement coffee, though. After I finished my latte from home each day, I got by without a refill.

It came as a huge surprise to me that Vivienne was the best artist among our little group. I was sure her sketches would be picked frequently — if she actually sketched clothing. Half the time she drew random objects, or did a portrait of someone at the table. Sometimes she didn't draw but filled her paper with words. Her writing was so cramped and she hunched over the sheet so secretively that I never saw what she wrote.

Felix had nearly as much artistic talent as Vivienne. His problem was that he refused to compromise his rough, distressed aesthetic. He ignored the current direction of trends and designed clothes that looked like *nothing* anyone was wearing. He pretended not to care and always scowled as Winnie passed by with the pile of selected sketches under her arm. Still, I had a hunch that he held out a little bit of hope each time. When a biker jacket of his was finally selected, he rolled his eyes and said, "I'm off — another exercise in futility!" But he didn't fool me. I watched him stroll to the elevator with a small spring in his step.

Kevin, Dido, and Randall had the opposite problem: they tended to play it safe. Again and again, I realized how tough a drafter's job was. To be good, you had to hit the center of this continuum — nothing too radical, nothing too familiar — every time.

Not that I planned to get stuck in a rut like Felix, but I started to think about my own design aesthetic. As a judge, I'd needed to keep an open mind to different styles, but now I was free to develop my own. Maybe it was all the time I was spending in the park outside my apartment avoiding Karen, but nature kept influencing me. A hummingbird whizzed nearby — and I sketched a blouse with wispy, translucent fabric. The rain dampened the ground one afternoon, and I came up with a mossy-textured scarf. A black cat skittered under the bushes, and I submitted a strapless dress with puma sleekness.

And then one day, four weeks after I had begun in the basement and one week after I'd really started submitting sketches in earnest, Winnie handed me a familiar piece of paper and patted my shoulder.

It was a one-shoulder, leopard-print dress with an attached gold belt. I'd submitted it along with my puma dress, thinking it might spin nicely off the safari line Torro was promoting. Feeling myself flush, I turned to Winnie. "What do I do now?" I asked.

"Head up to Garment Construction with your sketch. You'll advise a patternmaker on a prototype of your garment. Good luck!"

I rode the elevator with some drafters whose sketches had also been selected. When the doors opened, the bustle of Garment Construction electrified me. Patternmakers and drafters ran around the room, clutching giant fabric bolts or wheeling half-garbed dress forms. Everywhere, scissors snipped, sewing machines clacked, and people shouted over the fray.

Patternmakers approached the group of us as we emerged. I held my selected sketch tightly. One guy with a receding hairline and goatee nodded at me. "Come on then," he said. "What've you got?"

He introduced himself as Vaughn, glanced quickly at my drawing, and led me to the high shelf of animal-print fabrics.

I stood on my toes to look them over. "What if I can't find what I have in mind?"

"There's something there that'll work," he said. His voice was brusque but not unkind. "Trust me. Besides, you don't get to custom order your own fabric until you've had something like ten sketches approved."

Together, we settled on a print that I was happy with. The leopard's spots were the way I'd imagined — about the size of my thumbnail and densely packed. Then we found a stiff and shiny gold material for the belt. Vaughn's experience as a patternmaker was evident as he traced the dress's lining and positioned it on the dummy, asking me for input as he folded and puckered. In no time, we captured the silhouette I had created in my sketch. Honestly, I felt it was coming along even better than I'd hoped.

"How long do we have?" I asked as Vaughn dug into a bin of belt buckles.

"A week for difficult garments that require custom ordering. Everything else they like us to finish in under three days. Yours is simple — it should be ready for the fourth floor tomorrow morning."

I had to ask. "Do you think I have a good chance?"

Vaughn shrugged his shoulders. "You never can tell with these things."

I couldn't sleep that night. I envisioned people walking down the street in my dress, going to work, going out afterward in it. I thought what it would be like to wear it *myself* and casually mention that I'd designed it for the Torro-LeBlanc line. Even my mother would have to be proud of that. I woke Braxton up with a call to share my excitement. I chattered on, full of nervous energy, hugging the bear he had given me.

"Wow, Marl. I never thought you'd like being a drafter so much," he said when I finally paused.

"Yeah, I don't know why drafters get such a bad rap," I told him. "Creating clothes is fun."

After a drowsy goodbye, Braxton hung up. I lay on my back, clutching the bear, imagining my look coming down the catwalk again and again.

The next morning at work, Vaughn and I examined the dress with a critical eye and decided to raise the hem two inches to better reflect current skirt lengths. He steamed the fabric and added the finishing adjustments.

"I love it! Thank you," I exclaimed. I had the sudden urge to hug him but settled for an awkward arm squeeze.

"Good luck," said Vaughn. He smiled. "I hope to see you up here again soon. For ex–Superior Court, you're actually not insufferable to work with."

I laughed, pushed my creation to the elevator with pride, and headed to the fourth floor.

The rejection happened so fast I didn't have time to cry. Terrence, one of the three Junior Court directors I'd worked with, led me to the garment-judging room where Junior Court B sat. I wheeled in the dress form and maneuvered it to face the judges. I recognized one of them, a redheaded girl I'd been a sifter with. I tried to catch her eye and smile, but the girl didn't seem to remember me. I cleared my throat and opened my mouth to speak.

"Hoochie-tacky," said one judge.

"Totally crustaceous," said another.

"Sad, desperate housewife, fossil-in-training," announced a third.

Someone snorted.

"Defenders?" asked Terrence. A beat of silence. "All opposed?"

Each of the nine judges raised a hand.

"Thank you very much, Maria. We hope to see you again soon," he recited. And I was back outside, alone, my one-shoulder creation mutely mocking me.

Maria. He didn't even remember my name.

Trying to swallow the lump in my throat, I rode the elevator back down to the second floor, where, evidently, the news of my failure had already been delivered. Vaughn was nowhere in sight, but a woman grabbed my dummy and sliced down the carefully constructed seams with a small blade.

"What happens to the fabric?" I asked hoarsely.

"Scraps bin," the woman muttered before shooing me away.

I didn't want to return to the basement. I knew I had to, but I wanted to go home and have Karen make me chicken soup and fudge brownies. I rode the elevator down, walked to my table, and laid my head on my folded arms.

"P pill?" I lifted my head to see Dido offering the tin. I glanced at my colleagues. Vivienne was watching me intently. Felix was frowning.

"I'm not trying to tell you what to do." Randall's voice came from my other side. I turned, but he didn't look up from his sketch. "But those are incredibly habit-forming, you know."

"They're harmless, Randall," said Dido. She smiled, but there was irritation in her voice.

"Up to you, Marla," said Randall, "but I'd save them for when you *really* have a bad day."

I glanced at the little pink pill in Dido's palm. It looked like candy. I did feel pretty miserable — but I wasn't sure about trying placidophilus pills just yet. No one on the Superior Court used. My mother only indulged once in a great while for what she called "unbearably taxing moments," such as the days that

led up to my Tap. Randall was probably right — I'd have moments that hurt worse than this rejection. I could wait. "Thanks.
Maybe later," I said to Dido. "I should get my own, anyway."

Dido tucked the tin away in her bag. "Suit yourself. I can recommend a dealer if you want," she added.

Chapter Eight

J ennifer Tildy, *coming up on* your left," Naia whispered into Ivy's ear.

Ivy turned to see the actress approaching with her nymphs, the whole group in safari-inspired clothing. Jennifer's khaki hat hung around her neck by its drawstring and rested on her back. Ivy guessed there was no way Jennifer's publicist would have let her cover up her signature bob.

"*Love* the new album, Ivy," Jennifer said, a sheen coming off her hair even in the dim light of the ballroom. "*Super* prime." She pulled out her Unum. "Any chance I can get a shot?"

"No problem," Ivy replied.

Jennifer handed her Unum to one of her nymphs and positioned herself next to Ivy. Ivy draped her arm around Jennifer and smiled an aloof, close-mouthed smile at the Unum camera. There was something about having her arm around the actress's shoulders, not the other way around, that tilted the balance of power in her favor. She was the one gracious enough to give the hug. Jennifer, a huge star in her own right, was lucky to be around *her*. It felt good.

The Unum flashed. Jennifer thanked her, and Ivy continued gliding through her album-release party, thrown by Warwick

Records. The ballroom buzzed with celebrities. Actors, models, and other musicians mingled, grabbing hors d'oeuvres off trays. She felt a dizzy euphoria as they all clamored to spend a few minutes with her as she passed. She knew most of the guests personally, but if not, it was Naia's job to whisper names into her ear. Naia never missed.

It was the perfect event to distract her from Constantine's Tap failure. Even if she'd wanted to dwell on her visit home, she couldn't. In front of the crowd, as Fatima constantly reminded her, she had to be on. Spontaneous. Sexy. Wilde.

"Kev duPrince, action film star," Naia whispered in her ear.

"Duh," Ivy whispered back as he approached. "He's huge, Naia."

"Ivy Wilde," Kev said with a thousand-watt grin. "The girl of the hour."

"Hey, Kev," she replied, playing it cool. She'd always thought of Kev as a bit of a pretty boy — not her type, really — but she knew her nymphs thought he was prime. She felt Naia press against her side in an effort to get closer.

"I have a favor to ask." One of Kev's satyrs held out a felt-tipped marker. In a gesture that momentarily shocked Ivy, Kev ripped open his shirt, popping all the buttons off. He was a little on the skinny side, but he'd clearly been hitting the gym. "Sign my chest, will you, hot stuff?"

As guests and reporters raised Unums and cameras to catch a shot of Kev's bare chest, Ivy smelled an agent at work here. It was probably Kev's — though she could imagine Jarvis orchestrating the moment too. It didn't matter. She knew what she was supposed to do. First: Show that she wasn't, actually, shocked. She began fanning herself dramatically with her right hand, as if she loved what she saw, as if he were too hot to handle.

"Whoa, whoa, whoa. What's going on here?" Clayton Pryce stalked over, playful anger on his face. It was clear he wasn't really jealous . . . but Ivy could tell everyone was loving the show nonetheless.

"I mean no disrespect, man," said Kev. He took the marker from his satyr and held it out to Ivy. "I just want the primest pop star on the planet to leave her mark on me. You get her all the time. Let me have one moment."

Clayton crossed his arms. "Careful, now."

Second: Prove that she was a "Wilde" girl, wilder even than Kev. "Gimme that," said Ivy, snatching the marker and removing the top. "Clayton, I love you, baby. But you're going to watch"— she bumped her backside against his hip while the crowd whooped —"and you're going to like it."

On Kev's chest, in loopy black script, she wrote, *Stay wild!* ❤ *Ivy.* The marker glided over his sweaty skin, bleeding a little here and there. Kev's cologne made her eyes water, but she ignored it and gave him an affectionate bite on the neck as the cameras flashed.

Third: Patch things up with Clayton. Once Kev left, she snuggled up to him and sucked on his earlobe to show everyone there were no hard feelings. She imagined Fatima somewhere in the room, beaming.

All the while, her new album, *Laid Bare,* throbbed through the overhead speakers. Boys fighting over her, celebrities eating it up, gazing at her in her new Torro-LeBlanc minidress of beige silk — it was work, but it was fun, too. To have the spotlight for the evening, the theatrics were totally worth it. She was a pro by now, anyway.

And tomorrow she could sleep in and lounge around all day. Fatima had canceled rehearsal. All she had to do was get dressed up again and head to Scalpel for a club night. She thought again of her brother with a touch of sadness. Poor Adequates. Maybe her father really did like chemistry; maybe her mother was happy enough. But no matter what they said, their lives were so feeble compared to all this.

Chapter Nine

The morning after my garment rejection, to my surprise, Vivienne plopped down next to me, in Randall's usual seat to my right. She waited until Winnie was walking by to announce: "I'm switching seats with Randall for a few days so I can help you with your sketches. We'll get you in front of the Superior Court yet!" She even made a point of giving Winnie a fluttery finger wave. It was so out of character that I figured Winnie would be suspicious. But Winnie just returned an enthusiastic thumbs-up.

Was Vivienne actually going to offer me instructions? I took out a half-finished sketch of some black rocker jeans with chain embellishments I had begun the night before. I had yet to try boyswear and thought it was as far away from "fossil-in-training" as I could get. I studied the jeans, chewing the polish off my fingernail. Glancing down, I realized I'd really let my nails get into a terrible state. I remembered how I used to paint them each morning to coordinate with my outfit — but now, well, I wasn't around people who would notice or care. At least none of the clothes I was wearing had expired yet.

Next to me, Vivienne began sketching a sad clown. Fake

nose, big shoes, and all. I frowned. Surely she wasn't going to submit that.

"I wonder if the Junior Court gave you a fair chance," Vivienne said out of the blue a few minutes later. "They may have been told to reject you. It could be a power play. To make you remember where you belong now."

"That can't be true," I said. The entire year I'd served on the Junior Court, I'd never been told to vote one way or the other. But then again, I'd never had to evaluate a garment by an ex–Superior Court judge — because none who'd left had become drafters.

"I hope I'm wrong. For your sake." Vivienne added rainbow curls to the clown's hair with colored pencils. "So you were close with the other judges on the Superior Court? You think they would support one of your ideas now?"

I squeezed my eyes closed. The bench would endorse my garments, wouldn't they? I imagined going before them — and immediately had a vision of the faces at the semicircular bench looking at me with pity. Or maybe I'd be lucky if I got pity. They might think I was a talentless freak, just as the Junior Court had. And I had to be honest with myself: Julia had nothing to gain by making sure my garment got a fair chance. "I really don't know," I muttered.

Felix leaned toward us from across the table. "I have a question for you," he said quietly, looking at me. "Think before you answer."

"Okay."

"Who do you think are the most powerful employees at Torro-LeBlanc?"

I didn't hesitate. "The Superior Court judges. Obviously."

"And are the drafters the least powerful?"

I thought about it. The patternmakers weren't exactly royalty either. But they at least worked for salary, not commission. The other ex-Tap employees not involved in design — the PR reps, the runway-show producers, the court supervisors, all the departments I'd delusionally been convinced I'd join after my time on the court expired — all led if not fun then at least fast-paced and fashionable lives. There were some other dreary jobs: the budget and law offices were fully staffed with Adequates. But they'd never worked as children, so they probably didn't know what they were missing.

"What are you getting at?" I asked.

"Do you really think it's fair that the job of your dreams — and the most power you'll ever have — is behind you now?" asked Felix.

I looked down at my sketch. "You don't have to rub it in."

He leaned in farther. "I'm not talking about your own personal tragedy, princess."

"Felix." Vivienne shot him a look. "She's not the enemy."

His frown held a moment before breaking. "Right." He shook his head. "I'm sorry. But it makes me angry. This whole system is ass-backward."

My eyes widened — I couldn't help it. I glanced over my shoulder, but Winnie and Godfrey were well out of earshot.

"Think about it," Felix went on. "The creative minds are at the *bottom* of the pyramid, while a bunch of snot-nosed pre-pubes sit at the top, pronouncing their divine judgment on *our* ideas?"

"But it works. The styles the court picks sell."

Felix shook his head furiously. "It's a self-fulfilling prophecy. Everyone knows that kids pick the trends, so whatever Torro-

LeBlanc puts out must be what's in. That's the way the Silents have designed it."

I frowned again. The Silents held upper-level positions in the creative industries, but they mostly stayed in the background, overseeing things. I had never actually met a Silent, at Torro-LeBlanc or elsewhere. Growing up, they attended private schools and interacted mainly with one another. There didn't seem to be very many of them. There were always a few weird conspiracy theories floating around about them, but most people agreed they sort of kept things moving along efficiently, without interfering. "Oh, come on," I said. "The Silents aren't controlling people like that. The Superior Court judges actually have really good fashion instincts."

"So what happened to your instincts? Did they dry up on your last birthday?"

I couldn't believe his rudeness.

"Don't get me wrong," Felix went on. "I love designing. Always have. But why should I be obsolete at eighteen? *I* should be deciding what gets mass-produced. And I should be paid well for my ideas."

"You sound like a bitter fossil." I blurted out the insult. "Sorry," I added quickly.

"I got news for you," he replied, undeterred. "You have a choice. Become a bitter fossil with me, or spend your life believing in a system that has no real use for you anymore."

"Not so loud, Felix." Vivienne put her hand gently on my forearm. "You think the Superior Court has real power, but they don't. They're as exploited as we are. They're used and then discarded. We were all plucked out of school when we were too naive to protest. Did you think it was okay to be passed over in the Tap?"

"Of course not."

"I didn't either. And now I wish I'd been an Adequate."

I stared at her in disbelief.

"I do," Vivienne went on. "I wish desperately I'd had more than a seventh-grade education. It took me too long to get back to reading and thinking, to start questioning the way things are. I'm twenty-four, and I've just now figured out what I believe in."

"Vivienne's become something of a evangelist," Kevin whispered. "Convincing, too." Randall nodded. Next to me, Dido shook her head faintly as she colored in a denim jacket. I wondered whether the pigtailed drafter was on board with this craziness.

"So . . . you think the court should be made up of people like you and Felix?" I asked Vivienne.

She chuckled. "Felix and I don't exactly see eye to eye on the way Torro should be run."

"What do you mean?"

"I *loathe* trends," sneered Vivienne. "They're artificial and pointless. If it were up to me, we'd have a national dress code. I'll be generous. Four looks." She counted them off on her fingers. "Work. Weekend. Sleepwear. Formal. All breathable, durable fabrics, elastic waistbands, cuffs that could be let down as children grow." She smiled. "That's my heaven."

Dido smirked. "Why even bother with formalwear in your clone world, Viv?"

"I am not without sentiment," she replied wryly. "There will always be cause for celebration. People need something to get married in." She cleared her throat. "And to be buried in."

Everyone at the table laughed except me.

"Gosh, Vivienne," said Kevin. "You're such a softy."

"Wouldn't work," said Felix, shaking his head. "People want to be different. It's human nature. If we had uniforms, people would roll up their cuffs or add trim or dye the cloth. May as well capitalize on their need for variety."

"But . . . if people are so different, it's kind of funny that we follow trends," I said slowly. I was thinking of my floral lapel pin, which I'd scanned the evening after I'd been fired from the court, and which had indeed expired. There was something vaguely unfair about not being able to wear it anymore. "You'd think we wouldn't care so much."

Felix raised his eyebrows at Vivienne. "I think we made contact."

"Maybe we can't avoid trends completely," said Vivienne. "But it would be nice if we could all have a little more say in what we wear. To say nothing of what we watch and listen to. And, most important, what we do with our lives. Do you agree?"

I looked around at the drafters as I considered this. Vivienne, with her crusting makeup and funereal clothing. Bitter Felix. Forty-something Randall. Kevin, who thought that his jacket could disguise the fact that he'd worn the same shirt the day before. No. I wanted no part of whatever they were talking about. They were nice people and all, but I had been a Superior Court judge a month ago. I was *not* one of them.

"Please," I said, "leave me alone. I love fashion, and I love Torro-LeBlanc. All I've ever wanted is to work here. Just because I'm a drafter . . . doesn't mean I'm miserable like the rest of you." I felt mean and awful immediately — but I didn't take it back.

There was a silence. Randall cleared his throat and returned to his sketch. But Felix glared at me, his dark eyes insolent. "Remind me how that rejection felt again?"

"Felix, don't," said Vivienne. She turned her pencil sideways and shaded a pool of water where the clown's tears fell. "Okay, Marla. Fair enough. Just let us know if you change your mind."

I shoved my way out of the basement at five o'clock and sent Braxton a message telling him that I'd be riding home with some friends from the Superior Court. I looked around frantically and located Sabrina, chatting and laughing in a group of judges about thirty yards ahead. I followed her to the Fashion Row station, where the judges dispersed and headed toward their respective trains.

Sabrina was boarding my train with three other judges. Two of them quickly located some friends and waved a farewell. Ginnifer walked down the center aisle toward a middle seat. I caught Sabrina's arm before she could follow Ginnifer.

"Hey, Sabrina," I said. "What's up?"

She turned, and I watched her smile fall. "Marla." We grabbed the handrails for support as the train began to move.

Despite her obvious lack of enthusiasm, I tried to keep things cheerful. "How's it going? I haven't seen you on the train in forever. Are you taking an earlier one in the mornings now?"

"Oh. Yeah." She didn't smile.

I took a deep breath. "Do you have a minute? I thought we could catch up. I have so many stories about the *obsolosers* in the basement. You wouldn't believe it down there." I pointed at an empty pair of seats. "Want to sit?"

Sabrina glanced back at Ginnifer. "Look, Marla. No hard feelings, but we're not really friends anymore. I'm still on the court and you're ... not. So ..." She shrugged her shoulders.

My face got hot. "Look, I'm a drafter — but I'm not a *drafter*

drafter." I forced a laugh. "I mean, it's still me. I'm still Marla." I tipped my feathered hat at her. "No fossil in sight, right?"

Sabrina sighed. "I don't think you understand. And you need to. I feel bad about what happened to you, but it kind of changes things."

"You can't be serious." I couldn't help myself. "We're friends!"

Sabrina glanced back again. "Look," she said, lowering her voice, "how about this. I can get you tickets to the next Torro runway show."

I relaxed. "Oh. Prime. It'd be fun to go together."

"Oh no, you won't be sitting up front with the *judges*." I saw a ripple of guilt pinch Sabrina's face. "I mean, maybe you and some of your new drafter friends can go together. Okay?" She reached up to pat my shoulder — then seemed to think better of it and turned the gesture into a wave. "Stay young."

Sabrina walked away down the center aisle. She sat down with Ginnifer, and the two began whispering intently. Feeling sick, I stepped into the adjacent car to get away from them.

I caught sight of Braxton in the compartment. I was about to call out when he leaned over to the girl sitting next to him — leaned over until their foreheads touched. I froze. He whispered something, and the girl grinned and giggled. He reached up and stroked the girl's cheek with his fingertips, then grabbed a piece of her hair and twirled it around his finger. His eyebrows flicked up and down.

I blinked. The girl sitting with him was none other than Olivia, the youngest judge on the Torro-LeBlanc Superior Court.

Chapter Ten

Scalpel was already rocking by the time Ivy arrived. The remixed music was fresh, the nightclub dance floor packed. As the strobe light flashed, she moved and swayed with Clayton, transported by the raw rhythms. He was a great dancer.

Ivy wore a Torro-LeBlanc tunic of peacock feathers with purple leggings. It had a high neck, and she had to stop herself from scratching her chin. Her nymphs and many others wore feathers of some sort, too. Strays floated in the air and made the dance floor look like a snow globe — but with the flashing lights, it kind of worked. Every so often, though, one of the hard feather shafts pricked her torso as she moved.

She was catching her breath and taking a Sugarwater break with her nymphs when Lyric Mirth entered Scalpel.

A mob of flashing cameras and shouting reporters instantly jammed the club entrance. Ivy narrowed her eyes. There had been a scene when she'd arrived too — but she was Ivy Wilde, not some newcomer who'd had one feeble hit. She watched Lyric's bodyguards wrestle back the crowd so that she and her nymphs could pass.

Lyric was wearing a white dress so thin it looked to be made of rice paper. It had feather-embellished straps and feathers hanging in three tiers from the hem. On her head she wore a headband, from which shining gold feathers stuck straight up in a semicircle from ear to ear. It was supposed to evoke a halo, Ivy realized spitefully. Saintly little Lyric. She wanted to laugh at the stupidity — but the whole ensemble did succeed in making Lyric look like some kind of sun goddess. It was definitely eye-catching. Perhaps, Ivy thought darkly, even more so than peacock feathers.

From behind her, she heard Madison shaking the P pill tin questioningly. Ivy shook her head. "I'm fine," she snapped.

It was unavoidable; the club was one long tunnel, and even in the darkness, Lyric caught Ivy's eye. Ivy watched her gasp in surprise, wave furiously, and make straight for her.

"Here she comes," warned Naia, stiffening.

"Ivy!" said Lyric, displaying a dazzling white grin — Lyric was really all teeth, wasn't she. And so freakishly tall for her age, too. She bent over to give Ivy a hug and an air kiss, and Ivy gave her shoulder two weak pats. She sensed her nymphs tighten around her and felt a surge of fondness for them. They were ready to beat the smile off Lyric's face if she gave the word.

"It's really you! It's been so long since *Henny Funpeck!*" Lyric said. "You're one of my *heroes*, you know, Ivy. I went to five *Girl Gone Wilde* shows! And I *love* the new album. Love, love, love it!"

Slowly, Ivy nodded. At least Lyric was fawning appropriately. "Sorry — I haven't had a chance to listen to yours yet." It wasn't a lie; her nymphs knew to change the station every time "So Pure It Hurts" came on. "But I'm sure it's prime." Okay, that *was* a lie.

"Oh, no, well, of course not. You must be so busy," Lyric gushed. "I'm starting to know how it feels. We're gearing up for my first tour. It's so much work! Twenty-eight stops, with pub-

ELAINE DIMOPOULOS

licity events in each," she said. Ivy smiled through gritted teeth. *Girl Gone Wilde* had hit only eighteen cities.

"Yeah, well, you get used to it," she said. "The hotels are fun at first, but they get kind of old. You'll see how it is. Make sure you don't screw up the city name when you're onstage."

Lyric laughed. "No — that would be awful."

"I think Clayton's waiting for you, Ivy," Madison interrupted, pointing toward the bar. Ivy glanced over, but Clayton wasn't looking at her. He was talking to his satyrs. She realized Madison was giving her an out, but Lyric spoke before she could take it.

"Oh, I won't keep you. You're lucky — Clayton Pryce is super cute," she whispered, moving in closer. Her blond hair was curled into waves, and the curls shone with resin. Ivy wondered whether her hairdresser had always been lying when he said she'd look terrible as a blonde. "They're still deciding whether to give me a boyfriend," Lyric went on. "They don't want to spoil the 'pure' thing. I hope they do, though!"

"Good luck with that," said Ivy. "Well, see you around."

"Oh, I'll probably see you at the Pop Beat Music Awards, right? I'm performing — can you believe it? Stay young!" And with a wave, she walked into the crowd, her nymphs closing the gap behind her.

For a moment, Ivy stood motionless. She could feel her nymphs waiting for a reaction of some sort. There were other eavesdroppers watching her too, some of them reporters. She needed to stay composed.

"Nice kid," she said, shrugging. "A little virginal for my taste, though." Reliably, her nymphs snickered in unison. She turned to Hilarie.

"Hey, come to the bathroom with me, okay, Hil?" she said. She dabbed her lips with her middle finger. "I need a touchup. Tell Clayton I'll be right over," she instructed the other nymphs.

Passing the metallic basins, Ivy headed straight for a stall and pulled the door closed behind her. She was glad Scalpel was a classy place; the doors went all the way to the floor.

She unclasped her purse and pulled out her Unum. "Jarvis," she said into the microphone. A moment later, the words JAR-VIS UNAVAILABLE flashed on the screen. She swore in frustration. Tapping the New Message button on the Unum screen, she spoke into the microphone again. "Jarvis. Two questions. How many stops on my *Laid Bare* tour? And am I performing at the Pop Beat Music Awards again? I am, right? Reply ASAP."

She hit Send.

After emerging from the stall, she began freshening her makeup. She relined her lower eyelids and applied gloss until her lips shone like glass. Next to her, Hilarie and a few other girls were doing the same. Ivy could tell that the girls were staring at her while trying to look like they weren't. At least that felt good.

Her Unum buzzed.

Twenty stops on tour, the screen read. *Working on two more. We didn't get slot for Pop Beat Awards. Not to worry. You're going anyway. Have fun tonight!*

She could feel her face heating. Lyric would be on stage at the awards show, and she would be watching from the audience. *The audience.*

"You okay, Ivy?" she heard Hilarie ask. Ivy caught her nymph's gaze in the mirror.

"Fine," she said, motioning with her head. The two of them stepped into the handicapped stall together. Ivy locked the door.

"The Pop Beat Music Awards didn't book me this year. But they booked Lyric." She scanned Hilarie's face. It was sympathetic — but not overly so.

"Gross. That's totally wrong. Sorry."

"I kind of don't get why she's such a big deal. Her career is on *overdrive.* Twenty-eight stops on her first tour? What's up with that?"

"She's totally boring. Everyone'll be over her in a minute."

"That's what Jarvis says."

"He's right."

"Yeah, but did you see the reporters out there? They were crazy about her!" She pressed her back against the cold wall.

"So don't let her hog the spotlight. Do something wild. Fall down and let your underwear show again. Or slap one of the bouncers in the face. Get photoed."

Ivy let her nymph's advice sink in. "Yeah. You're right." She shook her head. "This is so annoying."

"Do you need me to pick a fight?"

"No. I'll figure something out."

As they exited the bathroom, Ivy threaded her arm through Hilarie's. They approached the bar where her nymphs were mingling with Clayton and his satyrs.

Farther on past the bar, directly in her sightline, Ivy saw Lyric sitting with her nymphs in one of the circular booths. The girls sipped Sugarwater demurely out of oversized tumblers. The nymphs were trying to keep the press from overwhelming their star, but Ivy noticed that Lyric made attempts to hold her smile for the photographers and answer a question or two if a reporter persisted.

As Lyric lowered her eyelashes to take a long, graceful sip from her straw, Ivy's plan came to her.

She dropped Hilarie's arm and walked up to Clayton. Ignoring the fact that he was in the middle of telling Naia a story, she ran her fingers through his hair and pressed her body against his. Naia quickly moved away. With both hands, Ivy began massaging the back of his neck. "Feel like getting frisky, Clay?" she asked.

Clayton raised his eyebrows at her.

"Photo op," she whispered. Vaguely, Clayton nodded in understanding. He put his arms around her waist, and Ivy began kissing him.

She wished she had wiped off the gloss. It tasted terrible, and she was smearing it all over poor Clayton's mouth and face. It was so sticky, too; stray strands of her hair were mixing with their kisses. She tried to pull them out and tuck them behind her ears without breaking contact. At least he had P pill breath this time and no beard to scratch up her face. She was aware of a few flashes behind her — good. The press had noticed.

She grabbed Clayton's shale bodyshirt and forced him backward a few steps. He flinched as she clutched some chest hairs, and she shifted her grip, still kissing him, still steering him in her desired direction. The two arrived at Lyric's table, and Ivy pushed Clayton backward onto its surface. Like bowling pins, the Sugarwater tumblers fell over, spilling their contents everywhere. Lyric and her nymphs cried out, and Ivy fell forward onto Clayton, squirming and kissing him hungrily.

The cameras flashed until it looked like daytime in the club. Ivy risked a glance at Lyric. Soaked, the front of her dress stuck to her wet skin. She was covering her chest with one hand and waving to her wet nymphs to go get her jacket with the other. A few feathers on her headdress drooped forlornly.

Bull's-eye.

She pulled the stunned Clayton to his feet. "Our bad. Really sorry," she mumbled over his shoulder. She jumped into Clayton's arms and swung her legs around his waist; luckily, he caught her. "Coat closet," she whispered. He carried her toward the club's entrance while she chewed on his ear. The cameras continued to flash. When they reached the closet, she yelled, "Out!" at the coat-check boy. He scampered. The two of them tumbled into the closet and shut both halves of the split door.

Ivy released Clayton and took a few steps back, catching her breath. Clayton blinked at her. He sat down on the coatroom floor, grabbed the hem of a coat, and wiped his cheeks and chin. Ivy sat down across from him and looked at her watch. "One eleven. Let's give it fifteen minutes."

Clayton nodded.

"Sorry about the gloss."

"It's okay. I'm used to it." The placidophilus gave his voice a calm, dreamy quality.

Ivy wiped her own mouth with her fingers and pushed her hair back. She held it in a ponytail for a moment, wishing she had a hair elastic, then let it fall. "So what's new?"

Clayton shrugged. "Not much. How're you?"

"Better now."

Clayton blinked a few times at her, but she didn't elaborate.

A minute of silence passed. Ivy scratched her neck. Clayton began humming "Swollen" absent-mindedly. He sat on his hands, widened his eyes in surprise, and began patting his backside. "My back is soaked!" he announced.

She laughed. "Sorry. I guess that's my fault, Clay. Well, Lyric Mirth's, really. Let's blame her."

Clayton pulled the coat he had used to wipe his mouth off

its hanger, folded it roughly, and sat on it. "Yeah, let's. 'So Pure It Hurts' makes my ears hurt."

"And *that's* why I love you," she said, hugging her knees to her chest. He grinned back at her.

Another minute or so passed in silence. Ivy wondered whether Lyric had left Scalpel altogether. She felt a small pang of guilt. It wasn't really Lyric's fault that her tour was scheduled so aggressively. And the girl *had* been decent to her tonight. She rubbed her temples. It was work to remain relevant. Sometimes . . . sometimes Ivy had to do things that would have shocked Evangeline.

At last, Clayton ran his fingers through his pompadour and spoke again. "Guess what? I'm actually taking a break before I go back into the studio again." He giggled. "I had a little meltdown a few weeks ago. In a restaurant."

"Really?" Ivy raised her eyebrows. She hadn't heard a whisper about it; Clayton's people had obviously done serious damage control.

Clayton nodded. "My agent was afraid I'd go all Skip McBrody on him, so he's sending me to Isla Del Sol with the fam for a vacation."

Ivy thought about how nice a trip with her own family would be. Maybe she should try flying off the handle. Constantine, especially, would appreciate the chance to get away. She had spoken to her family only once since visiting Millbrook, but Christina had reassured her that her brother was coping as well as could be expected. He had returned to school and seemed relaxed and at peace with the Tap outcome. Ivy was pretty sure she knew what was keeping him so calm, but she didn't mention the P pills. Christina was weirdly uncool about them.

"That's kind of prime, Clay. The vacation, not the meltdown. Is James coming with you?"

Even in the placidophilus cloud, Clayton's face grew somber. He shook his head. "No satyrs allowed."

"How are you guys?"

"Good, but . . ." He paused, removing another P pill from the tin in his pocket. He offered one to Ivy, who rolled it in her loose fist. "That's what the meltdown was all about," Clayton continued. He looked at the floor. "We got photographed, and Keane had to bribe the photographer, and I just kind of hit the roof." He popped the pill into his mouth and chewed. "Some days I'm just so sick of pretending," he said with a sigh.

Ivy nodded. Clayton was almost twenty. It had been a long run.

"No offense, Wilde. You're the best beard a guy could hope for." He knocked his knee against hers and hiccupped. "'Scuse me."

"Excused," said Ivy. "I'm really sorry about all that." She paused. "And tell James I'm sorry for that whole thing out there." She waved her hand.

"He understands. We know it's no picnic for you, either."

Ivy thought of the one and only boy she'd kissed before becoming a star. It had happened a few precious times, one being that strange evening after she'd been tapped, after the parties, hours before Fatima and Jarvis had helicoptered in. She'd gone outside to sprinkle rock salt on her front steps. She'd whined about it, but her mother had told her, "You're not famous yet." The sun had long set, and the snow was falling. Her friend Marisa's older brother, home to celebrate his sister's Tap, was salting his own walk. One of the Big Five fashion houses had tapped him two years before, but he'd been able to finagle vacation time here and there. He'd waved her over, then met her halfway and pulled her away from the streetlights, into the black gulf between their houses.

She remembered his hunter's jacket and his hat with earflaps. His nose had been red.

"Eva," he'd said. "You rock. You deserve *Henny Funpeck*. It's a feeble show — but I'll watch it for you, you know."

She'd beamed. And he'd kissed her. She remembered how warm it felt, how it cut the cold in an instant like a furnace.

"I can't wait until you get to La Reina," he'd said, his mouth a hair's breadth from hers. "It's going to be so prime. We can hang out all the time."

After a while, he'd squeezed her mittened hand and run back into his house. She'd been thirteen years old. He'd been, what, fifteen? After she'd moved to La Reina, she had seen him a few more times. But Fatima had been clear: To go solo after *Henny Funpeck*, Ivy needed to follow their instructions. Cut all ties. Rehearse all day long.

She'd done it.

She wondered what he was doing right now.

Ivy popped the P pill into her mouth and chewed in silence. "So, are you playing the Pop Beat Music Awards?" she asked Clayton.

"Yeah."

"Lucky."

"Keane keeps me relevant, but sometimes I wish he weren't so good at his job. But, as we all know, a contract's a contract." He gave her a too-bright smile.

"Be glad you have what you have," she said. "Jarvis could

definitely learn from Keane." She thought for a moment. "Maybe they need to reinvent me. Like they did you when your voice changed, and when you grew the goatee."

"No worries, Wilde. You're totally hot." Clayton stretched his arms above his head. "Is it time yet?"

Ivy looked at her watch. "Five more minutes." She felt the P pill's high begin to kick in. She had made a scene tonight, and Ivy Wilde's antics would be all over the papers tomorrow. Her new album rocked. That was all that really mattered.

Clayton shook out another pill from the tin and deposited it in his mouth. Chewing, he lay back on the floor and put his hands behind his head.

Chapter Eleven

When my *Unum buzzed* that evening after dinner, I knew it was Braxton calling to break up with me.

Sitting at my desk, gripping the underside of my chair with my free hand, I watched as he stumbled through his speech, filling it with the clichés I expected. "Look, you're a totally great person," he began, "but I think we've kind of drifted apart over the past few weeks. I just don't think we're into the same things anymore. You know?"

I wanted to tell him yes, he was right — I was into things like loyalty, and he was a two-timing snake. But I didn't want it to get back to the Superior Court that I was bitter. I couldn't give them that satisfaction. "This wouldn't have anything to do with my being made a drafter, of course," I said instead. I wanted to hear him deny it.

"Marla, *please,*" said Braxton. "Give me a little credit." He exhaled dramatically. "I've been feeling this way for a while. Way before you were demoted — uh, moved downstairs." On the screen, his eyebrows jumped. Suddenly, I despised the tic.

"Uh-huh," I said. I had never wanted to tell someone off the way I did now. The insults came thick and fast. *You're a big fat liar and a cheat,* I wanted to shout, *and I hope you and Olivia choke on chicken bones, and she's* gotta *be an awful kisser with those thin little vicious lips, so enjoy that, and I bet Denominator demotes* you *any day now, so don't come crying to me after Olivia dumps you cold.*

But I knew what Braxton would do after hanging up with me. He'd call Olivia to relay "how it went." I thought of Olivia, listening with that smug grin, wanting to know whether "poor Marla" went to pieces. I swallowed my anger and forced my lips into a smile. Braxton needed to see that I didn't care.

"You know, Brax, this is for the best. You're right. I think we are growing apart. I've fallen in with this group of drafters. They're a little crazy, but I think they want to change the world." I was surprised to hear myself say this. "Anyway, they're making me think about fashion — and everything, really — in a whole new way. It's like a fresh start."

"That's good — that's really good," said Braxton enthusiastically. I'd hoped he'd show a little more surprise at how quickly I was getting over him. Maybe he was just hiding it.

"Yeah. It is."

"So — stay young, I guess. I'll totally see you around," he said.

I'll do everything I can never to run into you ever again. "Yeah, see you." I pressed the button to disconnect and lay down on my bed, pulling my knees in to my chest. Perched on my pillows sat Braxton's gift, the stuffed bear. I jumped up, grabbed scissors from the desktop, and held them open around the bear's throat. But something held me back. I just couldn't decapitate it. It wasn't the bear's fault, after all. I put the blades together and gave it earring holes instead by stabbing repeatedly through the satin and stuffing.

Later, as I was brushing my teeth, it hit me that I wouldn't be giving Braxton a good-night call. I wouldn't be giving anyone a call now. I couldn't call Sabrina or anyone else from the Superior Court, of course. I could call someone from the local crowd — Emma, or one of the other daughters of Karen's friends — but the truth was, I didn't like them very much. When I'd been on the court, I'd stopped talking to them altogether. Come to think of it, if I did call now, I doubted they'd have a whole lot of sympathy for me.

"Don't cry," I ordered my reflection in the mirror. I whispered the command again and splashed cold water on my face. As I was drying myself with a towel, I remembered what was on the top shelf of the medicine cabinet, tucked discreetly behind a container of cotton swabs. I opened the cabinet, reached up, and found my mother's small tin. Taking it down from the shelf, I could feel that there were at least a half dozen placidophilus pills still inside. I turned the tin upside down and looked at the expiration date. The pills had expired four months ago. They were probably still fine. They wouldn't kill me, anyway.

I shook a little pink pill into my hand and held it between my fingers. It looked so small and harmless. What had Randall said — save P pills for a really bad day? Well, days didn't get much worse than this, did they? I was a drafter, I'd been dumped, I had no friends . . .

I put the pill in my mouth and started to chew.

The strawberry taste and smell were pleasant. It was just a piece of candy, really. I stood under the sharp vanity lights in the bathroom, watching myself chew in the mirror, waiting for something dramatic to happen, waiting for my sadness to transform to happiness with the flip of a switch.

Instead, the change came gradually. My rage at Braxton, my frustration, my self-pity — it felt as if something was tugging these heavy feelings out of my head. I found it harder to care that Braxton had left me for Olivia. But . . . I wanted to care. It *wasn't* okay. I resisted, trying to hold on to my outrage. But the some-thing kept tugging, stronger and stronger, until I had an image in my mind of Braxton caressing Olivia's cheek and it didn't annoy me, didn't bother me at all. I saw Braxton leaning in for a kiss, and even that was just fine, just fine, until their lips touched, and sud-denly, in a flash, a little part of my brain cried out that *no,* it was *not* fine. Although the something smothered the protest immedi-ately, it was enough. The pill had dissolved on my tongue, but I spat into the sink basin repeatedly. Reaching for the mouthwash, I gargled until the scent of strawberries disappeared.

Even so, my brain felt full of cotton. I shook my head to clear it and blinked at my reflection in the mirror. I didn't want this numbness.

Braxton was a jerk. The courts at Torro pitied me. My life was in the toilet. But I didn't want to stop feeling. My hands trembling, I replaced the tin on the top shelf of the medicine cabinet behind the cotton swabs.

"Name me something that would never become a trend," Vivi-enne said to me the next day at work as I was redrafting the rock-er jeans.

"What?" I said halfheartedly. I was trying to keep a low profile today. No eye contact with the other drafters. I felt aw-ful after what I'd said yesterday. Plus, I didn't want to deal with any remarks about my clothes, or about how I was a "princess." I couldn't take it this morning.

"Something no court would ever approve," Vivienne said. "Something you could wear on your body but has no chance of becoming a trend."

I thought. "You mean like shoulder pads?"

She shook her head. "Shoulder pads *have* been trendy. Something new."

"Why?"

Vivienne gave me a mysterious smile. "I want a challenge."

In my head, I went through the worst designs I had encountered as a sifter. Besides badly drawn sketches, mostly really ugly, sloppy-looking garments didn't make it past the selectors. But then I remembered when bohemian and grunge had merged into the homeless trend. Then, the uglier the design, the better. Torro had even sold pants that were moth-eaten and caked in mud.

"I don't know. Anything could get approved." I shrugged.

"Anything?" asked Vivienne.

"Well, maybe not something extremely painful, I guess. Like shoes that seriously damage your feet. Worse than high heels. Or something you couldn't move in or breathe in at all." I thought about some of the choices the court had made while I had served as a judge. "Actually, you never know, the stuff might be approved. But it wouldn't really catch on. People would never wear, like, something painful. Something that draws blood."

"They have before," said Vivienne thoughtfully.

I raised my eyebrows.

"But I agree. That would be a long shot." Vivienne reached for some blank sheets of paper. She tapped her pencil against her lips. "Mmm," she said. "Pain."

At noon, I walked to a food cart on Fifth Street. The air smelled like grilled meats, and the line for pita sandwiches curved like a fishhook. Usually, no one I knew at Torro got their food here —the reason I walked the extra couple of blocks—but today I caught sight of Felix about ten places ahead of me in line.

He was fiddling with his Unum but eventually lifted his head and looked around. Before I could look away, he caught my eye, held it for a moment, and, to my surprise, gestured with his head. "'Bout time you made it," he said loudly. "I've been saving your place for ten minutes."

It took me a second to get it. "Oh," I said, and walked up to meet him. "You didn't have to do that," I mumbled under my breath as I slid into line in front of him.

Felix tucked his Unum in his pocket and crossed his arms. "I guess even bitter fossils can have manners."

My words came in an awkward gush. "I shouldn't have called you that."

Felix shrugged. "Yeah, well. It's true. Being a drafter really unleashes the cynic. Not that what goes on in the other industries is any better. Sometimes, I get so angry I can't control what comes out of my mouth." He paused. "I should . . . try harder, though."

He was looking straight at me. His tone held a twinge of remorse, and I wondered if this was his version of an apology. For intimidating me, and calling me "princess," and all that. I took a breath. "I guess I have a control problem too. I was kicked off the Superior Court for saying something I shouldn't have."

Felix's dark eyes studied me. "Really."

We approached the cart counter and ordered our sandwiches.

"So what happened?" Felix asked while we walked back to Torro-LeBlanc.

Between bites of my sandwich, I told him about my final days on the court and about Julia's warning. I described the fateful day of judging, when I hadn't been able to conceal my admiration for Vivienne's dress. Felix listened without interrupting.

"That story says a lot," he said at last, holding open the heavy front door of the design house for me. "You know what Torro must like even less than a judge who's lost her touch? A judge who doesn't listen when she's told not to make waves."

I thought about his comment as we returned to the drafting table. Vivienne, Kevin, and Dido returned together, with doggie bags from Prehistoric Bistro. Randall came in a moment later, munching on a bag of potato chips. When everyone had settled in, I took a deep breath. "So, I just wanted to say," I began, "that I'm sorry for what I said yesterday about you — um, about drafters being miserable. It was really rude."

The others lifted their heads to look at me. My hands were shaking a little bit. I clasped them together and hid them in my lap. Vivienne kept her design covered by the crook of her arm and waited for me to continue.

"I think she finally woke up and realized we're all she's got," Kevin said, nudging Felix and smirking. Felix didn't reply; instead, he gave me a faint nod.

"Don't be a jerk," said Dido, tossing a crumpled sketch across the table at Kevin. "It's okay, Marla. Go ahead."

"Yes. Apology accepted," said Randall, giving me a small wink.

"Um," I began again. I felt Vivienne's dark eyes scrutinizing me and shifted on my stool. "I love fashion, and I love Torro-LeBlanc. I do. I was just thinking . . . it would be nice not to have my career end at sixteen, you know? Like you said. It's not fair."

Vivienne waited. She was making me nervous.

"So, just out of curiosity," I went on, "what exactly were you all getting at the other day?"

There was a pause. Vivienne flipped her sketch over in one swift movement and placed her palm on the paper.

"Here it comes," muttered Dido.

"We want to organize a strike." Vivienne said it quietly but with confidence. "If the Torro-LeBlanc employees unify, the Silents will have to listen to our demands. Basic labor theory. Some of the key patternmakers are on board. But we need the Superior Court to participate."

A strike? I had to think for a moment to remember what the term meant. It was when workers walked off their jobs illegally, I was pretty sure. The idea stunned me. A million questions popped into my head. I wondered where Vivienne had learned about labor theory — whatever that was. And why she thought the Silents would change anything. And why the Superior Court mattered.

"Are you serious?" Vivienne's face gave me her answer. "And ... why does the Superior Court have to be involved?" I decided to start with that one.

"Well, you won't have heard about them, but there *have* been attempts at drafter strikes before. The Silents crush them almost immediately, and they get no press, but you can find whispers about them online. The problem is," Vivienne continued, her finger pressed to the tabletop, "leverage. Drafters don't have much. We could get every drafter in here to walk out right now, and Torro would most likely replace us with scribbling monkeys within the hour. But if children on the upper floors were visibly involved in the strike, the company would be paralyzed. If it got out that Torro doesn't have its courts, the label would be dead."

I nodded slowly. Vivienne had a point. Everyone believed that the Superior Court and three Junior Courts were composed of elite trendsetters, tapped for their love of fashion, trained at Torro-LeBlanc, and assigned to serve only after they had perfected an eye for trends. If the judges decided not to work anymore . . . but this whole line of thinking was useless. Why would the judges *ever* stop judging? I wouldn't have quit for anything — I was sure of it. How on earth did Vivienne expect . . .

Vivienne looked over my head and cleared her throat meaningfully. I glanced behind her and noticed Winnie walking along the rows of tables, peering over the shoulders of the drafters. Vivienne hastily drew a model in a strapless sundress on the blank side of her paper. Once again, I was stunned at Vivienne's ability to throw together a breathtaking sketch. In just a few strokes, her figure looked ready to board the world's most exclusive yacht. This from someone who favored dress codes.

"Now, you can't forget that no matter what the season, people *will* want resortwear," she said loudly. "We haven't seen the sweetheart neckline in a little while, have we? That could work." She gave Winnie a close-mouthed smile as she passed. Winnie nodded approvingly, her cheeks radiating the same youthful, golden glow they always did.

Vivienne waited until Winnie had progressed far enough down the row to speak again. "Think, Marla," she said softly. "Who on the Superior Court might we be able to turn? Who on the court has the most influence right now?"

Turn the judges. So she *was* crazy. "I'm pretty sure that's impossible," I said. I thought of Sabrina. "I just ran into one the other day. She used to be my best friend on the court, and she would barely talk to me. She sent me passes to the Torro runway show out of pity."

"How generous," said Kevin.

"You have runway-show passes?" said Dido.

"Just give me a name or two," said Vivienne. "The judges who, you know, everyone tends to go along with."

I thought of Henry immediately. He had been there the longest and definitely had the loudest mouth. And . . . I knew the name of the other judge who had the most influence, but I couldn't bring myself to say it. I wanted nothing more to do with that little viper. Olivia did have power, though. She was young and decisive, convinced that anything she liked would become popular. I remembered thinking like that. It felt like a long time ago.

"Henry Sachs," I said at last. "He's been there the longest. The other judges follow his lead."

"Okay. Talk to Henry. He might be anticipating that it's not long before he's down here with us. You'll have to try to get into his head."

"Me?"

"Just approach him at first. Talk about your life now. Your garment rejection from the Junior Court. Tell him about the frustration you feel."

"Ask him if he's thought about what's next for him at Torro-LeBlanc," said Felix.

"Give him a cup of the lousy coffee," said Kevin.

"No, don't overdo it in the first conversation," said Vivienne firmly. "Just say hi, plant the seed, and we can work on building our case in stages."

I shook my head. "I don't think you understand. I'm like dirt under his fingernails now. He won't even talk to me."

"You've got to try," said Vivienne. "How about this. Put on a big act of needing his divine inspiration to guide your sketches. Appeal to his ego."

"It's not going to do any good."

"Please, Marla," said Felix. I realized it was the first time he'd called me by name. "You're it. You're our chance."

I opened my mouth to protest, but I could feel the weight of everyone's expectations. Even Felix looked sincere. He was pinning his hopes on me. They all were.

I shrugged hopelessly. "I'll give it a shot."

On the train ride home, I hid a few seats behind Henry like some pathetic spy, waiting for a chance to speak to him. He was sitting with Carmen Michelle and a couple of other runway models. How was I supposed to interrupt them without making an idiot of myself?

Finally, miraculously, the models got off together and Henry was left alone. I had my sketches half out of my briefcase when I saw him raise his Unum toward a girl in a Torro fringe dress standing by the train door. He then began tapping the screen with a little smirk on his face.

Of course. Why hadn't I thought of Henry's little side project before?

Quickly and quietly, I slid my papers back into the briefcase and pulled out my Unum. I snapped a picture of the girl in the dress. Then, I angled the camera to get both Henry and the girl in the shot. Feeling more like a spy but less pathetic, I zoomed in on Henry and his Unum and tapped photo after photo.

When I had some good ones, I called up the Maven Girl site. Sure enough, the girl's photo was there, cropped at the neck. FLAPPERFECTION the caption heading read.

I let my hair fall across my face so Henry wouldn't see me for the rest of the train ride. I had to think.

The next morning, Vivienne confronted me as soon as I settled onto my stool in the basement.

"Any luck?" she whispered.

"Sort of. I remembered something yesterday," I said, checking to make sure the drafters at the other tables weren't listening. "Henry is Maven Girl."

I looked around at their reactions and wasn't disappointed.

"But — no way," said Dido, frowning.

"He can't be," said Randall. "That's in violation of his contract, isn't it?"

I grinned. "Big time."

"Wait — then who's the girl?" Dido asked.

"There's no girl. He's the girl. I know it's hard to believe. A couple of people on the court know. I caught him posting a photo one time . . . and he admitted it."

I didn't tell them the whole story. When I first joined the court, I saw Henry updating the Maven Girl site and confronted him. I didn't think what he was doing was fair. The Big Five sanctioned the major online and print fashion magazines, but everyone checked out independent hotspots like Maven Girl anyway. Henry even critiqued celebrity style — he sold ads to pay for paparazzi photos. It would be a problem for Henry if Torro found out he was operating a rogue site as popular as Maven Girl and promoting trends from all the Big Five houses.

"You won't mind so much when your garments show up on the site," Henry had said with an acidic smile. "Trust me."

"But it's against the rules," I'd said. "What if Julia found out?"

"Marla." Henry had put his arm around me. "The nine members of the court — we're a team now. You understand? Torro hasn't been number one in the Big Five for a few years. Don't you want to see us at the top?"

"Of course."

"Good. You do your part, and I'll do mine."

So I'd told Sabrina instead of Julia. And Henry was right. Once I saw a few of my personal picks from the court pop up on Maven Girl and get a giant sales bump — well, it didn't exactly hurt Julia's opinion of me. Not surprisingly, Henry's own picks from the Superior Court made it on more often than anything else.

It was a point of pride for me that my longest-selling item, the knit shawl, had caught on *without* Maven Girl's endorsement.

"Yesterday I took some photos of him updating the site on the train," I said. "I don't think he'd want them printed."

"Stealthy," said Felix.

Vivienne's fingers tapped the handle of her coffee mug. "Maven Girl. Its readership is *huge*. We can use that. If he posts in support of drafters' rights, people will listen."

"Mm-hmm. So, I had another idea."

The night before, while my runway-show passes from Sabrina were downloading, I read a story online about Lyric Mirth. Apparently, Ivy Wilde had fallen onto Lyric's table at a club and spilled drinks everywhere. The headline read RISING STAR LEFT MIRTHLESS and featured a close-up of the drenched performer, her mouth open in shock.

The incident had inspired me. We could ambush Henry anywhere . . . or go for a little drama. The nice girl in me usually steered clear of drama. But this time, if we could pull it off, the drama would be mighty entertaining. I just had to convince the others.

At the table, I reached into my pocket, removed my Unum, and called up the ticket image. I spun the device around and put it in the center of the table so that everyone could see the show information printed on top of a light gray T-L logo. "I have four tickets to the runway show. We go. The judges will be wearing samples from the sample room, and I thought we could"— I inhaled —"leave a bunch of exploding-ink security tags near their chairs. The show is so packed, with everyone milling around beforehand, that I think we could get away with it." I paused, imagining Olivia, Sabrina, and Henry steaming with embarrassment as green liquid spattered their faces and clothes in the front row. What a beautiful sight.

"Tags?" Randall asked. The other drafters were all listening intently.

"You know, the tags that keep people from shoplifting. When I was a sifter, we used to steal buckets of them from the warehouse and explode them in the tunnels beneath the train station," I went on. "We tinkered with them until they'd blow with the slightest vibration, like when the train went by overhead. I *think,* if we get them really pressure sensitive, the music will make them explode once the show starts. Karisma's playing live. The amplified bass and drums should do it. And if that doesn't work, the applause at the end of the show on top of the music will."

"And then?" asked Vivienne.

I shifted on my stool and lowered my voice. "I know the code to the runway sample room. That is, if they haven't changed it. But it was the same the whole time I was on the court. Anyway, with their clothes wrecked, the judges will have to go back there to change. We could be waiting. We corner Henry and maybe some of the other judges. We let Henry know we're ready to tell everyone he's Maven Girl and refuse to let him go unless he cooperates with your strike — or whatever you want."

Deep down, I seriously wondered whether Henry would go along with Vivienne's strange ideas, even when facing blackmail. He might say what we wanted to hear in the moment, but I couldn't see him joining a revolt against Torro-LeBlanc. To see Maven Girl suddenly start writing about drafters' rights was even less likely.

I didn't really care. The urge to see him and the others publicly embarrassed overpowered the voices of reason in my head.

"Security will be everywhere," I said, "so we'll have to be quick."

I looked around. Dido's eyes were wide.

"You would do this, Marla?" said Vivienne. "You'd give your passes to us and take this risk — instead of going with your friends?"

I blinked. "I have no one else to go with." It was the truth. I looked across the table at Kevin defensively, but he didn't laugh. I avoided Felix's eyes.

"So, who's going?" asked Dido. I looked at Vivienne for help.

"It's your decision," Vivienne said.

I sighed. "Well, you, obviously." I looked around at the others. "Who else wants to come?"

"I pass," said Randall. "I'll leave the covert ops to the rest of you."

"Your skills could be useful, Randall," said Vivienne. *Skills?* What skills did he have?

"You'll be fine without me. Jeri needs help on the weekends with the kids."

"Um," Dido began, "I don't want to take someone else's place, but I've never actually been —"

"Oh, for God's sake, Dido, just go already," said Kevin. He looked at Felix. "You too. I can tell you want to be there. Just don't screw it up," he added.

Felix nodded solemnly. "I won't."

Dido picked up my Unum and stared at the ticket on its

screen giddily. I noticed the giant rings she was wearing today, remnants from the urban-gypsy trend that had expired in late fall.

"Only . . . one thing," I said. "We've got to fit in. Can everyone — uh — try to wear trends? Please?"

"Maybe I wear an expired piece now and again." Felix perked up his shirt collars and grinned around at the circle. "But tell me I don't look fine every damn day."

The other drafters laughed and rolled their eyes. "You do okay for a straight guy," said Kevin.

"Okay? I'm well groomed and working in an industry full of prime women, my friend. I'm living the dream."

I felt my face reddening and turned to Vivienne. "Anyway, maybe black isn't the best —"

"I've got some savings." She cut me off. "I'll buy something suitable. Don't worry." I wondered what Vivienne's definition of *suitable* was.

"Marla," Dido said. "Not to be, um . . . well, your clothes are so great, and we're sort of the same size, and I haven't had anything approved in a month so it's a little tough right now for my family —"

"You can borrow my clothes," I interrupted eagerly. The thought of having a friend over, trying on outfits together, was incredibly cheering. It had been a while. I looked down at my own outfit. It was current — though my trendchecker had revealed some expired garments just a few days earlier. Garments that I wasn't sure I'd be replacing. Still, I'd tossed them in the donation box immediately. Things weren't dire yet. I had more than enough to dress both Dido and myself decently for the show.

"You surprise me," said Felix. "I'll say that much."

I held his gaze. "You shouldn't underestimate princesses."

"Snap," said Kevin.

Felix's mouth twisted into a little smile. Randall gave me a wink, and we went back to work.

As usual, just after eleven a.m., Winnie made the rounds in the basement with her handful of sketches from the selector. I wasn't really paying attention. I hadn't submitted anything the day before, as my rocker jeans were still not quite right. So I was surprised to find Winnie standing behind me. I turned — but it wasn't my shoulder Winnie tapped.

"I knew you were just in a dry spell, Vivienne," she chirruped. "*Three* sketches approved today." She waved them under Vivienne's nose. "Gotta love those odds! Good luck." And with a wink, she was gone.

As if they were giant playing cards, Vivienne dealt the three sketches face up in front of her on the table.

I gasped.

Chapter Twelve

Each step brought pain.

The shoes — if you could call them shoes — were like a twisted punishment for a crime Ivy hadn't committed. From the surface of a stiff leather sole, thin elongated pyramids, painted a reflective red, grew upward like stalagmites. These dazzling protrusions were between three and five inches in height and rose northward into the flesh of Ivy's feet. The shoes stayed on with a series of transparent plastic straps, not unlike those on a gladiator's sandal.

"Distribution of weight makes these wearable," Fatima had told her, thrusting the ruby sculptures at her that morning. "Like lying on a bed of nails." But that was a lie. The points were arranged to achieve a platform heel shape, so the spiky pyramids at the rear were longer than those in front. As a result, the balls of Ivy's feet bore most of her weight. With each delicate step, she swore the points were going to pop through her skin and pierce bone.

The shoes would have been enough to keep her eyes perpetually watering at the Torro-LeBlanc runway show. But there was also the miniskirt of woven human hair, which itched like a rug of fleas. And the collar with the spiked spherical tassels that bounced against her back and released ticklish trickles of imitation blood when she moved. To catch the trickles, a detachable sponge had been snapped into her lace-up corset. The corset, black lace over red leather, with threaded boning, was bearable when she stood, but she swore it had rearranged her kidneys in the car ride over. She had no idea how she was going to bear sitting through the show in it — though at least she'd be off her feet then. The wrist shackles, thankfully, provided some movement. Although they were chained to metal garters locked onto her thighs, she could lift her arms to forty-five-degree angles. Not high enough to adjust the stretchy piece of shale that gagged her, but high enough to shake hands or sign autographs.

Ivy hadn't minded her original outfit for the runway show: a brown bodysuit embroidered with orange feathers, and a giant orange feather crown. *Much* taller than the one Lyric had worn at Scalpel, with stiff plumes exploding everywhere. Her nymphs had liked their feather dresses too. But Fatima had barged in with garment bags at the last minute and told everyone to strip. The feather craze was about to expire, she explained, and Torro-LeBlanc had sent over samples from their new line. It was unusual for anyone to debut a trend before it appeared on the runway, but "I convinced them to make an exception in this case," Fatima told Ivy. "Torture is going to be so big, and *you* are going to be the one who makes it famous. You could use that kind of publicity."

Ivy frowned. "What does that mean?"

"Nothing," said Fatima, smiling broadly. "Just doing my job. Keeping you current. Let me lace you in."

Ivy and her nymphs were certainly drawing stares in the theater lobby before the show. Her nymphs were done up in milder versions of the torture trend — no chains, no blood, and platform stilettos instead of the horrible shoes she wore. They all took cautious steps; the midday light from the tall windows made the already slick marble floor look like ice. Ivy waited for someone to raise an eyebrow, for someone to make a face or shake a head. No one did. People were studying her, but they nodded to their friends approvingly. The celebrities famous enough to talk to her passed on awed compliments as they inspected the corset, the chains, the hair skirt. Hilarie pulled the gag down so Ivy could reply, then pinched it back in place afterward. Ivy blinked away her tears and assured everyone that the clothes were a little painful, yes, but that the pain "kind of thrilled her." Fatima had said this answer would go over well, especially with the press. It seemed to.

As usual, the lobby swarmed with magazine editors, as well as performers and other A-listers who wanted first peek at the new midspring lines. Clayton wasn't with her today; he was still in Isla Del Sol. Ivy hoped the vacation was helping him. On the ride over, she had been dreading running into Lyric Mirth at the show, but now she wanted to see her. Ivy's clothes were grabbing all the attention in the room. The skewed headlines after Scalpel still rankled — but let that beanpole try to outshine her here. Ivy scanned the lobby, but Lyric didn't seem to be in attendance. She wondered why not. She had a moment's panic when she imagined a better Sunday afternoon event going on somewhere else that Jarvis hadn't been able to get her into. No — that was crazy. Lyric was probably just rehearsing or something. For her *twenty-eight-stop* tour. That girl got under her skin.

Ivy shook herself free of these thoughts. Her envy had distracted her momentarily from the mouth-to-toe pain. This was torture — literally. She stood on daggers; her waist and hips were starting to sweat, though her shoulders were getting cold.

But everyone was staring at her in the dimly lit lobby, everyone watching and snapping and judging . . .

From across the lobby, one face shifted into focus. Dark hair. Thick eyebrows. A face that didn't belong in these surroundings somehow. Recognition clicked.

Her mouth fell open — as far as the gag would let it.

It was her schoolgirl crush from Millbrook, who had kissed her in the snow that frigid night. What on earth was he doing here? Of course — he worked for one of the Big Five fashion houses . . . and yes, it had been Torro-LeBlanc that tapped him, hadn't it?

She squinted. Or was she imagining things? He looked so serious — not the way she remembered. Was it someone else?

She tried to call out, but her gag distorted his name. She tried to wave, but couldn't raise her arms. She jingled her chains in protest, and Hilarie worked the gag out.

"What is it?" Madison asked.

"I thought I saw someone I knew," said Ivy slowly. She took a few agonizing steps toward him but the lobby was packed full, and someone waved at her for a photo, and when she turned back after posing, his face had disappeared.

"I guess . . . I guess I was wrong," Ivy said to her puzzled nymphs. Hilarie maneuvered the gag back into place.

An usher appeared in front of her. "Miss Wilde, I'm here to escort your party to your seats — whenever you're ready — please take your time," he stuttered. Usually, Fatima had her wait until everyone was seated to make a grand entrance . . . but the thought of sitting down was too tempting. She nodded and said, "Now," through the gag.

The usher held out his elbow, which Ivy gratefully grabbed. Her nymphs followed. Ivy leaned on him to take some of the pressure off her feet, and the usher willingly flexed his arm to support her. They entered the long, narrow auditorium — and, oh God, she'd forgotten. There were stairs down to the front row. Not many, but each shift in weight, one foot to the other, brought a bigger lump to her throat. "Slowly, slowly, please," she tried to whisper through the gag, trying to smile, aware that people were watching her.

When they reached the bottom, Ivy collapsed into the chair at the end of the first row. Her feet instantly felt a wash of relief. That was it. She wasn't moving.

"Get this gag out of my mouth, Hil," she mumbled. The words were incoherent, but Hilarie understood and pulled it off.

"Thanks," Ivy announced to the usher. "We'll be fine here."

The usher's forehead creased. "Oh, but Miss Wilde, we have excellent seats for you right on the other side of the catwalk, if you'll just follow me." He gestured over the long stage. "These seats are actually for —"

"These seats are ours," said Ivy. She shifted to scratch her rear surreptitiously on the chair bottom. "I'm not moving. Sorry. Deal with it." She tried to cross her arms, but the chains prevented it. Annoyed, she settled for clenching her fists and resting them on her knees.

"Oh, but —"

"You heard her." Not bound by chains, Madison crossed her arms successfully and stepped between Ivy and the usher. The others cocked their heads at him, full of attitude.

With a forced smile, the usher mumbled, "Yes, Miss Wilde," and strode off, frantically scanning the room for an event coordinator. When he found one, he pointed and gestured, but the event coordinator was unfazed. Ivy watched the woman speak into her headset, nod, and dismiss the usher.

That was that. She wasn't Ivy Wilde for nothing, after all.

Delicately, she slid over two seats so she could sit surrounded by her nymphs. Hilarie reached over to fix her gag, but Ivy shook her head. "Leave it. It's hard enough to breathe as it is."

The catwalk rose up before her, a glowing, polished white. She hoped the models didn't skid in their heels again, like the disaster a couple months ago at Zhang & Tsai. To her left, in a small cluster on a platform at the end of the catwalk, the fashion photographers were grouped, readying their equipment. At the far end, Karisma was setting up on a small round stage to the side of the catwalk entrance. She was glad to see them. Shows with live music were always more entertaining.

Her insides were starting to cramp. Next to her, Naia began chewing a P pill. The pills had helped Ivy with the pain a little this morning, but she had chewed four in a row while practicing walking in the shoes. She'd felt strung out and sloppy, and she'd cut herself off. Even now, the faint scent of strawberries from Naia's mouth was giving her a contact high — or at least making her mushy-headed again.

"Can you chew in that direction?" Ivy asked, pointing away. She rubbed her hand over her stomach — or rather, over the stiff boning that pressed her stomach flat as a cutting board. With apologies, Naia switched spots with Madison.

Slowly, the seats around her filled in, and the buzz of voices in the hall increased. Ivy watched the Torro-LeBlanc Superior Court file down the stairs in the opposite corner. Light gray and turquoise cards with JUDGE printed on them hung from lanyards around their necks. They sat in a row directly opposite her and her nymphs, on the other side of the catwalk. They, too, wore items from new lines — a fringe dress, a gold jacket — although no one else was featuring torture, she noticed. Maybe that was

Fatima's doing. As always, the judges gave modest little shrugs and hand waves. Really, though, they radiated self-importance. *Feeble,* Ivy thought. Anyone could pick out clothes. It took *real* talent to do what she did.

The lights dimmed, Karizma's drummer clacked his sticks together twice, and the show began.

As the first model strutted down the catwalk, Ivy and her nymphs reached under their chairs for the provided Tabulas. Lit screens popped on throughout the darkened theater, although glare deflectors kept the glow to a minimum. Still, Ivy could see that most Tabula users were consolidated in the front rows. She entered her ID code on the intro screen, which sent her measurements and charge-account number to Torro-LeBlanc, and sat back to watch the show.

To her surprise, Karizma's sound wasn't as heavy as usual. They were playing one of their ballads, "To Love Is to Hurt." She saw that the models' steps were roughly keeping time with the light drumbeat.

The first models were showcasing some kind of superhero trend. It featured capes, leggings, underwear as outerwear, and vinyl bodysuits. Ivy thought it was a pretty obvious attempt on Torro-LeBlanc's part to capitalize on the popularity of Bancroft House's new shale fabric. The stretchy, sleek finish was definitely in. She still wore those ridiculous, squeaky pajamas to bed per Fatima's orders.

The male models were styled to look like Clayton Pryce clones. Their pompadours made Ivy smirk. The female models were the usual fare: No matter their real age, they had the bodies of twelve-year-olds. Long limbs, no hips, breasts no bigger than teacups. She recognized Carmen Michelle modeling the final superhero look: a shiny black catsuit stitched together with gold thread. Her figure was almost boyish. Looking down, Ivy wondered if her own breasts looked too large in the corset top. They weren't crazy big or anything, but they had gotten bigger every year since she'd been tapped. She shuddered at the thought of reduction surgery. She'd heard that an old model, Leena Elise, had bound hers at night to stop developing, but she couldn't remember if the method had worked or not. She should ask around. Maybe it was worth a try.

Her Tabula showed a grid of images of the individual pieces featured on the runway. Underneath each image were other colors the item came in and any variations. Temptingly, next to each item glowed a big green button that said BUY! Her revulsion for shale didn't inspire her to purchase anything from this collection. She clicked under one slate gray clutch and saw the coordinating purse and full handbag — but decided that she didn't really love any of them.

Her stomach gurgled unhappily. She sat up as straight as she could, trying to diminish the pressure. She felt the spiked tassels weep blood down her back as she shifted. She reached up to scratch the trickle — again the chain impeded her. Her face contorted in the darkness, and her eyes watered with frustration. *Keep it together,* she told herself.

Looks from the next trend were coming down the catwalk. Space-age was clearly still going strong. Unlike Zhang & Tsai's line, the palette was more gold than silver, but the looks resembled the outfits she and her nymphs had worn at Millbrook, with fresh tweaks and deviations.

The images on her Tabula flashed and tempted her, but how was she supposed to concentrate on anything when her organs felt like they were being slowly crushed in a vise? Her shoulders were still freezing, and the chains were now cold to the touch. She looked toward the stairs. Should she try to creep out to the lobby? But, oh God, that would mean walking on those spikes again. This was misery.

Some flapperish looks were coming down the runway now. The models wore boas and had feathers in their headbands and on their bags, but their garments were waistless and fringed. So the feather trend had morphed. Predictable.

"Ivy, you're not ordering anything!" Noticing her ignored Tabula, Madison spoke into her ear. "Are you honestly not into these flapper dresses? They're so cute!"

Ivy looked down at her Tabula and randomly pressed one of the BUY! buttons. A new garment replaced the photo of the dress she'd purchased. Her stomach again mewled in pain. She pressed another button and watched a boa get swallowed up and disappear. She hit the tab below a bolero jacket and bought it in black, navy, and brown. She got two headbands with feathers, one twelve inches high and the other fifteen. Soon she was no longer looking at the runway but tapping her Tabula screen as fast as she could, as if it were a video game. It *was* a game, this shopping by touchscreen. When no prices were visible, she didn't have to think about the waste, didn't have to think about Millbrook or Constantine or Clayton or Lyric, or the pain in her body. Tap it away. Buy! Buy! Buy!

The trends kept coming — punk, safari, mermaid — and Ivy made each piece vanish as soon as it popped on the screen. She sensed Madison looking at her but couldn't take her eyes off the garments, couldn't risk letting the peasant blouse get away before she purchased it in white, blush, ocher, *and* buttercup.

On her other side, Hilarie touched her arm. Aiko leaned

across Hilarie with a worried expression. *Are you okay?* she mouthed over the music.

"Just shopping. Like Madison said I should!" Ivy heard the words leave her mouth at a manic pitch. She shook her chains loudly. "If I'm not trendy, I'm dead, right?"

Her nymphs looked at each other.

"Do you need me to call Jarvis?" asked Hilarie, reaching for her Unum.

"No." Ivy grabbed her arm. "I'll be fine." She took a breath. "The show's almost over, isn't it? Get me out of here as soon as it ends."

Hilarie and Aiko nodded.

The new images on her Tabula screen stayed Ivy's hand. She looked up at the catwalk. The torture trend was the show's grand finale. Spiked collars, locked breastplates and corsets, ankle and wrist restraints, whips and weapons, and a rainbow of gags in different colors paraded down the runway. One unfortunate model skidded on her stilettos but waved her restrained arms to regain her balance.

Ivy examined the models' faces. Their eyes betrayed no pain, no dismay at what they had on. They looked the same as always — haughty and vacant.

Carmen Michelle was fifth or sixth down the catwalk, and she showcased the same corset and collar Ivy was wearing. Instead of a skirt, she wore a bikini bottom made out of hair. Ivy itched just looking at it. She also wore metal garters, with chains wrapped around her legs and attached at the bottom to ankle cuffs. Her hands were tied together behind her back. And she marched in the shoes, those horrible shoes, though the spikes were metallic silver, not red. Instead of a gag, a bridle secured her jaw, its leather straps attaching behind her head. A stiff bit stuck through her mouth horizontally. Ivy imagined how hard Carmen must be biting down on that piece of metal to ignore the lancing stabs of each step.

She scanned the crowd. No one was appalled. No one cried out that this trend was completely unwearable, was, in fact, *actually* torturous. She looked down the row. The attendees were hunched over their Tabulas, attacking the screens with their fingers. Across the catwalk, one of the judges crossed her arms and smiled. She looked smugger than ever.

Ivy heard a voice in her ear: "They should name this trend after you, Miss Wilde." She turned, and her stomach convulsed. Some middle-aged woman, probably a fashion-magazine editor, was leaning forward from the second row. "I bet you're going to wear these clothes on your tour, aren't you?" The woman smiled. "My daughter idolizes you. She's a singer too. I'm ordering the line for her right now." Ivy opened her mouth. "If anything will help her get tapped onto *The Henny Funpeck Show,* this will."

Slowly, Ivy turned forward, a dull roar like an underwater motor in her ears. The torture-trend models were still coming, one after another, like endless figurines from the mouth of a demented clock. She watched them for a moment — then turned over the Tabula and smashed it against the metal garter on her right thigh. Its screen shattered into pieces, three or four of them slicing her bare leg. She shivered in delight. The cuts siphoned the pain from the rest of her body and focused it in a few controlled spots. She watched the blood begin to drip with satisfaction. Laughing, she realized that she'd just improved her outfit.

Movement over her right shoulder caught her eye. A figure was awkwardly making its way through the row behind her, coming in her direction. It was a girl, hunched over like a fossil, annoying everyone she stepped in front of in her tight path to the aisle.

"Let's go," ordered Madison, pinching Ivy's elbow tightly with her fingers.

Ivy looked at her. "Now?" she asked. She realized that her three other nymphs were on their feet. They all looked funny. Naia's face was sober; Aiko's eyes were wide with alarm. Hilarie was mouthing something into her Unum while kicking the broken glass under her chair.

"All right, fine," Ivy said. With Madison's help, she struggled to her feet. Though her stomach relaxed, the relief lasted less than a second, as she balanced again on the spikes. If possible, they hurt even more this time, piercing the already sore spots on her soles. "Hold my elbows," she said to Madison and Aiko.

The person squeezing through the second row was in front of the editor woman now. Ivy turned to look and saw that the girl was around her own age, with flat-ironed hair the color of sand. The woman cried, "Hey!" as the girl bent over and grabbed something off the side of Ivy's seat. As she straightened up, she turned and looked at Ivy. She was holding a pile of little plastic things. They looked familiar — though Ivy couldn't place them. The girl's gaze shot over Ivy's shoulder to the catwalk. Quickly, Ivy turned her head. The finale was beginning — the encore procession of all the new trends in a long row. Around her everyone rose to their feet and started to cheer and clap thunderously.

In the roar of the applause, the girl looked at her with sad eyes. She mouthed, *I'm sorry.* Before she could speak, Ivy heard a popping sound and squeezed her eyes shut as something exploded all over her.

Chapter Thirteen

They'd handcuffed me. To the leg of a long U-shaped table in a dressing room at the runway show. "Bolted to the floor," the Corporate Security and Surveillance agents told me. "And we're right outside the door. You're not going anywhere." With my free hand, I tried to wipe green ink out of my eyes.

It had been so easy to smuggle the security tags into the Torro-LeBlanc runway show. Vivienne had stuck the tags and balls of adhesive putty in the bottom of her handbag. She'd flashed her pass and walked boldly through the front doors of the show with the rest of us. In her fatigue jacket and pants, no one glanced at her twice. She, Felix, Dido, and I shouldered our way through the mingling crowd in the lobby. I remembered what it had been like to work the room when I'd been a judge. Now, no one glanced at me. The three drafters followed me into the auditorium. It was still early and mostly empty. I pointed out the nine seats on the right side of the catwalk.

"Is this really where the Superior Court sits?" asked Dido, skipping down the stairs and plopping down in one of the first-row seats. I could tell she wasn't faking her excitement. She was wearing one of my feather-embroidered T-shirts with a black miniskirt and boots — the outfit she had chosen after trying on *everything* in my closet. "I just want to sit here for a few minutes and pretend," she said. "Tell me what it was like to serve. You were *so* lucky, Marla." She really was such a sweet girl.

Dido and I tried to chat casually and keep a lookout while Vivienne and Felix took seats in the second row. Vivienne took the putty and rigged cartridges from her bag and handed them to Felix.

Before coming, I had shown everyone how to snap each security tag open and, using pliers, delicately pull out the pin that separated the blue and yellow ink cartridges.

"Secret Agent Klein," Felix had said, grinning. "I like watching you work."

I had almost dropped the cartridge I was holding. "Thanks. I'm trying to concentrate," I said, attempting to keep my voice even. "I don't want this to go off."

"Didn't mean to be a distraction."

As I drew the pin out of the cartridge, I looked up and permitted myself a serene smile. "Nothing I can't handle."

Now, using the putty, Felix gently secured the tags to the sides of the nine plush chair backs in the front row, just above the armrests. They were visible, but only if you looked hard. I was counting on the adrenaline rush to distract the judges. The tags needed to be somewhat concealed but also placed high enough to have maximum impact when they exploded.

In a shorter time than I had anticipated, Felix and Vivienne were finished. The whole operation had taken no more than five or six minutes. We bundled ourselves up the stairs and back into the lobby.

Later, just before showtime, we'd taken our seats in the second to last row — thanks a lot, Sabrina — and realized that the

Superior Court was sitting on the opposite side of the catwalk. It was a devastating moment. Felix pounded his fist on his armrest and swore. We held a whispered conference.

Vivienne ended the discussion. "It doesn't matter," she said. "We stick to the plan. As soon as the tags go off, we run down and follow Henry."

Dido and I looked at each other. "But all those people —" I protested.

"Let it be," said Vivienne, leaning across Dido and giving me a severe look. "It's done."

Karisma's ballads hadn't generated enough reverb to explode the cartridges, however. I kept watching the show, kept waiting for the explosion that didn't come. I soon realized it wouldn't come until the finale. I peered at the inhabitants of the booby-trapped chairs.

"That's *Ivy Wilde* in the front row," I whispered to Felix.

"What?" Felix sat up and peered into the darkness. As he recognized the pop star, his mood seemed to shift. "Good," he said, crossing his arms. "Let the tags explode all over her."

I had frowned. And waited. And thought about how it wasn't fair to Ivy Wilde and to everyone else around her. I didn't love her new album, but she was still one of my favorite performers. I thought about how, if we used the gimmick this once, there wouldn't be another chance at a future runway show. Security would be alerted. The judges would escape untouched. Olivia wouldn't be humiliated.

"I can get them before they go off," I said, climbing over Felix. He'd grabbed my wrist and looked into my eyes. His frown softened.

"I'll help," he whispered.

"No," I told him. "Two people will just draw attention. I'm going to move through the row like I have to go to the bathroom."

He'd squeezed my wrist, just a little. "Good luck."

I'd almost made it. I'd palmed seven of the nine tags before the finale, before the thunderous applause set them off. I'd had time only to mumble a feeble apology at poor Ivy Wilde before the tags spattered over us both. Like locusts, CSS agents descended on me. And here I was.

The dressing room door opened. Ivy Wilde, her nymphs, and an older man with gray hair barreled in. Ivy and the nymphs looked as if they'd toweled off. In the vanity lighting, I could see that the ink had stained their faces and arms, though it no longer glistened. I looked at Ivy. I thought the singer would be furious with me — but while the nymphs and the fossil scowled, Ivy casually sat down on a chair next to me and began undoing the straps on her shoes. When she bent over, I noticed that her corset was unlaced. A two-inch strip of skin showed between the seams. I could see the outline of her hunched vertebrae.

A moment later, my old boss Julia arrived, followed by Godfrey, my current boss who oversaw the drafters. I had said no more than a few words to him since I'd begun working in the basement. He looked as he always did, vague and distracted in his long-expired suit, chewing away on what could only be a placidophilus pill. Still, he came over to me and patted a dye-free spot on my shoulder. "This is the end, sweetheart," he whispered. Panic enveloped me like a cold wind. What did that mean? Was I going to jail?

"Marla Klein, you're through," Julia said, flicking a glance over at me with no more care than if she were checking the time.

Still not raising her silky voice, she addressed the older man. "Jarvis, is it? Sir, is there anything we at Torro-LeBlanc can do to rectify this regrettable situation?"

"Yes. You can pay Warwick Records," said the man, looking up from his Unum. "We're suing."

My mind whirred as I tried to figure out what to say. I needed to stay calm and defend myself. "Julia, please listen to me. I was trying to fix things," I said, steadying my voice as best I could.

The adults glanced over, but Julia continued as if I'd not spoken at all. "I'm sure there's no need for legal recourse," she said to the man. "Certainly we can come to some kind of agreement. After all, Miss Wilde is our torture-trend spokesmodel now. We at Torro-LeBlanc have her best interests in mind."

I thought I saw a shiver ripple up Ivy's spine. The singer finally succeeded in removing her shoes. She crossed one leg and rubbed the sole of her foot with both hands. I noticed red welts where the spikes had poked the flesh. The shoes looked even worse in real life than they had in Vivienne's sketch.

Before the man could reply, the door burst open again. Felix, Vivienne, and Dido were hustled in by two CSS agents — followed by a petite figure I was relieved to see.

"Winnie!" I exclaimed. "Tell them to listen to me. You know I love working for Torro. I was trying to get *rid* of the tags. This is outrageous!" I rattled my handcuff against the table leg.

Winnie ignored me. "These three were at the runway show," she said to Julia. "They sit at the same drafting table as Marla. Thick as thieves. I'm sure they were in on it."

"*What?*" I said.

"Always watching," Godfrey mumbled next to me.

Ivy stood. She took a step forward, nudging her spiky shoes

out of the way with her bare feet. "It *is* you," she said. Everyone in the room looked up. She was staring at Felix.

Felix's mouth was closed in a firm line. He didn't meet Ivy's gaze.

"Felix?" Ivy said.

He acknowledged her at last with a cool nod. "Yes, hello."

"Felix and I both grew up in Millbrook," Ivy announced. From my seat, I couldn't see Ivy's face, but I assumed her expression matched the warmth in her voice. I wondered how well the two of them had known each other — and why Felix hadn't seemed to care when he'd discovered the ink tags would hit her. I was surprised he had never mentioned anything.

"Millbrook, yuck," one of the nymphs said, looking at Felix. "Sorry to hear it, buddy."

Felix cleared his throat. "It was a long time ago. Ev — Ivy was friends with my little sister." I waited for more, but it didn't come.

"So these three may have planted the devices along with Marla?" said Julia, eyeing the other drafters.

"No. That's impossible. You would never . . . Felix?" Ivy ended awkwardly, her defense fading into a question.

Julia approached me, her glossed lips stern. "Tell me who was involved."

I swallowed. For a second I thought of spinning the truth, of claiming the other drafters had hoodwinked me, of shifting the blame. But no — that wasn't an option. I couldn't betray Vivienne or Felix or Dido.

I worded my defense in my head. "I . . . heard a rumor that someone was going to put security tags on the seats. So I checked during the show and saw them. And I wanted to collect them and throw them away before they blew up all over the place. That's what I was doing when they exploded."

"You heard a rumor," said Julia, raising her eyebrows. "Really."

"Go ahead, Marla," said Vivienne. "Just tell them the truth."

I turned. Vivienne's face was stoic. She looked ready for combat in her fatigues, black cap, and boots.

"*I* planted the tags," Vivienne announced. "Before the show. I smuggled them in my purse and stuck them on with putty." She reached into her handbag and pulled out a putty wrapper. "See? Marla must have seen me. She obviously wanted to save poor Miss Ivy Wilde from the humiliation. Marla's the hero here."

There was a silence. I wondered how Vivienne was going to play this out.

"Why did you do it?" Julia demanded.

Vivienne shrugged. "Pop music is for conformists."

"I think she's telling the truth," said Ivy. She looked at me. "This girl said something right before the tags exploded. I think it was 'sorry.' I believe her—that she was trying to get rid of them, not plant them."

I vowed then and there to buy every new Ivy Wilde album, no matter what they sounded like.

"And you worked alone?" said Julia to Vivienne slowly. "These two"—she nodded at Felix and Dido—"weren't involved?"

"Them?" Vivienne snorted. "Those two couldn't operate a trendchecker. As if I would trust them. Search them. They're clean."

"Then you're fired," Julia said coolly.

"Yes, I expected as much."

"No!" I cried.

"Get her out of here," Julia said to the agents. They steered Vivienne out of the room by the shoulders. She didn't look back.

I stared at the closed door. Vivienne's dismissal stung like a slap across my cheek. She couldn't really be gone . . . could she? I looked at Felix and Dido for help, but both of them looked as stunned as I felt.

"Now then," said Julia, turning back to the gray-haired man.

"Ahem." Godfrey cleared his throat. I felt his hand on my chair back. "This drafter is free to stay on, to be clear."

Julia eyed me, then inspected Felix and Dido. "You three may continue your employment at Torro-LeBlanc in your present positions," she said with a feline smile. "But we'll be watching you closely. Please leave the premises immediately." She glanced at Winnie, who swung the door open with a smirk on her face. A CSS agent, blatantly trying to eavesdrop, took a brisk step back from the door frame.

Felix and Ivy lingered while the agent unlocked my handcuffs. Once freed, I rubbed my wrist and looked up at Godfrey. "Could I have a moment to clean up?"

This time he didn't look to Julia for consent. "Of course. The bathroom is out the door to the right."

The agent ushered us out of the dressing room. I saw Julia turn back to the gray-haired man and continue her negotiation. As I left, I cast a final backward glance at Ivy Wilde, but the singer didn't look up. She was staring at the floor, fingers massaging her temples.

Once in the corridor, Felix told me he and Dido would wait for me. But it was a long train ride back to my high-rise, and I didn't want to go the whole way looking like I'd been dipped in a vat of paint. "You should go on ahead," I told them. "I don't know how long I'll need in the bathroom."

But Felix shook his head. "We'll be outside," he muttered. He and Dido turned left and followed the agent down the hall.

I walked into the bathroom and turned on the tap. I looked in the mirror. Even though I knew what to expect, my green face still shocked me. Too bad it wasn't Halloween — I could go as a witch. Or a troll. In some places, where the ink had dripped, my skin looked like it was melting. My blouse was ruined — another trendy piece gone without a replacement — but I was wearing long sleeves, so the skin on my arms had been spared, at least.

I grabbed a paper towel, squeezed soap on it from the dispenser, and began scrubbing my face. The paper towel turned green — but the green on my face didn't seem to be fading. I scrubbed harder.

Suddenly the bathroom door opened. Ivy Wilde paused in the doorway for a second, looking at me, then disappeared into a stall. Her feet were still bare. Not knowing what else to do, I turned the water up so she wouldn't feel self-conscious. I soaped a new towel and returned to scrubbing.

Ivy came out of the stall carrying a heap of metal. She'd removed her linked wrist shackles and garters. Her spiked neckpiece was also gone, though the rubber gag still hung in a loose circle around her neck. She knocked the cover off the trash barrel and stuffed the entire heap inside. As she began washing her hands, she glanced at my reflection. "We're going to try rubbing alcohol at home," she said. "My mother always used that on ink stains. That or baby oil should take it off."

Fate was funny. This morning, if I'd told myself that Ivy Wilde would be giving me stain-removal tips in a runway-show bathroom, I would have questioned my sanity. I turned off the water. "Thanks," I said, trying not to trip over my words. "I want to get enough off so I can walk out of here without looking like a total freak."

Ivy smirked. "I'm letting my agent handle our escape plan."

In the silence, I scrambled for something more to say. After all, in spite of the awkward circumstances, it hadn't been that long ago that Ivy and I had attended some of the same events. "I'm not sure you remember me, but we met at Fashion Week last fall," I said, trying to sound casual. "I was on Torro's Superior Court then."

Shaking her hands over the sink, Ivy squinted at me. After a pause, she nodded and reached for a paper towel. "Oh, sure." Obviously, there was no recognition.

"I love your music," I blurted out.

"Thanks a lot." Ivy smiled a plastic smile. She probably heard that all the time. Now I sounded like a feeble fan-girl. Great. "Why did you throw your chains away?" I asked quickly.

Ivy stopped wiping her hands. "Do you know what it's like to wear that stuff?" she said, anger hardening her voice. "You work for Torro? How could you guys approve this trend?"

I swallowed. "Actually, the woman who was just fired? She designed most of your outfit. Those shoes were her idea. And the collar. And the chains."

"Is she out of her mind?"

"No — she, well, did it to make a point about trends, I think. How ... extreme they can be." I chose my words with care. I didn't want Ivy to report back to Julia that I was anti-trends or anything. "No one thought they would get approved." I certainly hadn't. I'd told Vivienne that the court never approved unwearable clothing. It wouldn't sell, and their job was to pass judgment on what would become popular. When she'd come back from the fifth floor, Vivienne had slammed her hand on the table. "It was unanimous!" she'd announced to the circle of our shocked faces.

"Oh." Ivy pursed her lips in annoyance. "Well, I'm glad she was fired. If it was a joke, it was kind of thoughtless. Apparently, I'm the spokesmodel for the trend now, and I'm supposed to prance around in this crap all day long. I don't know how I'm going to stand it."

I was surprised Ivy felt so irritated by the clothing. Sure, it was painful and all — but wasn't she used to crazy costumes? "Just . . . don't wear it, then," I said.

Ivy gripped the sides of the sink and leaned on it. "But I'm *Ivy Wilde*," she intoned, staring at her reflection in the mirror. "I have to be wild and edgy and sexy. *The* wildest and edgiest and sexiest. That's how I stay popular."

I looked at her reflection, at the pain in her eyes. "But . . . you're so famous," I said. "Most people would kill to be you."

"They shouldn't," Ivy said, still staring at her own reflection. "No one gets it. It's a fake life. I don't even know who I am anymore." She pulled at her gag, snapping the stretchy fabric against her neck. "I'm certainly not *this*."

I tried to grasp the meaning of her words. So she wasn't really a party girl. I never would have guessed. I thought about living and breathing a fake personality all day long. It had to be tiring. It might even break someone down.

I searched for something comforting to say. "Well, you should reinvent yourself then. Lots of stars do that, don't they?"

Ivy blinked and shifted her gaze back to me. "It's funny, I was just saying that to Clayton the other day."

Clayton Pryce. On second thought, maybe it *was* worth it. To spend time with Clayton Pryce, I would definitely consider strapping on the spiked shoes.

"I'd like to try something new," Ivy went on, almost shyly, "but my agent is pretty stuck on the whole 'Wilde' thing."

"Just do it yourself, then." The ink-tag plot, even with its miserable failure and Vivienne's getting fired . . . I had to admit that it had thrilled me to do something rebellious. Something without my mother or Julia presiding over every little detail.

"And be what? A slumber-party princess like Jelly Sanchez? Then I could wear pajamas all day long." Ivy sighed. "Though, knowing Fatima, she'd have me in a steel nightgown or something."

The idea came to me instantly. "No. You should go environmental. Your look could be all earth-mothery. Then you could wear flowing, comfortable trends instead of"— I waved at the hair skirt and corset, with its laces hanging loose —"this crazy stuff. And long, wild hair, maybe with a flower or two; that's always pretty . . ." I drew in my breath so quickly that I started to cough. *"Wilde,"* I managed to croak out, flapping my hands up and down in excitement. "It already works with your name. Instead of wild and crazy, you could be wild — like nature! *Ivy Wilde.*"

Ivy stared at me. "Ivy Wilde," she repeated.

I waited. It was a prime idea, if I did say so myself.

"That's kind of brilliant." Ivy's gaze moved glassily over the bathroom wall. I could see her mind working. Suddenly, she snapped out of it. "Are you any good?" she asked, turning to face me.

"Excuse me?"

"At designing?"

I widened my eyes. What? "Like I said, until a couple of months ago I was on the court at Torro. I'm a drafter now, but I can still design pretty well — I mean, I love to, anyway . . ." My words tumbled forth in a waterfall.

"Make an outfit for me," said Ivy. "Earthy and comfortable, like you said. Don't tell anyone else. Just make it and send it to me. Can you? Will you?"

I almost choked again. "Yes, definitely, absolutely. I'd love to."

Ivy smiled. "Let's see. You need to send it to me without Fatima opening it." She thought for a moment. "Give me your Unum."

With bumbling fingers, I rummaged in my bag and handed it to her. Ivy tapped the screen and spoke a strange-sounding name and an address into it. Then another name, another address.

She turned the screen toward me and pointed. "Put this as the return address. And don't send it to Ivy Wilde, send it to this name, at this address." I squinted at the screen and saw EVANGE-LINE VASSILIOTIS. "Everyone'll think it's from my family, and they won't bother with it. Send me a message when it's on its way, too, okay?" She spoke her Unum number into the device.

"Okay." I nodded, hoping I would remember everything. I hardly dared to believe what was happening.

Ivy handed the Unum back and smiled at me, a real one this time. "Our secret, okay?" She walked to the bathroom door and paused with her hand on the handle. "So . . . you work with Felix," she said.

"Oh. Yeah."

"How's that?"

"Um, fine, I guess. He was a jerk when I first met him, but I like him better now." Immediately I remembered the touch of his hand on my wrist and felt awkward. "I mean, he can still be a jerk sometimes," I added.

"Do you . . . have his number?" she asked, not looking up.

I shook my head firmly. "Uh-uh."

"Oh. Well, you can give him mine. Tell him he can call me if he wants. It's been a while since we've . . . hung out."

I noticed she didn't say she wanted to get in touch with his sister. I wondered exactly how much they'd hung out. "Yeah, sure," I said.

After a slight pause, Ivy opened the door and looked back at me. "Thanks for trying to stop the ink explosion. Stay young." She disappeared into the hallway.

Chapter Fourteen

Ivy Wilde. *The hallway floor* was cold on her bare feet, but thinking about her new image lightened Ivy's steps. She envisioned green ivy vines clambering up a brick wall. Could they be worked into clothing? She wondered what the designer would come up with.

The CSS agent who had been waiting outside the bathroom door escorted her back to the dressing room, where the other agent was still stationed. Inside, the crowd had thinned. Jarvis and the pinch-faced woman with the long black hair were gone, as was the fossil in the gray suit. She wondered if Jarvis had resolved things, or if he was going through with the lawsuit. It didn't really matter — either way, she'd probably hear nothing about it.

"Do you feel better?" Aiko asked, coming up to Ivy and putting a hand on her shoulder.

"Yeah." Ivy smiled at her most sensitive nymph. "Thanks." She looked around at Hilarie, Naia, and Madison, their concerned faces still spattered with ink. "Sorry I went all mental during the show."

The worry didn't leave Aiko's eyes entirely. "You should tell us if you're upset."

"My stomach just hurts so badly. I'll keep it together from now on. Promise." She grinned broadly, trying to put her nymphs at ease. "So what's next? When do we leave?"

"Fatima's off getting clothes for all of us," said Hilarie. "We have to wait, and then they'll bring the car around. Jarvis wants us to stay until most of the public has gone."

"Someone left to bring us Sugarwaters, but that was *years* ago," said Madison. She pursed her lips with annoyance. "I could use some food, too."

They would be there for a while. Unsupervised. It was an opportunity — one she might not get again. Ivy thought quickly. "Yeah, I'm hungry too," she said. "Don't worry. I'm on it."

She stepped into the hallway. Sizing up the two agents, she decided the shorter one, the one who had walked her to the bathroom, looked as if he had a better memory.

"You guys brought in three Torro-LeBlanc workers before," she said in a low voice. "One was the woman who got fired. Where are the other two?"

The agent looked confused. "The other two?"

"Yes. There was a guy with dark hair and a girl — I think she had pigtails."

Ivy saw recognition in his freckled face. "Oh. Right."

"Where are they now?"

"They're gone."

She bit back an expression of frustration. "Yeah, I can see that. Did you happen to see where they went? Or did they say anything?"

"They told the girl that got arrested they'd wait for her outside the building."

The other agent spoke, and Ivy realized she'd made the wrong judgment call. "I brought them out."

She turned to him gratefully. "Would you go outside and see if the guy is still there? If he is, bring him to me. I need to talk to him." She shook her head. "But don't tell him that. Just tell him he's needed back at the show or something." She looked down the hallway. "If there's another free room, keep him in there and come get me."

"We're not really supposed to leave our post," the shorter one said pointedly.

The taller agent flashed him an annoyed look and turned back to her. "No problem, Miss Wilde. What's his name, so I can identify him?"

"Felix Garcia."

"I'll be right back," he said. He paused. "Your voice is incredible," he blurted before hurrying away.

Fame was a burden, yes. But being Ivy Wilde did have its perks.

"Are they getting us food?" Naia asked when Ivy rejoined her nymphs.

"It'll be here soon," she replied guiltily.

Ten minutes later, the tall agent poked his head in. "Miss Wilde?"

Ivy strode to the door. "I have to use the bathroom again," she said, not bothering to look behind her to see if her nymphs were buying the lie.

Once she was outside, the agent pointed down the hall. "Mr. Garcia is in the room two doors down on the left."

"You're the best." Ivy pressed her cheek against his and kissed the air behind his ear. The agent's face crumpled into a dopey grin. "Oh, and you've *got* to call someone and get some food in there for my nymphs," she said as she walked backward down the hall. "They're dying."

She walked to the room the agent had indicated and opened the door.

It was a small storage room, dimly lit, full of metal clothing racks on wheels. They were about half filled with the fashions Ivy had just seen in the show, hung sloppily on hangers. There were no chairs. Felix was standing in the middle of the room with his arms crossed. When he saw Ivy, his mouth opened in surprise.

"Felix!" she exclaimed. She tried again with more control. "Hi."

Felix looked over her shoulder through the open door crack and then met her eyes again. "Hey," he grunted. "What's going on?"

"Nothing. I just kind of wanted to see you." She was suddenly and regretfully aware of her ink-stained face, and her hand rose to her cheek. "It's just so crazy running into you like this, isn't it? I can't believe that woman planted those explosives."

Ivy paused, but Felix's face didn't move. She looked around, wishing for a chair, or at least a table against which she could lean. "So how are you?" she asked.

"I'm okay." A slight scowl tugged at his mouth.

She tried to think of something to say as the pause stretched on. "How's Torro-LeBlanc?" she asked, swinging her arms uncomfortably. "You're a designer there?"

"A drafter."

"Do you like it?"

A crease in his forehead appeared. "Do I like being a hamster on a wheel? No. It's pretty crappy. But you wouldn't know anything about that."

"Excuse me?" she said.

"Nothing — sorry." He shook his head and sighed. "Just . . .

was there something you wanted to say? If not, I should probably get back to my friends."

Ivy stared at him. She thought of how distant he'd been in the Torro-LeBlanc dressing room as well. She'd often imagined reuniting with Felix. In her fantasies, he was always overjoyed to see her. He said things like, *I can't believe I found you again.* Once or twice, though she blushed to think of it, she'd even pressed the back of her hand to her lips and thought about their mouths coming together in more shy kisses. Okay — maybe her expectations were overblown. But this sullen person felt like a stranger.

"I know it was a while ago." She hesitated, then decided to go for it. "Sometimes I think about how we . . . you know . . ." She could feel her cheeks warming even more.

"We what?"

"You remember."

"Yeah, well, we all change, don't we."

The door swung open and two models appeared in the doorway, startling Ivy. They were in bathrobes, holding garments from the space-age line on hangers. Ivy knew one went by Anja, no surname; the other she'd met before at a nightclub but couldn't recall her name. They stopped their chatter midsentence and stared at her and Felix.

"Hey, what are you guys doing in here?" The nameless model's eyes locked with Ivy's. "Oh!" she said. "Sorry. I didn't recognize you with that stuff on your face." Looking at them curiously, the model walked over to a rack to hang up her outfit.

Anja hung hers up as well. "Are you guys getting samples?" she asked.

"No. We were just talking," said Ivy, trying to sound casual. "Avoiding press."

Anja's gaze shifted back and forth between the two of them

until it rested on Felix. "Hey, you're Adolfo from the new season of *Real Boys*, right?"

Felix's glare was chilly. "No."

Anja squinted at him. "You're someone, though, right?"

Ivy saw the skin on Felix's cheek ripple as his jaw clenched. He didn't respond.

The four of them stood there, looking at one another, until the awkward silence was more than Ivy could take. "Do you guys mind?" she said at last.

"Oh." Nameless didn't look pleased, but she moved toward the door. "Fine. Stay young."

"Yeah. See you, Ivy," said Anja, following, still looking at Felix as if trying to place him.

"Stay young." Once they'd left, Ivy turned to Felix. "Sorry. Ignore them. Where were we?"

"I think I was leaving," he said.

"No. You weren't. We were talking about the way things used to be," she said quickly.

"Oh, yeah. And how things change. Now that you're 'someone.'"

"You're someone —"

"Don't," Felix interrupted sharply. He paused. "How's the new name working for you, *Ivy*?"

"They change everyone's," she said. "Call me Eva if you want."

"It's not the only thing that's different," he muttered. "It's everything. Like the way you behave like a . . ." He grimaced.

"Like a what?"

Felix spat the phrase. "Like a big slut all the time."

Ivy stared at him in disbelief. Her instincts told her to turn and go, that nobody talked to Ivy Wilde this way. But it was impossible to leave without defending herself. "It's an act," she said, trying to stay composed, though her voice shook. "I thought you knew that. It's just an act."

"Really," said Felix. The sarcasm rolled off his tongue. "So someone holds a gun to your head while you suck face with your sellout boyfriend?"

"You mean Clayton?" She couldn't give away Clayton's secret, not even to Felix, not even to prove to him she wasn't what he thought. "Trust me. It's a manufactured romance. For publicity. He's *really* not into me."

"I don't believe it."

"Fine. Believe whatever you want." She didn't need to take this. She moved to the door and held it open. "You should probably get going."

"Yeah." He brushed past her into the hallway. Despite the anger that pulsed inside her, a little voice cried out for him to stay. So she was surprised when he stopped a few paces down the hall and turned around.

He walked right up to her and took hold of her shoulders. "I couldn't *wait* for you to get to La Reina, Eva," he said in an intense whisper. She felt the warmth of his hands on her bare skin. "It seems so stupid now — we were so young — but I can't get over it. We were going to be in the city alone, without parents, without anybody. I wanted to show you Torro-LeBlanc, and all the prime spots in the city. But then I barely saw you. And *then*"— his dark eyes grew pained —"you didn't want anything to do with me."

"I couldn't —"

"You were *Ivy Wilde*. You could have called me." His expression softened, and he suddenly looked once again like the boy in the silly hat with the earflaps. "And I had to watch Clayton Pryce and those other guys groping you. Every day. Think about it."

He let go of her but she grabbed for his hand and held it. "I'm sorry," she said, "but I didn't have a choice. I told you. To go solo after *Henny Funpeck,* I needed to follow their instructions. Cut ties. I couldn't even talk to Marisa. I hated it, but —"

"But it worked," said Felix.

"Yeah." He was just inches away now, and Ivy could see that his face was more manlike than it had been at fifteen, the eyebrows thicker, his cheeks shadowed in stubble. He was so good-looking it quickened her breath. No wonder Anja had thought he was a celebrity. With scorn she thought about the ridiculous outfit she had to wear at today's runway show, the outrageous things she had to do to convince the world she was a Wilde child. When all she wanted, really, to was curl up on her couch at home and watch episodes of *Clone Valley* with this person in front of her.

"I miss you," she said. She moved closer, willing him to lean in and kiss her.

Felix didn't move. "You should have called."

"I told you — I didn't have a choice." She took a breath and thought about her recent encounter in the bathroom. That would prove to him she wasn't a . . . what he thought she was. "I don't do everything they say, though. I have this idea for a new image. It's the complete opposite of party girl," she whispered. "It's going to be prime. My agent and publicist have nothing to do with it. The designer who almost got arrested is going to help me out."

"Marla?" To her disappointment, Felix let go of her hand and dug his fists in his pockets. His face remained soft, however.

They paused. Ivy could feel the moment passing, could feel him pulling away. "So maybe we could get together and hang out sometime this week," she proposed in a rush. She plucked at the hairs on her skirt nervously. "I could send a car. You could come to the house."

"Yeah, I don't know." He looked over his shoulder at the bare hallway. "Probably not this week. But maybe."

He was still wary of getting hurt. That was understandable. She needed to prove to him she was the same person she'd been in Millbrook, not a product created by her record label, and not a boy-crazy flirt. The atoms of a new plan began to quiver in Ivy's mind. The first part was revealing her new look, and then . . . did she dare? "Felix, make sure you watch me on television when I get my new clothes," she said, her voice rising with inspiration. "And follow my coverage afterward. Then we can talk more."

"What are you going to do?"

"I'm going to show you that I haven't changed."

He studied her. "All right," he said. He paused with his hand on the doorknob. "Well, take care of yourself, I guess."

"Yeah, you too," she said. "Stay young."

"Oh, and Eva?" he said quickly. "No matter what they tell you . . . you always have a choice."

She listened to his footsteps grow fainter as he walked away.

Chapter Fifteen

The next morning, around our basement table, Felix, Dido, and I shared the events at the Torro-LeBlanc runway show with Randall and Kevin. Everyone had a long face by the time we were through.

"Poor Vivienne," said Randall.

"It was horrible. Awful," said Dido, tearing up. "I tried to call her last night but she didn't pick up."

"I got a message from her," said Felix. "She's going to be fine. She misses us, but she's going on a little vacation to clear her head, so she doesn't want any contact."

Felix wasn't exactly telling the whole truth. Vivienne had sent her message to Kevin and me too. Her words had been mysterious. *Going underground for a while. Don't call. I'm fine. More than one way to skin a cat. F&K, share makeover with M soon. M, keep working on turning court. I'm counting on you guys. Will be in touch.*

What did she mean she was "going underground"? I thought of her in a tunnel with dirt and slugs — okay, I knew she didn't mean it literally, but I had trouble picturing where else she might be.

And a *makeover?* I wondered what that was about. I hadn't yet had the chance to ask Felix or Kevin.

"And instead of getting the boot, Marla comes out of the thing with a commission," Felix added.

Yesterday, standing outside the theater after the runway show, I'd told Felix and Dido about the encounter with Ivy Wilde. I'd also tried to give Felix Ivy's number, but he'd refused to enter it into his Unum. He claimed he had no interest in calling her. I wasn't sure I believed him. I asked him why not, but he said only that they hadn't known each other very well.

"Ivy acted like you guys did," Dido countered. I was glad I didn't have to say it. I watched his reaction carefully.

"She's an idiot," Felix told us. "A pawn. Look at her."

But ... she wasn't an idiot. Or she hadn't been when I'd talked to her. I tried to tell him how fed up she was with being a pawn. It was the whole reason she wanted a new look. But before I'd finished, a tall CSS agent came out of the building to retrieve Felix, claiming he was needed back at the show for paperwork.

"Just him?" Dido had asked. I had wondered too — it seemed weird that the two of us weren't called back. Dido and I had taken the train home together, and Felix hadn't mentioned anything about it at work this morning.

I shook away my questions and returned to the subject of Ivy Wilde's outfit. "I was thinking that I could ask Vaughn to help with construction — the patternmaker who did my leopard dress," I whispered to the others. "Do you think he'd make the garment with me? Maybe we could stay late — I don't really see how I can get away with doing it during the day."

Kevin nodded. "He's great. I bet he'd do it, too. We've worked together a bunch — let me ask him." He grabbed a blank sheet of paper from the table's center. "Do you want me to do some dress sketches, Marla? I've got some ideas."

"I want to work on it too," said Dido.

I hesitated. My briefcase was full of sketches. I had a pretty good idea of how I would turn Ivy Wilde from a sex kitten into a symbol of environmental awareness. It was some of the best work I'd done — and the most fun.

On my walk home from the train station yesterday, I'd stopped to visit the park near my apartment. It was dusk; the faded ink splotches on my hands looked like shadows. In addition to the regular winter plants, some red bougainvillea vines were just starting to bloom. As my shoes pressed into the soft grass, I thought about how the park was here thanks to the city's preservation efforts. People who cared about the environment had given me a place to play as a little girl. It mattered.

I'd stuffed fallen leaves and petals into my handbag and tacked them all over my bedroom wall at home for inspiration. Having locked the door in case Karen decided to come snooping when she got back from her cooking club, I pulled my expired shawl out of the closet once again. I wrapped it around my shoulders and began sketching.

Randall leaned over the drafting table. "Ivy Wilde asked *Marla* to do it. Marla, the look should be yours. We'll be your sounding board" — he smiled — "your own Superior Court, if you will. But too many cooks spoil the soup. Make it your own sketch, your own design." I could have hugged him. The guy was old, but he was the best kind of fossil. He totally got it.

Kevin agreed with only a touch of his usual sourness. Dido looked disappointed, but she gave me a nod.

A few minutes before the workday ended, Kevin and I left to find Vaughn. On the way to the elevator, Kevin dropped a stack of paper in the green recycling bin. I stooped and picked up the top sheet. "What is this?"

He looked at what I was holding and grabbed it out of my

hands. I grabbed it back and stared at it. "Kevin — this is incredible."

It was a picture of a girl underwater. Back arched, she was hurling a trident upward into two eels, while a giant octopus nipped at her ankles. The style was sort of cartoonish, but it didn't look silly. It looked graphic and powerful.

"Is that . . . Junie Woo?"

Kevin looked as if he'd been caught. "I was just thinking about her new flick. Designing a poster. I do them sometimes when I'm bored. Don't tell Winnie."

"You need to send this to Denominator." I thought for a second about sending it to Braxton. I hadn't heard a word from him since we'd broken up. The poster would be a nice excuse to check in, to show him how well I was doing, to maybe drop the news that I was now designing for Ivy Wilde . . . I hated myself for even having the thought. No. I didn't want to reach out to him now, or ever.

Kevin smiled sheepishly. He took the paper from me and laid it in the bin face-down. "Like Denominator would take art from a Torro drafter. It's okay. I just do them for myself."

The poster was far better than any garment sketch I'd seen him do recently. "At least don't throw it away . . ."

"I've got a full-color one I'm working on at home," he said, steering me into the elevator. "Come on."

In Garment Construction, we found Vaughn at a sewing machine, finishing a hem. Around him, patternmakers were packing up for the day. Trying to speak as quietly as I could, I shared with him what Ivy had asked me to do.

At first, Vaughn was reluctant. "I could lose my job," he said, while his machine clacked.

"Vivienne's been let go," Kevin said, "but she's not giving up on her idea. We think she's going to start recruiting. If this goes well, we'll have a connection to Ivy Wilde. That kind of star power ought to help us."

I was surprised. Vaughn apparently knew as much about Vivienne's subversive ideas as I did — if not more. He didn't exactly strike me as the rebellious type.

Vaughn paused for a long time, so long that I started to wonder if he was ignoring us. "Okay," he said at last. "But if it doesn't go well, I had nothing to do with it. Even if it does, don't use my name. Clear?"

I nodded eagerly, and we made plans to meet the following afternoon at five thirty.

The next day, I ran my final sketches by the drafters and, with their feedback, settled on the best idea. At 5:25, I grabbed my empty Sugarwater bottle from lunch and took the elevator to the mostly deserted second floor.

Together, Vaughn and I rummaged in the scraps bin and pulled out discarded fabric pieces in green and brown. When we heaped them in a pile on the table, I cringed. The whole thing looked too much like mud. We added some scraps of bright red and shimmering gold and silver. The effect was better. It had texture and depth now, like a mermaid's tail. Vaughn pinned a small circle of scraps on the dress form, tacking them to a lining cut in the pattern of a floor-length flowing skirt. We both agreed the randomness worked.

I discussed my vision for the lapel pin with Vaughn.

"That's original," he said. "Melted plastic." He turned the Sugarwater bottle around in his hand. "You know, I'm going to ask another patternmaker for help on it tomorrow. She's into green clothing design, and she's a pro at accessories. I won't tell her what it's for."

He strode toward an alcove in the right corner. "I'd better get a few more bottles, though, in case this one dies in the kiln. We've got some in the lounge," he called over his shoulder. I thought of the drafters' basement coffee bar. A whole lounge — the patternmakers were lucky.

When he returned, we cut the bottles into pieces the size of potato chips. Then we talked about the top. He said we could create the kind of fabric I was describing, though we would have to use the paper-processing plant a few blocks away. We agreed to meet there tomorrow after work. He would bring the pressed flowers. I would bring the newsprint.

That evening, after a few wrong turns, Karen and I finally located the *La Reina Times* headquarters. It was on the outskirts of town, near scrabbly desert hills. It had taken telling Karen that Ivy Wilde had commissioned an outfit from me for her to stop pestering me to quit Torro-LeBlanc. She even baked a sour cream coffee cake to celebrate. "This is your chance to get back on top, you know," she'd declared, almost giggling as she swept around the kitchen, measuring and mixing. "I *knew* this drafting business couldn't last." As there was a bowl of batter to snack on, I decided not to argue.

We entered the newspaper office to inquire about purchasing back issues. The *Times* was the one place in the city that still put out a print edition and kept fifty years of archives in an attached warehouse. The receptionist greeted us with a friendly smile.

To my irritation, my mother spoke first. "My daughter works for Torro-LeBlanc," she announced. "She needs some back issues from your archives. We can't go into details, but she's here on official design business."

Official design business. How feeble did that sound? I thought back to a time when my mother always said things like this to strangers — and how much I used to love it. "Could we visit the warehouse, please?" I asked.

The receptionist's face lit up. "Torro-LeBlanc? Oh my gosh, they were my first choice in the Tap. I didn't make it — obviously. I'm stuck here instead." She laughed nervously. "I *love* their clothes. Is it just amazing to work there?" She reached into her purse, which was hanging on the back of her chair, and withdrew a pair of black-feathered gloves. I recognized them as the same ones Olivia had been wearing in the elevator the day I'd started in the basement. "I saved up and bought these gloves," the receptionist said. "They tickle my fingers when I type, so I don't wear them much here, but I love the way they look." She pulled one on and modeled her hand for Karen and me. "Did you make them?"

I hesitated. "Not exactly. I did approve them for production, though."

"Oh my gosh, are you on one of the *courts*?"

I was saved from having to answer when a stern-looking man with glasses approached the reception desk. "What's going on here, Teri?" he asked.

"This girl is a Tap from Torro-LeBlanc, and she needs back issues for official business," the receptionist responded breathlessly.

The sternness didn't leave the man's face, but his tone became respectful. He nodded to me. "Excuse me. As you wish. Teri will be happy to show you the way."

The receptionist slipped on the second glove, then led us through the newsroom. Each reporter sat at a workstation with a mess of papers piled around a Tabula screen. Some dictated into microphones. Others typed into keypads. I saw a crumpled ball of paper sail through the air. The Adequate who tossed it and his ducking target both laughed.

"Poor things," Karen whispered.

I frowned. The Adequates seemed busy, maybe, but focused and happy. Everybody always talked about how Taps led glamorous lives in the creative industries and the Adequates were stuck doing dull work. I wasn't friends with any Adequates now, and from all accounts they were the first to admit how miserable they were. These people, though, didn't seem unhappy to me.

"Do you like working here?" I asked the receptionist quietly.

"Oh no," she said. "I mean, the hours are good and the people are pretty nice." She lowered her voice. "My boss can be a little tough, but he also gave me a couple extra vacation days this year." Her face twisted into a sad smirk. "But whatever. I work for the *Times*. I would *kill* to do what you do."

"Of course you would," Karen interjected.

I bit my lip. "Torro can be a tough place to work, too." My mother flashed me a look.

Once we reached the warehouse, the receptionist introduced us to the archivist, a stooped, white-haired man who looked nearly a hundred years old. A fossil of fossils. His name was Basil. He blinked his watery eyes at us in surprise and coughed. I wondered how much of the dust covering the shelves of newspapers nestled itself in his throat each day.

"How can I be of assistance?" Basil asked, as the receptionist excused herself.

I pulled out my Unum. "I have the dates of some issues I'd like to locate. Basically, I'm looking for headlines of environmental news. Like the day we enacted"—I read off my screen

—"the climate-change bill, single-stream recycling in La Reina, the mass production of electric cars, stuff like that."

"Delightful!" Basil rubbed his hands together. "Are you a science student?"

"No," I said. "I'm a . . ." I paused. "It's for a garment design. For an environmental fashion . . . project."

I was expecting more questions, but Basil just nodded enthusiastically.

Finding the newspapers took longer than it should have because according to a mandate from the *Times*'s legal department, Basil was the only one allowed to climb the wheeled staircase to the upper shelves. He creaked up the steps so slowly I thought I would scream. He did, however, manage to remember a few other important headlines my search had missed, including the devastating oil spill that had rocked the country. It had happened before I was born, but Karen remembered it. I was able to look up the exact date on my Unum.

During one of Basil's slow climbs, my gaze drifted toward a headline on top of a stack at eye level:

ECONOMY REVIVING: PRESIDENT CREDITS NEW STRATEGIST

There was a photograph of two men shaking hands. One was former president Wilcox — or was it Branbury? — I could never get them straight. The other was the first chairman, whose name, Rose, I did remember from school. Chairman Rose wore an easy smile, while the president's face was more serious.

We'd been taught that every organization was overseen by Silents — chief among them the chairman, who advised the president. The chairman didn't seem to do much, but he had the power to overrule the president on economic decisions. At least, I was pretty sure that was how it worked.

Reading a few lines of the article confirmed my general ideas. Apparently, adding children to the workforce had rescued the country from a long recession.

"Chairman Rose's vision for youth trendsetting has proven effective beyond our highest expectations," the president was quoted as saying. "We are indebted to the newly termed 'creative industries.' Harnessing the rapid shifts in tween and teen preferences has invigorated consumer spending. Let them be corporate models, and let us honor their contributions."

I read on. "Our nation's parents are already ferociously invested in their children's interests and development — admirably so. We must push this investment as far as we are able. Let us continue to add our sons and daughters — those who prove to be the most creative, the most ambitious, and the most talented — to the workforce. And let us support their pursuits at home with generous hearts. It is the next, natural step.

"I urge the chairman's critics to cease their protests. We greet the dawn of a new era, where the fountain of youth sustains us all."

"Marla! Look, February third! The day you got tapped," Karen announced, sneezing as she held up a newspaper. "I think I have the front page under the mattress at home, but do you want an extra copy?"

The paper had an ordinary headline about train repairs. Still, there it was, a souvenir from the day my life's path had turned and I had entered the fashion hive of Torro-LeBlanc. I glanced back at the other paper at eye level. Had I not been tapped . . . had there not even been industries that tapped at all . . . it was odd to think about what my life might be like today. Would I still be in school, like the Adequates? Would I be miserable? Or, not knowing what I was missing, would I be happy?

"I think I'm good here," I said, raising the stacked papers in my arms. I reached up to steady Basil as he descended the last few steps with a newspaper under his elbow, his three other limbs wobbling.

The following day, at the paper plant, I helped Vaughn pump a slurry of old paper and mulberry pulp onto a large screen mat that was gently vibrating. Vaughn explained that the mulberry would give the paper a texture closer to cloth and improve durability. At his command, I sprinkled the dried flowers on the slurry and gently added the newsprint headlines and articles. As the moisture drained away, I watched the fibers settle and interlock into a giant sheet. The plant workers took the sheet and passed it through huge rollers, dried it, and treated it to be flexible and water-resistant. It was returned to us in a cardboard tube, and Vaughn said he'd take it back to Garment Construction. Although he offered to split the cost with me, I paid for the processing myself. I was sure I still had way more in savings from my time on the court than Vaughn did — and he was already helping me so much.

After work the next day, Vaughn unrolled the paper-cloth onto a worktable. Its slight translucency made the natural fibers visible. The newsprint was blurred, but words from the headlines popped out here and there. The freckling of red flowers brightened the look. I took one corner between my fingers. It had a surprising flexibility, somewhere between tissue paper and silk.

"It came out nice, didn't it?" said Vaughn. Speechless, I hugged him.

Looking at my sketches, he traced the pattern for a wrap shirt, kimono style but with long bell sleeves, and cut out the pieces expertly. He accessed Ivy's measurements from the Tor-ro-LeBlanc database and tailored the shirt on the dress form accordingly. With a wrap style, he said, we had some wiggle room anyway.

Soon, Vaughn and I had put the finishing touches on both pieces. Together, we combed the embellishments room scraps bin and found a coiled strand of silk green leaves attached to a twisted velvet cord. I was pretty sure it was supposed to represent an ivy vine — if not, the likeness was close enough. We made a crown out of the silk plant.

"What do you think?" I asked, draping the crown over the neck of the headless dummy and stepping back to admire the full effect. The long skirt shimmered like leaves in the rain, and the combination of newsprint and flowers gave the top a hard-soft tension. The red accents in each garment drew the eye up and down. There were times on the court when I hadn't been sure about a look . . . but I was sure about this one. Both pieces looked beautiful and comfortable. I would wear the outfit myself. I hoped Ivy would.

"Am I late?" A patternmaker with blond hair and a freckled face was walking toward us from the accessories wing.

Vaughn looked sheepish. "Marla, this is Neely Syms, the patternmaker I told you about. Neely . . . knows what we're doing."

"I forced it out of him," Neely said with a grin. "Ivy Wilde. Super prime." She opened one of the two white bags she was holding and pulled out the floral lapel pin made from the recycled plastic. Its green and white petals, melted and distorted, sparkled like sea glass in the overhead light. As I had requested, the tip of each petal had been rimmed in metallic gold paint, adding to the shine. Neely pinned the flower on the garment's shoulder and held up the second bag.

"I made you an extra," she grinned.

"Thank you. I love it."

"No problem. I dig your aesthetic. Do you know about zero-waste manufacturing?"

I shook my head.

"It's when you incorporate every piece cut from a length of fabric into the design of a garment."

"Wow," I said, imagining the strategic cutting necessary to pull something like that off. The scraps bin would be practically empty.

"Yeah. I've tried to get Torro to try it, but they won't listen to me."

"They're not good at listening, are they," I said quietly. The three of us stood, looking at the completed design.

"They might hear this, though," said Vaughn.

When everything was ready and packed gently into a garment box, I wrote the appropriate addresses on the package and mailed it. I felt light-shouldered walking home from the post office. I took out my Unum and selected Ivy's number. "On its way," I spoke into the device. "Top is repulped paper and flowers. Bottom is discarded fabric scraps. Pin was plastic bottles. All recycled. Hope you like it." I pressed Send.

A message from Ivy appeared the next day. *Got it. Love it. Thanks. Plan to wear it on* Hot with Hyman. *This Saturday, three p.m.*

At Torro, we talked about what to do. Randall said he would stay home with his children and watch the show there. I considered inviting everyone over to my apartment but decided against it. When Dido had come over, Karen had been happy I'd made a friend — or she'd tried to act it, at least — but I wasn't sure how she'd feel about a living room full of drafters. Especially guy drafters. It wasn't worth the questions. In the end, we decided to meet at Felix's place. He lived in one of the apartments for tapped employees whose families lived far away.

That Saturday afternoon, I joined Dido and Kevin in Felix's common room. Felix introduced us to his roommate, Mike, who barely said hello before beating a swift retreat down the hall. From the looks of things, the common room was common to several bedrooms on the floor. It was pretty spare — there was industrial-looking furniture, a table, and a television. The linoleum had a layer of sticky crud on it that I tried to ignore. I sat down on a stained love seat. After tossing each of us a small bag of pretzels, Felix sat down next to me. It wasn't intentional — it couldn't have been — but then again, there was a perfectly good armchair next to us that no one was using. I could feel that place inside me, the little box in which I had sealed up all the pain from Braxton, open a crack.

Felix switched on the television.

Chapter Sixteen

laiming she felt cold, Ivy kept her long shale coat on
while she waited in the *Hot with Hyman* greenroom
on the second floor of the Pop Beat studios. Hilarie
knew what she had on underneath. No one else did.
Fatima, busy with her Unum near the sandwich table, dis-
tractedly called to Ivy to get ready. Ivy looked up at the giant
broadcast screen over the door. The digital timer beneath it indicated that she had one minute until her live segment on the
special Saturday edition of the show. Her stomach contracted.
She hoped she wasn't going to throw up.

She had chewed a couple of placidophilus pills on the way
over this morning, but she refused the tin Hilarie held out to her
now. No matter how nervous she was, she needed a clear mind
to make this work. No slurring or stumbling over her words. A
flawless performance.

"Don't worry. Everyone will love it," Hilarie whispered,
squeezing her hand. The chains from her torture garments rattled.

Aiko stood up from the couch, lazily swinging the spiked
shoes by their straps. Ivy had worn them into the studio and
promptly removed them, slipping into ballet flats. To deflect

suspicion, she'd put the gag on; it was now hanging around her neck.

"Here you go," said Aiko, placing them by her feet. "Don't worry — it's only for a little while."

"Fifteen seconds," a crew member in a red corset announced. Ivy drew in her breath and began unbuttoning her coat.

From her own jacket pocket, Hilarie withdrew a pair of scissors and snipped the gag from around Ivy's neck. She pulled the crown of silk leaves from her other pocket and fixed it on Ivy's head, fluffing her hair beneath it. Ivy peeled off the shale coat and unrolled her skirt band so that the hem fell fully to her ankles. She smoothed her delicate new top.

"*What* in the *world* — ?" Fatima's bellow made her jump. Ivy turned quickly to see the shock and fury contorting her publicist's face. Madison's mouth was hanging open as well.

"You're on, Miss Wilde," murmured the wide-eyed crew-member.

Ivy glanced sympathetically at Hilarie, knowing the interrogation would begin as soon as she left, and opened the door to the studio stage.

The lights were warm, the crowd on its feet and screaming. Unums filled the air, snapping her picture. Everywhere Ivy looked she saw gags, woven hair, chains, all the accoutrements of the torture trend. She waved, forcing her smile to last past the moment when the crowd's reaction shifted, when they began to realize she wasn't wearing torture, wasn't wearing anything sexy or provocative or Wilde in the old way.

Kressley Hyman hugged her like an old friend. He was his usual self: tanned, with dyed-blond hair and unnaturally white teeth. Publicly he listed his age at seventeen, but Ivy knew this had to be a lie. He'd had this gig for six years, and he'd definitely started after puberty. That forehead had to have some Creas-erase injections in it. Ivy swallowed as she realized he was wear-ing a slashed leather jacket and studded jeans from the torture line.

"Good to see you, girl," Kressley began.

"It's always good to be here, Kressley," she said, mustering her enthusiasm.

"First things first. I've got to ask what we're all wondering." He pulled her arm up by the hem of her sleeve. "*What's up* with the new rags?"

Ivy felt Kressley and the studio crowd holding their collec-tive breath. If she didn't pull this off, one, two, ten of them would begin to snicker, hisses of "obsoloser" and "crustaceous" would collide in midair, and her career would come tumbling down like a castle of blocks. But, for this moment at least, she was still Ivy Wilde. She could see Kressley and the crowd waiting for the explanation, waiting to be told why what she was wearing was something they all needed to own. Just like Millbrook, just like everywhere. She straightened up and fluttered her skirt so it shimmered.

"I refuse to wear torture anymore," she said, staring into the faces of the girls in the audience, their corsets cinched tight. "It's twisted and painful. I'm making a different choice." She hoped Felix was listening.

She took a breath and continued the speech she and Hilarie had gone over. "It's time for a new kind of 'wildness.'" Her voice trembled only slightly. "If you don't care about the environment by now, you're a huge obsoloser. What I'm wearing is all recy-cled. This pin used to be a plastic bottle." She looked down; the colored plastic and gold shimmered obediently under the studio lights. "Isn't it gorgeous?" To her relief, Kressley nodded. She could feel the crowd warming, examining the clothes, snapping more pictures with their Unums. One girl in the front row pulled her gag out of her mouth with a hooked finger and massaged her jaw.

"It's a tight new image," Kressley said, grinning. "So are the days of the 'Wilde' child over?"

"I'm as 'Wilde' as ever," she affirmed. "Just in a prime new way."

"So you're saying everyone should go all eco-conscious? Organics? Sandals with socks? Hemp T-shirts?" The slick grin was starting to irritate her.

"Not just eco-conscious." The term came to her so suddenly she almost snapped her fingers. "Eco-*chic*. These clothes are environmentally friendly *and* beautiful. And so comfortable, let me tell you."

She imagined the faces in the audiences contemplating their own pain, the points driving into their feet, the tightness, the itching. With any luck, torture would soon be dead. Thanks to her. The power made her fingertips tingle.

Next to the main camera, a crew member held up a Tabula with the words *Design House??* printed on its screen. Before she could puzzle out the meaning, Kressley spoke.

"No doubt. You've always been a trendsetter, Ivy. Can you let everyone in our audience know who you're wearing?"

"Oh. It's an original design by Marla Klein. She works for . . ." About to mention Torro-LeBlanc by name, she hesitated. They had been the ones behind torture, and, really, they deserved no credit for this outfit. ". . . one of the Big Five now, but I think she should split off and set up her own boutique, don't you?" she finished. The crowd worked their Unums, undoubtedly trying to locate Marla's online presence. *Good for her,* Ivy thought. The clothes really were prime.

"No doubt," Kressley said again. His smile sparkled. "So down to business. Before we see part of your new video, tell us about your *Laid Bare* tour. And you're filming for your reality show again, yes?"

She completed the interview in a happy fog. She had actually done it — gone and reinvented herself. Felix would see that the sluttiness was fake. Her old Wilde child self was now a dried-up chrysalis; she couldn't wait to stretch her wings and see how high the new Ivy Wilde could fly.

"I could murder you," said Fatima. She was pacing around the greenroom like a lion.

Ivy ignored her; not even a lecture from Fatima could kill her euphoria. She strode past her publicist to the sandwich table and began munching on veggie chips. With the interview over, her stomach had relaxed and her appetite had rumbled back to life.

"Do you realize how much damage control I have to do now?" barked Fatima. "For starters, the whole tour theme needs to be scrapped. We designed the stage to look like the circles of hell. *Hell,* Ivy. Do you know how much work it's going to take to change it to"— she motioned up and down in front of Ivy's clothes —"to this? From hell to Eden! All because you decided to grow an opinion!"

Ivy glanced at her nymphs for support. Arms crossed, Madison looked angry. Ivy guessed she felt excluded; Madison couldn't stand being on the fringe of things. Aiko and Naia stood by quietly with the rest of the *Hot with Hyman* crew, waiting for the storm to pass. Hilarie's eyes were still pink and watery. Ivy felt a twinge of guilt thinking of the way Fatima must have lit into her after she left. Still, it had been worth it.

She wiped her fingers on a cocktail napkin. "I'm sorry. But I kind of hated the torture trend." She remembered the Torro-LeBlanc runway show, how the pain had driven her to smash the Tabula against her leg. "No, I *really* hated it. You and Jarvis never asked me if I wanted to wear that stuff."

Fatima stared at her for a moment, then approached so that their faces were inches apart. "Our job is not to ask." Her voice was a low growl. "Our job is to know what's made every star before you popular and to give you the same treatment. This is what we *do,* Ivy." She tucked her thick black hair behind both ears, though it immediately resisted staying put. "Really, do you think your success happened by *accident?*"

That didn't seem fair. Fatima wasn't the one on stage at concerts, firing up the crowd, and recording tracks again and again until they sounded perfect. "I'm a good singer —"

"So are a million other girls and boys," Fatima snapped, then softened a bit as she registered Ivy's hurt expression. "You *are* a talented performer. But face facts. It took a lot more than talent to get you where you are. What do you think I've been doing for three years?" She stepped back and addressed the room, her arms spread. "Anyone around here who believes fame 'just happens' is sorely mistaken."

There was a beat of silence, and then Fatima's Unum buzzed so suddenly that everyone jumped. She grabbed it and thumped the screen with her thumb. "Jarvis! There you are. She's gone insane. Did you see the segment?"

Ivy heard Jarvis ask to speak to her. Fatima shoved the Unum at her and walked around to stand over her shoulder. To Ivy's surprise, Jarvis didn't look upset. He was actually smiling.

"You disobedient little minx." He shook his head. "First off, *never* do anything like that again. Okay? If you think of a new idea, tell us. Fatima and I are on your side, remember?"

Ivy glanced at Fatima. As she'd just made clear, Fatima obviously wouldn't have been on her side with the reinvention, especially with the tour approaching. But maybe Jarvis would have listened. It wasn't as if he'd ever openly rejected an idea of hers before. But he'd never asked for her opinion on anything either. Which didn't exactly encourage suggestions. "Uh-huh," Ivy said.

"It could have been a catastrophe. Instead"— his grin widened —"you may have worked a miracle."

"What?" Fatima spat.

"What do you mean?" asked Ivy.

Jarvis's face got bigger as he leaned closer to his device. "Kiddo, the hotspots are going crazy. Have you seen? You just got off the air and already everyone's buzzing. Look at these headlines."

Fatima's Unum screen divided into quadrants, each revealing an article. Fatima peered closer to look. Ivy read the headings:

NEW 'ECO-CHIC' LOOK FOR WILDE REFRESHING
WILDE TAKES GLAMOROUS STAND FOR ENVIRONMENT
WILDE ANNOUNCES: 'TORTURE OVER. ECO NOW CHIC.'
GREEN TREND COULD BE 'WILDELY' POPULAR

She glanced up at Hilarie and the others and read the last headline aloud. Hilarie's cheeks rounded in a smile.

The screen flashed back to Jarvis's image. "And that's not the best news. We just sold out Oreland. Ticket sales had been sluggish — I was afraid we were going to have to cancel the show.

Instead, and I don't want to promise anything, but if this gets big, we might be able to add another stop or two on the tour."

It was all Ivy could do not to jump up and down. Take *that*, Lyric Mirth. She grinned at Jarvis.

"Let me talk to Fatima. We've got to line up some publicity appearances for your new look. Get ready. Say — how did you come up with the environmental angle?"

Ivy thought quickly. It had been Marla Klein's idea in the bathroom, of course. But everyone was looking at her. Now was not the time to loosen her grasp on everything she had just seized. "I've always cared about the environment," she said. "It felt natural. And it kind of worked with my name already."

"It's *good*," said Jarvis. "Has real staying power. Okay, give me Fatima. Stay young."

At home, Ivy kept her new clothing on as the cook served dinner. She tucked a giant cloth napkin into the front of her shirt to catch any Alfredo sauce spatters. After corsets, the elastic waistband on the skirt was pure comfort to eat in.

Madison was slow to forgive Ivy for going behind her back with the whole eco-trend thing. "If it hadn't gone well, I didn't want to get you guys in trouble," Ivy explained, twirling pasta around her fork. "I told Hil only because I needed someone to help me out. You remember the story about CeCe Sunburst's nymphs helping her elope with the landscaper. Their careers were over afterward." The CeCe excuse was only half of the truth. She hadn't told Naia and Aiko because she didn't trust their poker faces. And she hadn't wanted Madison to know because Madison was bossy and might have tried to talk her out of it. Or worse, laughed at her. Fortunately, as she sweetened the excuse with apologies, Madison and the others bought it.

That evening, as usual, Ivy and her nymphs sat in front of the television for the primetime lineup. Chewing a placidophilus pill and studying the headlines on her shirt, Ivy suddenly decided that *Clone Valley* wasn't very interesting. She told her nymphs she was tired, but instead of heading to bed, she grabbed her Unum and sashayed in a haze down the red-wallpapered hall on the first floor. The fabric of her skirt brushed lightly against her legs. Maybe it was the pill, but she felt different — as if these clothes were rustling awake something inside her.

Ivy entered the music room and closed the door gently. It was within these insulated walls that her vocal coach, Suzette, went over new songs with her before she hit the studio. But tonight she didn't stand by the long mirror as usual. She sat down at the electric piano bench, raised the lid, and pressed the On switch. With her right hand, she played a G major chord.

She'd taken piano lessons in Millbrook but hadn't played much since. She didn't write the songs on her albums. Yes, she embellished them with runs and grace notes — but even those were mostly guided by Suzette.

She played the chord again, then lowered the third to make it minor. She had sung very few songs in minor keys, she realized. Pop was major. Majorly major. Minor sounded haunted. Disturbed. Right now, she liked it. Starting with her pinky on the fifth, she played four notes in a descending scale. And again, this time doubling each note. The blurred headline on her extended right arm caught her eye: MASSIVE OIL PLUMES PLAGUE GULF. She had some vague memory of studying the spill in class when she was younger. She tried to remember the photographs she'd seen of the toxic sludge, spreading like a blob in the water. Everyone took for granted that the environment mattered, but she didn't really give it much thought in her daily life anymore.

She probably needed to change that — especially given her new image. After thinking for a bit, she replayed her melody and sang along:

I wonder how they let the oil —

Tentatively, she played a C minor chord with her left hand and sang a new line:

Cover the sea in blackness

Her Unum on top of the piano buzzed, and Ivy whipped her hands away from the keys as if she'd been caught. Calming herself with a nervous laugh, she picked up the device. A moment later, Clayton Pryce's beaming face, deeply tanned, appeared on the screen.

"Wildness! What's up?" said Clayton. "I leave for a month and you explode! You're all over the hotspots tonight." He sounded good, better than he had in a while. His voice had lost its usual cloudiness.

"Yeah, I experimented with my look a little. It seems to have worked."

"I'll say. My agent's already talking about greening up my tour. Making the crowd bring refillable water bottles or something."

"Prime." She couldn't believe the eco trend was catching fire this fast. "So how was your trip?"

Clayton's grin grew even larger. Ivy noticed his nose was peeling at the tip. "*So* relaxing. I didn't want to come home. The beach was killer, and it was great to be with my family. I didn't realize how much I miss my brother and sisters. They're grown up enough to be fun now."

Ivy laughed, remembering the big smiling family photo that was the home screen on Clayton's Unum. "The press wasn't bad there?"

"*No!* The hotel management was amazing at sniffing them out. They have crazy laws there, like jail time for loitering or something. It was a sanctuary. You've got to go."

She imagined swimming with Constantine, alone, with no crowds and no cameras. That settled it. After the tour, once she'd secured her stratospheric status, she would insist on a family trip. Maybe she could get back in touch with Marisa Garcia and take her along too. And if Marisa was going . . . Ivy pushed the distracting thought out of her mind. "It must have been hard being away from James," she said.

"Yeah. But we talked every day, and we're definitely going to try to go down there together next year. He'd love it."

"I bet."

"So what's going on with you?"

The second part of the plan conceived at the Torro-LeBlanc runway show returned to mind. "I was going to call you, actually," she said. She paused for dramatic effect. "Clayton," she said, unable to prevent herself from giggling, "we need to talk."

Chapter Seventeen

vy Wilde was on Hot with Hyman. Wearing my clothes. *And she mentioned me by name.*

When it happened, the drafters in Felix's common room piled on top of me in a happy huddle. The full effect of the outfit had surpassed my expectations. In the studio lights, everything seemed to glisten and shimmer in such a beautiful way. Maybe my leopard-print dress had been a little tacky... but this outfit I would stand by forever. I hoped Vaughn and Neely had been watching.

That evening, Dido kept forwarding us articles that announced the sudden extinction of torture and the birth of a new "eco-chic" trend. One even contained a line about the "unknown designer Marla Kline" who had "dreamed up Ivy Wilde's new look." I could live with my name misspelled. It blew my mind that I might have single-handedly started a new trend even though I wasn't a judge anymore. But the articles also reminded me that the thing I had done was now very public.

Julia left a video message an hour after the show aired. She looked composed, her lip gloss perfect. Her voice sounded the way it always did, soft and silky and deceptively pleasant, as she told me I was fired. I sat at my desk, staring at my Unum in thick disbelief. I accessed my contract in the Torro-LeBlanc database and found the word TERMINATED visible across the top in red. But before I'd fully drowned myself in despair, Julia called again. I panicked and ignored the call, and Julia left another message, this time asking me to call her back. "We recognize your years of service and don't want to act in haste," she said. When I checked my contract again, it read UNDER REVIEW. I decided to avoid the whole issue by going to bed.

On Sunday morning, I awoke to find two news vans parked on the street in front of my apartment complex. Walter told me reporters from the Pop Beat channel and *Prime* magazine had called from the lobby. They were requesting interviews while I was still in my pajamas.

"Get some makeup on!" Karen yelled to me, hastily singeing the tips of her own hair with a flat iron.

I stared at the vans from my window. I thought about stepping out into the gray morning and answering questions about my designs. Maybe being photographed for a profile in *Prime*. Enticing — but it was too great a risk. I remembered that Torro-LeBlanc had a little provision in its drafter contract that prevented just this sort of thing. After yesterday's messages from Julia, I didn't want to draw any more attention to myself.

"Drafters aren't allowed to give interviews," I said to Karen.

She looked crestfallen, but only for a moment. "Well, *I'll* talk to them, then." She applied a coat of gloss, flipped her hair back, and exited the front door.

I didn't hear the particulars, but it was a short interview. I watched the reporters and camera operators climb back into their respective vans. They camped out on the curb for two more hours before driving away.

Later, Winnie called, leaving a chipper message: "I saw the show. Congrats on the eco-chic outfit! Give me a call when you get this, okay?"

Then Godfrey. His message was the nicest. He didn't ask me to call back, just told me he'd adored the clothes. He said the materials were some of the most innovative he'd seen. He ended with a definitive "I'll see you on Monday." I was tempted to call back and confirm that I was still employed, but I couldn't handle the bad news, even from him.

And the weirdest: Someone from Belladonna called. A crisply dressed woman wanted to set up an informational interview to discuss "lucrative career opportunities." I knew it was illegal to poach design-house employees. Once you were tapped, you were contractually bound to the house that hired you. Besides, design-house loyalty was fierce. But if Torro fired me, I would need to work *somewhere* . . .

Finally, the administrative assistant to Torro-LeBlanc's chief creative officer, neither of whom I had ever met, began leaving messages. I burned with curiosity — but he was a youngish man who had a brisk, dominating way of speaking that intimidated me. Fed up, I decided to face the entire mess in person on Monday. I powered down my Unum and left it off for the rest of the day. Every so often, I glanced suspiciously at its dark face.

Chapter Eighteen

I vy left her nymphs in front of Sunday night's primetime lineup and once again hurried away to the music room. She was supposed to be rehearsing "My Love Is Evergreen," a song the studio had rushed over. It was a potential opening number for her revised tour set list. Fatima and Jarvis hadn't wasted a moment. The venue sets were being reconstructed, and the choreographer was coming over in the middle of the week to work with her on some "environmentally inspired" dances. With amusement, Ivy wondered if she'd have to blossom like a flower or flutter like a bird around the stage. Both options were fine by her. Performing without chains or corsets was progress.

Sadly, the melody of "My Love Is Evergreen" conserved its resources, all right; it recycled the same three notes over and over. Ivy ignored it; she would sing it to death with her vocal coach later anyway. Instead, she tried to figure out the chord progression for a new song.

This time, she'd chosen a major key. The song was happy and upbeat. Four joyful, hummable lines of the chorus had come to her in a rush during dinner: "Forget yesterday / 'Cause today we escape / Come on, come on / Break free with me." Since her appearance on *Hot with Hyman,* she really did feel freer. Tomorrow's brunch with Clayton was on her mind too; they were both kind of breaking free, weren't they?

She was experimenting with the verse melody when she heard a knock and saw a knob turning.

Naia popped her face into the crack of open door. "What are you doing in here?"

"Nothing." Ivy folded her hands in her lap. "Practicing. What do you want?"

"There's a delivery for you. Flowers."

Ivy's mind flew to her eco-chic debut the day before. She felt a warm flush creep over her as she sat on the piano bench. Could they be from Felix? So soon? No, it was unlikely. Still, unable to help herself, she strode toward the door with expectation, brushed past Naia, and spotted the massive bouquet in the foyer. A young woman in a jumpsuit with *Mercury Florist* embroidered on the pocket was carrying it in, her arms hugging the giant base as if it were a small boulder. With considerable effort, she heaved it onto a bare table and took a deep breath. She then began perfecting the arrangement, adjusting the stems and greenery with an artist's touch.

Ivy walked up to the florist. "Who are they from?" she demanded. Naia followed her, half curious, half drifting toward the sounds of *Playground Crime Scene* coming from the living room.

"There should be a card stuck in here," the florist muttered, scanning the blooms. Her cap was pulled down so far over her eyes that Ivy didn't trust the woman's vision; she began looking herself. "That's funny," the florist said, patting her uniform and sticking her hands into her pockets. "Nothing." She glanced around the room awkwardly. "It probably fell out in the truck. I'll have to go take a look. I'm so sorry." Ivy twisted her mouth in impatience.

"Let us know who sent them," Naia called over her shoulder as she made her way back to the living room to join the other nymphs. Ivy stayed put as the florist headed toward the entrance. But instead of leaving, she paused at the door. She removed her cap and turned back to Ivy.

"Ivy Wilde," she said in a different voice. "Do you remember me?" She stared at Ivy full on, her mascara-laden eyes severe and unblinking, her hair falling darkly around her face.

Ivy felt a flash of recognition. She knew she had seen this woman before, recently, in an uncomfortable situation. There had been others around too. Like a struck match, the scene in the Torro-LeBlanc runway-show dressing room blazed in her mind's eye. This was the crazy woman who had planted all those ink explosives on the seats. And had been fired on the spot. She was here, in Ivy's house . . . for what? Revenge?

"*Don't* call your nymphs," the woman ordered, seeming to read her mind. "And don't touch your Unum." She pulled out her own and held it up between her thumb and middle finger, shaking it slightly. "I know what your brother did, and I know how disturbing it must be for you. If you listen to what I have to say, I promise to keep his little secret."

"Constantine?" Frantically, Ivy wondered what she was talking about.

The woman read her face and gave her a sad smile. "Ah. I figured you knew. I'll tell you in a moment. I want to talk first."

Ivy began to tremble as the woman advanced toward her. "What do you want?" Ivy asked in a tight voice. "Are you here to kill me?"

The woman halted her approach and began to laugh. Ivy waited, deciding the laughter sounded amused rather than evil. Still, she remained tensed and ready to run.

"Sorry," the woman said, wiping the corner of one eye and smudging her makeup. "We got off to a bad start, I think. My name is Vivienne Graves." She stuffed her cap into her pocket and extended her hand, which Ivy ignored. The woman continued, undeterred. "I used to work for Torro-LeBlanc, as you no doubt remember. *No*, Evangeline Vassiliotis, I am not here to murder you. Quite the opposite. I think you have the power to make a difference in an important movement going on right now." She glanced in the direction of the living room, where the young television stars' voices carried on a conversation about fingernail clippings. "Is there somewhere we can talk where we won't be disturbed?"

The tactical shift bewildered Ivy, as did Vivienne's use of her real name. She needed to proceed carefully. "The kitchen's this way," she suggested, leading Vivienne down three steps and around the corner. With its open design, the kitchen felt safe enough. After she found out what was on that Unum, she could easily run to her nymphs if need be.

"Perfect," said Vivienne, sitting down on one of the counter stools. She leveled her palms on the marble countertop. "Boy, does this remind me of drafting," she said. "Sit with me," she added, gesturing to a stool next to her.

"I'm good," said Ivy, remaining on the other side of the counter. It felt better to have a slab of stone between them. She patted her pockets but remembered that her placidophilus pills were in the living room. "What do you know about Constantine? Is he all right?" she asked, glancing at the device next to Vivienne's hands.

"Yes," said Vivienne lightly. "And I won't tell you any more until you listen to me. I promise, the sooner you hear me out, the sooner I'll leave. I want to talk to you about the eco-chic trend."

Ivy's face crinkled in bewilderment. "Huh?"

Vivienne reached into her florist's uniform and pulled out a medium-size manila envelope, which she placed on the counter-top. "I know Marla Klein designed the look for you. But tell me. Why were you willing to go along with it?"

Ivy shook her head, trying to understand what Vivienne was asking. Her head felt woolly. "Um, because I needed a new look."

"Why?"

She studied Vivienne, wondering how honest to be. "Performers need to change things up every so often. To stay relevant," she said.

"I see." Vivienne nodded. "Your single is number one on the pop charts for one week, someone else moves up the next . . ." She mimed the rungs of a ladder with her hands. "It's like a never-ending dance, isn't it? It must be hard work to stay on top."

One of Ivy's *Laid Bare* tracks, "Me First," had shot to the top spot yesterday, twenty-four hours after the Pop Beat exposure. Lyric Mirth was now sitting pretty at number three with "So Pure It Hurts." That was where she could stay. Vivienne seemed to be trying to read her with those dark eyes. Ivy scowled. "Tell me about Constantine," she said again.

"In a moment. I promise. What I'm really wondering is, why specifically did you and Marla decide on *eco-chic*?"

"I don't know. Because it's prime to care about the environment."

Vivienne paused. "Eva — do you *honestly* care about the environment? Or is it just a convenient trend to take advantage of?"

"Of course I care," Ivy blurted out. She thought about the song she had begun the previous night about the oil spill — if that wasn't proof, what was? "I care," she repeated.

"Your outfit, the one you wore on *Hot with Hyman*," Vivienne said. "Yes, it features recycled materials, but Torro is most likely in the process of mass-producing it. It will last as a trend for a few weeks and then something new will replace it."

Ivy could feel her waiting for a response, but she didn't give one. Vivienne went on. "Putting aside production for a moment, let's talk about waste. What do you think happens to clothes after a trend passes?"

Ivy thought. What does happen to clothes? She remembered her mother keeping a donations box in their house. "They're donated."

"Some of them are. Fifteen percent of textiles are recycled. Meaning they end up in a thrift shop, or are sold at a discount to other countries, or are turned into things like rags and upholstery stuffing. What happens to the rest?"

Vivienne wasn't looking at her unkindly, but Ivy felt stupid. "I hadn't really thought about it before. I don't know . . . they end up in the ground?"

"Yes. They're shredded and put in landfills. Or burned. In this country, we discard eleven million tons of clothes and shoes a year. That's seventy pounds per person — though *your* trend-setting contribution is four or five times that number, I'd guess." Ivy heard the edge in her voice. "What kind of environmental impact do you think that has?"

Ivy grew defensive at Vivienne's words. It wasn't her fault that trends keep changing and that Fatima would only let her feature outfits once. But the image of Millbrook came back to her, the legions of cheering people dressed in the armed-forces trend. That trend was surely over by now. She imagined all that expensive clothing stuffed into a hillside, torn and dirty, never to be worn again. Her hankering for a placidophilus pill increased.

Vivienne chuckled bitterly. "Torro was always so proud of

the way it recycled internally. It made everyone feel warm and fuzzy about corporate practices. So they wouldn't look too hard at the other ends."

Ivy put her elbows on the counter and massaged her temples. "You think I don't care, but I do. I can't stand walking through my own closet sometimes. And shopping's fun, but sometimes I feel sick looking at the price tags. Where I grew up, people shell out cash for trends they can't afford. In part because of me."

Vivienne sat up straighter, studying Ivy with her dark, deep-set eyes. "I underestimated you, Eva," she said softly. "Yes, there is a considerable economic cost for everyone."

Ivy suddenly remembered her conversation in the bathroom of the runway show. "So why did you design torture, then, if you're so against trends?" she demanded. "Marla Klein said those horrible clothes were your idea."

Vivienne seemed to consider her reply. "I thought someone ... important ... might be brave enough to point out the ridiculousness of the trend," she said at last. "And it might make people think harder about trends in general."

Even though Vivienne was an intruder, Ivy was finding it hard to stay angry at her. Here was someone who was comfortable talking about the wastefulness of trends. Some who maybe thought one hundred fifty-nine dollars for a pair of tights was ridiculous.

"The Torro-LeBlanc employees are going on strike soon," Vivienne said suddenly.

"They're what?"

"They're going to refuse to go to work. If all goes well for us, the production of official eco-chic clothing will be slowed or stopped." So that might explain it, Ivy thought. Fatima had spent the afternoon ordering a few things that could get Ivy through until they could shop properly. A recycled textiles site featured links to eco-friendly boutiques and repurposed clothing stores in the vicinity. After the success on *Hot with Hyman*, Ivy had hoped Marla Klein might be able to whip together some more great outfits, too, but she'd tried the designer's Unum all day without success. Was she refusing to design any more on account of the strike?

"I'm sure other design houses will hasten to fill the void," Vivienne went on before Ivy could ask about Marla. "But there is an alternative. The whole world will wear what you wear, Ivy. You know this. So making an environmental impact is truly within your grasp. Slowing consumer spending, too." A cunning smile crept over her lips. "And if that's not enough to convince you, while you're at it, you can make a certain competitor look absolutely villainous."

The opening theme song of *Real Boys of South Brunswick* drifted in faintly from the living room. Ivy heard her nymphs' voices and wondered for a moment if one of them would wander into the kitchen for a snack. Apparently, though, the latest episode proved more interesting than food, and, to her relief, she and Vivienne were left alone.

"Go on," Ivy said.

She listened to Vivienne's proposal. It involved even more renegade behavior. She didn't exactly want to turn herself into a crazy rebel or anything. Still, it wouldn't be hard to pull off, and if it worked, she could savor the victory for weeks. If it fell through, as Vivienne pointed out, she had little to lose.

"I'll think about it," said Ivy. She bit her lip, trying to seem noncommittal.

"Good," said Vivienne, standing. She picked up her Unum.

"I should be going, then." She turned the manila envelope over and pointed to a number printed on the flap. "That's my Unum, if you need to get in touch with me. I've got yours."

"What about my brother?" Ivy asked.

"Right." Vivienne looked at her solemnly. "Unfortunately, I don't think your brother has been feeling so great since being passed over in the Tap. He and a couple of other boys defaced a certain statue in Millbrook." Vivienne tapped her Unum screen. "Your parents are paying to have it cleaned. I heard they also paid a guy who caught the three kids on video not to release the footage to the media. Here, I have a photo."

She held her screen for Ivy to see. Ivy's first impression was of a boy who'd been in a paintball fight. But it wasn't a boy — it was the statue of Skip McBrody in the town square. *Obsoloser* was scrawled along the statue's base in red spray paint, just below the feet. Skip had a joker's wide smile painted over his lips and circles around each of his eyes. His body had been sprayed randomly with lines of paint, except — Ivy cringed inwardly — for a definite bulbous thing coming out of his crotch area. The sight of the marked-up statue, the monument that had always made her feel solemn and humble, sickened Ivy. What could have possessed her brother to do such a thing?

"I'm sorry you had to hear it from me," said Vivienne, pulling her cap out of her pocket and adjusting it on her head.

"I have to call him," said Ivy shakily.

"You probably should." Vivienne tucked her Unum away and slid the manila envelope across the counter to Ivy. "One last thing. Production waste and cost are bad enough. But if your resolve weakens, take a look at these pictures. They show where your clothes are made, and who makes them." She grinned. "My next task after the Torro strike is to unionize the Big Five's factory workers. I'll get the IGLF to bust down the factory doors. It's going to be beautiful."

"The what?"

"The International Garment Labor Federation. They determine which companies maintain humane working conditions and pay employees living wages. They've called out the Big Five manufacturing plants in print, but no one reads those articles. It's time to take action."

Her thoughts still with Constantine, Ivy nodded vaguely.

"We'll be in touch, then," said Vivienne, extending her hand across the counter. This time, Ivy shook it. "Oh, and sorry about the flower-delivery ruse." She pulled her cap down over her eyes. "I wish, for your sake, the bouquet really had been from someone exciting."

Envelope in hand, Ivy followed Vivienne as she walked back to the foyer and disappeared through the front door without a backward glance.

"I'm going to bed!" she shouted toward the living room. Her nymphs called back their good nights.

"Who were the flowers from?" she heard Naia ask.

"Christina and George," she replied, and headed up the stairs to her bedroom.

The door to her two-story closet was open, and she shut it firmly, not wanting to face the racks of clothes inside. She collapsed on her bed and looked at the clock. Was it too late to call her family tonight? Would Constantine even be awake? She decided to try them in the morning.

Shifting so her back was against the pillows and her legs crossed, she held the envelope Vivienne had given her and grabbed her Unum from her nightstand. She entered Vivienne's number into her directory, then bent the metal clasps of the envelope to release the flap. She pulled out a small pile of eight-by-ten photographs and studied them in her lap, one by one.

The workers were women and girls, some younger than she. The first shot showed them maneuvering mountains of fabric through sewing machines in a long row. The girl closest to the camera was focused intently on her work, her cheeks flushed pink and her brow moist. The neckline of her shirt was also ringed with sweat. Another photograph revealed women sleeping in bunk beds, two on either side of a small room. There were tapestries hung on the walls, but the effect wasn't all that cheering. Ivy noticed that the broken glass in one windowpane had been replaced with cardboard.

In another, a supervisor looked to be reprimanding a young girl of about ten, who sat in front of a table of buttons. A fourth showed a girl working a sewing machine with a bandaged finger. Her eyes drooped as she sewed a zipper onto a puffy silver garment. Ivy recognized it as the space-age jacket she'd worn to the Millbrook Tap. The girl herself wore a plain green T-shirt and small stud earrings — nothing remotely trendy.

Ivy stuffed the pictures back into the envelope. She knew what Vivienne was trying to do. She was supposed to feel bad for these girls who worked so hard to make everyone's clothes. And she did. It was just that their faces, their lives, seemed so far away from her own. They almost didn't seem real. She reclasped the envelope. She had so much to think about. Constantine, spraying paint all over a statue of a pop star. And then there was her brunch with Clayton. Her new songs. Lyric. Felix. She cared, of course, but she didn't have any more headspace to give to people she'd probably never meet.

Besides, her eco-chic image was already doing wonders. If

Vivienne's plan worked, Millbrook's residents would take a nice shopping break from designer brands. Thanks to her.

Ivy tossed the envelope in the trash barrel by her bedside — then thought better of it. She didn't want to answer questions if Fatima happened to find it. She got up and stuffed it in her purse. She'd throw it away outside, later.

Chapter Nineteen

M arla? *There's a boy here* to see you."

Karen's sharp call carried up the stairs to the second floor bathroom, where I was applying eyeliner. I paused with the pencil in my hand. A boy? At eight o'clock Monday morning? I hastily evened out both eyes and pulled my damp hair into a ponytail, teasing out some strands so that the mess looked purposeful. I'd get around to flat-ironing it again one of these days.

I grabbed the plastic flower pin Neely had helped me make and held it to my shoulder, judging the effect in the mirror. I took it away, then put it back. Pin or no pin?

"Marla?" my mother called again.

"I'm coming!" I shouted. I could decide on the train. I put the pin inside my briefcase next to my dark-faced Unum and latched it.

Half wondering if "the boy" was the creative officer's assistant who had called me yesterday, I descended the curved staircase. My mother was planted in the foyer with a travel mug in her hands. My father stood behind her, crumbs stuck in one corner of his mouth. From the doorway, a familiar face looked at me in relief.

"Oh, hi," I said, surprised. "Um, Karen, Walter, this is Felix. We work together."

"He told us," my father said, cluelessly chipper as always. "We've got extra blackberry muffins, Felix—would you like one?"

"I'm good, thank you," Felix replied.

Karen eyed Felix warily, then turned to me. "Is there something I need to know here?"

"What? No. Absolutely not. We just work together," I blurted out. Felix loudly overlapped with "Like I said, I just thought Marla might want company on her ride in this morning."

Karen studied us both in the silence that followed. She walked over to me, handed me the mug of latte, and put a hand on my shoulder. "This is a big day for you, honey," she said, looking me in the eye. "Don't let *anything* distract you. Okay?" I had shared only the good eco-chic press from Dido with my parents. They knew nothing about the contradictory messages regarding my job. Karen squeezed my shoulder. "Good luck. I'll be waiting."

"I know. Thanks," I said as politely as I could. "We should go." I half pushed Felix out the door. I didn't look behind me to see if my parents were watching us make our way toward the elevator.

"Sorry," I said, once we were outside. "Karen's a little intense."

"Well, showing up first thing in the morning is strange. She probably thinks I'm either stalking you or trying to steal your thunder."

"The joke's on her, then," I said, glancing up at my apartment building. "There's not going to be any thunder to steal."

Felix looked at me quizzically.

"I might be getting fired." I told him about the onslaught of messages and the red-lettered addition to my contract.

Felix laughed. "Are you crazy, princess?" I gave him a deep frown and he added quickly, "And I call you that only because you're about to become Torro-LeBlanc royalty again. Julia obviously made a mistake and was trying to backpedal. You drafted *the* couture piece that's started a huge trend. The creative director doesn't want to get in touch with you to fire you. Torro wants to claim ownership."

"But I ended torture. They can't be happy about that."

Felix drew his Unum from his back pants pocket and grinned. "No kidding. Did you see the piece the *Financier* posted yesterday?"

Marla shook her head.

"Let me find it." He touched the screen. "It was about the anticipated losses at Torro from torture changing overnight like that." I pushed him around a fire hydrant as he navigated his Unum. "Thanks. Here we go. They predicted first-quarter profits for the top fashion houses and ranked them. Take a look." He held out the screen for me.

I scanned the list:

1. Rudolfo
2. Zhang & Tsai
3. Bancroft House
4. Belladonna
5. Hidaya
6. Torro-LeBlanc

I gaped. *Hidaya.* If we mentioned the design house at all, it was only to make condescending comments about it. Every so often its court would get lucky with a trend, but it remained solidly second tier. Or so everyone thought. "Oh, God. Torro's not in the Big Five anymore?"

"They still are for now. It's just a prediction, but the lost revenue from torture is going to sting, and the *Financier* knows that. Torro's Silents must be steaming!" Felix's usual scowl was nowhere to be found. He looked as if he'd just stepped off the world's best roller coaster. Quite the improvement — not that I could appreciate it right now with my life coming apart around me.

"Then I'm definitely going to get fired — screw that, *sued*," I said, walking up the stairs to the train platform. "I've violated the non-compete clause in a million ways."

"No. Listen. *Ivy Wilde* ended torture. We saw it. You invented the one thing that gives Torro any chance of getting back in the game. They can't lose you now."

I wasn't convinced. But I didn't say anything as Felix stepped aside so I could pass through the turnstile ahead of him. We stood together on the platform, listening to the animated conversations around us. I caught snatches of "torture" and "eco-chic" emerging from the lips of the commuters. Just when I'd thought I'd managed to avoid getting recognized, I locked eyes with three Torro-LeBlanc drafters at the other end of the platform. They waved and began making their way toward me.

The arriving train saved us. "This way," I said, steering Felix into the rearmost car. We slipped into two facing seats and rested our briefcases in our laps. I was aware of my knees hovering an inch away from his. I took a gulp of latte and swallowed.

"So . . . *are* you stalking me?" I asked.

Felix's look turned mischievous, and I wondered for a second if the conversation was going to head someplace complicated. "Maybe," he said. "This morning the stalking happens to be work related. I had to see you before the Torro brass got to you."

"Why?"

Felix again took out his Unum and poked around the screen. "You remember Vivienne's idea? She and Kevin and I, and a couple of the patternmakers, talked last night. We tried calling you but couldn't get through. It's time. The company's vulnerable, and we can organize successfully even without the Superior Court's support. In a couple of weeks, we'll be ready to present the demands for our corporate makeover. And that's where you come in."

I stared at him, remembering Vivienne's message after the runway show. "Makeover?"

"Our vision for restructuring Torro-LeBlanc." Felix smirked. "Vivienne was calling it a 'manifesto,' but we thought that some rebranding might attract more people to the cause."

They wanted to *make over* the company. I had a feeling this meant more than repainting walls and hanging new curtains.

"You, Miss Eco-Chic, may soon be in a position to make certain demands of your own," continued Felix. "So we need to know if you're on board."

"On board? I told you I was," I said. "I think older people like us should still serve on the courts. It's not fair."

"Ah. But in our makeover, there are no courts."

Felix let his pronouncement sink in. He tilted his head toward mine and lowered his voice to a whisper. "You should read the demands"— he waved his Unum —"but I'll give you the gist. Torro, like all of the design houses, is massive. Monolithic. A very few people have creative authority, and a whole lot of others do the dirty work without much reward. Right?"

I had no idea what *monolithic* meant, but I didn't let on. "Sure."

"So we want to dissolve the tiered structure and break up the giant house. Create a whole bunch of small studio divisions within the organization. The divisions will have specialties. They can be grouped by item — like a handbag division — or by aesthetic, or just by people who want to work together."

I mulled over this idea. It was a drastic restructuring — but I admitted that it made some sense. Our own table sometimes felt like a mini studio, anyway. Of course, Felix would probably want to work with people who shared his aesthetic of tough, distressed-looking garments. That wasn't really my style. I could see it, though: a group of like-minded drafters collaborating. I wondered — maybe I could start my own "eco-chic" division? "Go on," I said.

"One representative from each studio will be elected to a leadership team that meets regularly with Torro's Silents. All the reps will serve brief terms and rotate members." Felix grabbed my mug and sloshed down some latte. I raised my eyebrows but didn't say anything as he handed the mug back to me with a grin. "Thanks. Your mother makes good foam."

"Okay, so independent creative divisions," I said. "Presumably, we wouldn't work on commission?"

"Nope. We'd set up a fair pay scale. I think there should be bonuses for high performance, but I haven't convinced Kevin yet," said Felix, shrugging.

"And no courts." The idea felt so foreign to me. "So what about sifters and selectors?"

Felix chuckled. "Vivienne didn't want children to be employed at all. She wanted the entry age to be eighteen."

"We wouldn't tap?" I exclaimed. I lowered my voice. "That's insane. Torro would lose all the good talent to the other houses."

"I don't know. I think the idea was that we'd get the other houses — and creative industries — to follow Torro's model eventually. Force reform from the chairman himself. But anyway, Viv lost that battle. We'd still tap. For the first few years, though, instead of sifting through sketches, children would rotate through a kind of . . . what did we call it?" He scrolled down his Unum face. "Apprenticeship program. The patternmakers actually have a good model where they shadow each other to learn techniques. We're going to make it companywide. Haven't you ever wanted to cut and drape your own patterns? And in case you haven't noticed, the patternmakers are desperate for creative input. There wouldn't be patternmakers and drafters anymore — there'd simply be *designers*.

"Anyway, the new Taps would apprentice in everything so they could have varied careers at Torro-LeBlanc if they wanted. Real art lessons. Patternmaking workshops. They'd spend time with sales and marketing. They'd get a little writing and math, too, so some of them could go into the business side of things. I've tried to teach myself basic accounting and statistics, but it's tough to do on your own."

I looked at Felix. Something clicked. His desire for a range of skills, his love of telling people what to do. "You're thinking you could run the place — Torro — someday, aren't you?" I said.

His scowl returned. "Well, why not? The Silents are practically mute — this place could use some real leadership from within. Like I say, people will always wear clothes. This makeover is about creating a design house where workers can be creative — and get paid for it. *And* have the opportunity to grow and lead if they want to."

I looked at his heavy eyebrows, so often knitted in frustration. "You're right," I said. I loved designing now — but who knew? Maybe someday I'd like to try something different. What was wrong with learning a few Adequate skills? I remembered the *Times* reporters buzzing around the newsroom. There had been furrows of concentration, but there had also been relaxed smiles and laughter. "I've started to wonder why there has to be such a lifelong division between Taps and Adequates," I said. "I think the whole misery-of-Adequates thing might be a myth."

"*Exactly.*" Felix was animated. "So you're with us, then. Here, take a look at the demands."

I put up my hand. "I'm with you in theory, yes. But I'm still hazy on how you plan to change the entire company. I don't want to lose my job."

Felix groaned and leaned back in his seat. "Are you serious? Torro abuses us, and you —"

"I know," I interrupted in a sharp whisper. "But I can't help it. I need Torro. Without them, I'm nothing. What am I supposed to do, design under my own label?"

"You could."

I pursed my lips at the absurdity. "Well, then, I'd better like wearing my own clothes, because I'd be the only one buying them."

"Ivy would buy them."

I paused. "She asked me to make her outfit because she knew I was a Big Five designer."

"That fear is what keeps us all in line." Felix shook his head. "How are we going to make Torro listen? We're going ahead with the walkout. We won't have the upper floors but about a third of the drafters and patternmakers have told us they're on board. With a little more time, we'll bring the rest around. We'll contact the mainstream papers and all the gossip magazines. This thing will be a media maelstrom. Vivienne's been working around the clock, calling the Torro employees who've left in the last ten years, convincing them to join the march."

I wondered if the protesters really would be a dense, angry mob — or if, when the moment came, everyone would get cold feet and Felix would end up addressing a scraggly, feeble bunch. It seemed so risky. "And how exactly do I fit into all of this?"

"Simple. Torro doesn't get you unless they agree to the make-over."

"They don't *get* me?"

Felix rolled his eyes. "Aren't you listening? They don't get to lay claim to Marla Klein, the innovator behind the trend destined for outrageous popularity, unless they cooperate. You'll take your mad skills elsewhere. They'll be left with no drafters, no patternmakers, a sixth-place ranking, bad press, and no prime trend."

"You're nuts. Eco-chic is not going to be that important." But even as I said it, I remembered the news vans and the strange call from Belladonna. Did they really want me and eco-chic? Maybe a threat to leave wouldn't be empty after all.

"It already is that important," Felix said. "In fact, when all is said and done, you'd better recruit me."

"Huh?"

"To your studio. If famous 'Miss Eco-Chic' will have me." The tinge of sarcasm wasn't enough to mask the sincerity behind his words. He shifted his gaze to the window. "The trend isn't just clever. You'll make an impact. I want to design sustainable clothes too."

"I figured you'd work with —" I began, but Felix spoke at the same time.

"I know sometimes I'm not the most approachable —"

Both of us stopped midsentence and laughed.

"You're as approachable as steel wool, Felix," I said.

"Yeah. Maybe." He shrugged. "But Ivy Wilde's outfit was prime. You're talented. You have been from your first day in the basement." The sarcasm was gone. I could tell he meant it.

"Thanks." I figured the door was open to return the compliment. "You know, I was on the court with people who were sweet on the outside but who turned into creeps the day I was fired. You're the opposite. You're steel wool on the outside, but underneath, you care about people a lot. About making their lives better. That's the best kind of person."

The smile he gave me transformed him into a really hot kind of person too, but I kept that thought to myself. I handed him my travel mug and opened my briefcase. I removed the floral pin, cupping my hand to shield it from the other commuters. "I didn't know if I should wear this today."

"Put it on. Everyone knows what you did anyway. Walk into Torro like you own the joint."

I watched the petals catch the morning light and cast a prismatic pattern onto the train car wall. I thought of the endless parade of trends I had approved for production while sitting on the Superior Court. "I have a demand," I said.

"Excuse me?"

"To add to the makeover. Change the number of seasonal releases from twelve to eight. It's too crazy the way it is. Let each trend have the chance to live a little. If I like something,

I want to enjoy wearing it for more than a few weeks before it expires."

"I don't know," said Felix. "The faster trends expire, the better for business."

I gave him a fixed look. "That's my demand. And I know Vivienne would agree with me."

Felix opened his mouth and closed it again, smirking. "Done. You drive a hard bargain, Klein." He began tapping his Unum face.

A world without courts. Even hearing the persuasive case Felix made, I had difficulty imagining it. I didn't see how the idea could ever catch on. The world was full of people like my mother, who worshiped the judges in every industry. Still, maybe we could change things somehow. A little.

Wondering how it was all going to play out, I pinned the plastic flower to my lapel.

The elevator doors opened and I stared at the figures in front of me: Julia, flanked by two large CSS agents in gray uniforms. Felix stayed by my side, both of us barriers to the packed elevator. We stepped out, and I was aware of the other drafters trickling around us in two forked streams. I felt the sidelong glances as they passed.

Julia had squeezed her curves into one of Torro's short flapper numbers from the midspring line. Her arms were crossed, but when she saw me, she opened them in a warm gesture and smiled broadly. "Marla! There you are. I left you some messages this weekend, honey."

Honey? I almost choked on my tongue. Trying to act genuinely surprised, I stammered: "Oh — really? My Unum's been a little fritzy. Sorry."

"Such a nuisance when they malfunction, isn't it?" Julia approached and wedged herself between me and Felix. She wrapped an arm around my shoulders. She smelled like an orange grove — she had evidently bathed in *Le Jus,* one of Torro's signature scents. "I wanted to catch you first thing," she intoned silkily. "Some very important people want to meet with you this morning." Her eyes flashed to my lapel pin.

What game was this? She knew I'd gotten the messages. I knew she thought more of sidewalk gum than she did of me.

Stepping out from behind Julia, Felix gave me an *I told you so* glare. He then tilted his head toward a nearby table. In addition to the customary stacks of magazines, I noticed glossy photos of Ivy Wilde wearing my design. That was somewhat reassuring. Were Felix and my mother right? Was I actually on my way to being respected again at Torro-LeBlanc? I spotted my own table, where Randall and Kevin stood, watching us. Dido must not have arrived yet. In a gesture as quick as a lightning crackle, Kevin brought the fingers of one hand to his forehead and gave a tiny salute.

"Who wants to meet with me?" I asked, turning to Julia.

"Come," Julia said, steering me toward the elevator door. The CSS agents approached.

"I'm going with her," said Felix.

Julia stopped. With dainty fingers, she took the travel mug from my hands and held it out to him with a cold smile. "You'll stay in the basement."

The hulking agents hovered. His face clouding, Felix grabbed the mug and took a step back. *"Remember,* Marla," he said.

Julia made a rude noise, something between a snort and a

cough, and said "six" at the voicebox. The doors whirred shut and he disappeared from view.

The sixth floor. I had never been there. No one I knew had ever been there. It was supposed to be where a bunch of Adequates crunched numbers and where the Silents had their offices. The doors parted to reveal a central corridor and two others leading left and right. As I stepped out of the elevator, my shoes sank into dense, rose-colored carpet. The decor was classic and old-fashioned, but somehow it managed not to look feeble.

Along the side corridors, men and women — Adequates, I presumed — sat at a number of sleek, wide office desks, arranged in pods of two or four. They were talking on their Unums or working on Tabulas. Natural light poured through broad square windows. As in the *Times* office, it was a lively, upbeat atmosphere — until they spotted Julia, at which point they lowered their heads and grew quiet.

Julia dismissed the agents, who disappeared down the right hallway. I followed her down the central corridor. On my left and right was a series of doors, whose gold labels had titles such as Vice President of Human Resources, Vice President of Manufacturing, Vice President of Recruitment, and Vice President of Operations. At the end of the corridor, two polished desks of dark wood faced each other. At the left desk sat a young woman; on the right, a young man I recognized from my Unum messages. It was the chief creative officer's assistant. They weren't incredibly young, but both were really good-looking, and both wore Torro's latest trends — though not torture, I noticed. The woman's hair was done exactly like the star of *Pillow Party's*, right down to the pink grosgrain ribbons.

In front of them, I suddenly felt like an awkward lump in

my sweater embellished with feathers. I was pretty sure it had expired, though only just. I hadn't been trendchecking my own outfits as regularly as I used to, and in my rush this morning I hadn't bothered. I wondered if the flower pin helped or made the whole thing worse.

Julia turned to the young man, whose chiseled torso was wrapped in one of the superhero-trend bodysuits. "Are they ready for us?"

The assistant didn't answer her but looked at me. "Are you Marla Klein?" he asked.

"Yes." I stood while the man evaluated me, pausing, as Julia had, on the lapel pin. He turned to Julia. "The Silents would like to see Miss Klein alone."

"Oh. Yes, of course. Happy to deliver her." Although she recovered smoothly, it was clear Julia had expected to be involved in whatever was going on. She inclined her head toward the line of empty chairs next to the man's desk. "Should I wait, or —"

"They'll call you if they need you."

It was a firm dismissal. I almost felt bad for her. Visibly gathering her dignity, she nodded at the man. "Very well. Tell them they can call me anytime this morning." He nodded once in return. Without a final look at me, Julia headed back toward the elevator.

"I'll let them know you're here," the man said to me. "Can I get you anything?"

"Uh — no, I'm fine, thanks." My fingers traced the edges of the flower pin. Catching myself, I dropped my hand to my side.

The man pressed a button on his desk.

"Go ahead, Cam." It was a deep male voice.

"Miss Klein is here," said Cam.

"*Wonderful,*" said the voice. "Send her in."

Chapter Twenty

Her hair styled but still in her bathrobe, Ivy closed the door to her room. It was only nine fifteen — she had a few minutes to try Constantine before she had to dress for brunch. She called his Unum and listened to it ring, wondering what she was going to say. Maybe he would talk first.

The Unum rang five times and went to voicemail. She had a crazy thought that he'd seen who it was and ignored the call. Or maybe it wasn't crazy? Maybe he didn't want to face her?

"Christina," she said into the Unum microphone.

Her mother answered on the second ring. "Eva! Hello! What a nice surprise."

Even in her bleak mood, Ivy warmed at the sight of her mother's face. "Where's Constantine?" she asked.

A pause. "He's in school."

Oh. Right. Of course he was in school on a Monday morning. He probably hadn't heard the call. Teachers tried to keep Unums out of the classroom — as best they could.

Ivy decided not to beat around the bush. "Why didn't you tell me about the statue?" she demanded. "Did you think I wouldn't find out?"

Her mother sighed. "Oh, Eva. Hang on a minute. George'll want to speak to you, too."

They conferenced him in. George and Christina consoled her, apologizing for not calling, claiming they hadn't wanted to distract her before her tour. This outraged Ivy — she was sixteen, not a child — but her parents wearily informed her that they'd had their hands full. No, there wasn't going to be any trouble, as far as they could tell. Yes, she could try again tomorrow.

"But you might want to wait a bit," her mother said gently.

"Why?"

"The therapist said there are a lot of cases of kids acting out after failing to get tapped," George explained. "Constantine picking that statue was no accident, we think. We need to understand if he's not ready to speak to his . . . famous older sister."

In a way, she was glad her father had said it so she knew she wasn't inventing things. It wasn't just the shock and tastelessness of the vandalism that bothered her. The attack felt so . . . personal. "Okay, yeah. I'll wait. But he's okay otherwise?"

There was a long pause. Her father pursed his lips together grimly. "He's skipped a little school."

"Oh."

"He stole some video games from the mall," said her mother. "We've returned them. The clerk was very understanding."

Ivy felt ill. Why wasn't Constantine taking the placidophilus pills? Had he run out already? She would send him more, but Christina was sure to open any package that came to the house. They couldn't be that hard to secure, even in Millbrook.

Wait — was that why he had stolen the games? To sell them for P pill money? Or did he want to play them in some twisted, post-Tap exercise in masochism?

"Tell him we're all taking a long trip to Isla Del Sol after my tour," Ivy said. "Just the family. I promise."

"That sounds lovely, sweetheart," said her mother. Her parents promised they would encourage Constantine to call her when he was ready.

Ivy hung up. Poor Constantine. A trip away — they could all use one. What was her money for if not to help her family and relax a little bit once in a while?

A knock on the door cut through her thoughts. Hilarie poked her head in. "I have your new outfit," she said. "Ready?"

"Come in," said Ivy, again glancing at the clock.

Hilarie carried in a garment box and laid it on Ivy's bed. The box top said *Greenery* in flowery letters. Ivy liked the sound of that. Yesterday, when Fatima had placed rush orders at the independent boutiques, Ivy had overheard one proprietor exclaim through her publicist's Unum speaker: "'Eco-chic' is nothing new! We've been selling environmentally conscious clothing for years."

"Yes, yes, just get the samples here by tomorrow at nine a.m." was her publicist's sharp response.

"Comfortable waists only!" Ivy had yelled at the device before Fatima hung up, flashing her an aggravated look.

Now, from the *Greenery* box, Ivy withdrew the clothes packed in brown tissue. Both items were soft, shimmery, and definitely comfortable-looking. She held the skirt up to her waist and looked in the mirror. "Prime, isn't it?"

Hilarie nodded. "It's pretty. I'll go get my stuff on. I think I'm in some kind of tea-length number."

Alone, Ivy pulled on the outfit. She gathered her focus, checking her reflection in the mirror. Humming the chorus of the new song she was writing, she picked up the plastic flower from her bureau and worked it into the updo. The whole effect was a little fancy for brunch, but then again, the point this morning was to attract attention.

Chapter Twenty-One

Trying *not to let* the two assistants see, I wiped my sweaty palm on my skirt. I turned the knob to the office at the end of the sixth-floor hallway of Torro-LeBlanc.

It was a strange room. For starters, it was oval, with the door at one end of the thin tip. A row of sleek rectangular screens, each about a yard in length, encircled the entire room at eye level. They had been built into the walls. Most were black, but not the dull black of a dead Unum face — the live, crisp black of a screen powered on. In fact, three of them displayed the phrase NEW MESSAGE in small red letters at the bottom.

Gray carpet covered the floor, and the walls behind the screens were a deep teal. In the center of the room, black leather chairs surrounded a rectangular granite conference table. The T-L company logo had been etched into the center of the polished gray stone and stood out in dull relief under a ceiling spotlight.

At the head of the table, facing me, stood a middle-aged man. Despite his light gray hair and the few lines on his forehead, his face was tanned and his features youthful. A blond woman and an older man sat to his right, their heads turned toward me. Surprisingly, the seated man was the only one of the three wearing trends.

"Come on in, Marla." The standing man pushed back his chair and advanced on me with an easy smile. He held out his hand, which I shook. "Hugo LeBlanc, chief creative officer of Torro-LeBlanc," he said. So this was the descendent of the original LeBlanc who had founded the company. An actual Silent. I couldn't believe it — he wore a black T-shirt, jeans, and dark gray athletic shoes. It was the approximate outfit Walter wore while repainting the kitchen ceiling, while my mother yelled at him not to get near the window in case someone in an adjacent building saw. These were the garments of choice for the man who ran Torro?

"This is Adele Nash, our board chair and chief executive officer," he continued, gesturing to the woman. Adele reached across the table and shook my hand primly. Another Silent, I guessed. I was surprised to see that she wore a simple black sheath dress. It wasn't a trend, but I found that I liked it. It reminded me of Vivienne's prototype that I had defended in front of the Superior Court. "And Jonah Leavitt, our general counsel." Counsel — that was a lawyer. Why was he here? Again, my mind spun with thoughts of contract violations as I shook his hand. He was dressed in a black studded jacket from the new punk line. It didn't quite close over his stomach bulge.

"Sit down. Make yourself comfortable," Hugo said, gesturing toward the chair to his left, opposite Adele and Jonah. I sank into the soft leather. Across the table, a Tabula was propped on a stand in front of Jonah. He was tapping something on it. "Have you eaten, Marla?" asked Hugo, easing himself into his own chair.

"I had breakfast at home." I placed my briefcase on the chair next to me.

"How about something to drink?"

"Uh — Julia had me leave my latte downstairs."

"That's ridiculous." He pressed a button on the conference table. "Cam? Four lattes, please. One with sugar." He looked at me. "I assume you take sugar?" I nodded. Who didn't? "Immediately," he continued. "And, oh, some of those cinnamon buns and strawberry croissants, I think, too." He released the button. "I know you're not hungry, but I always like a little something with my coffee in the morning."

I tried to smile. So far, so good.

"So." He clasped his hands together and leaned forward on the table. "We meet the creative genius behind the eco-chic trend."

He didn't sound sarcastic, but I didn't trust my ears. "Sorry?" I said.

"How does it feel to be the girl of the hour? You drafted the outfit that everyone's been crazy for all weekend. Torro-LeBlanc's been flooded with inquiries asking if Marla Klein is one of our own." He nodded at my lapel. "That's a smart pin you're wearing," he added with a wink.

I glanced down at it. "I thought you might be upset," I said carefully. "Considering it competes with torture . . ."

"A good trend endures in the face of competition." Hugo's eyes grew playful. "I'm reminded of a certain shawl that featured prominently in the bohemian trend a few seasons back. It kept selling even as other trends matured. Remember?"

Of course I did. It was draped over the chair in my room these days. Hugo certainly knew a lot about me. I glanced at

Adele, who gave me an impassive, tight-lipped smile. Jonah kept his eyes focused on his Tabula.

"Now *that's* a sharp eye," Hugo went on. "An eye like that shouldn't be relegated to drafting."

I remained silent. The office door opened and Cam appeared, carrying four drinks on a tray. "The latte with sugar," he announced as he handed me the tall ceramic mug.

"Thanks," I said, and took a sip. The flavor of the latte reminded me of those delicious concoctions I used to make on the fifth floor. The sixth floor no doubt had its own shiny gold machine. Cam finished serving the drinks and closed the door delicately behind him.

Hugo took a generous swig of his. "Good?" he asked, grinning. I nodded and took another sip.

"I'll get to the point, Marla," Adele said, ignoring the steaming cup in front of her. "We convened an emergency board meeting yesterday. The Superior Court has unfortunately proven itself ineffectual, and we voted to place its current members in new positions within the company. To start fresh. We believe we have a unique opportunity to offer you here at Torro-LeBlanc."

The whole court fired at once. I reeled from the news. Had this ever happened before, at any design house? Were Henry and Olivia now drafters? I felt a flash of glee. Whatever came next, this news healed a wound that had been stinging since I'd left the court.

"We'd like to create a new position," continued Adele. "Chief justice of the Superior Court. There hasn't been a clear leader on the court, and we think it's high time one existed. We'd like to offer you this new position."

I stopped breathing. The power was mine again, for the taking. Immediately, I hated myself for having the thought, after everything I'd been over that morning with Felix. I couldn't accept — could I? I reached for my cup and took a long, slow sip of latte.

Hugo leaned back in his chair. "The main perk is that you, as chief justice, will work with the court director to select the other judges. Whomever you like, Marla. We trust your judgment. We've heard that you're friends with a young drafter named Felix Garcia, and some others? Imagine them sitting next to you on the bench. Running the show at Torro. Shaping the seasonal lines."

The fantasy materialized in front of me like a frost pattern blooming on a windshield. A court made up of friends, kind people who could work together to develop beautiful, wearable trends. Felix sitting next to me every day, no longer bitter and scowling, his hunger for power satisfied. My mother proud again. Prime seats at every runway show, movie premieres, studio parties . . .

"We also believe we may have acted hastily in the recent dismissal of a drafter named Vivienne Graves," added Adele. "We'd be happy to extend employment to her once again, if you'd like her on the court."

I almost laughed. They had gotten that one wrong. Vivienne the rebel would never sit on the Superior Court. *Yes, she would,* a voice inside my head seemed to tell me. I tried to focus on the preposterousness of the idea, but my thoughts seemed strangely jumbled. Suddenly, I had a mental picture of Vivienne on the court, her mascara actually tasteful, wearing trends and happily judging drafters' designs. I could talk her into joining. It wasn't so crazy, after all.

The female administrative assistant, the one with the *Pillow Party* hair, entered bearing a tray heaped with golden-crusted croissants and buns drenched in icing. She deposited it on the conference table with a smile. The pastries filled the room with a buttery smell.

"Thank you, Kendra. Have one," Hugo said to me, though he didn't help himself. "From Starling Bakery — delicious. Now, we've already started production on the garments you made for Ivy Wilde. We'll do them in a number of palettes. And the drafters are downstairs this morning with orders to take the ecological theme and run with it."

The drafters were at work on eco-chic. Strangely, I felt a pang of envy. Even with all the risk, even with the potential for cruel rejection, I had to admit that dreaming up garments was the most gratifying work I'd ever done. Again, my mind clouded. *No, I was misremembering.* Telling other people whether or not their designs were good enough was the best part of working for a fashion house. Drafting was for obsolosers. I'd always thought so.

And yet, that didn't seem right. What was wrong with my brain this morning? I hadn't felt this addled since I'd chewed my mother's placidophilus pills in the bathroom . . .

My hand cupping the mug of latte froze. I pressed my tongue against the roof of my mouth and swallowed. Yes, I could just make it out. The faintest aftertaste of strawberries.

I stared at the drink, fighting to keep the horror off my face. There was no other explanation. I'd almost not tasted it over the sugar — they'd probably counted on that. I considered the tray of sweets. No one had touched them. Were they laced with placidophilus as well? Slowly, I slid my hand back from the cup and rested it in my lap.

"If I may?" Jonah, the general counsel, spoke for the first time. Hugo nodded in his direction. Through my haze, I wondered what it was like to be an Adequate working with Silents. How did they treat him? Did he have to ask permission to speak all the time? "Julia Atkinson acted rashly," he said. His voice wavered, but I figured that could also be because he was so old. "We apologize, and we hope you'll continue here at Torro-LeBlanc. Have you spoken to another design house?"

I struggled to think clearly. My mind was starting to conjure up excuses: *They didn't mean harm. They probably figured you used already. They just wanted to relax you.* It was hard to resist the pleasant feeling that accompanied these thoughts. *Focus,* I ordered myself.

"I'm sorry, what?" I said, buying some time.

"Have you spoken to another design house?" he repeated.

Felix had been right. Torro-LeBlanc needed me. I could get away with asking for anything right now. And if I wanted to leave, Belladonna, and who knew how many other houses, would probably offer me a job. I needed to play this right. "I've been contacted," I said with a casual shrug.

The Silents shared looks. I heard a dull beep and looked in the direction of the sound. Across the room, one of the screens in the ring, previously blank, now read NEW MESSAGE.

"We want you, Marla," Hugo said. "We have a vision for what eco-chic could be, and we need you at our helm."

He paused, and Adele jumped in. "Julia assures us that she has great personal respect for you and that the two of you enjoy working together. If, however, you feel differently, we'd be happy to appoint a new court director."

They would be willing to fire Julia to keep me. Once again, a charge from the power they were offering me crackled through my body. But no, the placidophilus was enhancing that feeling.

I remembered the new company vision Felix had shared that morning. *Hold on to it,* I ordered myself. Imagine running a sustainable clothing studio. With Felix. And an end to drafting and judging as it currently existed.

"I need to think about it," I said.

Adele's face fell, but Hugo kept grinning. "Of course, of course," he said. "The thing is, we were really hoping to make an announcement today. Set the tone for the week, the month, the season, you know. Jonah has your new contract drawn up." He nodded to Jonah, who turned the Tabula to face me. Under my name, I read POSITION: CHIEF JUSTICE, SUPERIOR COURT.

I stared at the title. "I have to weigh my options," I said, fighting the protesting voices in my head. "I want until the end of the day."

"Why wait?" said Adele sharply. "Your decision won't change. What does your gut say to do right now?"

I looked at my lap, holding an image of Ivy Wilde's garments in my mind's eye. "I need time," I mumbled.

"Adele, please," said Hugo, waving his hand. "If our new chief justice wants the day, she can have it. Whatever you like, Marla. Look around — get an idea of whom you might like to serve on the court with you." He chuckled. "*Under* you, that is. We'll expect you back here at five p.m. Come and see me anytime today if you have questions."

"The tickets, Hugo," Adele muttered.

"I almost forgot." He snapped his fingers and withdrew two glossy stubs of paper from his pocket. "Passes to the *Creatures from the Fog IV* premiere. The first of many. Gabe Foxxman himself will be there." He winked at me again. I stared at the tickets stupidly, then slotted them into my briefcase.

Hugo stood up and extended his hand, and the others followed. "Sure you don't want some pastries for the road?" Adele asked, lifting a corner of the tray.

"No. Thank you," I said, shaking hands all around and heading for the door. "Stay young," I said awkwardly as I turned the knob. In response, Hugo, who had reseated himself at the table's head, raised his mug to me in a toast.

Chapter Twenty-Two

I vy slid into a cream-colored booth. The reporters and photographers, feebly disguised as diners at nearby tables, craned their necks and snapped pictures of her without much discretion. The high white ceiling and yawning windows left few places to hide anyway. Saltimbocca was a place to get noticed.

The host had let her know that Clayton Pryce hadn't arrived yet, so she ordered an orange juice and looked around. Her nymphs were dining nearby at a separate table, with empty seats for Clayton's satyrs to join them. In one corner, Jelly Sanchez was in a booth with Selma Crisp, her costar on *Pillow Party*. They were dressed in designer pajamas. There was a giant ice cream sundae on the table in front of them; Ivy wondered how they could eat something so sweet first thing in the morning. But maybe they had ordered it for show. It sat between them, ignored, the whipped cream runny, while they balanced spoons on their noses. Each time one fell, they giggled and cameras flashed.

She was trying to figure out if the guy in the back was Johnathyn "Rottweiler" Dupree, a new hip-hop artist the Pop Beat channel had been featuring recently, when someone across the aisle spoke.

"Look at those little bitches. Don't it make you sick?"

Ivy turned sharply. A woman was sitting in the booth across from hers. She was dressed in a fancy maroon and black dress: lacy, low-collared, and accented with spangles and feathers. It wasn't anything from the feather trend, though; Ivy hadn't seen an outfit like that for a long time. The woman had a heaping plate of eggs and pancakes in front of her, but it was pushed to the center of the table. She was sipping a glass of Sugarwater and staring at Jelly and Selma with a surly look.

Even though the name Bernadette Fife came to her immediately, Ivy didn't believe her own eyes. This couldn't be Bernadette. Maybe it was Bernadette's mother. This woman looked as if someone had grabbed her scalp at the pinnacle of her head and yanked hard. Her eyebrows and eyes rose at the corners, and her skin was tight over her bony cheeks. And the mouth. Lips plumped like shiny balloons. Ivy had to work hard to keep the shock off her face.

"Bernadette?" she said tentatively.

The woman took a long sip of Sugarwater, then burped. She grabbed her glass and slid awkwardly out of her booth. Carrying her drink with care, she sidled into the seat across from Ivy, who was immediately aware of a pungent smell.

"If you order a hot fudge sundae," the woman said, "I'm gonna have to kill you." She slurred her words together: *hot fudge sundae* came out "hahfejsundie." Her stretched face was even more grotesque close-up. It really was Bernadette. Ivy remembered listening to her nonstop as a child, her music a sassy blend of pop and country. She'd even seen her in concert twice. She quickly did the math — Bernadette couldn't be much more than thirty now. What had she done to herself?

Ivy searched for something to say. "How've you been?"

"Oh, honey," Bernadette said. She hiccupped. "How *you* been, that's the question." She wagged her finger at Ivy. "Everybody cannot stop talking about how Ivy Wilde's wearing trash."

Ivy was taken aback. "It's not really —"

"*Traaaaash,*" Bernadette said loudly, waving her hand in the direction of Ivy's clothes, as if wiping them away. "Now this," she said, plucking one of her black shoulder straps, "was a *dress*. From the saloon trend." She hiccupped again. "Skip's favorite."

Ivy noticed Madison glaring at their booth. Madison gestured to ask if she should come over, but Ivy waved her off. She had always felt a small degree of connection to Bernadette because she and Skip McBrody, from Millbrook, had been girlfriend and boyfriend. Rumor had it that Bernadette had been the one who found him after his suicide. Ivy remembered the way she'd sobbed at the televised funeral. Funny — until now she hadn't put together that their relationship must have been manufactured. But maybe they were one of the rare celebrity pairings that had actually developed romantic feelings. The woman was wearing Skip's favorite dress in Saltimbocca ten years after his death — that said a lot.

"It's nice," Ivy said warily.

"Damn right it is." Bernadette gulped for her straw like a fish and finally managed to locate it with her sausage lips. Her sip sputtered into coughing, making her eyes water.

It dawned on Ivy what the sharp smell was. The coughing, the slurring, the rudeness — only one thing could explain it. That wasn't Sugarwater in her glass; Bernadette was drinking alcohol. Ivy's nose wrinkled. Alcohol had gone out of style before she was born. Who wanted to deal with puking and hangovers? Placidophilus pills were so much neater: you got a pleasant little lift, but you could still function perfectly well. Plus, they fit in your pocket. Sneaking alcohol into a Saltimbocca glass was as high on the obsoloser scale as calling your parents "Mom" and "Dad."

"So whose idea was the trash?" barked Bernadette. "Your agent's? Or did it come straight from Miles Jackass himself?"

Ivy assumed she was referring to Miles Jackson, the Silent who served as executive producer of her record label. She'd met him only once, right when she'd gotten the green light to record her first solo album. He'd seemed very nice — not like a jackass at all. She wondered why Bernadette didn't like him. "No," she said. "It was my idea."

She could feel Bernadette straining to focus her gaze. "Your idea's garbage," she deadpanned, then burst into laughter. Her head flopped down on the table; with her hair fanned out, Ivy could see her dark roots.

Madison appeared at the side of the table. "Everything okay?" she asked, frowning at the pile of hair.

Bernadette flipped her head back up and looked at Madison. "What do you want, nympho?"

"I think you'd better go," said Madison.

Bernadette let out a cackle. "What, am I tarnishing your precious image?" she said to Ivy.

"Yes," said Madison. "Now get up or I'll call security."

Bernadette's face grew sullen. She sipped her drink. "Don't worry. I was just leaving anyway." Ivy wondered if she was used to being kicked out of places. "I have a full day ahead. If anyone needs me," she slurred, as she lifted herself out of the booth, "I'll be watching my old concert footage." She picked up the glass and jiggled the ounce or two of liquid left at the bottom. "But first, I have to mix myself a nice, big Sugarwater." She winked at Ivy.

"Bye, Bernadette," said Ivy. "Take care of yourself."

Bernadette leaned over Ivy's side of the booth, the alcohol sour on her breath. "See that?" she whispered, pointing to the lamp hanging above the table. "That's your spotlight. Enjoy it while you can." She looked into Ivy's face, her freakish features as solemn as the face-lift would allow. "It goes out, you know."

She left the restaurant, carrying her glass with her.

Madison turned to Ivy, lips pursed. "Why didn't you get rid of her right away?"

"I think I was in shock," Ivy replied. "Did you see her face?"

Madison stared at Bernadette through the restaurant's front windows as she wobbled her way down the sidewalk. She shook her head. "Bernadette Fife is the obsoloser poster child. What a hag."

Ivy felt repulsed by the encounter, but Madison's comment made her want to defend Bernadette. She was pitiful now, but she'd been talented once. Lyric Mirth had given Ivy a tiny taste of what losing your fame could feel like, and it had left her angry and frustrated. She could understand Bernadette's desperation —to a point. *She* would never go to such an extreme, drinking and carving her face up and living in the past. But Madison didn't get it at all.

Chapter Twenty-Three

Back in the sixth-floor hallway, I walked past the Silents' assistants Kendra and Cam. I glanced at Cam's face, searching for recognition — or guilt, or something — over the drugged drink he'd served me. But he barely looked up from his Tabula as I passed. I wanted to shake him and ask him how he could work for such creepy people.

Instead, I continued down the hall of labeled doors and past the branching hallways of Adequates to the elevator. "Down," I whispered at the voicebox. The doors opened, and with relief, I saw that the elevator cab was empty. "Basement," I said, stepping inside quickly.

The doors closed. Inside, a stale smell — body odor and perfume, presumably from the morning's commuters — continued to clear the traces of fog from my head. What Hugo and Adele had offered me glittered with all the fun of my old life. I would be lying if I said I wasn't tempted. Chief justice — who wouldn't like the sound of that? But I knew what would happen. I'd already lived it. I'd serve for a year, maybe two, and then get transferred somewhere else, just like before. Just like the current court had been. Nothing would change. I didn't want to go back.

I wanted to go forward. To find a way to do what I loved for as long as possible.

No Superior Court. I saw the nine empty chairs in my mind's eye, the current judges shocked, brokenhearted, furious. Furious enough to march in a strike? It might be the perfect time for the makeover Vivienne and the others had come up with.

I hesitated. So I was making my choice. Committing to marching and protesting and coming out publicly against Torro. I thought about the possibility of a new Torro-LeBlanc, then pressed my tongue to the roof of my mouth again and thought of the alternative. What, really, did I have to lose? And there was so much to gain . . .

We needed to act fast. I juggled the various pieces in my head, trying to fit them together. It would take Vivienne, the drafters, the patternmakers; even the Junior Courts might see things our way . . . And then I had a flash of genius. Ivy Wilde could help us out. The question was, would she?

Before the elevator could finish its journey, and before I could lose my nerve, I called out "one." The doors to the lobby opened and I stepped out. I found the quietest corner I could, took my Unum out of my briefcase, turned it on, and dialed a number. "Pick up, pick up," I whispered.

"Hey." Ivy Wilde's face filled my screen. Her hair was all done up like she was someplace important. "I was wondering what happened to you."

"I'm really sorry if I'm bothering you," I said.

"You're not. I'm just at brunch. I tried to call you after *Hot with Hyman* to thank you for the look. You probably saw — it went over well."

"Yeah. You looked amazing. Thank you for mentioning my

name." I could do this. Just get the words out, I told myself. "I thought you might be able to do something for me."

Ivy tilted her head to the side.

I took a deep breath. "I was wondering — since you liked the look so much — if I continued to design for you, would you stop buying Torro-LeBlanc clothing? And let people know that you aren't?"

The screen went black, and for a second I thought that she had hung up. When her voice returned, I realized she had switched over to the private audio setting.

"What do you mean?" Ivy's voice came faintly through the speaker.

"I will personally continue to design anything you want if you don't buy from Torro anymore," I said, holding the Unum to my ear. "They don't treat their Taps fairly. People get fired and demoted left and right. No one has any say in what job they hold and for how long. And the drafters — the people actually designing the clothes, you know? — work really hard and don't get any recognition." I remembered Hugo raising his mug to me. "They have some twisted ways of getting their workers to do what they want. I was hoping you could not wear their clothing ... for a little while." I paused nervously, hoping I'd made a good enough case.

Finally, Ivy spoke in the softest whisper. "Did Vivienne Graves tell you to call me?"

"What? No. I haven't talked to Vivienne in a while. Why?"

"She came by last night."

"What?" What was Vivienne doing at Ivy's? I tried to think of possible explanations. Did she know her through Felix?

"I can't really talk about it," said Ivy in a louder voice. "But yeah, I'll do it. What you said. I love my new look, and I'd love to wear anything you design for me."

I unleashed a massive stream of gratitude that I knew made me sound like a fan-girl, but I didn't care. I said goodbye to Ivy and ran back to the elevator.

"Marla!" Her fringe swaying, Julia advanced on me as soon as the doors to the basement opened. "I thought we could have lunch and talk about —"

"No, thank you," I cut her off. The things I wanted to say filled my head, but I held them back. I needed Julia to leave quietly, not report my frame of mind to the Silents. "Nothing's decided, I mean." I leveled my voice. "I have an offer to consider. They've agreed to leave me alone to think about it. I need some time."

Julia leaned in. "Hon, what's to think about?" Her eyes flashed seductively.

"Please, Julia. Hugo said I'd have the rest of the day to make my decision." I lowered my voice. "He said I'd have complete control over who gets to stay on the fifth floor." The threat was cruel, I knew, but I needed to get rid of her.

Julia paused to chew her glossed lip. "Take your time, dear," she said. "I'll be on five if you need me."

I made my way past her and the drafters, some craning their necks to watch me. I ignored them and headed toward my table. Felix, Randall, Dido, and Kevin looked like owls marking my approach. I leaned in as the circle of heads drew tight.

"What happened?" whispered Randall.

"How quickly can Vivienne get the former employees ready?" I asked.

Everyone exchanged glances. "I don't know," said Felix.

"You were right," I said to his questioning expression. I looked at Kevin. "You all were."

"What happened?" Randall repeated.

"They offered me a new position. Chief justice of the Superior Court."

Dido gasped.

"I can pick all the other judges. And then they drugged me to make me say yes. Placidophilus in my coffee. I could taste it."

Randall's eyes got large. Felix's expression didn't change, but I could feel him watching me carefully.

"Did you accept?" Dido sputtered.

I glared at her. "I have till the end of the day to decide. But no. I'm not going to."

"Right," said Dido, shrinking a little.

"P pills," said Kevin, shaking his head. "That's messed up."

I pressed both hands on the table. "So what I want to know," I whispered, "is what's stopping us from getting up and walking out right now."

For the first time since I'd known him, Felix appeared to be at a loss for words. He opened his mouth.

"Torro fired its Superior Court this weekend," I went on. "If we walk out this morning with the patternmakers, and get the ex–Superior Court judges to join, that's the majority of the tapped workforce. The Silents have got to listen. Who knows? We might convince the Junior Courts to walk too. And the best thing — Ivy Wilde has agreed not to buy from Torro-LeBlanc for a while. I just called her."

"Really? You know her that well?" said Dido. "That's totally prime."

"Leverage," muttered Kevin.

"Yes, leverage," I repeated. "Call Vivienne. Tell her to get down here with the fired workers. Call the media, too."

"Now?" said Kevin.

"The way these things usually work," said Felix, finding his voice at last, "is that we present our demands. The board sees them so they know what we want, then we threaten a strike if they don't comply."

I thought about this idea for a half second. "That seems like a feeble waste of time. I've been up there. The Silents are never going to listen to us unless we show them we mean business." I picked up Felix's Unum. "You said about a third of the drafters and patternmakers are on our side? Can you send the makeover demands to them? And to the fired judges, too?"

"I can, but —"

"Felix." I looked at him hard. "There's *no* Superior Court. Tomorrow, though I won't be on it, the Silents will appoint a new one. There's not going to be a better time to do this. It might blow up in our faces; it might not. But if we have this chance to get rid of the courts once and for all, how can you sit around? I personally can't stand the thought of sitting here in the basement one more minute."

In the silence that followed, the atmosphere in our circle changed. It became real, the crazy gamble of what I was suggesting. I watched as a deranged grin broke out on Randall's face, then Kevin's. "Can we really do this?" whispered Dido.

"You win." Felix's eyes flickered at me. "Let's do it."

I could feel my adrenaline spiking. "Send out the demands," I ordered.

Felix turned to Kevin. "You have the addresses saved?"

"I'm on it." Kevin spent a few moments on his Unum. I sent him the addresses of my former bench mates so he could include them as well. "Done," he said. Around me, in the silence, I heard the simultaneous buzzing of Unums. This was it.

"Oh, jeez," said Dido.

"No turning back now," Felix said gleefully. "Kev, go outside and call Vivienne. We'll start things off with current employees. Her recruits can join us later today, whenever they can get down here. Then start calling reporters."

Kevin nodded. "Prime. Good luck." Quickly, he clasped hands with Felix and jogged toward the elevator.

Around us, I noticed people were looking at their Unums curiously. Felix saw it too. "Okay, we've got to rally the drafters," he said. "Go ahead, Marla. Tell them your story. Ask them to follow us."

I almost expressed surprise, almost asked why Felix was willing to let someone else be the spokesperson for the new Torro-LeBlanc. But the protest died on my tongue. I *wanted* to speak. The company I'd loved so much had crushed the dreams of so many. It made me angry.

"I will," I said. Feeling brave, I grabbed Felix's hand in the same clasp he'd exchanged with Kevin. I clasped Randall's and Dido's hands, too. I clambered on top of the drafting table, kicking the pencils to the floor with a clatter as I stood.

I cleared my throat. "Excuse me," I began loudly. Every head in the basement swiveled toward me. Out of the corner of my eye, I saw Randall nodding encouragingly. "My name is Marla Klein. I'm a drafter," I continued, trying to project my voice as best I could. "I've worked at Torro-LeBlanc since my Tap, just like all of you. I designed the eco-chic look that Ivy Wilde wore this weekend." A hush settled over the room. I thought about what to say next. The truth would work. It was enough. "This morning, Hugo LeBlanc, Torro's chief creative officer, told me that I could be the new chief justice of the Superior Court. I would get to pick the other eight judges."

Immediately, the room filled with angry murmurs. I put up my hands. "It's not fair, is it?" I said loudly. "Every day, we draft until our fingers cramp. And our designs are picked at random by strangers. And if we do get picked, most of us don't even have the money to buy the outfits we draft."

Some of the drafters, the ones I figured already knew about the makeover, started to nod. "Damn right!" one shouted. The others stared at me expectantly.

"So, I've decided to turn down Hugo's offer, generous though it is." I let sarcasm coat my words. "Just because design houses have drafters, patternmakers, sifters, selectors, and judges, it doesn't mean that's the only way it can work. On your Unums, you have a proposal for a new way to structure Torro-LeBlanc. A company makeover." I thought back to the details of my conversation with Felix that morning. "A way that lets people work together in creative teams. A way that lets us share leadership. And a way that lets us get paid fairly." I saw a few drafters craning their necks to read their neighbors' Unums. "If someone at your table didn't get the message, please send it along," I added, glancing down at Felix. He gave me a nod.

"This morning, the Silents I met with bribed me and drugged me to get me to agree to their plan." I ignored the shocked murmuring. "I think a better way to get people to do something is just to ask. So I'm asking you to put down your pencils right now and walk out with us. Don't let Torro take advantage of you anymore. If we all walk out right now, they have to take notice. They have to listen to our demands. We have the support of —"

"Get down from there!" A shrill voice cut me off. I turned and noticed Winnie Summers moving toward me through the maze of tables. "Do you really think you'll get away with this?" she yelled, looking around the room. "You'll all be fired. Is that what you want?" Her usually neat bangs were split like curtains in the center of her forehead.

"Winnie, how can you be happy?" I asked as I stared down at her. It was a question I'd wondered since my first week in the basement. "You judged for three years, and now you don't work with fashion at all. You just manage really unhappy people."

Winnie ignored me. "Godfrey? Godfrey, I assume you're going to let them know about this upstairs?" She cast about and finally located the director of the Drafting Division standing near the elevator, holding a white cup. Winnie put her hands on her hips. "Well?"

Godfrey tilted his head and looked at his assistant. After a pause, he walked over to a free stool and sat down. He took a sip from the cup. "I'll get to it," he said slowly. "No rush. I intend to finish my coffee while it's warm." And he looked up at me, the side of his mouth twitching up in a smile.

More than half the drafters clapped and cheered. I beamed at him.

Winnie made an exasperated face. "Fine," she said over the noise. "Then *I'll* go tell them. And I advise you all to stay down here," she chirped. "Or there'll be big trouble."

As she made her way to the elevator, a handful of drafters followed in her wake. Tess Peterson was one. I guessed the others, like Tess, were the most successful drafters, the ones whose ideas got approved most often. They would be loyal to the old Torro. It was a small group, but the sight still discouraged me. Other drafters hovered behind uncertainly. Felix and I had the support of many, but not all.

Below me, I was surprised to see Randall make his way toward the elevator. I almost cried out to him, but the elevator door closed before he could board. Randall kept moving. He headed for a control panel to the right of the elevator and jimmied the cover off with what looked like a pocketknife. He pressed something that I couldn't see. Randall nodded at Felix, who hoisted himself on top of the table next to me.

"That ought to hold them for a minute," Felix said. Whoa. Randall had stopped the elevator car. Now *that* was a useful trick.

"We want everyone to join us," Felix continued. "Please take a look at the new organizational model we're proposing." He went on to explain the creative studios and the elected representatives. Again, I was impressed with how perfect it sounded. The other drafters seemed to be warming. A few shouted questions, which Felix answered. "Let us know if you have ideas," he finished. "This isn't one person's vision. Everybody has a voice."

"And another thing," I added. "Ivy Wilde has agreed to support us. If we strike, she'll refuse to wear Torro-LeBlanc. Publicly. Who knows what other celebrities will add their support?" I threw in at the end, hoping I wasn't getting carried away.

This news seemed to satisfy the drafters' final doubts.

"I'm with you!" one woman shouted.

"Me too," I heard from all corners of the room.

"Let's go!" someone bellowed, and the room erupted in cheers and whistles. I felt goose bumps shoot up my arms. I couldn't stop smiling.

Felix was grinning too. We exchanged a look. "Okay!" he shouted, holding up his hands. "Those of you who have especially good relationships with the patternmakers, follow Marla. Go up to the second floor and get them to join us. Most of them have already been sent the makeover demands, so they should be ready to go. The rest of you, follow me. We'll start marching outside the building and block the entrance in case they decide to lock it. Got it?" The room cheered and stomped again.

Felix hopped off the table and offered me his hand. I took it and jumped down. "You shouldn't have any trouble. Just say what you said here. They love you." Still holding my hand, he pulled me toward him. "You're a warrior, Klein," he whispered coarsely. "I hope you know that."

"Um, we'll go first," I said giddily, nodding toward the stairwell entrance. "You follow."

Felix flashed me the best smile in the world.

"I'm coming with you." On my left, Dido slid an arm through mine. "Great speech." Drafters swarmed around us as we walked toward the door, cheering and patting me on the back. With a final glance at Felix, I pulled open the door and began leading the crowd up the stairs. When I passed the first floor, I glanced quickly through the little window that revealed the elevator bay. I wondered how long it would take for someone to notice us snaking up the stairwell. The truth would be out soon.

Chapter Twenty-Four

C layton and his entourage finally paraded into Saltimbocca. Ivy watched the female heads turn in adoration as they passed. Even Jelly and Selma were whispering. She gave James a little smile as the satyrs sat down with her nymphs.

"You look prime," Clayton announced when he joined Ivy in her booth. She heard a few cameras snap.

She thanked him and filled him in on the strange encounter with Bernadette. Over brunch, they talked more about his vacation. She told him how great the tan looked. He showed her pictures on his Unum. Ivy could feel the warmth of the water just by looking at its turquoise surface dappled with sunlight. The sand on the Isla Del Sol beaches was dove white. Clayton was right; it looked like paradise.

Shyly, she told him about her songwriting attempts. Clayton practically roared his encouragement; looking over her shoulders, she had to tell him to keep it down before they were overheard. "Do it, Wildness," he whispered. "Even if they don't let you perform the songs, who cares? Write them if it makes you happy. You know, that's a good idea. In spite of all the performing, it never even occurred to me . . ." He trailed off into thoughtful silence.

When the bill arrived, Ivy nodded at Clayton, and the charade commenced. Ivy cleared her throat.

"Now, Clay, babe, you know we've had a lot of fun together," she began. She said it loudly — unnaturally so — but this wasn't a private conversation.

"We sure have," Clayton responded, also in a megaphone voice.

She sighed. "I've been thinking, though — it's kind of time for a fresh start. I know you've felt it too."

"I'm glad you brought it up," Clayton said, looking solemn. "I'll always love you and everything. But yeah. Things have run their course."

The reporter across from them actually fell out of his booth trying to listen. Ivy focused on her fork so she wouldn't burst out laughing.

They continued, reminiscing about a couple of "dates" they'd had at nightclubs and concert venues. *Dates*, Ivy thought wryly. Why couldn't people see through the fakeness of it all? Wasn't it obvious that dates with the world looking on didn't count?

She could hear the camera clicks increase in speed. They upped the volume.

"So we're okay?" said Clayton. "No hard feelings, no regrets?"

"Definitely. I'm grateful for the times we've had . . ." They sounded like a soap opera. She bit the inside of her cheek. "And I'll never forget you."

When it was over, they rejoined their respective entourages. Reporters bombarded them outside the restaurant.

"Miss Wilde! Mr. Pryce! Is it true your relationship's over?" they screeched, the now uninhibited camera flashes lighting up the foggy morning. *What bloodsuckers,* thought Ivy. What if I'd really just had a breakup?

Clayton put his arm around her. "Yes, but Ivy and I are going to stay friends."

She chose her words deliberately. "Clayton is an amazing guy, and he's going to make someone very happy." She kissed Clayton on the cheek, and the two groups parted.

Not wanting to relive the *Hot with Hyman* aftermath, Ivy had run the breakup by Jarvis and Fatima beforehand. Fatima threw up her hands and said there was so much image reinvention to manage she didn't care if Ivy decided to date a flagpole. Jarvis was less ambivalent; he liked the idea. "Your new persona is concerned with saving the planet, not hooking up all the time. It's better if you're single." Ivy choked out her thank-yous. Being listened to was a new feeling.

Clayton had checked with his agent, Keane, as well, who was less than thrilled about severing the connection to Ivy Wilde just as Ivy's popularity was on the rise. But Keane had come around when Clayton began talking about staying more focused and balanced if he didn't have to fake a relationship. Still, Keane wasn't going to let him come out or date James openly — yet. "I think we both know that my career isn't going to last forever," Clayton told Ivy, when they had made plans to meet at Saltimbocca. "I just have to wait it out. It won't be too long now." Ivy wondered how he could so readily envision the curtain closing on his fame. The thought made her queasy. Seeing Bernadette that morning had only underscored the importance of keeping her own spotlight shining.

As soon as Ivy and her nymphs returned to the urban utility vehicle after brunch, Fatima pounced. "What were you doing talking to Bernadette Fife?" she demanded. Ivy wondered how she knew about their conversation. She'd been outside the entire time, hadn't she? "Bernadette's the plague. You'll catch career death, Ivy," Fatima warned. "Stay away."

Ivy ignored Madison's *I told you so* look. It didn't matter. She was single again, privately and publicly. The gossip magazines would blow the breakup out of proportion, of course. A friendly split didn't draw readers. They'd probably say that Ivy cheated on Clayton with Kev duPrince. Or that he couldn't handle her new image. So what. It meant that she was free and that Clayton no longer had to live a demeaning lie. She would definitely finish writing her song for them both. And maybe start a new song for someone else, who she hoped would be giving her a call any day now.

In the meantime, she needed to focus her attention on another matter. Namely, using the idea Vivienne Graves had given her to drive a nail in the coffin of a certain pop singer's feeble career.

Chapter Twenty-Five

*A*s Dido and the other drafters and I approached the second floor, I remembered how cautious Vaughn had been about helping me with Ivy Wilde's look. The patternmakers didn't make much money, but they also didn't work on commission like we did. Felix seemed confident, but would they really risk their jobs to join us?

I pushed open the door to Garment Construction. A surprising sight met my eyes. The patternmakers weren't scurrying about as usual. They stood clumped in a large mass in the center of the workroom. Each face turned to me expectantly as I entered with Dido and the mass of drafters behind me.

Everywhere, there were banners of fabric, some carried by four or six hands, some stretched between two poles in the air. On each, a slogan had been printed in some kind of paint or dye. I read:

LET PATTERNMAKERS DESIGN
WE SUPPORT STUDIOS
TIME FOR A MAKEOVER, TORRO!

OPPRESSING WORKERS IS
NEVER IN FASHION

One young woman in rainbow bell-bottoms near the front even carried a sign that proudly declared **I DESIGNED MY OUT-FIT.** It hung like a flag from a yardstick. I wondered if these banners had been made in the last fifteen minutes or if they'd been stashed somewhere in preparation for this day.

I scanned the crowd and found Vaughn. He had one hand on the **LET PATTERNMAKERS DESIGN** banner. With the other, he waved at me.

To my left, near the lounge, a man sat on a rolling chair. His mouth was gagged with knotted fabric scraps. Scraps also bound his wrists and ankles to the chair. He struggled, rolling jerkily in one direction and another. No one helped him. The patternmakers had apparently made short work of their floor director.

The bell-bottomed woman stepped forward. "We've been ready for this for a long time. Is Vivienne Graves with you?" she asked in a husky voice.

"No," I said. "She's calling the employees that Torro fired. They'll join us soon."

"Good," said the woman. "I'm Gwen Manning. When do we begin marching?"

"I'm Marla Klein." This degree of cooperation threw me off-guard. I hadn't expected it. "So you've . . . read the makeover demands?

The woman snorted a laugh. "Read them? I helped draft them. We're ready. What's the plan?" Around her, the patternmakers nodded.

I thought fast. "Felix has a group guarding the entrance for us. We need to leave the building before they lock us in."

"We want some signs too!" a drafter behind me shouted. There was a hum of agreement from the others.

Quickly, some fabric and brushes were produced, and the drafters got to work on banners of their own. I made my way to Vaughn, stepping over signs that read NO MORE COURTS and FAIR PAY. "I wasn't sure you'd risk your job for this," I said quietly.

"And I never thought you'd be one of the ringleaders," Vaughn replied, laughing. "Strength in numbers," he went on. "That's the only way something like this will work. Gwen made sure it was all of us or none." I nodded. We had probably left a few uncertain drafters in the basement, and we'd lost the ones in the elevator, but from the looks of the crowd in the room, not many were unsure here.

"Marla!" I turned to see a freckled patternmaker hopping over the signs toward me.

"Neely!" I gave her a hug and touched my flower pin. "Have you been following the Ivy Wilde stuff? Our pin is famous!"

"It's incredible," said Neely. "We need to work together after all this is through."

I smiled at her and made my way back to the front of the room. "Okay, we should go," I announced. "Everybody follow Dido and Gwen down the stairs to the first floor."

"Aren't you coming?" Dido asked me.

"Yeah, I'll be right behind you. I want to make two quick stops." We'd spoken to most of the tapped employees . . . but not all of them.

"We need a chant," Gwen announced, holding her flag high. "Something that captures what we're marching for."

"How about 'Kill the courts'?" someone yelled out.

"It's a little violent," I said quickly.

"I agree," Gwen said. "Let's keep it light. What about 'Torro Needs a Makeover'?"

Around the room, the drafters and patternmakers approved the slogan. Almost immediately, the chant began. The rhythm of the line got everyone's feet moving, and Gwen took the lead down the stairwell. I followed the crowd through the door, but instead of heading down, I raced up a floor. I entered the third-floor Sifting Room, where the sifters sorted through hundreds of sketches on long rectangular tables. Selectors paced behind, overseeing the sifters and approving or vetoing their choices. I'd forgotten how young and small they were. The new additions from February's Tap were only twelve or thirteen years old.

My entrance didn't cause much of a stir, so I stood on a chair near the door and clapped my hands. "Could I have your attention?" I shouted. "You should know that Torro-LeBlanc's employees are striking. Walking off their jobs. Hundreds are gathering outside the main entrance right now." I looked around at the faces that were frozen in puzzlement. I thought back to the bliss of those first few years of employment. Explaining to the sifters and selectors that life down the road got disappointing would be a tough sell. Instead, I said: "We're asking for better conditions and better pay, and we welcome you to join us. Even if you don't, there will be no need for you to work anymore, as no more sketches will be coming in, and there's no Superior Court to judge them. Your workday is over. You can go home."

Without waiting to see if any of them actually left, I hopped off the chair and continued up to the fourth floor.

Poking my head into the Junior Court judging rooms, I announced the strike, then gathered the judges in the waiting room. I expected the court directors to spring into action, but they regarded me with a mix of confusion and amusement. The drafters who were waiting with their dress forms didn't make eye contact with me.

Still, here I thought I had a shot. Surely, there were some judges who had been hanging around for a few years without a promotion and who could see the writing on the wall. But my speech was met with sneers. Desperately, I explained how the Silents had pressured me to take charge of the new Superior Court that morning.

"You're not going to run the court?" one of the judges asked.

"That's right. I'm not."

"What kind of obsoloser gives up that job?" The boy narrowed his eyes at me in disgust.

"There are *nine* free seats on the Superior Court right now," said a girl, talking to me like I was a baby. "We're sticking around."

"You should leave," another said.

Their words deflated me. I had never been like these kids . . . had I?

"Just wait," I said. "You won't have jobs anymore when we win." But my words sounded weak. I turned and headed down the stairs alone.

My uneasiness disappeared, however, when I emerged from the marble lobby and caught sight of what was happening outside. On the sidewalk and halfway into the street, slowing traffic, Torro-LeBlanc employees marched together in a giant circle. Protest signs fluttered in the wind. They were now chanting:

"One, two, three, four,
We won't take it anymore!

Five, six, seven, eight,
Torro must negotiate!"

Media vans lined the sidewalk. Cameras and reporters flittered about trying to capture footage of the strike. Kevin had done his job.

Just as I was wondering about the size of the crowd, about how it seemed larger than I'd expected, I heard the clatter of the elevated train coming to a stop around the corner. A moment later, a mob of reinforcements came into view. People, faces red from hustling, swarmed toward the circle. Its members absorbed them with welcoming handshakes and hugs. These additions were mostly older than I was. A couple of the women had babies in carriers on their backs.

I caught sight of Vivienne standing on a milk crate, directing her recruits. She wore the same fatigue jacket and pants and black military cap she'd had on at the Torro-LeBlanc runway show. She looked like a general.

I felt a hand on my shoulder and turned. It was Felix, beaming at me. He looked exhilarated. And so . . . good. I pulled him back into the lobby. My arms slid around his neck while he hugged my waist.

"We have work to do," I whispered.

"I know." His face was six inches away, then two. "But if you don't kiss me, I'm going to lose my mind."

I leaned in. Everything fell away except the lovely feeling of his lips, slightly chapped, against my own. When we finally broke apart, both of us were grinning like idiots. We ran down the steps to join the march, my lapel pin shimmering in the midday light.

Chapter Twenty-Six

I hear you're ready to take 'eco-chic' to the next level."

Savannah Brown, the host of the popular morning show *Up & At 'Em*, sat in an armchair facing Ivy. She had on a red bubble dress, which Ivy knew Rudolfo had released recently. When Savannah had first come on the set to shake hands, Ivy had thought immediately of a walking lollipop.

"Yeah, that's right." Ivy took a sip of tea from her *Up & At 'Em* mug. "Eco-chic is more than a trend. We kind of have to get serious about the environment. I mean, not kind of. We do. There's a lot of waste." She stopped there. *Don't lecture,* Jarvis had warned her. It had been hard enough to convince him and Fatima that her splashy announcement on the morning show was a good idea.

"So you have a task for everyone tomorrow, yes?" prompted Savannah.

"Yeah. Tomorrow, show your support for conservation. Wear your favorite expired trend. There are vintage stores everywhere, some right here in La Reina. I got these prime clothes from one." She crossed her legs and patted the linen pants, which she wore with a stretchy gold tank top. The plastic flower glittered proudly on her shoulder. A week ago, she wouldn't have been caught dead appearing at multiple events with a repeat accessory. Now it was her signature. "Or better yet, wear that look you have in your closet right now, the one you never threw away." She leaned over and pushed Savannah's shoulder lightly. "You know what I'm talking about, Savannah. We all have them!" The host grinned uncomfortably. "Don't be afraid to mix and match," Ivy continued, looking into the camera, hoping everyone in Millbrook could hear her. "Create something new. Be eco *and* chic!"

"Usually, we're all trying to *avoid* that red light on the trend-checker." Savannah gave a toothy laugh. Ivy could see the silver braces on the backs of her teeth.

As if by magic, the perfect quip landed on her tongue. "Well, maybe it's worth considering which is more important — a green light or a green earth?"

Savannah's smile dissolved. Repositioning herself in the cushy armchair, she cleared her throat. "Everyone's talking about the Torro-LeBlanc strike that began yesterday. Any thoughts?"

Ivy had seen footage of Felix and Marla on TV last night, marching in an endless circle with their giant cloth banners. She chose her words carefully. *Definitely* don't take sides in the strike, Jarvis had warned her. It was too inflammatory. But she remembered her conversation with Marla, and her promise. "I've heard the workers have good reasons for striking. I hope they can come to an agreement," she heard herself say. It wasn't enough. She thought of Marla and the other eager design-house employees, waiting for her words of support, and of Vivienne, who had given her the idea of a day celebrating expired trends. She thought of the waste in her closet. She thought of Felix, watching her. "Some friends and I have decided not to buy clothing from Torro-LeBlanc while the strike is going on," she blurted out. She couldn't see Fatima from where she sat but imagined her publicist's gaze searing the back of her neck.

"Oh?" Savannah shifted and looked at her producer standing next to the camera. Ivy saw him give a wide-eyed shrug. After an awkward silence, Savannah's training kicked in; she gazed straight into the camera and smiled. "Well, we here at *Up & At 'Em* are on board with Ivy Wilde's 'Eco-Chic Day,'" she said. "We look for ways to support the environment whenever we can. In fact, take a photo of you and your friends in your outfits, and send it to the show. We'll put the best looks on the air!"

"That's prime," said Ivy, nodding her approval.

Savannah switched gears. "Now, I know it's a sensitive subject, but your relationship with Clayton Pryce has recently ended. Is that correct?"

Ivy put on her best serious face and continued the interview.

After the lights came up and a stagehand unclipped Ivy's microphone, Fatima barreled toward her. She held up her Unum. "Torro-LeBlanc just called. I didn't pick up, but I'm sure they want to know why you and 'some friends' have decided not to buy from them after modeling their clothes for years."

Ivy didn't want to explain things to anyone, least of all to Fatima. She cupped her hands around the now cold mug of tea and took a sip. "I think I'm coming down with something," she lied. "My throat hurts."

"It does not. You sound fine."

"It was all I could do to finish that interview." She rubbed her neck. "Besides, what does it matter if I pissed off Torro? I'm wearing vintage stuff anyway."

"For now," said Fatima. "Believe me. You do not want to alienate one of the Big Five design houses."

"Tell them I'm still mad that I got sprayed with ink at their runway show."

"Ivy." Fatima put her hands on the arms of Ivy's chair and looked her in the eyes. "I think we need to have another talk about the way things work. The blindsiding has got to stop."

Why? Ivy wondered. Why was it that every little thing that came out of her mouth needed Fatima's stamp of approval? She put her hand to her forehead. "Can it wait? I really think I'm getting sick."

"Don't lie to me."

"I'm not! I'm thinking about my tour. I want to be in good voice for all the rehearsals coming up." It was an easy lie. She really did want the new eco-themed tour to be phenomenal.

Fatima stood up and regarded her with a skeptical expression. "Fine," she said, after a long pause. "I'll call a doctor. Go wait in your dressing room. I'll send Madison in."

Ivy had no interest in listening to Madison's opinion of her *Up & At 'Em* interview. "Why? I don't want to get her sick."

Fatima's scowl deepened.

Ivy figured she had pushed her luck far enough. She left, moving as quickly as she thought someone sick would move.

The doctor was a young, thirtyish woman with thick, curly brown hair. When she entered the dressing room, she treated Ivy the way that some people did — deliberately not staring, as if Ivy weren't a big deal, and then stealing a glance or two when she thought Ivy wasn't looking. The doctor removed her designer coat to reveal blue scrubs and a stethoscope.

Ivy wondered if she should admit she'd been faking.

"So, a sore throat?" the doctor said, and began feeling Ivy's neck before she had the chance to say anything. She took Ivy's temperature, inspected her throat, looked in her ears, and listened to her breathe.

"It's not bacterial," she said after completing her examination. "So no antibiotics. I can give you a decongestant or an expectorant, but truthfully, I'm not hearing much congestion at all."

Ivy gave her a weak smile. "Maybe I'm not actually sick. Maybe I'm just tired."

The doctor studied her. "But your throat hurts?"

"Um, not really." She suddenly felt stupid. "I feel okay."

"What am I doing here, then?"

The doctor's blunt tone surprised Ivy. People who attended to her were usually nauseatingly polite. "Uh, sorry," she said. "Here . . ." She hopped up from her chair and grabbed a signed headshot from the pile on the dressing table in front of the lit mirror. The producers of *Up & At 'Em* had slipped one under every audience seat. She held it out to the woman.

The doctor stared at the black-and-white photograph. Just when Ivy was certain she was going to say she didn't want it, she took it. "You know, I have four siblings whose families would love these too," she said.

"Oh, yeah, sure," said Ivy, grabbing a small stack and handing them to her.

The doctor tucked them gently in her medical bag. "My niece got passed over in the last Tap. She loves you," she said without smiling. "I hope this cheers her up." She draped her coat over her arm.

Ivy's thoughts went to Constantine. She wondered how he was holding up after the vandalism and theft. Those had to be low points. It got better for him from here, didn't it? She looked at the woman in front of her. "You're an Adequate, right?" she asked, slipping back into her chair.

The doctor's eyebrows went up. "Of course I am."

This woman was put together and seemed to have a decent enough job. "And you're happy?"

The woman frowned at her. "Excuse me?"

"I mean," Ivy said quickly, "you liked school and everything? You like working as a doctor now?"

The woman looked at her for a long time. "I'm going to pretend your condescension isn't intentional. I'm going to pretend it's an unfortunate side effect of idle curiosity."

Ivy wasn't sure she understood. "What?"

"Why are you so interested in my life?"

She could feel herself beginning to blush. "It's my brother. He didn't — he just found out he's an Adequate too, and he isn't handling it very well."

"No kidding."

"So I want to know he's going to be okay."

The doctor stared down at her. "You want to know what it's like growing up?" She laughed unpleasantly. "We sit in classes during the day and go home and watch Taps like you on television at night. Some we might even know. Do you know what it's like to watch kids your own age performing everywhere? To think, *That could be me right now, but I wasn't good enough*?"

Ivy had never heard an Adequate be this direct. The doctor's response upset her. Constantine wasn't interested in performing, of course, but with every new video game released he might feel the frustration of knowing other kids got to work on it. "But did classes get interesting, eventually?" she asked.

"Biology was," the doctor said. "That's where I first started to think about medicine as an alternate career once I was passed over. I had a great teacher who made us do a lot of work on cell structures, and I got hooked. So when my friends were settling down and having families, I kept working. Still not married." She held up her left hand. "But you never forget what you wanted to be pre-Tap," she continued. "You spend your first thirteen years obsessed with the creative industries. It's a long time before anything else excites you in the same way."

Ivy wondered if something would strike her brother's interest in school. She tried to remember what classes there were: science and language arts and math. Maybe he would develop an interest in chemistry like her father had. It would take time, of course.

"Well, as you seem to be in fine health, I should get going," the doctor said. "Stay young."

"Sorry," said Ivy, "but *are* you happy now? I'd really like to know."

"Happy," the woman said as she put her coat on. "I work a seventy-five-hour week. What I make all year, you and your little Tap friends probably make in a couple of days. Good thing I have the added perk of being exposed to infectious diseases." She paused, bag in hand, and her tone became less cynical. "The days I keep my head down and focus on the challenge of diagnosis and treatment, I like the work. A lot. If I turn on the TV or go online, though, the reality of my life comes rushing back. Sometimes, it's almost too much to bear." She sighed and patted the shiny shale fabric of her coat. "At least I can afford my rent and one or two trends per season. No, I wouldn't say happy. But I . . . get by, I suppose."

Though it wasn't a rosy picture, at least the doctor was honest. Ivy considered offering her some placidophilus pills but immediately checked the impulse. They were, technically, illegal — and it wasn't as if the doctor couldn't score some if she wanted. "Thank you for telling me this," she said, rising. Another thought occurred to her. "Do you ever get over thinking it's unfair that you became an Adequate?"

"But it is fair," the woman said simply. "I had a shot to get tapped like everyone else. I wasn't good enough." She shrugged. "That's life."

Ivy received an Unum message from Vivienne Graves that night. *Thank you for the endorsement,* it said. *We invite you to join us on the steps of the Torro-LeBlanc design house anytime tomorrow. We know you're busy, but your presence would help our cause greatly. In the meantime, good luck with your confrontation.*

Fatima and Jarvis would never let her go to the strike, of course. As she drifted off to sleep, she thought about possibilities. Maybe she could call and talk to everyone through speakers or something. Maybe — and she got a thrill as she thought it — it was the perfect excuse to talk to Felix. She would have to make sure that happened somehow. She was a little surprised he hadn't called yet, seeing as her breakup with Clayton was now thirty-six hours old. She rolled over and hugged her pillow. She hoped Marla had remembered to give him her number.

Ivy had suggested Monterey Drive in front of the Pop Beat studios for the eco-chic photo op, and Fatima set it up without suspicion. Of her nymphs, Madison was crankiest about wearing old trends. As they dressed for the day, she chose a green-feathered blazer that had only just expired. "I don't know how long this eco-business is going to last," she said, "but we may need to schedule an intervention soon. What's the point of being in an entourage if we don't get to wear prime clothes?"

"I like my vintage shoes," said Aiko, pulling on a pair of fringe-topped moccasin boots from an old Plains Indian trend.

"Ugh — boots that someone else has stuffed their smelly feet in. Nasty."

"Quit whining," said Hilarie. "You could have gone to the vintage store with us and found something nice."

"*Vintage.* Right," Madison scoffed. "Face it, Hil, it's a store for poor people. I will *never* like dressing like a tree-hugging hobo."

Ivy glanced at Fatima, but her publicist thumbed through a magazine, ignoring them. Ivy wondered whether she was actually distracted — or still peeved about the spontaneous announcement on *Up & At 'Em* and letting her take some heat. Someone needed to stand up to her most outspoken nymph. "That's too bad, Madison," she said sharply. "Because eco-chic is here to stay. Watch."

"Sure, sure," mumbled Madison.

"You've got something on your face," said Naia. As she reached over to brush Madison's cheek, Madison jerked away. Ivy saw a tiny flash. What looked like a little piece of gold thread seemed to be attached to the skin near her nymph's ear.

"What *is* that?" Ivy demanded. Madison was covering her cheek with her palm and staring at Fatima. No longer perusing the magazine, Fatima's attention was now fully focused on the conversation at hand.

"It's a treatment," the publicist said after a pause. "Madison's cheeks were starting to hollow out, so we gave them an extra burst of collagen." She put down the magazine and rose. "Leakage is a side effect. Let's get that fixed." Steering Madison by the shoulders, Fatima led her out of the room.

"Gross," said Hilarie.

Ivy's hands went to her cheeks that the same time as her three nymphs prodded their own, as if testing for ripeness. Her cheeks were still firm, weren't they? She didn't have time to worry about treatments, on top of everything else.

Chapter Twenty-Seven

W e'd passed the twenty-four-hour mark and the strike was still in force. Twenty-four hours — it felt like a hundred. Life since the walkout had whirred with activity. I couldn't get enough of it.

Monday's spontaneous marching had lasted until the sun began to set. Vivienne told everyone to go home and rest up for another day. That night, I called each of the fired Superior Court judges, inviting them to protest Torro-LeBlanc and answering their questions about the makeover. They all seemed a little dazed, but angry, too, so I was hopeful they'd join us.

Henry had been the angriest. He'd made me listen to a fifteen-minute rant about how, through Maven Girl, he'd been personally responsible for prolonging certain trends and generating massive profits for Torro. He'd told Julia all this when she'd called to demote him.

"And you know what she says? She says, 'Honey, we've known it was you for years. Time to power down.'"

I told him that the ultimate payback would be for Maven Girl to come out in support of the strike.

"The site's *vanished,* Marla. They've pulled it offline. After four years, it's gone."

Wow — they could do that? All his work . . . ethically questionable work, but still. He'd never found out that I wanted to blackmail him at the runway show. I was glad the exploding security tags plot hadn't happened the way we'd planned. The idea seemed sort of petty now. "Come march with us," I told him.

Henry's expression turned resolute. "I'll be there."

I'd even sucked it up and called Olivia. Relieved when she didn't pick up, I left a very short message. And although Sabrina had blown me off, I tried her number — but again, I had to leave a message.

On Tuesday morning, I wore my bottle pin again and joined the protesting crowd outside Torro-LeBlanc. There were even more signs. Kevin and a bunch of other people were holding a wordless poster with a fist clenching a giant needle. I thought at first that Vivienne had drawn it, but Kevin proudly disclosed that he was the artist.

I noticed Henry carrying a sign that read **OVER SIXTEEN AND STILL A CREATIVE GENIUS**. I gave him a huge wave.

We sent the demands to the Silents that morning from Vivienne's Unum. We also asked for a meeting. Vivienne ended our message with these words: *If you consent to our makeover, Marla Klein will lead a studio devoted to an eco-chic line. If not, Marla will take the trend elsewhere.* It was a little nervy, but I didn't argue.

We will not negotiate, came the first Unum reply. *Return to work now or lose your jobs.*

I imagined Adele, the chief executive officer, as the mind behind the words — or maybe it was Hugo, showing his true nature. Either way, the reply made me feel the weight of what we were doing. The strikers were real people, some, like Randall, supporting families. They were in danger of losing their income. It had to work.

"This is only the beginning." Felix squeezed my hands when we stole away for a moment together. We didn't think the others had figured anything out yet, but he kept giving me looks that made me want to sneak us both into the abandoned Superior Court judging room. "Our contracts don't say *Terminated* yet, do they? They could have fired us all after work yesterday. They're afraid of even more negative press. They'll listen eventually."

We tried: *Negotiate, or Marla will go public with your attempt to drug her.*

We will not negotiate, was the response. *This allegation is false. Furthermore, you have no proof.*

Vivienne said it was unfortunate I hadn't taken a blood or urine test yesterday morning. Placidophilus stayed in the system for only a few hours. Felix pointed out that the Silents didn't know whether I'd gone and tested myself, but I didn't think it was smart to try to bluff them. But since they had called ours . . .

"I say we go public," I said to Vivienne. I had some idea that she would send the *Times* a note about the drugged coffee to put in the paper.

"Good. We're putting you onstage," she said instead.

So I spoke to the strikers. At the top of the steps, I stood behind a raised podium that Vivienne had ordered. I was glad I could clutch its sides for support. It was one thing to address drafters in the basement — it was another to speak when there were TV cameras around. Once again, I told the story of my meeting on the sixth floor. Speakers Randall had set up broadcast my voice up and down the block. I tried to ignore my dry mouth and the strange way the echo made me sound. As it turned out, the crowd made it easier. They booed robustly, then cheered when I told them that I preferred better pay and better working conditions for everyone than the highest seat on the court for myself. It was prime, the way everyone seemed to be on my side. After a while, I forgot about the cameras and mikes.

When I finished, the other drafters gathered around to congratulate me. "Well done," said Vivienne, her black-rimmed eyes regarding me with fierce approval.

"That was kick-ass," said Felix. He would have said more, I think, but some reporters requested follow-up interviews with me. This time, I figured I had nothing to lose and answered their questions. Afterward, Felix twisted his fingers in mine. "You're a rock star," he said.

Later in the morning, news of Ivy Wilde's appearance on *Up & At 'Em* reached us. We sent a clip of the video around to the strikers and to the Silents. *Ivy Wilde just announced on national television that she is boycotting Torro-LeBlanc on our behalf,* Vivienne wrote. *Negotiate with us or lose her and other celebrity clients forever.* Again, I knew that the last line was a bit of an exaggeration, but it sounded so good. And we'd come this far.

End the strike by nine a.m. tomorrow and there will be no repercussions, the Silents replied.

"Steady," said Vivienne. "They're giving us the day? And no sign of the CSS? I think they're starting to get nervous."

I pictured the Corporate Security and Surveillance agents I'd seen around the building. "I didn't think about that. Do you think they'll shut us down?"

"Don't worry. Torro won't call those fascists in yet." She snorted. "They want to maintain the illusion that they are not an evil corporation."

Vivienne told me that a *scab* is the name for someone who

goes to work during a strike. I watched the sifters, selectors, and Junior Court judges attempt to pass the picket lines throughout the morning. The strikers didn't it make it easy to get into the building, jeering at the scabs. Then I noticed Olivia, walking into the building with her nose in the air. Now *there* was a true scab — scabby heart, scabby brain, scabby everything. As I watched her pass, I wondered what job she'd been given after her demotion. I hoped it was cleaning toilets.

I didn't feel any love for Olivia, and probably never would, but I realized I wasn't jealous of her anymore either. I understood her. It hit me that I was standing outside the building, not walking in, precisely because I had been made a drafter. Otherwise, I might have ended up like Olivia. Ignorant. I would have had nothing to do with a strike.

I remembered being surprised when Vivienne told me she wished she'd never been tapped. Well here I was, thankful that I'd been kicked off the court. Life is funny.

I was listening to Gwen the patternmaker rally the strikers when I felt someone touch my arm. I turned to find Sabrina standing next to me. As usual, she was dressed impeccably, but her concealer didn't quite cover the gray hollows under her eyes.

"Hi, Marla," she said.

"You came."

"I can't believe you had the chance to lead the court and you turned it down."

I couldn't tell if Sabrina was impressed or if, like the Junior Court judges, she thought I was crazy. "Yeah, well. Once you're a drafter, you realize how unhappy everyone else is."

Sabrina nodded. "They assigned me to the mailroom," she whispered after a pause. "I almost didn't come to work on Monday, but I couldn't face staying home with my mother and my cat."

I wanted to stay mad, I really did. But I couldn't help but feel real pity for her. To go from Superior Court judge to mail sorter . . . I didn't know exactly what the mailroom was like, but I imagined that the job didn't involve much creative expression.

"I just wanted to tell you that I'm sorry for being such a jerk that time on the train." Sabrina spoke in a rush. "It was feeble of them to kick you off the court. Ivy Wilde's eco-chic look was killer. Obviously, they made a big mistake."

I looked back at Gwen at the podium. "Maybe. I'm glad they let me go when they did."

"No — er, right." She gave me a small smile. "What you guys have done is really amazing. People are saying the sixth floor doesn't know what to do about us. That we might win." She leaned in closer to me. "If we do win, maybe you could recommend me for one of the studios in the makeover? They sound prime."

I was surprised that Sabrina so readily saw herself as part of *us,* the protesters. I looked into my old friend's hopeful eyes. Despite all that had happened between us, I didn't have any appetite for revenge. "Of course."

"Thank you. I mean it. You're the best," Sabrina gushed.

Around lunchtime, an Adequate named Georgia Johnson from the Torro-LeBlanc Finance and Accounting Department stood beside Felix at the podium. Georgia, whom I judged to be forty — at least — talked about her interest in clothing design, which hadn't blossomed until she was an adult. She didn't think it was fair that she had no chance to follow her passion and change careers under Torro-LeBlanc's current setup. Felix, in turn, shared that he loved designing but also wanted to know more about business and finance. "After the makeover," he said into the booming microphone, "Georgia and I will have the opportunity to share our skill sets. The gulf between Adequates and Taps will diminish. We hope other Adequates who think like Georgia will join us in our fight." He spoke with knit brows, staring down the cameras. It was risky, a Tap coming out in support of Adequates. But he sounded outrageously confident.

Torro's Adequates hadn't joined us in one big swell, but some of them had trickled into the picket lines yesterday afternoon and today. From the cheers, I could tell his speech touched the crowd.

Afterward, I gave Felix a quick hug. "Did you see how intently everyone was listening?"

"Were they?" He shrugged. I knew he was pleased.

He introduced me to Georgia and we shook hands. "Thank you for starting this whole thing," she said. "I'm beginning to think we might get through to some of the other industries watching at home, too. You never know."

I nodded. "What you guys were talking about makes so much sense."

At the end of the day, Vivienne shared some news with us. "A small group of workers from Bancroft House and another from Belladonna walked off their jobs today," she announced into the microphone. I exploded in cheers, as did everyone around me. "We will welcome our compatriots if they choose to march with us tomorrow, and we support them in their fight. They are our brothers and sisters in revolution." Again, cheers erupted. "We will *keep on marching*"— she pounded the podium —"until *all* of the design houses realize they cannot treat us like indentured servants. We are creative professionals who deserve fair pay for our hard work."

Vivienne's ability to inspire stunned me. As I rode home that night, my mind swam with possibilities about what tomorrow would hold. The Silents had given us until nine a.m. to end the strike. If we made it past nine, would they break down and negotiate?

They wouldn't — couldn't — fire that huge crowd of people. I refused to believe it.

Karen drove away my daydreams in short order when I arrived home. Yesterday evening, though I'd tried to sound sure of myself, I had haltingly, ramblingly told her I'd turned down Torro's offer to lead the Superior Court and had instead led the workers in a company walkout. I knew she'd be upset — but I hadn't anticipated that the news would unhinge her in the way it did. At first she stood staring at me, completely speechless. That was the good part. Then she began screaming about all she had given up to raise her only daughter and how I was crushing both of our dreams with this "unfathomable decision." Finally, she threw some food on a plate, thrust it at me, and told me to go to my room. I ate my dinner alone.

Tonight, Karen kept at it. She banged around the kitchen preparing dinner. "Disgrace" seemed to be the core theme of her ranting, which revealed she'd watched the news all day. Rebellions were disgraceful. This talk of Adequates and tapped employees working together was disgraceful. I had disgraced the family by giving that speech today, by *admitting* that I was feeble enough to give up a seat on the court, and by "spouting lunacy," as she put it, in all those news interviews. And then, the kicker:

"Who's going to want to marry someone like that?"

I thought I hadn't heard her right. "You're worried about my *marriage* prospects?" I said.

"Like it or not, it's your future," she said, wiping her forehead as she stirred the string beans. "I'm sure this seems like a fun little adventure, but it will end badly. Trust me. God knows after today you'll never *work* in this city again," she muttered. "Calling off this strike nonsense now is the only way of preserving any shred of a reputation." She replaced the pot cover. "I'm only thinking of you, Marla. You've got to listen to me. I've been around longer, and I know the way things are."

I looked at my mother standing in her apron by the stove. "Karen, marriage is the furthest thing from my mind right now. Maybe I don't even want to get married."

She groaned. "It's like talking to a brick wall."

Matters didn't improve when my father came home. "Marla, did you know you were on the news today?" Walter asked cheerfully. "I was doing invoices, but some of the folks at work were saying you made a speech or something?" He turned to my mother. "And last night you were worried that she'd made a bad decision!"

Karen looked as if she wanted to beat him with the meat mallet.

The next morning, I ignored the death stares from my mother and headed back to the strike. We all watched nine o'clock come and go. Torro-LeBlanc did nothing. No one came out of the design house to talk to us. All our contracts were still intact. Felix and I ducked behind some sound equipment and I slid my hands under his T-shirt, up his warm back. He twitched as I tickled him.

"Their silence has to mean fear," he said.

I wasn't entirely convinced, but pressing my lips to his, I felt dizzy with hope.

Chapter Twenty-Eight

The fans were alerted; security was in place. Ivy and her nymphs emerged from their urban utility vehicle at the Pop Beat studios on Wednesday afternoon to a wall of screaming fans cordoned off behind a long rope.

Ivy wore a long green and yellow tie-dyed sundress from an old flower-child trend. She topped it with a denim jacket with MILLBROOK CHORAL ENSEMBLE printed across the back. Her mother had overnighted the jacket from home. Its arms were a little short, so she rolled them, and she could no longer button the front, so she wore it open. Since Fatima had thrown out her Millbrook sweats, it was the closest thing she had to an old favorite, and she insisted on wearing it. The plastic flower from Marla she pinned to an elastic band and wore around her wrist like a corsage.

The variety in the crowd was stunning. There were people in outfits like Madison's, complete trends that had only just expired. But others had dug up old looks Ivy hadn't seen in years. There was a football jersey from the athletic trend, a slinky dress from disco, polo shirts and plaid pants from the golf look . . . and on and on. So many different looks, like the world's best costume party.

And that wasn't all. Ivy squinted at a few strange-looking attendees. They might have raided their junk drawers or a sanitation facility for their outfits. One close to the front seemed to be wearing a garbage bag cinched at the waist. A mother-daughter duo had on vests that resembled armor; when Ivy looked closer, she saw they were plated with flattened Sugarwater cans. She marveled at the creativity. Around another woman's neck glittered a necklace with the same melted look as her flower pin.

A small group of people carried signs with **K.U.T.** printed on them. Ivy wondered what that was about.

She advanced toward the crowd a few steps and from her drawstring purse withdrew a trendchecking gun. Fatima had secured the latest model, platinum and sapphire-encrusted, with a long, shiny barrel. Ivy flicked it on and brandished it in the air with both hands like a sword. The crowd roared.

"Now, let's see who's *really* eco-chic!" Ivy yelled.

She approached one of the golf-trend fans and aimed the barrel at the back of her neck. The gun hit the tag through the fabric, and the light turned red. Grinning, Ivy shook the girl's hand and held up the trendchecker for the whole crowd to see.

She went down the line, scanning and shaking, as the crowd cheered. There were several moments when she could tell from the sheepish look on someone's face that some garment of theirs — their boots, or their jacket — hadn't yet expired. She simply passed them over. The point was to gain support for eco-chic, not to shame people. With one notable exception, of course.

"Scan us! Scan us!" two girls screamed at her, each holding a **K.U.T.** poster. Ivy approached them with the trendchecking gun.

"Careful," Hilarie muttered.

"Oh my gosh, it's so amazing to see you again," the first girl gushed. "I don't know if you remember, but Sandra and I"— she grabbed the arm of the girl next to her —"are co-managers of the Wildefan Chatlist." Ivy recognized the round-cheeked smiles; these girls were a frequent presence in the front row of concerts, stretching their arms toward her as if they were starving children reaching for bread. She proceeded warily. There were always those who took fandom to a scary place, who styled their hair and wore colored contacts to look like her, or who stalked her family, or who, upon learning she liked polar bears, sent her a stuffed animal once a month. Once, in an autograph line, one had tried to snip a piece of her hair. Her bodyguards evidently had the same fear and moved closer.

"What's K.U.T.?" asked Ivy.

The first girl held the posterboard above her head. "You'll have to *kut* the shirt off my back!" she exclaimed.

Ivy raised her eyebrows, and Sandra clarified. "We've decided to make eco-chic a lifestyle choice, just like you did, Ivy. *K-U-T* stands for 'Keep Until Threadbare.' It's an online movement started by this superfan named Vivienne Graves. We've chosen four outfits, and we pledge to wear them as long as the clothing holds up."

"It's for *real* environmentalists." The first girl grabbed a television camera lens with both hands and pulled it toward her face. "Go to keepuntilthreadbare-dot-fan. Do it for Ivy Wilde and the environment!"

"That's insane," Ivy heard Madison whisper to one of the other nymphs.

"Wow, you guys are really committed. Keep it up," said Ivy, moving quickly down the line.

In talking to them, she realized how much the eco-chic momentum could snowball. She smiled to herself as she considered "superfan" Vivienne's insidious tactics. K.U.T. — a pledge

ELAINE DIMOPOULOS

to hold out against trends permanently. The majority of people would never go for it, but a little side group could still make a lot of noise. This crowd proved there were more people willing to ignore trends than she'd thought possible. What it meant, at the very least, Ivy thought happily, was more publicity for eco-chic and for her.

A black limousine pulled up in front of the guest entrance to the Pop Beat building. The entrance was roped off, and security kept the fans in line, but Ivy was free to go where she liked. Leaving her nymphs behind, she positioned herself in front of the stage door, holding the trendchecking gun ready.

Following Vivienne's advice, Ivy had gone over Pop Beat's broadcast calendar carefully. The publicity event was no accident. Lyric Mirth had an appearance on *Hot with Hyman* this afternoon.

Behind her aquatic-looking nymphs, Lyric emerged from the limo. She fluffed her blond hair, whose streaks of green and blue coordinated with her mermaid outfit. Ivy recognized it from Torro-LeBlanc's latest runway show. Lyric waved her arms high and the crowd roared.

Ivy seethed.

Before she could advance, another figure emerged from the limousine. A boy waved at the crowd and lifted his chin to give Lyric a quick but deliberate kiss on the cheek. So they had her dating the middle Angel brother, Danny. Ivy almost snorted. That feeble rock trio, with their cornball music. Good. They deserved each other.

Ivy took a deep breath. *"Lyric Mirth!"* she yelled, opening her arms wide from her perch on the stage door step.

Lyric, Danny, and her nymphs turned at the sound of her voice. Lyric's smile held, but her brow creased in surprise.

258

"Lyric, it is *so* good to see you here," Ivy said, projecting as loudly as she could. "Thank you for coming and supporting eco-chic. Lyric Mirth cares about the environment, everyone!"

The crowd cheered again, but she could see a few people frowning and pointing. Clearly, they had previewed the new Torro line. Ivy didn't waste time. "Come over here and let me scan you."

Lyric's smile faltered. She glanced at her publicist, an older woman who was just emerging from the limo, speaking into her Unum. The disengaged look on the woman's face told Ivy that she hadn't processed the situation yet.

"Come on! Don't be shy. Those expired trends are prime!" cried Ivy. She held the gun in her right hand, high above her head, and advanced toward Lyric. Danny Angel and the nymphs stood around her helplessly.

"I didn't think you meant — this is my first Pop Beat spot!" Lyric whispered. Her eyes searched Ivy's face, and Ivy felt their desperation, their plea for pity. But as in Scalpel, when she'd toppled over the Sugarwaters, her heart hardened. Lyric was the fly in the ointment; she had to be flicked away.

Ivy moved around Lyric and aimed the gun at her back where the dress zippered. She held the trigger until the gun beeped.

"Look everyone, it's — *oh.*" Staring at the gun, Ivy gasped dramatically and returned to the stage door step. She held the device at her side, shaking her head.

"Show us!" someone shouted. The crowd chorused in agreement.

Ivy filled her face with brokenhearted pity. Slowly, she lifted the green light high for all to see. Gasps punctuated the crowd, followed by a few jeers and boos.

By now, Lyric's publicist understood what was happening.

She hustled the party toward the stage door as the boos crescendoed. Lyric masked her face with one hand. The fishtail skirt bound her ankles so that she moved in stiff, wobbling strides. Ivy hopped off the step to let them pass.

"You little brat," the publicist hissed at her before disappearing into the building.

Ivy risked a glance at Fatima. Her publicist had a smirk on her face. Good. She had bought herself some credibility.

Her Unum buzzed suddenly, and when she saw the caller, she waved to her entourage to form a shell around her. They stood with their backs to her, and she pressed the button to answer. "Constantine?" she said.

"Hey." Ivy blinked at the screen. Her brother had one giant black eye and a scratch under the other. He looked like a sad panda.

"What happened to your face?" she asked, trying to keep the edge out of her voice.

"Nothing. It's nothing."

"It was obviously something."

"Just a fight."

"With who?"

"My friend Colin's cousin. He works for Arcadia, and he's a royal ass-wipe. He started it."

Ivy sighed. She seriously doubted that Colin's cousin, whoever he was, had taken the first swing. "Constantine, I heard about the . . . statue."

"*Please* don't give me another lecture. I've heard it all from George and Christina. We're going over and over it in therapy, too. The doctor's helping me find"—he raised one hand and mimed air quotations—"positive ways to express my frustration." He snorted.

Ivy hoped the black eye was enough proof for the therapist that her brother was still full of anger. She wouldn't bring up the connection between Skip and herself now. Maybe later — much, much later, when they could laugh about it all. "I just wonder why you're not . . . *calmer*," she said meaningfully.

Constantine glanced over his shoulder. "Working on it," he muttered.

"If there's a friend I can mail —"

"I got it covered." He changed the subject. "Hey, I saw you on *Up & At 'Em*."

"I have a signed photo from Savannah Brown for you." Constantine had always watched the show attentively; Ivy suspected he had a little crush on the host.

"Oh. Prime." He coughed. "We've been watching the fashion strike here too."

"Yeah?"

"Yeah. That's why I called, actually. They're saying — they're saying stuff about Adequates getting prime jobs in the company, if they want. Have you heard anything about that?" He looked at her intently. "Do you think it might happen for other companies? Like for gamers, too?"

Ivy knew nothing about what the Adequates were up to or the state of the gaming industry. But she thought about the prospect of Adequates like Constantine getting to work in the industries they wanted to, instead of spinning out of control when their dreams were shattered. She remembered the doctor who had examined her, who had seemed convinced that the system was fair. Maybe . . . maybe it could be fairer than it was. Her brother looked so hopeful that Ivy didn't hesitate. "Absolutely." she said. "A lot's changing right now. Keep watching, okay? And take care of yourself."

"Yeah. I will."

Ivy gave her love to him and to her family and hung up the Unum. With Constantine's words ringing in her head, she looked around at the crowd. She was done here. Lyric was humiliated. What if . . . what if she just took off? She could help her brother *and* accelerate an overdue reunion. To dodge security, she'd need a massive distraction. Having already proved useful once today, the trendchecker in her hand gave her an idea. She'd have to time the thing just right. But if it worked . . .

Emerging from her makeshift cocoon, she once again began trendchecking along the rope of fans. Eyeing security and Fatima, she looked for a section where the fans seemed especially rabid. She found one and lingered, trying to work up her courage. She'd taken so many risks recently — what was one more? She took a breath and yelled: "Whoever catches this gets free tickets to my tour opener!" Then she hurled the trendchecking gun into the air.

Ivy had a half second of distraction as the crowd, necks craned, stretched hands toward the gun. Running to the stage door, she whipped it open. She bolted down the long hallway, pushing her way past bewildered technicians and assistants. She turned right, then left, then right again, as the hallway meandered toward Pop Beat's lobby.

She heard clacking footsteps behind her. She turned expecting security, but it was Madison, pumping her arms and pursuing her in high heels. "I can see her! I can see her! She's almost to the lobby!" Madison shouted wildly. *Traitor*, Ivy thought. She waited for more people to follow, but, strangely, no one else appeared behind Madison. Who was she talking to?

Ivy crossed the flashy lobby and spun through the revolving door. Outside, still sprinting, she wriggled out of her jacket and put it over her head to shield her face. She crossed the street and took off running down a narrow alley between two buildings. Grateful for her dance-rehearsal conditioning and her practical shoes, she didn't stop moving until she reached a train station. Finally permitting herself to glance over her shoulder, she saw that she was completely alone.

Even so, Ivy didn't stop to catch her breath. She climbed the steps, bought a ticket for the Fashion Row station, and boarded the train.

Chapter Twenty-Nine

On Wednesday afternoon, the parade of speakers continued as the cameras rolled. While Vivienne stood at the podium introducing a drafter from Belladonna who had walked out, I noticed a clump of people holding signs that said **K.U.T.** The clump waved them high in the air and cheered when the Belladonna drafter took the stage.

I turned to Felix. "K.U.T.?"

He looked where I was pointing and shook his head. "You've got to be kidding me."

"What is it?"

"One of Viv's side projects. They're pledging never to buy new trends again. Come on."

We made our way to the podium, and Felix beckoned Vivienne over. "We saw the posters, Viv," he hissed into her ear. "What are they doing here?"

Vivienne gave him a placid smile. "Apparently, I'm not the only radical out there," she whispered back.

"How does that help our cause? Huh?" he demanded. "Encouraging people to believe that fashion is worthless? We want to return to work and design new looks. This whole K.U.T. business will hurt us, if it ever catches on."

"I'm fighting the good fight," Vivienne said. "Having the K.U.T. fanatics on one end of the spectrum shifts the balance of the whole debate." She smiled and tilted her head back toward the speaker from Belladonna. "Suddenly, what the strikers are asking for seems reasonable."

"I know you, Viv. You're recruiting them hard. I saw the site." He snorted. "Never knew you were such a big Ivy Wilde fan."

I wondered how Ivy was involved.

"You want them to be a force, not some little fringe group," Felix went on. "If we get our way, Torro's sales need to be *through the roof* to show the new system works. We need people buying our stuff!"

Vivienne glanced at the K.U.T. sign holders in the crowed and shrugged. "Sorry, Felix. It's done. It's who I am. You've always known that."

"And *you've* never understood the way —"

"Felix." I put my hand on his arm gently. "I haven't seen the site you're talking about. But you're worried that people will stop buying new designs?" I paused, hoping he'd hear how absurd the words sounded. "Think about it. Do you really think trends will ever stop?"

He didn't answer.

"Early on, you said something to me about people always wanting to be different, about it being human nature," I continued. "You were right. Fashion will always be changing. Personally, I hope it doesn't change so fast under the new system. But trends are safe. They're never going away."

"Unfortunately, she has a point," said Vivienne. "But there

should be a place for those who want to resist the constant change. That's all I've provided. So relax." She stepped away from us and turned back to the podium.

Felix's frown softened. "For the sake of everyone here, I hope you're right," he said.

"I am," I declared.

Later in the afternoon, while marching in the circle of protesters, I chatted with Neely Syms. I liked the patternmaker's warm intensity. She had ideas about everything: unraveling old sweaters for yarn, repurposing coffee sacks into handbags, annealing silverware into jewelry . . .

We were brainstorming plans for our eco-friendly design studio — it was getting a little pie-in-the-sky, I had to admit — when my Unum buzzed. I pulled it out, prepared to ignore the call, but as I glanced down, I saw a name I hadn't seen in a while. "Excuse me for a sec," I said to Neely. I scurried away from the marchers and pressed the button to accept the call. "Hello?"

"Marl! What's up?" Braxton's obnoxiously grinning face appeared on the screen.

"Braxton," I said. "This is a surprise."

"You're everywhere," he said. "You're all over the news. It's crazy."

I looked at him. He was in front of some kind of building. I could see bricks behind his neck. "What exactly do you want, Braxton? I'm sort of busy here."

"I've just been thinking about you, that's all," he said. "I thought we could get together sometime and hang out." His eyebrows flicked up and down.

"Really," I said. "Olivia would love that, I'm sure."

Braxton laughed. "Please. Livy and I are ancient history."

"Ah." I didn't need to hear more. "Well, I'm sure you need to get back to judging. I've got to go too."

Braxton's lips gathered into a knot. "I'm not really on Denominator's court anymore," he mumbled. "But I got a cool promotion. Movie-premiere design. You know, like I decide which posters we should put up, and where the life-size cardboard cutouts should go. It's a really important job."

And that's when Olivia dumped you, I wanted to say. *As predicted.*

"You know," Braxton continued after an awkward silence, "one of my friends from Denominator told me last night that your little drafter strike is giving people ideas. Apparently, some people are talking about making the same kinds of changes over here. A couple of the storyboarders are starting a petition or something. I hope it works — just to see the judges' faces."

This was news. I was eager to tell the others. Braxton's take on the whole thing, though, aggravated me. "You know, change doesn't just happen. You could do something about it yourself."

"Oh, yeah, definitely, I think I will. But it would be great to hang out in the meantime. What are you up to this weekend?"

This weekend? I thought ahead to how busy I would be. Braxton didn't have the first concept of what we were trying to accomplish. "Well, if the Silents don't agree to the makeover, we'll have to keep visiting the homes of other design-house employees to convince them to join the protest. And making signs. And scheduling more press appearances. And if they do, we'll be in negotiations. I don't think this weekend's going to work."

"Maybe you could come over tonight, then? I really, really want to see you." His eyebrows hopped again.

I sighed. Talk about pathetic. Even if he hadn't left me for

Olivia, and even if I'd never met Felix, I couldn't imagine being his girlfriend. "Braxton, it's not going to happen. We've drifted apart." I recalled his words during our last Unum conversation. "I just don't think we're into the same things anymore," I said with an edge to my voice. "You know?"

"What are you talking about? We're totally into —"

"Stay young, Brax," I said, and hung up the Unum.

Around half past three my Unum buzzed again, this time with a message from Vivienne. *Just heard from Torro,* she wrote. *Looks like we broke them.* The forwarded message appeared farther down the screen: *We will speak with you today at four p.m.*

I left the protest and ran to Vivienne.

"I think we might have done it," she said in a rush. For the first time since I'd known her, she looked jubilant.

Gwen and Dido appeared next to us. Randall waved from where he was standing near the sound equipment.

"Do you think they'll really listen?" Dido asked.

"If they don't, we walk out of the meeting," said Vivienne. "It's that simple." I nodded.

"This is incredible," Kevin said, jogging up to them with his Unum out. "Is it for real?"

"Believe it, baby," said Gwen, clapping him on the shoulder. "It's our time."

"Aren't you going to send it to everyone?" Kevin asked. I looked down at the addressee list and noticed that Vivienne had forwarded the message only to our inner circle.

"Of course. But I just got a message from our last speaker. She's on her way, and we don't want an eruption quite yet." She glanced at her watch. "I'll make the announcement right after her speech."

I saw Felix running through the crowd toward us. He was whooping with abandon. It was . . . adorable.

"Of course, that one might give away the whole thing," Vivienne muttered with a smirk.

"We did it!" Felix yelled, waving his Unum above his head crazily. When he reached us, he hurled his arms around me, then lifted me off my feet and spun me around several times. I could see the others shaking their heads and laughing at us. Only Dido looked surprised.

When he finally returned me to the earth, he kissed me. "I think I'm delirious," he said, following it up with four more quick kisses on the cheek. Even though it was a little embarrassing, I couldn't stop smiling.

I broke away and turned back to the group. Before I could say anything, I caught sight of someone behind Vivienne's shoulder.

Ivy Wilde was standing there, watching us.

The expression on Ivy's face lingered only a moment, but I recognized it. It was the look I was sure I'd worn when I'd noticed Braxton and Olivia sitting together on the train. Pained eyes, a crestfallen mouth. I knew instantly that Ivy had come here unprepared to find Felix kissing another girl.

Her expression slid back into neutrality as the group turned around to greet her. I glanced at Felix, wondering if he had seen. He was looking at Ivy, but his face was unreadable.

"You came," said Vivienne. As Ivy shook hands around the circle, I saw the plastic flower affixed to her wrist. My own was pinned to my lapel — it was the third day in a row I'd worn it.

When it was my turn to say hello, my heartbeat quickened. Ivy gave me a cool handshake. "Hey."

It was hard to know what to say. *Sorry I kissed Felix? I should have guessed from our bathroom conversation that you had a thing for him?* "Thanks for helping out with the boycott," I said instead. "We all watched the *Up & At 'Em* clip. That was so prime. It made all the difference. Thank you." I meant it.

Ivy's gaze dropped to my pin. One side of her mouth broke into a little smile. "Design any chic looks recently?" she asked.

I gestured to the strike and laughed nervously. "I've been a little busy. But as soon as we get back to work, you're my first commission."

Ivy brought her wrist to my clavicle so that the flowers glistened next to each other. "Nice," she said.

I smiled. She moved on to Felix and shook his hand quickly without meeting his eyes.

"So, we'd love it if you could say a few words . . ." Vivienne led Ivy over to the podium steps, relaying instructions. She spoke into the microphone to call for attention and began her introduction. The protesters who realized the pop star was in their midst began to yell and whistle.

Across the street, I noticed something strange. A group of kids — preteenish — were walking along the sidewalk. They quickly and neatly grouped themselves in a rectangular formation the length of the block and about four bodies deep. They faced the design house.

"Who are they?" I asked Felix. He was standing next to me.

Felix squinted at the crowd and frowned. "No idea."

"Another one of Vivienne's projects, you think?"

He shot a glance at Vivienne's back and shrugged uncertainly.

Ivy took the podium. A full minute of cheering followed. Repeatedly, she put up her hands to stop it, but I could see she was enjoying the attention.

In the midst of the noise, I moved closer to Felix. "Ivy likes you, you know," I said pointedly.

I had caught him off-guard, and he shifted his stance. "What can I say? I'm pretty irresistible."

"Felix." I didn't smile. "You guys knew each other when you were little. I can tell there used to be something there. And she's *Ivy Wilde.*"

"So what? You're *Marla Klein.*" Felix turned to me. "Look. I was never more interested in someone than I am right now. Eva's okay, but she spent too long as a corporate puppet." He leaned in and whispered in my ear. "You blow me away. There's no comparison. Believe me."

I felt the hairs on the back of my neck tingle. I threaded my fingers through Felix's and listened to Ivy talk about her decision not to buy any more Torro-LeBlanc clothing while the workers were striking. "I actually think she's pretty great," I said.

"... and one of your own designers created my new look. Marla Klein? Come up here." As Ivy turned back, I dropped Felix's hand. A bit guiltily, I made my way toward the podium. Ivy made room for me on the raised platform, and I stepped up beside her.

"Marla called me and told me about the stuff that goes on here," Ivy announced to the crowd. She articulated her words perfectly. She was obviously a pro at press appearances. "I'm with you guys. You've got to break free and get what you want!" She paused for cheers. It did surprise me that Ivy was showing such aggressiveness. She sounded a little like Vivienne.

"Also, I heard you think Adequates should be able to have jobs people are usually tapped into?"

Ivy was looking at me for confirmation. "That's right," I said quickly, thinking back to Felix's speech from the day before. "We think there shouldn't be such a divide. If someone's good at a job, that person should be able to do it. That's what our makeover is all about."

"I agree. It should happen everywhere, in every creative industry." Ivy moved her gaze from one news camera to the next until she had stared down every lens in the vicinity. "Together, we are going to change things!" Ivy grabbed my right hand with her left and held it high in the air.

I felt weightless. This was happening. We really were going to win. I gripped Ivy's cold hand tightly.

Four CSS agents in gray dress uniforms and sunglasses jogged up the steps toward the podium. They surrounded Ivy, wrenching her hand from mine and shoving me aside. "You're coming with us, Miss Wilde," I heard one of them say in a low voice.

"No," said Ivy, struggling in their grasp. Her bag fell from her shoulder.

"Yes," said the man, securing her. The four surrounded her in a diamond and jostled her down the stairs and away from the crowd. They were gone before the cheers had stopped.

As I stooped to pick up Ivy's handbag, a booming voice filled the air.

"EMPLOYEES OF TORRO-LEBLANC." It was Adele. Powerful speakers amplified her voice. I glanced around but caught no sight of her. "PLEASE DIRECT YOUR ATTENTION TO THE CHILDREN ACROSS THE STREET."

Slowly, the strikers swiveled around. I stared at the wall of kids. Felix appeared by my side with a worried look.

"We have selected these potential employees from the second tier of our most recent Tap list," Adele continued. "They were just below the cut. All of them are now prepared to begin work as drafters and patternmakers, sifters and selectors and judges. We will train them."

I looked at the serious young faces. They probably thought they had caught a lucky break. I felt sick.

"It's them or you. Your choice. As of this moment, all of your contracts are terminated. If you log in and check them, you will find this to be true."

Swiftly, Felix tapped his Unum face. He nodded at me.

"There is one way to reverse the termination. Return to work today and register with your floor director. If you are registered by the end of the day, you will be welcomed back. If not, one of these children will take your position. Either way, tomorrow morning, we will once again be a fully functioning design house."

My heart sank.

"Finally, as an added incentive, we have decided to select a new Superior Court. Every employee is now eligible for one of the nine seats. We intend to recognize hard work and talent where we have seen it in the company. How quickly you return to work at the end of this announcement will be taken into consideration."

"It's the same old structure!" Vivienne flew to the podium and shouted into the microphone. "Marla resisted them, and so can you!" But I heard the edge of desperation in her voice. The workers' faces looked uncertain, as the temptation hovered in the air.

"One final thing. There will be no more organizing. We have enlisted Corporate Security and Surveillance troops to secure our building and grounds indefinitely. At five o'clock, they will remove you from the premises.

"Thank you for your time. We hope many of you will continue to work at Torro-LeBlanc."

Instantly, a security presence encircled the perimeter. Resembling a colony of beetles, these CSS troops wore gray combat fatigues and black helmets with chin straps. They carried nightsticks. Two of them pulled open the heavy doors to Torro-LeBlanc and stood on both sides of the entrance, holding them. The glass cases with their garbed mannequins glittered silently from inside the marble lobby. No one else could be seen.

For a moment, no one stirred. Across the street, I watched a light wind flutter the children's clothes and hair. I felt I ought to say something but found my mouth had gone dry.

"Hold fast," Vivienne ordered from the podium.

The first movement came from nearby, on the steps. Her head cast down, a familiar figure advanced toward the mouth of the building.

"Dido, what are you doing?" I cried.

"I'm sorry," Dido said, turning her head slightly. "But I could be a judge, you know?" She shrugged and gave a sad half smile. In shock, I watched her disappear into the building.

More of the strikers followed, one straggling after another, their faces heavy with defeat. "They got us," one mumbled to me as he passed by. I saw Vaughn meander his way into the building without meeting my eyes. The block of strikers that remained kept glancing over at the children, as if trying to make up their minds.

"Torro-LeBlanc!" Vivienne suddenly screamed from the podium. "You may think you own us, but we will never be your slaves! You stole our childhoods, but you cannot take away our humanity!"

She barreled down the steps and grabbed a long wooden

broomstick out of the hands of one of the strikers. Ripping off the attached banner, she shoved her way to the line of troops. With a cry, she swung her weapon down on the shoulder of one of the officers and began bludgeoning him over and over.

Chaos erupted. A ring of troops closed around the fight, and soon the crowd was pushing in all directions and yelling.

"We've got to help her," I said. As a herd of strikers dashed up the steps, I fought my way down, Felix at my heels. Around us, suddenly, handcuffs glinted like tinsel in the crowd. The troops were cuffing the wrists of the protesters, even as they kicked, even as they insisted they were trying to go back to work at Torro.

I gave Felix a panicked look.

"Come on," said Felix. "We're getting out of here."

We ran.

Chapter Thirty

*I*vy was alone.

The back of the urban utility vehicle into which she'd been thrust had no door handles on the insides. There were no window controls either. She ran her hands over the smooth leather and metal. She found it strange, as if it were a space capsule instead of a car.

She'd figured Fatima or Jarvis would eventually show up at the strike and bring her home. The four CSS men, though — had Jarvis sent them? Why? They'd handled her so roughly, digging their fingers into her upper arms as they steered her away. Two were sitting up front in silence. She had watched the other two enter a vehicle parked behind the one they'd put her in. It was now driving behind them.

"Where are we going?" she asked the men for the third time. No answer. Though he had on sunglasses, she thought the driver was eyeing her in the rearview mirror.

Idly, she fiddled with her seat belt shoulder strap. She didn't have her purse or her Unum or even one nymph for company. No placidophilus pills, either.

It had been prime, though. To stare down those cameras — so many of them, all focused on her — and talk about breaking free. To stand up for Constantine and tell everyone that Adequates matter too. To be filmed without worrying about someone from Millbrook spending money on something she was wearing. To hold the spotlight, on her own terms. What a high.

But then — Felix and Marla. Felix swinging Marla around, kissing her, holding her hand. Ivy's mood plummeted. She'd reinvented herself and broken up publicly with Clayton for Felix. And he didn't even care.

She wondered why she didn't want to crush Marla in her palm, the way she wanted to crush Lyric. She did, a little. But love wasn't the same as fame. When someone took your love away, you couldn't fight back. You couldn't force it to happen. You just had to watch it go. And it hurt so much.

She blinked back the tears from her eyes. *Think about the cameras,* she told herself. *They loved you.*

The vehicle twisted and turned through city streets and finally pulled up in front of a curb. Ivy peered out the window. She recognized the Warwick Records building.

She'd been to her record-label headquarters only once before. It was the day the court at Warwick had approved her solo album deal. She'd entered the top-floor conference room wide-eyed, shaken Miles Jackson's hand, and sung for him there and then, a cappella. Then he'd asked her to answer some questions about herself as if she were giving an interview. "You've got it, girl," he'd said afterward. "Warwick is going to make you a recording star. Are you ready?" She'd replied with an eager yes and signed her contract.

The agent in the passenger seat emerged from the vehicle and opened the rear door far enough to put his hand through. He grabbed Ivy's wrist tightly and swung the door open the rest of the way. "This way, Miss Wilde," he said, unclipping her seat belt with his free hand. "There's no point in trying to run."

Ivy hadn't been planning on running, but the man's words made her nervous. Why would she need to run? Or was it just that she'd bolted once outside the Pop Beat studios and they didn't trust her?

She swung her legs out of the back seat. The man, joined by another from the vehicle behind him, escorted her into the Warwick Records building.

Chapter Thirty-One

By some miracle, *Felix and I* made it to his apartment complex. We'd elbowed our way through the mob without getting arrested and sprinted all the way there. We ignored the crowd glued to the TV in the common room and headed for his bedroom. Now, sitting on Felix's bottom bunk, I kept glancing toward the locked door.

My mother had left four messages on my Unum. Shaking my head, I'd silenced the device and tucked it away. I could face the lectures later.

We stayed until it grew dark, talking about the stunning turn of events. Speculating about what had happened to Vivienne. And Kevin and Randall and Gwen and Neely. And cursing out Dido. Felix paced back and forth in the narrow room like a wolf. He stopped only when I caught his hand. "You're making me nervous," I said.

"Sorry." He sat down and put his arm around me. It felt nice — but awkward, too. Neither of us was much in the mood for kissing.

At one point, the lock turned and I panicked, but it was only Felix's roommate. A huge grin broke out on his face when he saw me. "Just dropping off my stuff," he said, planting his briefcase by the door. "Let me grab a jacket and you guys can get back to doing ... whatever." He said it in this smarmy way. "Hey, Felix, you need me to crash at Gavin's tonight?" I really did not like this kid. I wondered if roommates were assigned in Tap housing.

"No. Just go," Felix muttered.

The roommate paused with his hand on the doorknob. "Oh, heard about the Torro-LeBlanc strike. Sorry. But it's pretty much what everyone expected would happen, don't you think?"

"Get out!" Felix barked at him. After the door closed, he got up and locked it again. "Sorry," he said, turning back to me. "Mike's a dick."

"Agreed." I poked at Ivy's bag with the toe of my shoe. I'd kept it with me even as we fled. "I wonder if Ivy's okay. Her Unum's probably in here."

"Let's take a look." Felix grabbed the bag and loosened the drawstring.

I didn't feel great about going through her purse. I would never want anyone to see the stuff in mine—like oil-blotting paper for my face and emergency tampons. "That's her private stuff," I protested.

"Eh, she's not going to sue us." He looked at me playfully. "Well, maybe you. But she likes me. I'm safe."

I rolled my eyes.

Felix had it open in no time, but we found only an Unum, a couple of dollars, a pile of cosmetics, and a manila envelope. Felix pinched the metal clasp open and withdrew a handful of photographs. He handed them to me. I looked at the faces of the girls, but I didn't understand what they were.

Felix scratched his ear. "Vivienne showed these to me once. They're workers at one of the Torro-LeBlanc factories."

"What?" I examined the crowded sleeping quarters, the factory workstations. "This isn't in La Reina, is it?"

Felix shook his head.

"And I thought being a drafter was rough," I said slowly. I'd never thought much about how clothes were mass-produced. No one on the upper floors at Torro talked about it. I'd had this weird mental image of a bunch of adult men standing around drinking coffee in a clean, spacious factory — the floors and walls were white — and sort of supervising as machines did all the cutting and sewing. Finished garments flew off a conveyor belt and folded themselves into shipping boxes. All the workers had to do was punch the clock, check some boxes on their clipboards, and enjoy a nice long lunch break.

Looking at the pictures, I realized how naive I'd been. There wasn't magic involved in clothing production. Buttons and zippers might be sewn by machine, but someone had to maneuver the cloth. Loose threads needed to be clipped. Fabric had to be pressed. Labels needed to be added. For each and every garment of each and every trend.

I scanned the faces in the photos. If Torro-LeBlanc treated its Taps as replaceable, disposable employees . . . how did it treat these workers? "What's Ivy doing with these pictures?" I asked.

Felix shrugged.

"Well, she obviously was going to do something with them if she had them in her bag. Maybe she was trying to give them to a reporter. You see, you underestimate her."

Felix frowned at the pictures. "Maybe."

I picked up the Unum. "She's definitely missing this."

We put everything back in the bag. After a while, once I got up my nerve, we ventured into the common room, which had mostly emptied out, and turned on the television. The news reporters declared the strike over, with Torro-LeBlanc offering terms "able to please most." The cameras panned broadly over the brawl, but every channel broadcast a special clip of Vivienne's attack on the agent. The footage also showed workers streaming back into the design house through the open doors. It was hard to watch.

"Disgusting," Felix said.

He rode the train with me back to my apartment. To my great surprise, a teary-eyed Karen embraced us both when she opened the door. She alternated "I'm so glad you're safe" with "I've been worried sick." I immediately felt terrible for not having called. She invited Felix in, but he said he ought to get home before it got even later. I waved an awkward good night to him. Once the door was closed, Karen hugged me again and started crying fresh tears.

"I'm okay," I said, patting her on the back. "Really."

"I made flan." Karen gestured to the custard on the table and wiped her eyes. "I didn't know what else to do. I went down to Torro to try to get you, but they'd closed off the street. Your father is still out searching."

I felt another surge of guilt. "I'm sorry I didn't call. We barely got away."

Karen led me to the kitchen table. Suddenly feeling hungry, I dug into the flan. After a brief call to Walter, Karen joined me.

Less than ten minutes later, a loud knock at the front door startled us both.

"That can't be your father — he was all the way down at Yardley Station," Karen said, standing.

Plus, I thought to myself, *he wouldn't knock.*

Karen tightened the belt of her bathrobe — Torro-LeBlanc's, I noted wryly — and answered the door.

Behind her, I could see a male CSS agent and a woman in a white lab coat in the doorway. "Karen Klein?" the woman said, flashing a badge. "We're from Corporate Security and Surveillance. We have orders to speak with your daughter, Marla."

I set down my spoon. I'd been a fool to think hiding at Felix's would make any difference. They'd probably been watching the apartment. I swallowed and steadied myself for whatever was coming.

The intruders asked to sit down in a way that made it impossible to refuse. They stationed themselves next to me at the kitchen table, and Karen joined them.

"The short of it, Miss Klein," the woman began, "is that you have been identified as a threat. Numerous witnesses have confirmed your part in organizing the Torro-LeBlanc labor strike. Your actions were unlawful. We will not tolerate another uprising."

Through my anxiety, I felt an odd glint of pride. Yes, I had been an organizer. They had needed an army of troops to bring us down. They were right to be threatened.

"Our organization aims to avoid litigation and incarceration whenever possible," the male agent said. "We have found a sixty-day monitoring period using legal surveillance methods to be highly effective. Once we confirm that you have ceased to engage in disruptive behavior altogether, you're free to continue your life."

"She has stopped," Karen said firmly.

The man smiled at her. "Then she has nothing to fear. First, Marla, please retrieve your Unum and Tabula for us."

"Why?" I asked.

"Do what they say, honey," Karen urged.

"If you do not cooperate," the man said, still smiling, "we will have no choice but to arrest you."

Wouldn't you at least try drugging me first? I wanted to say. But I figured now was not the time to be smart. I retrieved my devices and watched as the agent placed his own Unum in between them. He turned everything on and waited until a blinking light on the central Unum stopped flashing and remained lit.

"There," the man said. "You are prohibited from communicating on devices other than these two for the sixty days. We'll be receiving all communications. We will also be monitoring your whereabouts using the Unum. You must keep it on you at all times. Odds are, you already do."

"Am I not allowed to go certain places?" I asked.

"Go wherever you like," the agent said. "But know we'll have a record."

I didn't like the feeling of my messages being read, but I was already thinking of ways around the restrictions. Would they really be able to tell if I made a call from someone else's Unum? And how would they know if I went somewhere without my Unum?

Then again, if they had been watching the house, they might keep tracking me by sight, too. I thought about asking — but wondered if I could trust their answer.

The woman stood. She walked to the kitchen sink and washed her hands. "We're also installing subdermal floss for sixty days."

"No," said Karen. I had never heard of subdermal floss, but my mother looked stricken. "You'll be listening to her Unum," Karen pleaded. "Why do you need to do that?"

"We have our orders," said the man. "If she has nothing to hide, it won't matter."

The woman returned to her seat and withdrew medical gloves from her bag. "On the upside, the floss stimulates collagen production," she said, pulling on the gloves. "She's getting a face-lift for free."

Karen didn't smile. I looked at the gloves apprehensively. "Karen? What's going on?"

While my mother hesitated, the woman ripped open a packet containing a small piece of wet gauze and ran it along my jawline. From the smell, I guessed the gauze was soaked in alcohol. The woman gave the alcohol a moment to dry; she then opened a tub of cream and rubbed it vigorously into my cheeks. "Anesthetic," she said simply. She pulled the gloves off inside out and put on a new pair.

"Karen?"

From a sealed bag, the woman pulled out a needle about four inches long and curved like a rainbow. Attached to the end was sparkling gold wire.

"This floss picks up everything you say and everything said to you. It's fine to curse us for an hour after it's in — we've heard it all before. Go ahead and talk freely. We're only interested in discussions of potentially subversive activity."

Breathing fast through my nose, I backed away from the sharp point. "Mom? Mom, please?"

"This is *unnecessary*," my mother said. "Marla's a good girl. She's learned her lesson."

I nodded crazily. "Don't put that thing in my face."

The woman sighed. "We can't leave until the floss is installed."

After a pause, my mother leaned forward and held both my

hands tightly. "I'll be right here. It's not supposed to hurt, honey. I saw something about it on *Hardline* once."

The woman gripped my chin with one hand and tilted my head to the side. She picked up the needle. "Your mother's right. This may feel awkward, but it shouldn't hurt. Don't move."

I forced my head to stay motionless. Out of the corner of my watering eye, I watched the needle penetrate the flesh near my ear. It didn't hurt, exactly, but the tugging sensation as the woman worked the needle under my skin turned my stomach.

The needle emerged near the side of my mouth, and the woman pulled it through until the gold wire poked out. She clipped both ends close to the skin.

"Perfect," the woman said, patting my cheek. "Now for the other side."

The woman packed up her materials after she finished. "You might bruise a little in the next couple of days, but go ahead and apply concealer. If either end of the floss starts poking out, give us a call. Otherwise, we'll be back in sixty days to remove it."

Gingerly, I touched my cheeks. The flesh was still numb, but I thought I could feel the hardness of the tiny wires beneath the surface. Every word I uttered, every burp, every snore, every kiss — they would be listening.

"Now comes the fun part," the woman said.

The man, who had left in the middle of the floss insertion, came in through the front door wheeling a trunk on a dolly. He set it down in the middle of the foyer.

"Here's your new wardrobe," the man announced, patting the trunk. "As a public show of faith in our design houses, we expect you to wear trends for your surveillance period. Here are the latest styles from the Big Five." He clicked open the lock and lifted out some garments wrapped in tissue paper. "If you point me to your room, I'll be installing a metal plate in your mirror to monitor your clothing choices."

"Well, that could be worse," said Karen, patting my knee. She gestured up the stairs toward my room.

The man approached and held out his hand. "Of course, we'll be taking your flower, too," he said.

It took me a moment to realize he was referring to the plastic flower on my lapel. I touched its petals. Eco-chic wasn't going to be a real trend — at least, not my version of it. But they didn't have to take everything. "No."

"*Marla*," my mother said.

"It's my design. I want to keep it."

My mother grabbed my lapel and detached the pin herself. As she handed it to the man with a weak smile, a raw feeling — a mix of despair and exhaustion — suddenly overwhelmed me. "Are you done yet?" I blurted out. "I'd like to get some rest now."

Turning away, the man climbed the staircase without answering.

The woman stood. "There's one final thing. You should know that you have been added to the national Do Not Hire list. No established corporation with a branch on domestic soil will employ you."

"For sixty days?" I asked.

"For life," the woman replied. "Be quick, Agent," she called up the stairs. "We have a few more houses to visit."

Chapter Thirty-Two

The CSS *agents, or kidnappers* — whichever they were — had escorted Ivy out of the elevator on the top floor of the Warwick Records building. They'd walked her down the hallway with its rose-colored carpet and shoved her through the door at the end. Here she was in the oval conference room, two years after entering it for the first and only other time.

Miles Jackson, looking as imposing as she remembered, sat at the end of the granite table. He was leaning back in his chair, resting his steepled fingers against the bridge of his nose. He glanced up as they entered.

A man sat to his left, deeply engaged in his Tabula.

Ivy wasn't surprised to see Miles and an assistant. She hadn't, however, expected the shouting.

The screens that girdled the conference room were all live, each broadcasting a man's or woman's face. Everyone looked irritated. Ivy's head swung back and forth, following the conversation thread as the accusations escalated.

"You've got to get your house in order, Hugo," a heavyset man bellowed. "Our floor managers at GameTech have reported that the kids have been watching the strike on their Unums in the bathrooms. God forbid the same thing breaks out over here."

"Mine actually circulated a *petition*, Hugo," an older man said. "In all my years —"

"It's *over*, Larry." A man with light gray hair and a tanned face spoke wearily. He touched a tissue to his forehead. "I told you. We needed time to recruit the replacement Taps and fly them out. We ended it this afternoon."

It dawned on Ivy who these people were. The Silents. Like Miles, the rarely seen heads of each company. So many of them, communicating together. And being, in fact, not very silent at all.

"It had better be," snapped a white-haired woman. "Yesterday — in one day — the Sargent Malls lost seventeen million in revenue."

"That's nothing." A younger woman with glasses cut in. "We had to bump a film release because of this disaster. People weren't going to line up to see *Shopaholorific*, not with Miss Anti-Trend spouting her nonsense. Now Candimax has nothing opening this weekend." Her glare narrowed. "That's on *your* head, Miles."

Ivy looked to Miles, but he didn't move.

A man Ivy recognized spoke next. His voice was smooth and authoritative. "Torro-LeBlanc has fixed their end. The strike is over." She remembered him from the few government news broadcasts she'd watched, hovering behind the old, tired-looking president. He had gelled hair, graying temples, and a well-proportioned face. "Let her go, Miles. We'll use what's-her-name, the other one from RedLight Records. The Mirth girl. She'll promote trends. That's all we need for now. In the meantime, you can build up a new face."

Ivy's heart began to hammer.

"You're right, Mr. Chairman," another man added. "If it's any indication, Sugarwater's sales have increased by ten percent since we gave Lyric Mirth the campaign."

The chairman nodded. "The Wilde girl and this eco business are in the way. Force the obsolescence."

Miles Jackson cleared his throat. "Welcome, Ivy."

"Oh, she's there?" The woman with glasses squinted. Ivy wondered if the cameras would stay on Miles or pick her up. She shrunk her shoulders self-consciously.

"Good," said the agitated-looking tanned man. "Fire her now."

Miles flashed a gleaming white smile. The first time she'd met him, his smile had struck Ivy as kind. Now the grin looked sharkish. "Have a seat," he said.

Unable to stop shaking, she moved away from the agents. She lowered herself into a chair halfway along one side of the conference table.

"You've been busy, sweetheart, haven't you," Miles began. It wasn't a question.

Ivy sat, frozen, feeling the scrutiny from the ring of hostile eyes.

"As you just heard, some folks feel I ought to release you from your contract."

She felt tears coming and blinked them back furiously. "No," she whispered in protest.

"Problem is, Ivy," he continued, "I pride myself on my good judgment. I saw that you had the makings of a star. My friends"— he pointed his finger in a circle around the room —"seem to think I was wrong." Miles studied her. "Was I wrong?"

"No, sir," Ivy murmured.

"Really." Miles seemed to be making up his mind about

something. "I think we'll continue in private," he announced. "Sorry to deprive everyone of the public execution. Mr. Chairman, I'll be in touch shortly. Warwick out." He hit a button on the table. Instantly, the screens went dark. Miles nodded to the agents, who left the way they'd come in. The man with the Tabula remained. Even though the dismissal of their audience brought some relief, Ivy remained tense.

Miles leaned back in his chair. His gold necklace caught one of the overhead lights and glistened. "Here's the thing, sweetheart. Great success requires great sacrifice. You don't seem to have learned this lesson."

"But I didn't —"

Sharply, he held up a hand and she stopped. She watched him through watery eyes.

"You see, Ivy, Warwick establishes a path." He slid the edge of his hand along the conference table's smooth marbled surface. "We fund your development, and you agree to stay on the path. You sing our songs. You dance our dances. You go where we tell you to go. And you certainly wear what we tell you to wear."

With a shudder, the look and feel of the torture trend came back to her. She felt the prick of the spikes on her soles, the hug of the corset, the itchiness of the hair.

"This path leads to stardom. We know. We've been leading young singers down the path for generations."

Fatima had said something similar during her tirade in the Pop Beat greenroom. What was it? *Anyone who believes fame "just happens" is sorely mistaken.* Ivy knew all this, of course — but couldn't it be both what Warwick wanted *and* what she wanted? Shouldn't she have a say? She was the performer, after all.

"But sometimes a singer gets a little voice in her head, a little serpent that worms its way into her brain," Miles continued. "It comes along and tempts her. *Step off the path.*" He whispered the last line. "And when you step off, it might even feel good for a while. Problem is, there are consequences, Ivy. Consequences you can't anticipate. Consequences that affect Warwick. And others."

Ivy shifted her gaze toward the black screens.

Miles nodded. "So here's what you do." He held out his hand, and the man to his left placed a black stylus on Miles's open palm without looking up. Miles squeezed it in his fist. "You grab that serpent by the throat and strangle it. Every time. That's what you have to do to succeed in this business."

Strangle it. Strangle the urge to write her own music, to dress the way she wanted. To kiss the person she wanted to kiss.

Miles's voice turned kind. "I get it, sweetheart. The constant changes. The pressure. The exhaustion. I understand. It's hard."

He didn't get it. He didn't get what it was like to enter the wasteland of her closet, to see her hometown spend its savings on trends they saw her wearing, to see her brother break down and be unable to help him. Never mind the vigilance it took to keep an eye on threats like Lyric. *Exhaustion* didn't cover it. Miles didn't get something else, either — how good it felt to disobey her agent and publicist and follow her instincts.

"It takes a special kind of person with a special kind of strength." Miles went on. "I saw it in you, Ivy. You have it. I can feel it when you sing. You know you belong on top. Thing is"— he tapped his chest —"*we're* the ones who keep you there." He paused. "This eco-chic business will be gone tomorrow. You know that, don't you, sweetheart?" he said gently. "It's just a trend like everything else. You'll be left wearing recycled rags and singing to yourself in the mirror. You'll lose it all."

As security had dragged her away from the Torro-LeBlanc design house, Ivy had seen the troops in gray arriving. From the conversation in the conference room, it sounded as if the strike had failed. But maybe there were those, like Marla Klein and Vivienne Graves, who had ideas about what to do now. They would keep fighting, somehow.

But how? Ivy wondered. And, more important, what was her own next move? If eco-chic was really dying . . . well, then, she was dead, wasn't she? It made no sense to keep talking about the environment if nobody cared. And she could keep writing her own songs, but if she didn't have a major label to produce them, who would listen? Silently, she recounted the lyrics she'd written: *Forget yesterday / 'Cause today we escape / Come on, come on / Break free with me.*

Was it a lie? Was there really no breaking free?

Glancing at the man to his left, Miles cleared his throat.

The man looked up and nodded. "All set, sir."

"Now, it's time to make a decision, Ivy," Miles said. "We've put together a revised contract for you. We've included some provisos we neglected the first time around."

The man swung the Tabula stand in a half circle and pushed it toward her.

She scanned the text, trying to interpret the legalese. The first sentence that she understood made her eyes sting with tears again. "I don't get to see my family for a *year*?" She thought of the vacation she had promised Constantine. She thought of the sensitive state he was in right now, how much he needed her support.

"It's a show of your commitment, sweetheart. We need your focus to be on your work. Besides, you'll still have an Unum. We're only partially restricting conversations."

She read on. "Keane Kelly will represent me?"

"We've released Jarvis and Fatima. Obviously, they're no longer effective. You've met Keane, Clayton Pryce's agent. He's agreed to take you on and rework your image.

A new agent. She hadn't exactly loved Fatima — especially in recent days when her publicist had freaked out over the littlest thing — but she would miss Jarvis. He was firm but also patient; no matter what was going on, he always calmed her down. Keane had done wonders for Clayton — but he'd also been partially responsible for his meltdown, she remembered. Ivy wondered what Keane's vision for her would be. Would he take her back to her Wilde child days? Clubbing, kleptomania, gags . . .

The prospect made her feel as if she were underwater, breathing liquid into her lungs. She tried to take in the remaining points of the contract, but the letters bobbed indecipherably in front of her. She dug her nails into the flesh of her palms. The last time she'd felt this way, she'd cracked a Tabula. She could do it again, right now.

"Let me be clear, sugar." Miles again leaned back in his chair. "If you're not willing to make the appropriate sacrifices, we'll find someone who is. Millions of girls dream of a chance like yours. We picked you because we believe in your talent as a performer, but you have to decide what you want. We're offering you everything. Or you can go home and it ends. We don't force your hand here." He smiled. "It's your choice."

Choice. The last real thing Felix had said to her was that she always had a choice. Felix, who had kissed Marla so triumphantly at the strike. The image sharpened again in her mind's eye, and she fought to forget it. After all that hoping and waiting . . . she'd lost him. Even if she walked away now, he wouldn't be waiting for her.

Could she really choose to leave? She thought of returning to her warm family kitchen, eating Christina's incredible cooking and rolling her eyes with Constantine at George's boring stories. She could lie on the couch and watch TV and just *rest*. Ivy closed her eyes for a moment, imagining the peace. She could reassure Constantine. She'd show him that getting tapped sometimes wasn't worth it.

But — and her breath caught — stepping aside meant being replaced. It meant letting Lyric Mirth win. There would be no more screaming fans, no more exhilarating concert performances. Ivy Wilde would be a has-been, a fossil, no better than Bernadette Fife, the old country pop star. She'd have to watch Lyric dominate the airwaves and ads and television spots day after day. Who knew what that would do to her?

To stay or to walk away? There was one person who had chosen a third option. She thought of the statue on the green in Millbrook. Had Skip McBrody sat in this room? Had he been told the story about strangling the serpent of independence and self-expression? How hard had he been pushed before he put a gun to his temple? Could she . . . would she end up like him if she stayed?

Miles slid the stylus across the table to her.

What future did she want?

Chapter Thirty-Three

The next morning, I knew without scanning that every piece of clothing I wore would turn the light on my trendchecking gun green. I'd gotten dressed in the steamy bathroom after showering, afraid of the eye behind the mirror plate.

I still couldn't shake the dense cloud of exhaustion. My cheeks were purple and tender. I wasn't ready to call Felix and hear about his own wires just yet. How could I talk to him — or Kevin or Randall or Vivienne, for that matter — knowing someone was listening in?

Eventually, Felix called. I hadn't planned on leaving the silent cocoon of my room for a week, but he convinced me that there was one visit we needed to make.

A few days later, tucking my damp hair behind my ears, I stepped into the cavity of a body scanner at a minimum-security prison. The guard studied the screen for a moment. Instead of gesturing me forward, though, she motioned for me to return to the starting point.

"You have subdermal floss installed," the guard said, coming closer to stare at my cheeks.

"Yes. He does too," I said, nodding at Felix.

The guard peered closer at both of us, and I saw the recognition hit her face. "You're two of those Torro-LeBlanc kids, aren't you?"

"Yes, but we just want to visit our friend and make sure she's okay," I pleaded. "You can even listen in on the conversation."

The guard chuckled loudly and put her hands on her hips, right above her holster. "If you're under surveillance, I don't have to do a thing. They're hearing it all. Go ahead through."

Felix passed into the scanner next and received a nod of approval.

The guard led us both down a white corridor with walls that shone as if they had been freshly scrubbed. The only sounds were the loud taps of our steps and the muted roar of the rainstorm outside. On either side, we passed white doors with tiny windows at face level. I kept expecting to see eyes flashing through the diamond-scored glass. Thankfully, none appeared. If the rooms held prisoners, they were busy. Or just not interested in us.

"Recreation hour," the guard announced as she unlocked the door at the end of the corridor. She held it open and we passed through.

I understood why the cells were empty. The prisoners were all in this large room. A few of the women stood around a foosball table. Some played cards. Some attempted to get exercise by performing basic calisthenics like sit-ups. The large windows dripped with rain.

I scanned the room. Near the window, I saw a solitary figure with black hair turned away from us, sitting in front of an easel.

"There she is," I whispered to Felix.

"Fifteen minutes," the guard ordered. I thanked her.

As we approached, I drew in my breath. On a sheet of paper

clipped to the easel, painted with watercolors in a narrow plastic tray, the scene through the window had been brought to life. The painting captured the cornflower-colored fountain in the middle of the grounds, the green lawn, and the hedges on the perimeter. Best of all, from the way the colors ran and dripped, it was clear the scene was being viewed through a rainy window.

"It's beautiful, Vivienne," I said gently.

Vivienne stiffened but didn't turn to face us until she had finished adding some orange highlights to the fountain's base. Still holding the brush, she glanced over her shoulder. "Hello, you two." A yellow bruise above her right eyebrow made me wince.

"How're you doing, Viv?" Felix asked, pulling up two nearby chairs and sitting down. I joined him.

Vivienne again touched the paper with her brush. "I get to paint landscapes. Life could be worse." She gave a little shrug.

"Your head," I said.

She touched the spot with her knuckle. "It's nothing. Doesn't even hurt anymore."

Without a word, Felix ran his finger from his ear to his lips.

"Ah," Vivienne said, nodding.

I couldn't help myself. "What's it like in here? Being in jail, I mean?"

Vivienne dipped the paintbrush in a cup of water, swirled it clean, and turned to us. To my surprise, a smile danced around her lips. "Look around. I finally got my wish." She swept her arm around the room. "A dress code. One single look for work, sleep, weekend, *and* formal." I looked. Every inmate was clad in a matching light blue short-sleeve jumpsuit.

Vivienne pinched a bit of the fabric from her pant leg between her fingers and rubbed it. "Comfortable, durable material, like I always wanted." She laughed and shook her head. "I had to go to jail to find my heaven. I should have figured this out a lot sooner."

I glanced at Felix. Had she cracked up? "I'm so sorry this happened. We tried to come help you, but they started arresting people . . ." I trailed off, waiting for her to say something.

"I'm glad you two got away." Her voice was calm. She again flashed a smile at me as she dabbed some black and then blue paint on her brush.

"Kev's in the hospital," said Felix. "Someone hit him on the head. He has a concussion, but he'll be okay."

Vivienne nodded and added some gray to the sky. "And Randall?"

Felix and I looked at each other.

"He went back," I said. "Jeri stays home with the kids, so they need the money. He called afterward . . ." I looked at Felix again. "He feels terrible."

Felix frowned and shook his head. He thought we should stay angry with Randall. I'd been arguing that a person could take only so many risks, especially where his children were concerned.

"They've released most of the people they arrested by now," said Felix. "Gwen and a bunch of patternmakers are out. Blackballed by the corporations, and under surveillance, same as us." He nestled one fist in the opposite palm. "If only your officer hadn't sustained injuries —"

Vivienne waved her free hand. "It's all right."

"We're trying to raise enough for your bail," I said, choosing my words carefully. "I have savings from being a judge, but the bail's steep. My parents won't help, and between us —"

"I won't take a dime," Vivienne said, cutting me off. "You should keep any money you have. There are better things you can do with it."

"What do you mean?" I asked.

"For the first time in your life, you're free," she said slowly. She put down the brush and took my hand in both of hers, looking at me hard. "For the first time, you can do anything you want."

Free. I had gold wires in my cheeks. I couldn't work. Now that the strike was over, though I kept telling myself I'd be okay, I knew I wasn't. It felt like a gray fog had settled over my life. To have gone from having so much hope, so much purpose, to ... nothing. It was worse because I still felt this incredible anger at what had happened, to me and to everyone Torro-LeBlanc screwed over. But I couldn't do anything about it. So it festered, and the gray fog grew thicker.

At least I'd made a sort of shaky peace with Karen in the past few days. The marriage talk had been tabled. I knew she was doing her best to cheer me up, telling me how great I looked in the designer clothes and offering to make all my favorite foods. I tried not to make cracks — even to myself — about her obsessive cooking. I'd realized a couple of nights ago, after a particularly delicious cassoulet, that if you looked at it a certain way, designing complicated meals was sort of like designing clothes. It took creativity — it even went through trends. Only, in our house, nobody paid you for it.

The days dragged, the hours empty. Even Felix didn't serve as a distraction. We'd make out to pass the time — quietly, aware that the floss was capturing every smack, rustle, and whisper. Things had happened pretty fast with Braxton, but Felix and I had sort of leveled off during our monitoring period. I was self-conscious, and he didn't want "to give those perverts any more satisfaction." Afterward, he would lie back and stare at the ceiling, and my restlessness would return.

I pulled my hand away. "I don't know how you can be so calm," I said, trying to keep the frustration out of my voice. "Actually, we *can't* do anything we want. And in here, you definitely can't do what you want. We're not free." I stopped, wondering if what I'd said would make the surveillance people suspicious.

Vivienne picked up the brush and twirled it between her fingertips. "You think we lost, don't you?" she said, still smiling.

I looked at Felix again. He was studying Vivienne curiously.

Suddenly, she leaned toward me and spoke in a whisper. "Change doesn't happen overnight, Marla. Sometimes it takes a hundred years, sometimes more. Believe me, people saw what we did. For three days, the whole world stopped and paid attention. So they shut us down — so what? I'll do my time, but they can't lock me up forever for giving an agent a couple of broken bones. And if they do, then there will be someone else to pick up the fight, and that person will make another small dent. And so on. We pound and we pound until everything comes crashing down."

She scanned the room. "In the meantime, I'm here — surrounded by lawless women with a bunch of time on their hands. It presents . . ." She drummed her fingers on her lips. "Interesting possibilities." She grinned, then leaned in so close to my cheek I thought she was going to kiss it. "You get all that?" she said loudly.

I stared back into her triumphant face. Maybe she was crazy — but right now, I felt nothing but awe for her. She was Vivienne, and she'd always be. Nothing, not even jail, could break her.

Still, I didn't know what to say, now that she'd basically

incriminated us. If that didn't qualify as a discussion of "potentially subversive activity," I didn't know what did. Before either Felix or I could find our voice, though, Vivienne twirled the brush between her fingers, dipped it in the green paint, and quickly painted the word *disavow* on the bottom of her landscape. I didn't get it right away, but Felix did.

"You're nuts, Vivienne," he said. "The strike is over, and we accept that. If you're going to keep talking like this, we can't have anything more to do with you." He gave her a quick wink.

Both of them looked to me, and I raced to think of the right words. "I agree. Stop saying those things. I want to cooperate. Sorry you're in jail, but maybe it's the best place for you."

"Eh, get out of here, both of you," Vivienne said, her face full of mock disgust. "You make me sick. Your hearts were never in the movement." She took her hand and blew us both a silent kiss.

"Bye, then." I watched Felix rise and give her a quick squeeze on her shoulder. I did the same.

Before we left, we watched Vivienne turn back to her painting and blur out the word she had written.

Vivienne's words in prison, about finally being free and about the strike having mattered, rolled around in my head for two months. They sustained me in the grayest moments of my CSS monitoring period. Through the slow days at home with my mother. Through knowing someone was listening to every word I said. By the end, I didn't say much.

But through the long and silent hours, my ideas kept growing. One day, I wandered into my local branch of the La Reina Public Library. I didn't get a card or check anything out, fearful that CSS would monitor it. I passed the kids gathered around the public Tabulas and ignored them — the CSS guy had told me not to use any Tabula but my own. I didn't know how they'd be able to trace a library Tabula, but I wasn't going to take the risk. So I did a search and got actual books from two sections of the library: self-employment and sustainable clothing. I sat and read them behind *Prime* magazines just to be safe. I was still nervous.

I realized I hadn't read a whole book since I was twelve. It was slow going at first. It helped that I didn't have anything better to do. I came back every few days or so until I'd finished.

By the time the sixty days were up and the woman in the white lab coat returned to extract the subdermal floss, Vivienne's words had bloomed into something ferocious. The woman congratulated me on an incident-free monitoring period. She also complimented me on the firm condition of my collagen-enhanced cheeks. The man in uniform removed the plate from my mirror. He claimed the surveillance on my Unum and Tabula had ended as well. I listened to their condescending praise. They had only silenced my tongue. They had no idea what had taken root in my head.

Chapter Thirty-Four

Ivy's eye caught something on the Wildefan Chatlist. She was scrolling through the hundreds of notes left since the Torro-LeBlanc strike, the notes of inquiry, of confusion, of support. Among them was a different comment.

Hi, Ivy. You left your handbag with me by mistake, and it has your Unum in it. If you need it back, let me know. The message poster was *YourFlowerFriend.* Ivy checked the date — it had been left a few weeks ago.

Whom had she left her handbag with? What handbag? She reread the message and paused on *YourFlowerFriend.* In her head, she saw Marla's earnest face and the flower pin glittering on her shoulder. Ivy remembered she had gotten a new Unum after the visit to Miles Jackson's office. Because she'd dropped her bag at the rally. Marla must have picked it up.

Marla. Ivy liked her too much to hate her — but still. They weren't "FlowerFriends" any more. After a few seconds of indecision, she tapped the button to reply directly to the poster.

Saw your note. Keep the Unum. I got a new one.

Within a minute, she received a response.

In the bag there were also some photos I thought you might want.

Photos? Ivy wasn't sure what she was talking about. They were probably old signed publicity photos.

Ivy's fingers hovered over her Tabula screen, but a knock on the doorjamb made her look up. Her boyfriend poked his head into the room.

"Ready?" he asked. "Wait — you're not even dressed yet!"

Chapter Thirty-Five

L*ate, late, late, late.* I tried to take deep breaths and control my frustration. This day, of all days, for the stupid trains to be fussy . . .

Mine was the last stop, all the way out in Blackburn. When the train finally wheezed into the station and I got off, I gripped my briefcase and ran through the gravelly alley. I found my brick building and turned the knob of the heavy front door. It stuck, as usual, and I yanked it open with both hands. Heading down the cement staircase, I passed a sculptor, Milo, who kept his studio on an upper floor. We exchanged a quick hello. The temperature dropped as I finished my descent. Even in midsummer, it stayed cool in the basement.

The gray door in front of me had an index card taped to it, on which, weeks ago, I'd written "U.G." in blue pen. I grabbed the key dangling from a cord around my neck, fit it into the eye-level lock, and let myself in.

"I'm here! The trains were awful this morning," I announced.

Four faces briefly looked my way. Each person nodded or smiled, then returned to work.

It was dim in the basement, as usual. The narrow rectangular windows close to the ceiling let in a stingy amount of daylight. We had brought in standing lamps and workstation lights, but it was just one of those rooms that seemed to resist artificial brightening.

My coworkers sat on metal stools at their own folding tables. Kevin was working on a Tabula, Gwen was talking on her Unum, and Neely was sewing a jacket together on a dress form. Georgia, the former finance and accounting Adequate from Torro, was sketching. Felix's table was unoccupied.

Around the room, I'd taped the photographs from Ivy Wilde's bag to the cinderblock walls. Ivy had never asked for them back. I remembered her in the Torro-LeBlanc bathroom, miserable and tossing her trends into the garbage. I wondered how she was doing these days.

Other photographs and images torn from magazines decorated the walls of the room as well: a river, wildflower fields, three trees gnarled together. I had even glued dried leaves and petals to one wall in a giant *UG* pattern.

I walked to my workstation and laid my briefcase on the table, startling a cockroach on the corner. It scuttled down one of the legs and disappeared. I sighed. The space wasn't perfect. But it was ours.

The underground design studio had been my idea. The day after they'd removed the subdermal floss from my cheeks, I'd met Felix and Kevin, also newly floss-free, at a coffee shop. Kevin had recovered from his concussion, though the poor guy still got headaches occasionally. The three of us agreed that there was no way to know whether we were still being watched.

"But we can't live afraid," I said. So I drank a latte and tried to appear casual and carefree as I laid out my proposal in a voice hoarse from lack of use. No company would hire us now. So why didn't we start our own label? We could run it fairly and also keep the spirit of eco-chic alive. Repurposed garments, each one lovingly made. It would take some startup cash, as I'd learned from my reading, but I had my Superior Court savings. My parents would freak, but too bad. And each person could maybe put in a little. We could work cheaply, too, in a small space, with minimal materials to start. Buy used clothing and rip it apart for the fabric, rent old sewing machines. That sort of thing.

Felix got so excited he knocked his drink off the table. He grabbed my shoulders. "I *knew* you were a fighter," he said. "This is brilliant. Brilliant!"

"I'm in only if you two control yourselves," said Kevin.

We had recruited the others and found the studio space. We'd scrubbed the walls and cement floor as best we could and brought in the tables and lamps. Every day that I made the journey to Blackburn on the train, I expected CSS agents to be there, blocking the door to the building. Technically, starting our own business wasn't illegal, but I wondered if creating a non–design house clothing line could be considered "subversive." It definitely *felt* subversive. But so far, it seemed our little company had been overlooked.

We had needed a name. I'd wanted Eco-Chic, but the others had convinced me to start fresh. For our own safety as much as anything.

Felix had come up with Underground. "We're literally stuck underground, our clothing line isn't mainstream, we're a subversive organization — it's perfect," he said one day.

I went home and mulled it over that night in bed. When I thought of Underground, I thought of worms, dirt, and death. It needed something more.

"I think we should call ourselves Underground Garden," I announced the following day. "It's not just about being secret.

It's about our creativity blossoming and growing, despite the darkness."

"I love it," raved Gwen.

Felix nodded. "It's better." The others agreed.

But the spirit of eco-chic was still alive outside our lair. A week after we'd started working, I opened the studio door in the evening to find a giant box of good-quality, usable fabric scraps sitting at the bottom of the stairs. The box had a T-L logo printed on the side. Two more boxes arrived the following week. One evening, when Felix and I decided to head out a little early, we opened the door to find Randall coming up the alley with a box in his arms. His expression didn't change as he approached us and handed Felix the box. "From Vaughn, too," he whispered, before turning and heading back the way he came.

Of the others, I'd heard Sabrina had gone back to Torro, though I had no idea if she still worked in the mailroom. Henry was at home, living off his savings and trying to build an audience for his new fashion hotspot, Judgmental Diva. I asked him to feature garments from our startup company once our first line was ready. He agreed to — if he liked them. So far, the Judgmental Diva had liked *nothing* Torro-LeBlanc had designed.

Today, as I unpacked my briefcase, I watched Kevin work feverishly on his Tabula. He was making last-minute changes to our new company site. He had consulted with some Adequates and designed it himself. Now that the money and time had been invested, now that we had judged our first items as a team, it was time to see who might be brave enough to wear our line. The finished garments hung from silver racks along the back wall, zipped in impenetrable garment bags to protect against the roaches and the damp.

What I had seen so far of the site looked beautiful — black, with iridescent anemone-like flowers that changed from green to purple. Kevin, who had never been a standout drafter at Torro, was a natural at bringing Underground Garden to life on the screen.

I looked at my watch. Nine thirty. The site was going live in two and a half hours. I exhaled and ran my hand over the mirror fragments on my table. I had found the shattered mirror at the dump, and a glass worker upstairs in the building had softened the edges of the pieces for me. I was using them as neckline embellishments for a line of twenty dresses, all similar but each an original. I held a piece up to the navy-blue material on the form, turning it this way and that to determine the best angle.

Gwen ended her Unum conversation and dragged her stool over to my table. She crossed her legs, her wide bell-bottoms brushing the floor. "I was going over our specs with the manufacturers. They thought we wanted two thousand T-shirts, not two hundred."

"Seriously? Good thing you caught it in time."

"Yeah." Gwen rubbed her forehead. "I looked at the order form again — Felix's handwriting is a little messy. There's this squiggle next to the zero. I'm not surprised they read it wrong. But they were super nice about it."

I nodded.

From the beginning, everyone had committed to creating garments that included used and repurposed materials, as I had done with Ivy's outfit. It was a way to unify ourselves as a studio while preserving our individual styles. Felix could keep his rougher aesthetic by patching together old denim, while my clothes could have a softer, more refined feel.

But soon Gwen decided that some of our clothes, mostly

casual sportswear pieces, would need to be manufactured. I resisted until I saw Gwen's prototype for a T-shirt: organic cotton with a large silkscreened chrysanthemum on the front.

"We can silkscreen the flowers ourselves, but we'll save time if the shirts are ready-made," she explained.

I would wear that forever, I immediately thought to myself. The flower brought to mind my forfeited lapel pin. The chrysanthemum was a literal bloom from the new Underground Garden. I gave in.

With Georgia's help, Gwen found a manufacturing plant that was approved by the International Garment Labor Federation. I learned about the IGLF from Gwen and Felix, who had heard about it from Vivienne. The organization made sure garment workers were treated and paid fairly. Even Felix, the most profit-focused of any of us, wanted only an IGLF-approved company to manufacture our clothing.

The craziest step, at least for me, was our decision not to put trendchecking labels in our clothes. I actually proposed the idea, with my favorite expired shawl in mind. But it still felt strange to create a garment that would, in theory, *never* go out of style. I could wear Gwen's T-shirt forever. Felix had wanted the labels to encourage sales in each new season, but he was overruled. Instead, we attached a little brown card to each garment, explaining what Underground Garden stood for.

After chatting briefly with me about the rest of the specs, Gwen returned to her station. We sank into our work for the day. With some feedback from me, Neely decided to cut fresh jacket sleeves that were an inch wider, allowing for better bend at the elbow. Georgia, whose technical knowledge of budgeting and strategy had been a huge help in the first days, was transitioning to design work more and more. Neely and I watched over her as she traced and cut a dress pattern in some old bed linens she had dyed beet red.

"I'm so nervous I've traced the pattern wrong," she mumbled, biting her lip as she cut.

"Ridiculous," said Neely. "You can remake anything. We had a saying in Garment Construction. 'Cut with confidence!'"

A short while later Felix burst through the door, out of breath. "Two boutiques in La Reina will carry our line!" he announced. "*Two* of them!"

He explained as we put down our work and gathered around him. "One's called Greenery; the other's Duke's Rag Bag. They're independent stores that specialize in environmentally conscious clothing. I got the sense from the owners that they struggle, but they've managed to hold on to a tiny local clientele." He grinned. "Jaded ex–design house employees mostly."

"Felix, that's incredible!" exclaimed Neely. "So what happens now?"

"We deliver Underground Garden's first garments next week."

Georgia gave him a high-five. She had explained how Torro-LeBlanc sales reps pitched their lines to department stores, and he'd wanted to try it. Last week he had returned each day demoralized. He'd shrugged off my attempts to comfort him, berating himself for not being a better salesperson.

Even now, as the others congratulated him and returned to work, he softened his expectations in front of me. "I mean, we can't get too excited. We'll probably still lose all our money."

I shook my head and smiled. "I don't care. It's worth it." It was. We had lost our fight. Torro-LeBlanc had held on to its place in the Big Five, which still controlled the fashion industry.

The Silents still treated Adequates and Taps and clothing manu-facturers badly. But despite circumstances we couldn't change, our little band had found a way to do what made us happy.

"Two stores in one day," I said. "That's so prime, Felix."

"I thought they were joking when they said yes. You know, both times it was your rag skirts that convinced them. They lit up when I brought them out." He grabbed my hand and played a tune on my palm with his fingers.

"Thanks. Sometimes I wonder if you love me just for my de-signs."

He looked mischievous. "Your designs *are* pretty hot." He touched his cheek to mine, and his whisper tickled my ear. "But you're wrong about that."

"PDA warning," muttered Kevin from his table. "Take it out-side."

I brushed a quick kiss on Felix's cheek before he pulled away.

"It's crazy to think about," he said. "Next week at this time, people could be wearing our line."

I imagined a scene in the boutique: a girl picking one of my skirts off a rack, rubbing the uneven texture between her fingers, slipping it on and smiling at her reflection in the dressing room mirror. Maybe even twirling around. And then buying the skirt and taking it home.

"Okay, back to work." Felix rubbed his palms together. "I've got to get cracking on that old tire. I *know* I can get it into a gar-ment somehow!"

At ten minutes to noon, Kevin called everyone to gather around his table.

"I think we're good," he said. "We should come up if people are doing a search for 'eco' or 'environmental clothing' or anything like that. I'm planning to link to every independent hotspot that will let us. And I fixed the glitches, too. Here, take a look."

He scrolled through the site slowly. The pages that showed our garments were clean and uncluttered — mostly, I thought with amusement, because we didn't have that many pieces to offer. We had worked hard on a few strong looks. I saw my rag skirts, Felix's distressed jeans, Gwen's T-shirts, Neely's outerwear. Dresses incorporating repurposed prints and materials. All chic, all eco.

"We need a toast," said Gwen. Quickly, we grabbed our travel mugs.

"To Underground Garden!" Neely proclaimed, raising hers.

"To Vivienne," said Kevin. There was a moment of silence.

"Yes," I said. "And to freedom." We clinked and sipped.

Kevin entered commands on his Tabula. He glanced at his watch. "That should do it." He opened a browser window and typed the address. Shivering with anticipation, I peered closer and watched the Underground Garden home page fill his screen, dark and alive.

We were open for business.

Chapter Thirty-Six

Y ou're lucky to wear something so beautiful. The little voice in Ivy's head repeated what her agent, Keane, had told her earlier. *No one has ever worn live butterflies before.*

The legs of the insects had been removed, and their bodies were affixed to the surface of her strapless dress with special glue. The iridescent blue and black wings fluttered, straining against their bonds, sending ticklish shivers over Ivy's body. She wasn't supposed to touch them, but she couldn't resist brushing a finger against her side now and again. A powdery residue came off on her fingertip. The wings felt like velvet. She *was* lucky.

A stole of wolf fur coiled around her neck. She walked high in iguana stilettos. As for her headpiece, it rivaled the dress. Stuffed snakes sprouted from her scalp like winding dreadlocks. She brushed a stray asp over her shoulder, and the rat-tooth bracelet on her wrist rattled.

"You look *so* hot," Madison whispered in her ear from behind. "People are going to freak."

Ivy nodded her thanks.

Her entourage stood behind a black curtain set up outside the renovated Torro-LeBlanc flagship store. The curtain concealed them in front of one corner, and a short red carpet led to the entrance. Ivy peeked out to see the new exterior design. Before, the storefront had been all rough and warehouse-edgy; now it looked sleek. Black overhangs on a clean white background.

She peered inside the windows. The stuffed racks were all the same, of course. Heaps and hills of expensive clothes.

"P pills," she called out. Hilarie reached into her purse and quickly shook three placidophilus pills out of her tin. She handed them to Ivy, but they fell through her unsteady fingers and rolled away. Ivy pursed her lips at her nymph.

Hilarie extracted three more pills. This time she pushed them directly into Ivy's mouth. Ivy began chewing, and the burst of strawberry scent clicked her back to the place where she had been a few moments before. *High-end design houses make clothes. Superstars like me wear them. How else would it be?* Aiko rubbed her shoulders lightly to calm her.

"Thanks, Aiko," she said. Feeling a swell of love, she grabbed Hilarie's and Naia's hands. "You guys are kind of the best."

Her boyfriend approached, flanked by his brothers and a cluster of satyrs. Danny Angel looked so cute, sipping a Sugarwater, a coonskin cap on his head.

"They say it's time," he said.

It had been a genius move of Keane's to steal Danny away from Lyric. "You're channeling animal wildness now," Keane had said to her, his arched eyebrows coming together in seriousness. "You follow the laws of the jungle. That means taking the best lion in the pride for your mate." She had repeated the phrases in her interviews with the gossip magazines. To make things even more delicious, the rumor Keane made sure the magazines spread was that Lyric was a prude. Danny had left her because he, too, wanted a lioness.

Almost overnight, Ivy watched Lyric lose popularity in the fourteen-to-eighteen-year-old demographic. Her record sales were slowing. It had been almost too easy.

Ivy tilted her head to the side and watched Danny's dimples pucker as he sipped. He was so sweet. Of course, he was also a year and a half younger than she was, and his voice hadn't fully changed yet. The two of them wouldn't be sharing any smoldering kisses anytime soon.

She turned to Hilarie. "One more."

"You won't forget what you're supposed to —"

"Jeez, she'll be fine." Madison grabbed the tin and shoved another P pill into Ivy's mouth. "We're right behind you, Ivy."

Ivy took Danny's arm and he led her onto the carpet. They stopped and posed for the press. So many camera flashes, like the twinkles on a mirror ball. All for her. The butterflies were doing their part, flapping in the light. She looked prime. Keane and Madison said so. She knew so. She stared down the cameras and stretched her smile as wide as it would go.

After a generous minute, they continued toward the small group of people who were gathered at the entrance. Ivy stumbled slightly on her heel as they approached, but Danny held his skinny arm firm and she steadied herself.

In front of the double doors, a red ribbon tied in a giant bow was suspended between two standing brass posts. A couple of Torro-LeBlanc representatives met her behind the ribbon and shook her hand. The latest crop of Superior Court judges stood proudly in a line behind them. Ivy didn't recognize any faces — but then again, she never did.

A blond judge stepped forward and handed her a giant pair of scissors. Ivy wasn't expecting them to be so heavy, and she struggled to get a firm hold. Again Danny came to her rescue, grabbing the scissors and supporting them so she could simply rest her hands on top of his. Her grip was strangely unreliable these days.

"Oh." Before she made the cut, she was supposed to recite the lines Keane had made her memorize. She looked out into the crowd. "This is a great day. Torro-LeBlanc is one of my favorite designers. They've designed the looks for my *Wilde Kingdom* tour." Her voice sounded unusually loud. Had she been miked? She couldn't remember.

"Thirty-one cities, sold out," Danny added on cue.

Keane had told her to lower her eyes at this point, bat his arm, and say, "Oh, Danny." Instead, she couldn't help it. She let out a giggle. "Yup, that's right.

"I want to . . ." she continued. What was the next part? She paused. It wasn't her fault she couldn't remember. Her brain felt so mushy.

She heard Madison's voice whispering in her left ear. "You want to congratulate —"

"Oh, right, right. I want to congratulate Torro-LeBlanc on its new flagship store. I kind of can't wait to go in and check out the prime trends." There. Almost done.

She and Danny opened the scissors wide around the ribbon and posed for more shots.

"One, two, three," Danny whispered.

"Ready, set, shop!" they shouted together.

The giant scissors made the slice.

Everyone cheered, the crowd a colorful blur of fashionable fans.

Ivy couldn't believe she had ever wanted more than this.

She remembered the past couple of months hazily. What had she been thinking? Wearing old clothes was gross, not prime.

And the environment . . . well, they were doing so much already. Cleaner fuel. Recycling and all that. The earth would be fine. Like Miles Jackson said, she was an artist. Her job wasn't to save the world. It was to entertain billions of people.

She shifted her weight from one stiletto to the other. Her family was probably watching proudly from home. She didn't need to visit them. She'd done more for them with her fame than she could ever do in person. The three of them could take a first-class vacation together. Thanks to her. And her parents could afford to send Constantine to the top shrink in Millbrook. Lots of Adequates turned out okay — like that nice doctor she'd met.

Besides, how could she be lonely? She beamed at her nymphs, standing to her left, mingled with Danny's satyrs. Madison caught her eye and gave her a small wink. They had all been through so much. Just like family, her nymphs and Keane would do anything for her.

She was, indisputably, the number one pop star in the world. She was wearing butterflies. Every eye in the crowd was fixed on her, studying, admiring, and envying her. She had it all.

"Stay young!" she called to her fans.

More Information

For more information on sustainable clothing and ethical manufacturing practices:

WEB RESOURCES

The Clean Clothes Campaign, dedicated to improving working conditions and supporting the empowerment of workers in the global garment and sportswear industries: *cleanclothes.org*

The Council for Textile Recycling, whose goal is to achieve zero textile waste going to landfills by 2037: *weardonaterecycle.org*

The Environmental Protection Agency's statistics on textile waste: *epa.gov/osw/conserve/materials/textiles.htm*

Etsy, the online marketplace for handmade and vintage items: *etsy.com*

Green America's National Green Pages for consumers: *greenpages.org*

The IndustriALL Global Union, which represents 50 million workers in 140 countries, including textile, garment, and leather workers: *industriall-union.org*

The Institute for Global Labour and Human Rights, which promotes and defends human rights, and specifically women's, and workers' rights, in the global economy: *globallabourrights.org*

SMART, the Secondary Materials and Recycled Textiles Association: *smartasn.org*

Books

Bartoletti, Susan Campbell. *Kids on Strike!* Boston: Houghton Mifflin Company, 1999.

Leonard, Annie. *The Story of Stuff: How Our Obsession with Stuff Is Trashing the Planet, Our Communities, and Our Health — and a Vision for Change.* New York: Free Press, 2010.

Walker, Rob. *Buying In: The Secret Dialogue Between What We Buy and Who We Are.* New York: Random House, 2008.

Acknowledgments

Material Girls would never have become a book without the help of so many. Enormous Greek bear-hug thank-yous to . . .

- the Associates of the Boston Public Library, who generously provided the space, time, and resources to complete the novel;

- the incomparable Margaret Raymo, who gave *Material Girls* the best kind of makeover, and everyone at Houghton Mifflin Harcourt for bringing it into the world with so much care and attention;

- Edward Necarsulmer IV, agent extraordinaire, who guided the journey with infinite wisdom, patience, and resolve;

- the members of the Saint Botolph Club, especially Kathryn Lasky, for encouraging my writing in its early days;

- the fabulous Griper girls, Jane Kohuth, Kirsty McKay, Sonia Miller, Jean Stehle, and Laura Woollett, who read every word of *Material Girls* and urged me on;

- my writing partner, Amitha Knight, for accountability and friendship;

- my mentors at Simmons College, including Cathryn Mercier, Susan Bloom, Hannah Barnaby, and Jackie Horne, who taught me what children's literature is and what it could be;

- the incredible writing community at Grub Street, especially Christopher Castellani for bringing me on board;

- my parents, who gave me the best of everything, and my brother, Tom, for not teasing me too much about writing in cafés;

- and finally, Nicholas, who brings me joy every day, and John, the finest copilot, counselor, and champion I could hope for.